JUMPER!

Bathed in the glow of a dying afternoon, an emaciated male, no more than twenty years of age, teetered on the building's edge.

As if on cue, the crowd slowly, softly, began to chant: *"Jump. Jump. Jump."*

Harry Porter dove across the roof, just as the boy blithely stepped off the edge. Sliding on his stomach towards the precipice, Harry managed to latch onto the jumper's left ankle with both hands. The boy found himself dangling head first from the top of the brownstone, swinging in a pendulum-like motion over the ground six stories down.

Harry gaped at the crowd below. He wasn't crazy about the view.

Rave reviews for Ed Naha's
THE PARADISE PLOT:

"The novel jumps with shoot-em-up action, nonstop drinking and some of the best sleazy dialogue this side of *The Long Goodbye*."

—The Boston Real Paper

The Suicide Plague

Ed Naha

BANTAM BOOKS
TORONTO · NEW YORK · LONDON · SYDNEY

THE SUICIDE PLAGUE
A Bantam Book / October 1982

ISBN 0-553-22588-X

Published simultaneously in the United States and Canada

PRINTED IN THE UNITED STATES OF AMERICA

O 0 9 8 7 6 5 4 3 2 1

In memory of David Harold Meyer

Special thanks to pep squad '81:
Robin, Joyce, Diana, Ken, Cynthia
and Karen.

I

"Men of action, when they are without faith, have never believed in anything but action."

Albert Camus

1

"Harry. Can you ever be sure someone is trying to kill you?"

The speaker, William Pratt, sat in the faded blue hotel room. He was short, stocky and worried. He riveted his attention on the face of Harry Porter, flickering on the videophone's tiny screen. "Well," Porter laughed over the phone, "if the someone in question is a real pro, by the time you're sure, it's too late to worry about it."

The man in the hotel room did not smile. A barely perceptible tremor worked its way through his body. "Jesus!" Porter exclaimed on the video screen. "You're serious, aren't you."

William Pratt cradled the phone in his left hand. In his mid-thirties but possessing the stomach of a senior citizen, he hunched over the phone. "I guess so. I'm pretty sure that someone's been following me since I got into town."

"I thought you just checked in."

"Uh-uh. Two days ago."

"You should have called me sooner, Bill. We haven't seen each other in, what, six years?"

"Mmmmm." Pratt's mind was elsewhere. "I was waiting until I got set up in my new office." Pratt and Harry Porter went back a few years. They had met during the last war. Two hard-drinking, unarmed men, Pratt a medic and Porter a war correspondent, they had taken turns keeping each other's backsides intact. If Pratt could confide in any human being about his present fears, it would be Harry.

The televised face of Harry Porter remained motionless for several thoughtful seconds. "Who the heck would want to kill a medic?"

Pratt flipped a strand of blond hair off his pockmarked forehead. "I can't be sure. I've been getting quite a few job offers, ultimatums really, from most of the larger chemical firms. Maybe they're upset that I want to remain in the health field."

Porter grunted. "When did you first spot your shadow?"

"As soon as I got off the planetran. We made it from Dallas

2

to New York early. Thirty-nine minutes. I was walking through
Penn Station when I just had this premonition, you know? I
turned around and spotted him, a runny-nosed kid. Sixteen
years old. Seventeen at most. Very normal looking. Clean cut.
Totally unexceptional . . . except for a crescent-shaped scar
under his right eye."

Pratt slid a forefinger along a jagged blotch on his neck. "I
notice scars these days."

"Better than noticing earthworms, pal," Porter muttered.
"You've seen this kid again?"

"Every time I turn around. I half expect him to hold the
soap when I shower."

Porter took that in. "Could just be a case of big city
paranoia, Bill. It happens. I just can't fathom a big firm hiring
a hit *kid*. Hell, the poor bastard probably wouldn't know
whether to squeeze a trigger or a zit when it came down to
it."

Pratt bit his lower lip. A light layer of sweat had formed on
his forehead. "Always the optimist, Harry. I suppose you
could be right."

Porter nodded. "I mean, the kid could just be staying at
the same hotel. There could be a lot of reasons for running
into him. Tell you what. Why don't you meet me for a drink
at Mecoy's tonight? Remember that dive I used to love?"

Pratt forced a smile. "Seemed unrequited at the time."

"The best kind of affair," Porter grinned. "Saves you the
heartbreak of parting. Why don't you meet me there after
you leave the office. Just tell me what time is best. I'll work
around it."

"Around eight."

"Those are some long hours you're pulling, doc. What are
you up to these days?"

"I'll tell you all about it tonight. Gotta go." Pratt babbled a
hasty good-bye and hung the phone back on its receiver. He
hadn't meant to be so vague with Porter, but he had nothing
concrete to base his fears on. He didn't know who could be
following him or why. He couldn't even be sure that someone
was tailing him. He had no explanation for it, just a feeling in
the pit of his stomach that he should expect the worst. It was
the same sort of twinge he used to experience seconds before
someone yelled "incoming wounded."

Bill Pratt slipped into a faded blue sport coat, picked up his
briefcase, and headed for the door. He'd tell Porter every-

thing tonight over a drink. Perhaps he was just being para-
noid after all. In the back of his mind, however, lurked the
hope that Harry, with all his years of investigative legwork,
would be able to zero in on some casual detail of the story, a
detail ignored by Pratt, and come up with some answer.

Pratt left his room and walked to the elevator bay. The
hotel corridor was lined with holographic artwork and small
laser displays. Pratt suppressed a nervous smile of content-
ment. He had certainly come up in the world since the days
when he and Porter traveled together. Back then, the hotels
they frequented were somewhat less posh. Every floor seemed
to have its own set of stray cats and the term "with or
without" referred to mosquito netting.

The elevator door slid open, and Pratt stepped inside.
There were three other passengers also heading for the
lobby—all young. A blond boy stood on the left of the car. A
red-haired girl stood on the right. In the center was a
short-haired male with light brown hair. He had a crescent-
shaped scar under his right eye. The carmine coloring of the
crescent contrasted sharply with the dull glisten of his pale
skin. The boy seemed almost feverish.

Pratt did not know whether to back out of the car or hold
his ground. He hesitated, mesmerized by the sight of the
wide-eyed teenager. The scar face flashed a wide grin. It was
a move that conveyed both sincere pleasure and utter insanity. The pit of Pratt's stomach lurched violently.

He heard the elevator door close behind him with a "snap"
of finality.

2

In the distance, sirens wailed, amplified banshees heralding
the arrival of another lost soul. Harry Porter emerged from
Mecoy's Bar and Grille and squinted at the brown, setting
sun disappearing behind the battered skyline of Manhattan.
Sirens. There were always sirens to be reckoned with in this
city. Sirens for fires. Sirens for smog alerts. Sirens designed
to worsen hangovers.

Harry retreated two steps into the darkness afforded by the

building's awning. Two listless citizens, traveling in opposite directions, paused in front of the bar.

"What's going on?"

"There's a jumper down the block."

"How high?"

"Six stories."

A smirk affixed itself to the first speaker's face. "Let's go. Could be fun."

The two pedestrians stepped onto the motorized walkway and undulated down the block. Harry stepped back into the tarnished sunlight and glared at the twosome making their way crosstown on the lower East Side.

"Let's hear it for the welcome wagon," he muttered half aloud. Another jumper. Another suicide. Hell. It was beginning to seem like the national sport. The latest polls showed an average of fifty jumps a week. All successful. Mostly kids, too. Dispirited. Despondent. Swan divers.

Harry trembled involuntarily. He took a small, rectangular communicator from the inside pocket of his artificial cotton blazer. "May ten. Six-thirty P.M. Possible jumper in the vicinity of Twenty-third and Second. Save me at least eight inches in the A.M. edition. Will trim graphs to fit. Acknowledge."

The communicator hummed for several seconds. A green light flashed at its top right corner. "Acknowledged, Porter," the gadget belched.

Harry stuck his hand inside his coat. He attempted to replace his official apron string, missed his pocket and dropped the communicator down into the torn lining of his jacket. Damn. In order to retrieve the thing later, he'd have to take off his coat and shake it upside down as inconspicuously as possible. It was a ritual he performed at least a dozen times a day. His clothes just didn't seem to wear very well.

He glanced at the moving sidewalk crawling before him. Illogical annoyance. The city of New York had installed a whole system of these wriggling buggers throughout Manhattan on the twenty-fifth anniversary of the city's bankruptcy. Now, only a year later, hardly any of them worked. And the few that did emitted noises that sounded somewhat like a large yak caught in a small kitchen garbage disposal unit.

Rumor had it that the city itself was sabotaging the pedways. When the local politicos came up with the idea, they had failed to take into account the general lack of agility possessed by the populace. This absence of dexterity soon manifested itself when people began attempting to get on or off the sidewalks. Within weeks of installation, it became clear that only the bravest and most athletic of souls would attempt to take leave of the walkway in the middle of a block. The risk of misjudging one's exit and slamming into an ill-placed store-front was too great. Places of business located mid-block, hence, lost quite a bit of revenue. A flurry of lawsuits against the city ensued.

Harry hated these automated walkways. They had a pecu-liar habit of assaulting his feet and stealing the soles of his shoes with alarming regularity. He had surrendered four pairs in the last eight months to these leather mashers and would be damned if he would sacrifice another.

Stepping over the sputtering sidewalk, Harry made it to the safety of the street. Following the moans of nearby sirens, he walked quickly on the firm macadam for two blocks. He didn't have to guess where the action was. On the corner of Lexington and Twenty-third, a crowd of nearly thirty people stood transfixed in front of a soot-encrusted brownstone, their collective gaze focused on the rooftop. Harry tilted his head skyward. Bathed in the glow of a dying afternoon, an emaci-ated male, no more than twenty years of age, teetered on the building's topmost ledge.

As if on cue, the crowd slowly, softly, began to chant. "Jump. Jump. Jump."

Harry clenched his fists and marched across the street towards the mob. The tableau conjured up eerie visions of a primitive native tribe staving off an angry god with the hasty offer of a human sacrifice.

A howling ambulance pulled up behind Harry, taking its place next to a pair of electric police cruisers. Harry began to shove his way through the sea of lowlifes. The fatalistic voyeurs huddled together, their voices growing stronger, their passion escalating with each additional spark of flesh-to-flesh contact within the ranks. By the time he reached the front of the mob, Porter was thoroughly winded. At age thirty-six, he was not as athletic as he once was . . . which was never all that limber to begin with. To this day, his idea of an action sport was checkers.

He pushed a lock of brown hair from his forehead and set his heavily lined face into a halfhearted mask of objective concentration. He wouldn't react emotionally. He would merely observe the facts. Commit them to memory. Analyze the situation. Dissect it. Stay out of it. File the story and forget about it.

To the right of the crowd, he noticed a gaggle of impassive technicians clutching porta-pack video units. The television team had beaten him to the scene once again. He sighed to himself. In this age of satellite communication, print journalism really didn't stand a chance.

"Aha!" snickered an idolized voice from behind him. "So the print media has sent its resident celebrity into the fray."

Harry turned to face the grinning visage of Marty Clay: newsman, game show host, and all around video king. A former actor, Marty possessed a mountain of good looks and a molehill of intellect, his swelled head being nature's way of filling a vacuum. He was, however, the acknowledged master of the meaningless news "tag," that final "twist" utterance that kept dull-witted viewers out in videoland hanging on through several deodorant commercials. Harry offered the curly-topped personality a sneer and, mentally, envisioned the prefabricated ending of tonight's tragedy-in-the-making.

"And so," Marty would intone solemnly into the all-seeing eye of the camera, "yet another senseless death has occurred in the streets of this great city. Police can offer no explanation as to the young victim's motivations. Friends and family can only shake their heads in shock and disbelief. Perhaps, only *we* can really understand what drove this innocent boy to a premature end. And perhaps, only *we*, by our everyday actions and kindnesses to those we consider social misfits, can prevent future (victim's name here) from imitating this horrid act. From Lexington and Twenty-third, this is Marty Clay saying 'May all your news be happy news.'"

Poetic. Solid. Utterly inane. Harry stared blankly at the blue-eyed commentator, still lost in thought. "How's the writer's cramp coming, Porter?" Marty smiled, flashing a Michelin guide to the wonderful world of dental caps.

Harry attempted to sidestep the video crew without incident. He posed no threat to their story, but his local status irritated the hell out of the television boys. Both his fame and the competition's jealousy stemmed from a space habitat scandal he had uncovered a few years ago, an event that would prove both his crowning achievement and Waterloo.

Clay dogged Harry's footsteps. "Is it true what I hear about guys who write longhand?"

Harry slowed his gait and exhaled. "May I ask you a personal question, Marty?"

"Well, sure, I suppose."

"Would you like a ruptured spleen?" Harry continued to walk.

Clay stepped in front of Porter. "Listen, pal. My crew got here first. I don't want you interfering with any of our shots, all right? I don't want to see your face on our tape tonight. This is *my* story. That kid up there is *my* meat. You lucked out once, but don't think that entitles you to mess with the big boys."

Harry pushed his way past the indoor-tanned Adonis. "I bet you guys just can't wait until those three-V units are perfected," he grunted. "You could all stand right under the poor slob as he fell. Imagine how your ratings would soar. You could send him splattering into the laps of millions of chip 'n' dip lovers."

"I don't deserve that!" Clay bellowed at Harry's back.

"You're right," Harry admitted, a warm glow of satisfaction beginning to spread throughout his chest. "You deserve a lot worse. Remind me to come back later for another cheap shot."

Harry glanced nervously above him. The boy still teetered on the ledge. He didn't have much time to act. He trotted up the six concrete steps leading to the building's shabby entranceway. A granite-faced patrolman barred his way. Porter flashed his holographic ID mechanically at the cop, more out of ceremony than necessity. "Can I get up there, Frank?"

The cop kept a tight rein on a laugh. "You gotta be kidding me."

"Come on, Frank, it's my job."

Patrolman McGann smiled sweetly at the reporter. "And my job is to keep you out."

"Give me a break, Frank. You don't want me to get japped by those video vampires do you?"

The red-haired policeman regarded Harry's well-worn visage in silence before turning his attention to the freshly made-up face of Marty Clay. He moved to the side in a single, casual step. "Just don't make any trouble, okay?"

Harry swung open the front door. "Do I ever butt into police business?"

The cop's eyes widened. "Your stunt with the midtown rapist almost had me back on foot patrol."

"Someone had to lure him into the open."

"But hiring a dozen transvestites?" McGann wheezed, still in obvious awe. "Harry! The publicity we got!"

"You caught the rapist, didn't you?"

"Sure. And got stuck with the bill for all that torn clothing."

"Be thankful they bought off the rack, Frank," Harry shrugged, closing the door and starting up the five flights of stairs. By the second landing, he was nearly winded. Why had he given up jogging? Gasping for the last three flights, he remembered why. He hated gasping.

At the top of the final landing, he came to a dented metal door, slightly ajar. He pressed his shoulder to its surface and, pushing it open gently, stepped out onto the roof.

Four figures stood atop the building, seemingly frozen in time. Surrounded by a fiery red sky and buffeted by a gentle, westernly breeze, the quartet glared at one another in silence. The two policemen and the priest confronting the boy didn't bother to take note of Harry's entrance.

The jumper stood poised on the edge of the rooftop. He was a clean-cut youth, perfectly normal in appearance, more than perfectly normal, in fact. His hair was impeccably styled: close-cropped, brown, and shiney. His skin was clear, unblemished. His eyes were alert although glassy. He was dressed in casual, but faultlessly arranged apparel, loose-fitting slacks and immaculate white tunic. He was every mother's son: the quintessential all-American boy. He'd tug at the nation's heartstrings on tonight's videocast, no doubt about it.

Harry squinted his eyes in the sunlight, noticing one last detail about the boy. He stifled a gasp. The boy had a bright red scar beneath his right eye. It was in the form of a crescent.

The police officer nearest the jumper, a round man in blue, purred softly. "At least give us a chance to talk to you about it," he pleaded. "Just step back from the ledge. Take two steps towards us. We won't move. We won't touch you. We won't do anything you don't want us to. We just want to discuss this, that's all."

The boy stared impassively over his shoulder at the man in uniform. A small dribble of water dripped from his right nostril. He wiped it away with the back of his hand. "There is nothing to talk about. It's far too late to talk. Nothing can save me now. I am an alien in this world . . . in *your* world."

The voice was wistful yet firm. The kid did not intend to go anywhere but down.

The priest, a Roman Catholic apparently trained at Hollywood High School, padded forward dramatically; a tall, angular fellow with short sandy hair, he had a cross the size of a space shuttle dangling from his neck. "My son," he intoned haughtily, "if you value your life one tenth as much as I value your soul—"

"My soul?" the boy laughed, his grin twisting into a sneer which contrasted with his otherwise angelic face. "My soul was lost long ago. We are all lost, father. We're trapped in a stagnant, putrefying world created by fear and hatred. We are aimless. We are leaderless. We move neither forward nor backward but in small, senseless circles. We never gain. Only lose. To die, father, is the only honorable way to put an end to this farce that you call *life!*"

Under normal circumstances, Harry would have interrupted the youth with a sudden burst of false optimism, any line of snappy patter to turn the angle of the conversation away from visions of doom and despair. The boy's melodramatic eloquence hit a nerve. In a demented way, the kid made sense. During the course of the past decade, the United States *had* tumbled into a state of total lethargy.

The economy was stable but there was no growth. The populace was seemingly content but their docility was spiritless, closer to stupor than satisfaction. President Sonny Walker never made waves but was, at best, a totally inept leader. Harry theorized that the only reason America's citizenry hadn't risen up in a massive show of displeasure was due to their tranquilized mood . . . in the literal sense.

The Drug Decriminalization Act of '97 had mass marketed bliss, making it possible for citizens to partake of the sedative of their choice in local tranx bars. Today, nearly the entire globe was in a state of cerebral stultification. Creativity was on the downswing. Advances in science and the arts had slowed to a trickle. Hell, America had even let its only space habitat, *Island One*, float into obscurity. It was now jointly run by The Peoples Republic of China and Walt Disney Enterprises.

Harry could understand why a sensitive, idealistic youth would feel trapped, futureless in such an environment. He had seen this sort of melodrama unfold countless times before. But that didn't make it right. Harry had lied to the patrolman below. He *was* going to butt in. Summoning up all his powers of fast-fading glibness, he would try to talk the kid out of all this nonsense.

Porter eyed the jumper. He noted the anxious positions of the cops and the priest. A nonchalant entrance on his part would not upset the delicate balance before him—as long as he kept his presence very-low-keyed. Accordingly, he placed one foot forward, the beginning of a leisurely, self-assured step. The jumper shot a look in Harry's direction, his face a portrait of total acquiesence. If the boy felt that Harry was a potential threat, he certainly didn't betray that fact.

So far, so good.

Harry began to bring up his other foot when something awful exploded inside him. A shocked look on his face, he froze; his foot still in midair. He began to sweat. The tips of his fingers turned cold, icey. His foot trembled in space.

Before he could cover any more distance on the housetop, he consciousness unexpectedly began to swim. Harry cursed himself silently as the nausea whirled within his stomach. His legs felt like lead weights, his arms as agile as tree limbs. Unable to move forward, he clumsily backed up against the roof's brick chimney. Damn it all. He would have been able to railroad that kid. He felt it intuitively. Not only would he have had been able to save the boy's life, but he could have gotten some answers for Bill Pratt as well. The source of Pratt's phobia, was less than fifteen feet away.

Fighting off unconsciousness, Harry Porter slid into a hapless sitting position on the tar-papered surface of the brownstone. His current weakened state could mean only one thing.

A peeper was on the way up the stairwell.

Peepers. Parapsychs. An elete group of psychotherapists well trained in the telepathic arts. Harry clutched his forehead, still extremely sensitive to their presence after an unrequested bout with a few PSI-laden shrinks three years ago.

Harry managed to focus his eyes in time to see a stately white-haired man dressed in a one-piece molded suit and sporting Coke bottle-bottom glasses emerge from the portal. The newcomer stood in front of the metal door as if he were laying claim to the contents of the lower half of Manhattan. "I am a parapsych," he announced somewhat regally.

Harry refrained from applause.

The peeper immediately attracted the attention of both the policemen and the man of the cloth. Harry wrapped his arms around his knees and sighed. He knew the routine from here on in. The peeper would lock onto the kid's thoughts, see what the obvious trouble was and, then, telepathically transmit his own counter-imagery in an attempt to short-circuit the death wish. Even though PSI-therapy had been in existence for over two decades, it was still a highly controversial practice still in its medical infancy. Sometimes the antisuicide riff worked splendidly. Sometimes it did more harm than good.

The parapsych marched to a point within ten feet of the boy. The jumper calmly turned his entire body around to face the man. The peeper locked his pale green orbs on the boy's perfectly relaxed face. "You don't want to die," he stated.

The jumper offered a lopsided leer for an answer.

Then, something began to happen. Harry felt it start as clearly as if he had heard a large twig snap. The buzzing in his head stopped abruptly. His sense of awareness was turned back "on."

The white-suited peeper's face drained of all color. His eyeballs shot upward, hugging his eyelids. Without warning, his torso arched back. Just as suddenly, it pitched forward, nearly slamming the peeper's forehead into the roof. The man remained doubled over for a split second before flailing backward a second time. The peeper shuddered into a series of such exaggerated convulsions, pitching back and forth like a metronome gone haywire. Harry watched in complete fascination as the psychiatrist's convulsions picked up speed. The parapsych rocked to and fro wildly, uttering not a word, not a sound, not a cry. The white-haired fellow gritted his teeth, his face now blood red from exertion. Finally, the peeper's glasses took leave of their perch and flew onto the rooftop, shattering upon impact. The tinkle of the plastic against the surface brought both the ominous silence and the fit to an end.

The man in white straightened suddenly and began to rip at his eyes with his hands. Face contorted, he let loose with a single, shrill, inhuman shriek. As the shout echoed throughout the nearby side streets, the disheveled psychiatrist collapsed in a heap on the housetop. Harry shuddered. No wonder Pratt felt this kid's presence. The young suicide-to-be turned his back on the physical wreck and once again faced the street below. The policemen and the priest rushed to the aid of the whimpering peeper, momentarily ignoring the boy.

Scrambling to his feet and abandoning all earlier plans of logic and cunning, Harry trusted his reflexes this time out. He dived across the roof just as the boy blithely stepped off the ledge. Sliding on his stomach toward the precipice, Harry managed to latch onto the jumper's left ankle with both hands.

The youth tumbled forward. Harry held onto the foot, effectively stopping the fall. The surprised jumper found himself dangling headfirst from the top of the brownstone, swinging in a pendulumlike motion over the ground six stories below. Harry tried to pull the boy's leg back onto the roof with no success. The jumper, not at all pleased with his current tentative statistic status, swung his right foot up toward the roof's edge, aiming a few desperate kicks in Harry's direction. One pass caught Porter square in the nose. Harry heard an unfortunate "pop" as the foot made contact with the tip of his snout. Within seconds, he felt warm fluid dribble out of his nostril and onto his lip. Hell. He had just put on a clean shirt, too. A second kick grazed his right hand, leaving a red patch of skin in its wake.

"Knock it off," Harry grimaced. "Are you crazy or something?"

A third kick whizzed by his ear.

"Look who I'm asking," he muttered.

The youth continued to sway back and forth in Harry's grip. The crowd below applauded, whistling and hooting with each spasmodic movement. "Let him go! Drop him!" they cheered.

Starved for entertainment tonight, Harry noted. Must signal the start of summer reruns. He tightened his fingers around the boy's leg. The jumper, still determined to accomplish his task, twisted and turned maniacally in response, emitting shrill, feline sounds as he did so. Harry swore softly as he felt his body begin its inevitable slide across the tar paper. His arms moved slowly over the edge of the roof. Then, his head. A quick twist executed by the jumper pulled the top portion of his chest over the precipice as well. Harry gaped at the crowd below. He wasn't crazy about the view.

He tried to slow his rate of movement by digging his knees into the rough surface of the roof. It was no use. With his two hands wrapped around the youth's ankle, he had no leverage with which to remain stationary. He was doomed to glide off the housetop.

The boy wriggled determinedly. "I don't want to disturb you guys," Harry barked at the three men somewhere behind him. "But in another couple of seconds, I'm going to be joining this kid on his trip to the sidewalk!"

The boy whinnied and slammed his back into the side of the brownstone.

The unexpected violence of this movement caused Harry's body to bolt forward. His waist tipped over the edge of the building. If he didn't let go of the jumper now, he would indeed embark on the cosmic belly whop. "Shit!" Harry hissed, still clinging to the youth's leg. "I'm not going to let you die, you asshole!"

Before his body could plunge into space, Harry felt the welcomed pressure of strong, masculine hands on the back of his knees. It must have been the two cops.

The men began to slowly pull Harry back onto the roof. It was delicate work. Harry's hands, arms, and back ached with each yank. Pressure tore at both ends of his body. His midsection slid onto the housetop. Harry exhaled, relieved to find something solid under him. His entire chest soon skimmed across the sandpapery surface. His arms began to make contact with the roof. His elbows throbbed with pain. His fingers were numb around the jumper's ankles.

Apparently sensing that survival was at hand, the boy began wriggling furiously. "In death there is freedom!" he bleated. He sent his body into a paroxysm of wild vibrations. Harry could maintain his grip no longer. "Goddamn you!" he hissed as the jumper kicked free of his hold.

Harry watched, speechless, as the youth cartwheeled to the street below, striking two windowsills on the way down. Harry shut his eyes before the kid struck bottom. An enthusiastic roar wafted upward from the crowd. A sick feeling enveloped Harry's insides.

Porter wobbled to his feet, his reddened hands quivering violently from the strain they had just experienced. "Thanks guys," he muttered to the two puffing policemen. He staggered towards the steel door, leaping over the still-prone peeper en route. He stumbled down the five flights of stairs, burst through the front door, and skidded to where the boy had landed.

A middle-aged man knelt next to the jumper, his hawkish countenance a welcome sight to Porter. Dr. Andrew Cade nodded perfunctorily as Harry teetered over the boy. "I tried to save him," Harry wheezed.

Cade was strictly business, tearing furiously at the boy's tunic, feeling his chest with his hands. "I should have known," he remarked casually, noting Harry's frantic state. "I was on my way home from the center when I saw two idiots dangling from a building. I should have said to myself then and there 'one of them has to be Porter....'"

"How is he?"

"How does he look."

Harry knelt across from the doctor. Cade did his best to avoid Porter's gaze. "You're still angry about your ambulance?" Harry huffed.

"You stole it."

"Borrowed it."

"Ruined it."

"But returned it," Harry pointed out.

"Minus an axle," Cade said. He relaxed his body, sitting on the back of his heels. His permanently arched eyebrows betrayed no hint of any emotion but disgust. "There's nothing that can be done for him, Porter. It's not your fault. You did the best you could under the circumstances."

"I always do," Harry said. He stared glumly at the boy's twisted body. The youth's blood-flecked lips began to twitch. His eyes opened suddenly, sending the crescent scar twitching. He stared heavenward with an incredible sense of purpose. "It's all over..." he rasped.

"He's trying to say something." Harry bent over the jumper's face.

The boy smiled faintly. "Over...soon...we'll bring... country to knees...."

The boy convulsed wildly. He coughed up a mound of thick, red liquid and solid matter. Harry pulled his head back automatically. The jumper trembled, his broken arms and legs twitching like fish suddenly tossed landward by the sea. Presently, all movement ceased. The boy shut his eyes. His battered form grew still.

Harry tipped backward, sitting on the roadway with an undignified thud. "Ever have one of those days?" he asked no one in particular.

"You have an uncanny knack for saying precisely the wrong thing at the wrong time," Cade said.

A patrolman walked to the scene and pointed an accusing finger at Harry. "Are you a doctor?"

"Uh-uh," Harry said. "Necrophiliac."

"*I* am the physician," Cade declared.

The patrolman turned his attention to Cade, ignoring Harry. "We have a sick man on the roof."

Cade stood and glowered down at Porter. "Duty calls."

"Guess I'll just wait here," Harry said.

Harry crossed his legs and watched the satisfied crowd dwindle in number. The show was over. They'd have to find some other source of diversion now. The ambulance backed slowly to the curbside. Two attendants emerged and sprayed the boy with a quick-drying body bag jell. Clamping handles around the upper torso and feet, they lifted the corpse, carried it to the back of the vehicle, and drove off. The mournful cry of sirens filled the air once again. The banshee had claimed another victim.

Harry gingerly got to his feet and walked back to the front steps of the brownstone. He sat down on the lowest one, the back of his neck a tangle of knotted muscles. Nerves. Sometimes he hated his life, his job, his tenuous connection with the human race in general. He chipped a blotch of crusted blood off the tip of his nose. His life. His job. The two seemed synonymous these days. Hell of a way to wind up.

Fifteen feet to Porter's left, Marty Clay stood, pontificating for the benefit of his mini-cam operator. "Perhaps only we, in our every day actions, can prevent further tragedies such as this one from occurring in the future. From Twenty-third Street and Lexington Avenue in Manhattan, this is Marty Clay saying 'May all your news be happy news!' Ciao."

Harry rubbed his eyes with the thumb and forefinger of his right hand. "Ciao?" He felt a sinus headache coming on.

Moments later, Cade emerged from the building, his thin lips pressed tightly together. Cade stood next to Porter, the personification of aristocratic medicine. His custom-tailored, three-piece suit was as unruffled as the man within. He watched the news team load their equipment back into their electric van with undisguised disdain. Harry couldn't be sure, but he thought he heard the word "cretins" drift through the breeze above his head.

"Anything I can use up there?" Porter asked, straightening his body.

"It's police business, Porter," Cade replied curtly, his tone more authoritative than usual.

"Oh come on, Andy. It was only an *axle!* One axle. Besides, you know I'll only wheedle it out of one of the guys at the station house anyway. Look. I promise I'll even spell your name right."

Cade gazed at the grit-laden cityscape before him with a look of bittersweet dismay on his face. In Porter's eyes he was a symbol of a wistful time long gone: a time of aristocracy, of romance, of easily definable castes. Harry scratched his head, briefly taking into account the difference between the two of them. Porter fancied himself a man of the people who, somewhere along the line, had lost any and all sociological groupings to latch onto. He was a solitary figure, by trade and by choice. He considered himself almost as out of step with the times as Cade professed to be. Yet, there they stood. Two men of two different worlds surrounded by death and confusion.

"Feel like having a drink?" Cade finally offered.

"You buying?"

"Don't I always?" Cade replied, walking past Harry. The doctor stepped on the moving walkway. In a moment of intense bravura, Harry did the same.

"What happened on the roof?" Cade asked, too nonchalantly. His squinted eyes betrayed more than a glimmer of interest.

"I was trying to get the kid on the ledge off the ledge when the peeper showed up. He tried to probe the boy."

"And then what happened?"

"The kid jumped."

Cade shook his head angrily. "Must I prod you for every detail? I assume since you used the word 'tried' that the parapsych's telepathic endeavor failed?"

"Since the boy jumped, I think that's a pretty safe assumption," Harry acknowledged. "The shrink made contact. I could feel it. He then took a stab at that perennial party favorite, the Saint Vitus's dance, and I decided to take a crack at saving the kid myself."

"Interesting," Cade murmured.

"What's interesting?" Cade rode the pedway in silence. Harry nearly stuck his face into Cade's. "Must I prod you for every detail?" he mimicked.

Cade was immersed in thought. His reply was slow in coming and monotoned. "That professional parapsych, that

highly trained master of mental resources, is now lying on
that rooftop babbling like a two year old. He appears to have
suffered a stroke of some kind during the mind-meet. What a
bizarre coincidence."

Harry began grinding his teeth, recalling both Bill Pratt's
uneasiness and the surrealistic scene on the housetop. "Too
bizarre a coincidence."

"HAPPY FEET MEAN A HAPPY DAY! USE THE AP-
PLE'S ZIP PEDWAY!" proclaimed a billboard situated next
to the motorized sidewalk.

"Suppose it wasn't a coincidence," Harry posed. "What
could have set the peeper off like that?"

Cade remained silent.

The two men traveled the length of a single city block
before Harry felt the bottom of his left shoe tear loose.

3

Porter disregarded the derelicts huddled in the storefronts
adjacent to the pedway. In his mind, he saw only the contorted face of the young jumper. The helplessness that had
welled up within him as the boy plummeted to the street
echoed continuously within his chest causing a tightness.
Harry, the hotshot reporter, had failed to keep the boy alive.
Harry, the hotshot reporter, had failed at quite a bit of late.

One marriage gone sour. One life on the slide. He wrote
news stories for a public that didn't read; the only challenge
was the intellectual process of the hunt. All he had left was
the hope that, somehow, in some strange way, a small bit of
good came from his seemingly endless legwork. Depending
on how much alcohol was in his system, Harry's outlook
swayed from outright pessimism to existential serenity.

Porter saw the familiar doorway loom closer and staggered
off the pedway. He limped inside Mecoy's bar with Andrew
Cade in tow. Despite their somewhat mutually antagonistic
banter, the two often frequented the establishment together;
both were the victims of professional hours that could, at
best, be called highly irregular.

"Back so soon?" the cherubic face behind the bar called as

Harry limped stiffly to his regular table in the back. "What happened to your foot?"

"I threw a shoe in the last furlong," Harry muttered. "They disqualified me from the race."

"I would have had you shot," the proprietor cackled.

"I hope I live long enough to become a burden to you," Harry said. "Two tequilas. Gold if you have it."

Harry and Cade sat at the left rear corner of the bar. Harry slumped down into his chair and shut his eyes, the faces of nameless dead and dying encountered over the years suddenly appearing. Every fiber of his body ached. Every muscle longed for the soothing touch of sleep. He blinked several times, exorcising his ghosts while focusing on the room before him. Mecoy's was what was commonly considered a "dive" by the young and stylish.

It was decidedly out of fashion. No chemicals were served on the premises. No drugs were offered on the menus, just plain, old-fashioned booze. The interior was, appropriately enough, a holdover from the twentieth century. Drab. Devoid of holographic go-go girls and gyrating jump-suited youths bumping, grinding or vomiting to the latest hedonistic hits.

Simple, synthesized ambient sound wafted through the air. Mecoy's sole nod to progress was the presence of a wall-sized video screen at the far left of the room where potted patrons could watch the latest sports event, variety extravaganza, or porn sit-com. The rest of the room was pre-2000. Old-fashioned high tech.

One of Mecoy's barhops placed two small plastic containers on the table. "Put it on his tab," Harry instructed. The two men drank in silence. "What's your problem?" Harry asked.

Cade narrowed his reptilian eyes into slits. "As usual, I haven't the faintest idea what you're talking about."

"You've been staring at the front door since we sat down. Expecting the Messiah?"

"For a mere print journalist, you're alarmingly perceptive," Cade answered. "Actually, I'm waiting for a companion of the opposite hormonal persuasion. I was on my way here when I saw the accident."

"That was no accident." Harry signaled for another drink.

Cade frowned. "It was suicide, Harry. Plain and simple. There are a lot of them."

"Too many."

"Granted. It's the zeitgeist we must contend with, the spirit of the times. We are living in an age of unrest."

"Bullshit." Harry allowed the full effect of the shot to take hold. His face was growing flushed. "It seems that we've entered the age of the erudite manic depressive. I've covered a dozen of these local leaps in the past three weeks, and it doesn't add up."

"People are tense, Porter. Jobs are scarce and leisure time isn't. There's not much room to move around in. There's an undercurrent of anxiety brewing. People under that kind of pressure crack. Honest."

"People don't crack en masse, Andy. There's something unnatural about it all. I've been covering crime and violence and generally repulsive goings-on for over ten years. I've never seen anything like this, Andy. Never. A flood of suicides. And they're all too damned calm. Too precise. They're not normal."

"Brilliant observation."

"I'm serious, Andy. There's something missing in these suicide scenerios. Something the public doesn't know about."

Cade attempted a smile but was quite unsuccessful. "So I've gathered from your stories. I've found them fascinating—to a degree."

Harry's mouth tried to twist itself into a responsive grin. It had no more luck than Cade's. "You and six other readers."

"May I surmise that there's trouble brewing on Fleet Street?"

"There is always trouble on Fleet Street," Harry smirked. "It's a veritable hotbed of ghetto activity." Porter's wisecrack was closer to the truth than he cared to think about. Since the arrival of the news satellite service ten years ago, the world of print journalism had fallen into a state of terminal decay—no pun intended. Most of the global public was perfectly content with receiving their hard news in handy, easy-to-read headline form via a subscription service. Newspapers weren't necessary when abbreviated items snatched from the four corners of the earth could be beamed into one's home, receivable on either video newscreens or the more old-fashioned, but exciting, print-out units.

Print journalism was almost dead.

In all of America only the *Herald-Times-News* remained; a newsprint cooperative made up of the skeletal remains of twenty-one major dailies. United, shakily, under a common logo and a ruptured sense of purpose, they presently catered to the whims of the rapidly dwindling number of eccentrics who preferred their news in detail as opposed to in absentia. Adding to the general hilarity of it all was the fact that almost no one was willing to financially support the *HTN*. During the course of the past two years, the paper had gone through three ownership changes. Rumor had it that a fourth was in the offing. Such was not the stuff morale was made of.

Harry slid out of his jacket and rested his chin on his hands. "Damn it, Andy. If things get any tougher, maybe I'll go out on a ledge myself."

"I doubt that," Cade said, tossing him a napkin. "It appears that you get nosebleeds from high places."

Harry stared at the blood-spattered shirt. "Damn. This is one of those chromotropic numbers. It's suppose to change color according to your mood."

"Congratulations. You are in a hemoglobin frame of mind."

Harry dabbed the shirt gently with the napkin. "If the job doesn't get me up on a ledge, this cleaning bill might."

"No, Porter. You're much too stubborn a pain-in-the-ass to just roll over and die."

Harry tossed the napkin down and slapped the table with the flat of his hand. The unexpected activity caused Cade to visibly shudder. "That's my point exactly!" Harry declared.

"Translation, please."

"During the past four months, the suicide rate in this country has almost quadrupled. Especially in the major cities: New York, Los Angeles, Chicago. Most of the victims have been kids, young people. All right, so this isn't the greatest of worlds right now. So what? Times have always been tough in one way or another. Things have always gone wrong. And it's always been the kids of this country who have stood up in the face of convention and said 'This stinks! Change it!'

"They haven't always been listened to at the time they were shouting, but that fact didn't shut them up. Why the sudden change? What's going on here? For no particular reason, we suddenly have a large segment of the youth population turning belly up. They're spiritless. Suicidal. That is not logical, Andy. It's just too weird for me to accept as being a natural phenomenon."

Cade loosed his tie. His arched eyebrows lowered somewhat, his face sagging under the weight of a long day and a short drink. "Harry. Despite your blatant eccentricities and inconsistencies, you are one of my closest associates. If I've imbibed enough, I would even go so far as to call you a friend. But you are crazy.

"You watch events unfold before your eyes, yet you refuse to *see* them for what they are if they go against your own personal value system. You talk about these suicides as if they're linked to some philosophical conspiracy. That, in a word, is balderdash—"

"Are you sure that's only one word?"

"All right. There has been a flurry of suicides of late. The television hucksters are referring to it as an epidemic—a suicide epidemic. As much as that label smacks of sensationalism, there may be a shred of truth to it. Medically, I know of dozens of cases of mass—"

"I don't buy that mass hysteria theory, Andy. And, if you used your head, you wouldn't either."

"Those years in charm school have paid off in spades, Porter."

"Will you listen to me for a minute?" Harry pleaded. "There's something more to all this than mere mass-hysteria-cum-depression. A friend of mind told me about that kid we saw tonight, said he'd been acting weird for a couple of days."

"How odd for a suicide."

"And how about his last words? 'We will bring this country to its knees?' What kind of last words are they for an ordinary jumper?"

"Nonsensical," Cade admitted through pursed lips. "But, while I bow to your obviously superior knowledge of the world of medicine, you might be surprised to know that dying people sometimes utter the darndest things—things that make no sense whatsoever. People on the way to meet their maker can chat about anything they so desire. Who's going to tell them to stop? They talk about God. They talk about lights at the end of tunnels, football games, sex, lack of sex, their pet dog Froofy."

"Whoever would name their dog Froofy deserves to die."

"Porter!"

"Okay. What about the peeper on the roof? What caused Mr. Wizard's mind to enter fudgeland?"

"I'm not sure. A stroke can cause temporary—"

"Now you're talking stroke. Right. Just another routine occurrence. A trained parashrink makes contact with a barely post-pubescent jumper, and his brain turns to farina. Perfectly natural. Happens all the time."

Cade ran a hand through his silver mane of hair. "I didn't say it was perfectly natural. But, until I have any reason to suspect otherwise . . ."

Harry pointed a finger at Cade. "Well, tomorrow I'm going to check in with that peeper. I know what kind of mental resources those men have. They worked me over for quite a while when I was in—therapy." Harry used this polite term when referring to his treatment in a state hospital following a rather inopportune breakdown. "I know that it would take one hell of a lot of force to make one of those cerebral citadels crack!"

"You can visit the peeper all you want, Porter, but unless you're planning on reading his mind, you're not going to learn too much. He's *out* there."

The faintest trace of a smile played across Harry's face. "Read his mind . . . not bad."

"And when you're finished doing that, I've got some tea leaves in a cup at home that could use some scrutiny."

"Be smug," Harry shrugged. "I'm telling you that there's something going on, something entirely perceptible, so obvious that we just aren't noticing it."

Cade pounded his container on the tabletop. "Your sense of self-righteousness is beginning to make me ill, Porter. Do you think you have the personal calamity market cornered? Do you have any idea of how many inexplicable, dire incidents occur in this city every day? It may surprise you to know that even *I* have my share of mysteries. Two of my finest new men disappeared from the burn unit today. Vanished. Walked out. Not a word. Not a note. Not a wave bye-bye. Nothing. I worked a double shift because of it."

Harry stared at the untouched lime and salt sitting next to his plastic vial, slightly intrigued. "Technicians?"

"Oh no," Cade said, raising his eyebrows to full mast. "That would be too simple. Technicians I could replace. These were two of my best syntheskin men, expert in both research and application. Two men of genius!"

Harry's interest waned. "What's the big deal? Syntheskin's been around for years?"

Cade began to fume. "Remind me to give you a lecture on the constant development and improvement of medical techniques throughout the ages and how any fluctuation in research and development, no matter how small, can cause intolerable delays. Right now, however, I will not go into the realm of speculative fiction and try to analyze why these two men would abandon their chosen field of endeavor. I will not bore you with any tall tales of espionage, high adventure or intergalactic intrigue because I wish to underscore the fact that people can actually behave illogically without any Machiavellian machinations hovering about in the background. Witness your own fluctuating behavior patterns should you need further proof."

Harry watched Cade slip from a simmer to a full boil before smiling. "Did anyone ever tell you you're beautiful when you're angry?"

Cade rolled his eyes in despair. "Why do I bother to talk to you? A genetic malfunction, perhaps?"

A warm flush made Harry's forehead throb. Drinking on an empty stomach again. He'd have to leave Mecoy's soon and file his story. Why break tradition and be totally sober when he wrote it? Hell. Some rewrite idiot would only transform it into a slice-of-life fable anyway. Porter glanced at his watch. It was slightly after eight. Pratt would show up soon and, more than likely, there'd be a lot more drinking done before the story would be hammered into shape. Maybe he could do it as a stream-of-consciousness feature. A news first.

Porter noticed Cade's bleary eyes suddenly focus. Both men turned to view a young woman with blazing red hair enter the bar. She was young, at least ten years Harry's junior and fifteen Cade's. Harry sighed to himself. Cade's taste in women astounded him. For the most part, they were all exceedingly beautiful but had IQs that you couldn't find with a searchlight. Harry shrugged to himself. Maybe he was simply jealous. The closest thing he'd had to a sexual experience lately was two weeks ago when his doctor told him to cough.

The woman bounded towards the table. Dressed in a spandex jump suit, she gave the impression that she had just purchased her outfit at an automobile spray paint emporium. As she bounced closer to the men, Harry suddenly noticed that the air in the bar was growing warm and uncomfortable.

"You're tardy, my dear," Cade offered, obviously not willing to work himself up into serious anger.

"I couldn't help it, Panda-bear," the woman said, slipping into the seat next to his.

"Panda-bear?" Harry exclaimed before lapsing back into silence under the weight of a withering glance from Cade.

"My meeting went on longer than I expected," the woman said.

"Meeting?" Cade repeated uncertainly.

"The Reverend Kapps' sermon at the Garden."

"Not Reverend Ashley Kapps!" Harry blurted.

Cade saw trouble coming and intuitively attempted to avoid it. "Harry, this is Mitzi Smythe-Lewis. Mitzi, this is Harry Porter. Please like each other. This is all I request. It has been an exceedingly trying day."

"Yes, Reverend Ashley Kapps," the woman replied evenly, ignoring Cade's entreaty. "And I'm not sure I like the tone of your voice."

Harry shrugged. "Excuse me. I was just surprised. I've never met anyone who has actually swal—participated in that stuff."

Cade placed his face in both hands. "I don't think I ask for so much out of life. I work hard. I *do* so look forward to what little leisure time I am able to purloin..."

"Stuff?" Mitzi gasped, her red lips beginning to form a distinct snarl. "The Reverend Kapps is a brilliant and spiritual man!"

"Not a bad bookkeeper, either," Harry replied. "He's made a few million dollars out of rewriting the Bible, changing the pronoun 'Him' to 'I,' hasn't he?"

"He is a man of the gods!" the woman stated. "He and his Church of the Ancient Astronauts are the sole beacons of sanity to be found in today's world. Where others offer apathy, he offers leadership. Where others offer despair, he offers hope."

"Where others offer freebies, he offers a bill," Harry added.

Mitzi prodded the bewildered Dr. Cade in the ribs with a taloned forefinger. "Are you going to let him talk about the Reverend Kapps like that?"

Cade slid his hands away from his face. He had seemingly aged a century or two. "Of course not, my dear. Harry. We are leaving this establishment right now. Ms. Smythe-Lewis and I are walking out that front door, and I trust you will not utter one more syllable about our most Reverend Klax—"

"Kapps," Harry corrected.

"Not another word," Cade reemphasized. "I will smile

politely now and take Ms. Smythe-Lewis by the arm. You will remain seated. Should you follow us, I will be forced to call upon the nearest local law enforcement agent and have you arrested for harrassment."

Harry turned to Mitzi. "Have you ever noticed how beautiful he is when he's angry?"

"Pervert!" the woman bellowed, leaping to her feet. Without waiting for her escort, she bounded toward the door.

"You can never leave things alone, can you Porter?" Cade complained, scrambling out of his chair.

Harry rested his chin on his palm. "It's the little things in life that give me the most pleasure."

Cade shambled towards the door. Harry slouched in his chair. "Hey, Panda-bear. Just in case there's a story in it, let me know if those missing technicians turn up, will you?"

"Researchers!" Cade yelled. "And, for the record Porter, I detest you!"

"Hey, Andy. What are their names?"

Cade burst out of the exitway. "Joseph Weiner and William Pratt!"

An explosion went off in Harry's chest, his stomach transformed into a bottomless pit of fear and confusion. Bill Pratt wouldn't quit a newly acquired job. There was no way that would happen...unless. Unless someone frightened him off. Could that someone have been the scar-faced jumper? Harry glanced at his watch. It was eight-thirty. He'd hang around Mecoy's for a while in case Bill decided to resurface. He had a bad feeling about all this.

Maybe Pratt's paranoia was spreading.

Harry picked up his empty vial. The barhop was staring at him uncertainly, glancing furtively at the still-fuming figure of Cade outside the bar. Harry motioned for a refill. "It's all right," he assured the boy, nodding toward the door. "We're brothers. Mom gave him less milk."

The barhop nodded dumbly and backed away from Harry's table. Harry settled into an uneasy drunk. Pratt's phone call echoed in his mind like a footstep on an empty stairwell. He had told Pratt to relax. Suppose Bill had been right about the assassin? A flood of activity hit the stairwell. No. That amounted to no sense whatsoever.

On the viewscreen across the bar, the evening news materialized. Porter grimaced but held his stand, watching with a vague sense of fascination. The American Pedestrian Association was still petitioning for louder audio tapes to be declared standard features in electric vehicles in order to give the nearly silent cars the sound of locomotion, thus alerting unsuspecting citizens on foot of their approaching presence.

A peaceful antinuclear march in protest of a cancelled meeting with the President dovetailed into a mercifully truncated report on the evening's young suicide. ("He must have dived one hundred feet, at least, Chris." "Cleared the sidewalk, too, Chet. Flew clear into the street." "How about that!"). Harry's presence on the roof had carefully been excised from the taped tale.

After several scintillating stories about lost dogs, minor acts of antisocial behavior, and a topless/bottomless bar closing because of prickley heat, a short feature on the Reverend Ashley Kapps flickered onto the screen.

Harry slid even further down into his chair, his chin nearly level with the table top. He watched the blue jump-suited preacher ascend the massive stage at New York's New Madison Square Garden. Jeez. Some people would put their faith in anybody or anything just to get through a day. Harry smiled to himself. He had once believed in people. He had once believed in ideals. Now, he believed he'd better leave Mecoy's before he got too inebriated to get any work done.

Cade had given him an idea about unlocking that peeper's mind. If the good psychotherapist wasn't able to bring the details concerning the jumper out into the open, then Harry would have to get inside the shrink's brain and drag out the information himself. Harry couldn't personally carry out such a complicated cerebral task, of course, but he knew just the man who could—for a price.

Maybe the peeper saw something in the kid's mind that could help explain the rash of suicides, or something that could have caused Bill Pratt to bolt.

Harry got to his feet. It was ten-thirty. He noticed the barhop staring at him again. Harry glanced at himself in the polished surface of the wall nearest him. His once clean and wrinkle-free suit was a wad of crazy quilt creases. His pants were soiled around the knees. The bottom of his tie was shredded and there were droplets of blood on the front of his shirt.

Harry limped out of the bar, feeling self-conscious under

the barhop's stare. "I'm going to a costume party, all right?"

Stepping into the night air, he gingerly hopped over the pedway.

He hailed a monocab. The vehicle pulled up alongside the curb. The joint-smoking cabbie inside glanced, first, at Harry and then at his watch. He refused to unlock the passenger door. "Sorry," he said. "Off duty. I'm on strike."

"Since when?" Harry demanded.

The cabbie consulted his computer dash for accuracy. "Forty-five seconds ago . . . right about the time you flagged me down."

"I thought it was the tramway that was on strike!"

"That was this afternoon," the hack replied. "They settled a couple of hours ago. Now, we're out."

"Jesus Christ!" Harry shouted, turning away from the burly driver. "What next?"

"Sanitation workers," the cabbie called after him. "Tomorrow morning."

Harry walked to the corner of the block. He stood on the curbside, staring at the smog-laden night sky. Hourly strikes. Suicide epidemics. Missing friends. Phony saviors. He was beginning to long for the good old days when he worked the mid-East beat and the most he had to worry about were acts of terrorism and the outbreak of war. He embarked on the long way back to his office, one shoe flapping sloppily on the cracked concrete of the New York City streets.

4

Porter stood in the middle of Times Square surrounded by outtakes from a Fellini Film revival. A slim woman in see-through slacks sidled up to him, uttering a romantic "wanna go roun' da solar system." Porter peered into her rose-colored eyes. She had the kind of charm that rubbed off with a damp cloth. He passed her by and walked towards his destination: a seedy tranx bar that featured uppers, downers, hallucinogens, and exotic dancers of both sexes on its menu.

He knew he'd find Saint-Crispen there.

Porter spotted him immediately after walking through the entranceway. In the back of the bar, a pair of dancers, one male and one female, danced a *Kamasutra* inspired bump and grind on a dimly laser-lit table. Saint-Crispen was their sole appreciator; the rest of his companions were resting face down on the heavily padded floor next to his table. Saint-Crispen had a high tolerance for drugs.

His unkempt hair and badly trimmed moustache quivered slightly in the breeze generated by the dancer's swaying limbs. He had small, ferret eyes and a face that showed he trusted no one. Saint-Crispen was a professional hustler. A curly-haired character frequently referred to by the local police as "slime-mold," he was well known as a street mercenary ever ready to turn a con with the highest bidder.

Saint-Crispen valued money and loyalty, in that order. This outlook on life made him an ideal contact for Harry. Saint-Crispen also was an orthodox coward. This latter personality quirk made him less than an ideal fellow to rely upon in a tight situation—as Harry had indeed found out on more than one occasion. In fact, Porter's left buttock still bore a cherry-colored laser scorch as a result of one of the Saint's speedier and more unexpected exits and one of Harry's slower, more bewildered ones.

Porter took the seat next to Saint-Crispen and, attempting to avoid staring directly into the crotch of the woman undulating above him, whispered into the Saint's ear for not more than a minute.

"You want to break into a hospital?!" Saint-Crispen snorted, nearly spilling the spoonful of white powder in his hand. "You're crazy!"

"I know," Harry replied, watching the Saint's orbs do a quick bit of mental calculating.

"Okay. It'll cost you one hundred dollars."

Harry leaned over the cheap plastic table illuminated by a lava light in its base. "How can you charge me one hundred dollars when I haven't even told you what it is I want you to do, yet?"

The Saint deposited the powder up his snout with a porcine intake of air. "You're right. It could cost you more."

Harry leaned back in his seat with a sigh. "Marion, what can I say?"

The Saint sputtered to life, looking to and fro, his rodent eyes dilating and his lower lip trembling beneath his badly kempt face fur. "I told you never to call me that!"

"Marion, Marion, Marion," Harry smiled, spreading both

hands, palms up, on the table before him. "You're truly a
mystery to me. Why, for instance, do you persist in denying
your given name?"

"Nobody knows that it's my name, and I want to keep it
that way, all right?"

"But, Marion, why on earth—"

"Because it's bad for my kind of business, that's why! You
know that and you promised never to mention it in public.
Who the hell is going to trust a guy to pull off some illegal
score in a back room when he had a name like, well, like, you
know—"

"Like Marion?"

"I told you not . . ."

Harry shrugged. "Forgive me, old buddy. I guess the talk
of all that money just addled my memory a bit."

The Saint ordered a tranx cocktail from a passing druggess.
"All right. All right. Forget the hundred dollars. We'll prorate
it when you tell me what the gig is. But this isn't going to be
a freebie. I have to make a living, you know? I'm not some
charitable institution. You want freebies, you go to the Sisters
of Mercy."

Harry watched the bosomy druggess bring two yellow pills
and a cup of fruit juice to Saint-Crispen. He felt uncomfortable in the midst of this jump-suited and tunic-littered night
spot, Fantasyland. It was one of the first tranx joints to have
opened in Manhattan way back when. At the time, legal drug
intake was still in its experimental stage, so the club was
deliberately constructed in an admittedly seedy area of town
in order to avoid adverse public reaction. Before long, however, it was the most popular night spot in town. Soon, other
tranx joints were springing up all over the city. Fantasyland's
lustre faded, somewhat, as the tranx club movement blossomed.
The years had made the area even seedier.

Surrounded by weird holographic and laser-light effects,
Harry felt like he was sitting in someone's sweat-drenched
phantasm. The glistening bodies meshing pelvic regions above
his head didn't put him any more at ease, either. Jiggling
anatomies danced and collapsed around him on the padded
floors. The druggess leaned over the table. "Anything for you,
hon?"

Harry hated to pop pills. It seemed unnatural. He preferred a good, solid drink. Alcohol, of course, was prohibited

in a drug club. Americans might be pleasure oriented but they weren't totally suicidal... yet.

"Oh, just a little, um, codeine for me," Harry said, embarrassed.

"Codeine?" the tranx waitress replied, her voice barely hiding her amusement.

"Just a tad, yeah."

"Okay," she shrugged, walking toward the bar. "We need a Shirley Temple at table eighteen."

Harry slouched in his chair.

The Saint popped his pills. "What's the scam?"

"No big deal," Harry stated. "I have to break into the university hospital tonight to visit a patient after visiting hours. The guy witnessed a death and may have some information that could prove vital to a piece I'm working up. I've already made arrangements to get inside. We use my press pass and a fake one I've had printed up for you to gain access to the front entrance. I'm roaming their halls a few times a week on routine, police blotter stuff anyhow, so we really shouldn't be noticed. Besides, their security stinks.

"When we get inside, we take the freight lift to the second floor. There will be two male nurse outfits waiting for us in the linen closet off the main corridor."

"How'd they get there?"

"I know a couple of female nurses."

The Saint's eyes began to cross slightly. "Whew. This stuff packs a whallop. Pretty smooth setup you have there, Harry-boy. What do you need me for? Sounds like everything is taken care of."

"Well, it's this particular patient I have to see, the one I want to question—"

"That's small potatoes, my man. Mini-spud city."

"Well, this guy had some sort of breakdown while watching a jumper. So, it may be a little tough for *me* to communicate with him—verbally."

"So? Who do I look like, the president of the Berlitz School? I still don't see why I—" The Saint stopped mid-sentence, putting two and two together and not at all caring for the final tally. "Oh no. Count me out."

"Yeah," Harry nodded, "the guy's a peeper."

"No way, José. You want to communicate with a twisted peeper? You handle it."

"He's sedated."

"Fine. The guy's under. You handle it."

"I can't."

"Yeah? Well, neither can I."

"Oh, come on, Saint-Crispen, you can con everyone else around here into thinking you're just another street-wise huckster, but I know your background."

"Yeah? And I know yours. You're sensitive to these creeps. You absorb their telepathic punches like a pansy palooka. You don't need me in there to help!"

"I can only pick up what they're sending out. And if this parashrink isn't broadcasting, I can't do any receiving."

"Forget it, Harry," the Saint fumed. "You can pick up the tab and say adios to the Saint, here."

"Marion!" Harry exclaimed as the druggess dropped off his codeine. "No," she corrected. "Agnes."

She shot Saint-Crispen a quizzical look before walking away. The Saint held his ground. "It won't work, Harry-boy. You can call me Lou-Anne the whole night and I wouldn't do it. Not me. Forget it. Fat chance. Uh-uh."

Porter remained silent.

"Do you know what I'd be exposing myself to?" Saint-Crispen continued. "This guy had a breakdown? He's lying there sedated? JESUS! Do you know what the AMA does to peepers when their mental machinery moves into the Twilight Zone reality section of the paper? They give them a quick laser-lobe. They short-circuit the ol' fine tuning. And do you know why they fuzz them out? BECAUSE A PEEPER GONE CRACKERS IS FUCKING DANGEROUS!"

"I figured," Harry shrugged.

"You figured? Do you know how powerful PSI power can be? Telepathy. Telekinesis. Precognition. In the right hands, this is all great stuff, you know? But give PSI powers to some lameass and you have real problems, pal, if you catch my drift. Give 'em to a candidate for the laughing academy, and you really get some chuckles. Tables tossed. Chairs chucked. Minds in the immediate vicinity melted. And this mind is the only one I've got. So, as for my participation in your little picnic, erase the thought from your head, babycakes."

Harry ignored Saint-Crispen's emotionalism. "I wasn't aware that any peepers had cracked before."

"It's not public knowledge," Saint-Crispen said sullenly.

"But I still have a couple of sources at Rhine. They keep me informed."

"That's exactly why you're the perfect man for the job. You're knowledgeable in this area. You trained at the institute."

"I was a guinea pig. There's a difference. Besides, you can't connect me with those experiments."

"I have your files."

"Blackmail's illegal."

"Effective, too."

"Let's look at this situation objectively, Harry. This is *your* problem, "your" being the key word in that statement, denoting possession of a problem on the side of this table unaffiliated with yours truly. Since I'm not the curious type, it can stay on your side of the net."

"You'd be doing your country a great service! Perhaps stopping a suicide epidemic!"

"Can't hear you. Check, please."

"You could be saving a lot of innocent lives."

"Nobody's *that* innocent. Oh, miss?"

"You'd be earning two hundred dollars."

"Three hundred."

"Two-fifty."

"Four."

Harry blinked in astonishment. "Four?" The druggess handed the Saint the check. "Nothing personal, Harry, but it's a jungle out there. I have to plan for the future. In my line of work you don't have medical plans, workman's compensation and all that stuff."

Harry scooped up the check before the Saint had a chance to inflate the figure and split the extra cash with Agnes. "You're a thief."

"And a damned good one," the Saint said, pointing to his smiling mouth. "I specialize in high-paying, low-risk jobs these days, Harry. These choppers cost me three grand. I have no intention of walking away from a gig looking like a jack-o'-lantern. Not even for you."

"The peeper is going to be sedated."

"The security guards won't be."

"I told you everything was taken care of," Harry replied, paying the check.

"You told me that when we were up in Montreal, too. I wound up getting two fingers sprained."

"Hey, I'm the one who wound up eating six feet of shag rug."

"It was your own fault."

"My fault? I almost got my ass scorched to cinders when you ran off."

"I didn't run off," Saint-Crispen said, heading for the door. "I simply tried a diversionary tactic."

"Yeah. Running off."

"I did not."

"You did too," Harry said, following the Saint.

The Saint held the door open for Harry. "Didn't."

Harry stepped out into the night air. "Did."

Saint-Crispen let the door swing closed and headed for the sidewalk. "Didn't."

Fifteen minutes later, the two men walked up the front steps of New York University Medical Center, located but a few blocks from the suicide site. "Did," Harry mumbled fishing into his pocket for his press ID. He flashed it at the security guard at the front door. Saint-Crispen held up his bogus badge with a smile, following Harry into the lobby.

According to plan, Porter and Saint-Crispen entered a service elevator, emerged on the second floor, and donned two white jump suits left (for a considerable fee) in an empty linen closet.

Harry emerged from the closet first. "All right. It's clear."

The Saint stumbled into the hallway, his tousled hair and walrus moustache contrasting sharply with the neatness of the white uniform. Harry led Saint-Crispen down the alabaster corridor. "Two-oh-one, two-oh-three, two-oh-five," he read, passing the doorways of the second floor rooms. "Here we are. Joanie said he was in room two-oh-seven."

Harry's head began to throb. "On the button. They may have sedated this guy, but he sure as hell is still cerebrating up a storm." He rubbed his eyes with the palms of his hands. The pain was most intense above his lids, his eyebrows feeling as though there were large needles jabbing into them. The nape of his neck, too, was beginning to ache. He was suddenly very glad he had ordered codeine.

"Are you okay, man?" the Saint asked.

"Fine." Harry evoked a false air of calm and eased open the door to room 207. The two men entered the room cautiously. The chamber was dark. Harry lit a small wall light near the door. He walked to the front of the bed and removed the computer-chart hanging there. He hit the "on" switch. A small, green readout appeared on the flat, black screen. "Our boy's name is Hardy Flowers."

"You're kidding," the Saint smirked. "Can you imagine the abuse he must have taken when he was a kid? Man, I can empathize."

"Age: fifty-two."

"That makes him one of the original peepers, I guess," Saint-Crispen theorized, doing a quick bit of math. "Makes him around twenty-two when the program first started. Wonder why such a big gun got mixed up with a nobody jumper? Just a kid, you said, right?"

"Right."

"These guys can make millions in private practice, Harry. Some of 'em have even become in-house shrinks for major corporations. Big bucks."

"Educated at Rhine, then the Steckler School." Harry glanced at the sleeping figure in the bed. "You're onto something, Saint. Our Doctor Flowers does seem to be too important to be messing around with an ordinary suicide— unless he was just passing by." He returned to the chart. "His medical history seems pretty routine. It doesn't look like the folks here know just why his head short-circuited as yet, though."

"Great," the Saint muttered. "Not only am I stepping into numb-numb land with this guy, I'm going without a road map."

"I just want you to take a short peek inside."

"What is it that I'm looking for?"

"Anything strange."

"Great." The Saint moved next to the white-haired patient's pillow. He leaned over the parapsych's forehead. Straightening suddenly, he faced Harry. "This is really important to you, isn't it?"

"You know it is."

"Right. It'll cost you five hundred."

Harry clenched his fists. "You agreed on four."

"I forgot to include expenses."

"What kind of expenses are going to cost me an extra hundred dollars?"

The Saint leaned over the patient again. "Aspirin, man. This guy is going to pack quite a punch."

Harry sighed and leaned against the door. "Okay. Five

hundred. Just peep him a bit, okay? Find out what set him off, what he saw in that suicide's mind."

"Is that all? Are you sure you don't know what brand toothjell he uses?" The Saint placed his hands on the parapsych's forehead. "I'm not a professional, you know. I don't have the real gift. The most I can do is pry open a small corner of what's up there. I just hope I remember how to do this right."

Saint-Crispen stood above the bed, swaying gently in the weak glow of the wall light. He furrowed his brow over the sleeping Flowers. The throbbing in Harry's head increased in intensity. The Saint clutched the peeper's forehead. The patient's right foot began to twitch. Then, his left. Harry watched in fascination as the electronic monitoring unit above the patient's headboard fluttered into a state of frantic action, the various lines and dots beginning to pulsate madly.

"Is it working?" Harry hissed.

Saint-Crispen didn't speak. His face was drenched with perspiration. Flowers' body began to thrash frantically in the bed, a being reliving a horrible dream. Saint-Crispen dug his fingers into the man's head, giving Harry the impression that this action reflected a desire to hang on for dear life as opposed to an attempt at increasing the cerebral bond between the two.

Flower's nightmare suddenly exploded into reality.

The Saint screamed. He released his grip on the patient and sailed across the room, over the bed and into the wall next to Harry like a pellet discharged from a slingshot. Harry rushed to Saint-Crispen's aid. "What happened."

"Let's get the hell out of here," Saint-Crispen wheezed. "Make tracks, Harry-boy!"

The wall unit above the bed went berserk, lighting up in a rainbow of pulsating colors.

The chair next to Flowers' bed broke loose from the moorings imposed by gravity. It shot straight up and smashed into the ceiling, splintering into a half-dozen plastic shreds.

A vase of flowers exploded.

The bed containing the parashrink assumed a life force of its own. It rumbled slowly back and forth in an arc across the surface of the floor. Harry could have sworn the bed was zeroing in on him and Saint-Crispen, huddled by the door.

"He's after us now," the Saint whispered. "No doubt about it. Open the goddamn door. Fast!"

"You're overreacting," Harry replied, seconds before the bed rushed toward them.

Quickly reconsidering his philosophical stance, Harry tore the door open. Saint-Crispen dived over him. Harry rolled out into the hall just as the bed slammed into the threshold, wedging the door shut with a bang. The sound of shattering plastic reverberated throughout the nearly abandoned corridor as the bottles hanging from the i-v racks hurled themselves against the floor.

Saint-Crispen remained face down on the hallway floor. "Jesus Christ, Harry! I could have been killed in there. He could have charbroiled my brain!"

"Will you be quiet?" Harry admonished, picking his companion up off the linoleum. "We're still trespassing on hospital grounds. Straighten up and act like a nurse."

From inside the room, Harry heard the bed back away from the portal. The commotion inside seemed to slacken off. Slowly, Harry's head stopped throbbing. "I think he's gone back under."

A wide-eyed doctor ran down the hallway? "What's the commotion?" the doctor demanded.

"Patient in two-oh-seven," Harry replied in a clipped, militaristic tone. "Having a seizure of some sort."

"I'll take care of him," the doctor said, pushing past Harry and Saint-Crispen. He entered the room and shut the door behind him. There was silence from within. Harry and Saint-Crispen waited outside until the doctor emerged moments later. "He'll be fine, now," the white-smocked samaritan said reassuringly. He blinked his heavy-lidded eyes three times in rapid succession. "He needs a good deal of rest. You'd better leave him alone for a while."

With that, the doctor turned on his heel and hurried down the hall. Porter stood outside the door, a frown on his face. "Let's split," the Saint advised.

"Let's check Flowers first." Harry said.

"What for? We got what we came for! I got the picture. Now, let's get out of here. Is there a law against impersonating a nurse?"

"I have a bad feeling about this," Harry said. He opened the door to room 207 and flicked on the wall light to the right of the entrance.

"Don't be so suspicious. The doc shut him up, right?"

"That's one way of putting it," Harry said, hoarsely. Saint-

Crispen peeked into the room over Porter's shoulder and gagged. On the bed inside the room was the body of Dr. Hardy Flowers, still smoldering from where the laser had begun its swift arc in his chest. Where his face had been was a mound of molten flesh. His forehead was nothing more than a gaping hole, dripping ooze.

Harry slammed the door. "And we just let the son of a bitch walk out of here!"

"Let's not get into a guilt trip, Harry-boy," Saint-Crispen babbled. "We can discuss the karmatic implications of this later. Right now, let's take off. I don't want to be around when someone discovers the barbecue in there. I don't know about impersonating nurses but I *know* there's a law covering the topic of murder."

"I bow to your superior logic," Harry said, running for the linen closet.

The two men slipped out of their white jump suits in the darkened room. "Someone might remember our being in the building and question us casually tomorrow," Harry said. "Don't panic. We didn't see anything. I'll get Joanie to find a friend who'll swear we were on a different floor."

Porter discarded the suit in a laundry chute, thankful that hospital employees were grossly underpaid. "Well," he whispered. "Let's have it."

"Have what?" Saint-Crispen answered innocently.

"What you found out in there. What was Flowers thinking about?"

"Oh, you know. This and that."

Porter's face grew crimson. "Come on, Saint-Crispen. What was it he saw up on that roof?"

Saint-Crispen crinkled his nose. "It'll cost you."

"I'm paying you five already."

"Yeah. But we're talking about long term mental trauma here. That's an extra hundred in anyone's book."

"I swear, Marion, you're going to need at least that much to get your bones reset."

"All right." The Saint leaned against a metal shelving unit in the shadows and shuddered. "It was wig city, Harry. Really bizarro stuff. It even shook *me*. There were a whole bunch of images flashing at once. It was like watching a schizoid TV set. Kids were swan diving off rooftops. It was like a tape loop or something. The same action, over and over again. Atom bombs were going off, too. Flames and smoke were everywhere. Bodies rotted in the streets. Real Dante stuff. And all these people were marching around, too. Weird. Faceless: no eyes, no noses, no mouths, no—nothing. They were sort of blurred out, soft images. The strongest image was pretty clear, though. It was the President."

"Walker?"

"Yup. The Prez of the U.S. of A. himself. He was standing there like an idiot with all these blank-o's surrounding him. They were moving towards him like zombie marathon runners, clawing at his head and stuff."

"Then what?"

"I don't know, man. Flowers in there started dancing the telekinetic twist. He shut off the video portion of the show pronto. That's when the 'please stand by' sign tossed me across the room. I tell you, Harry, I could see why that guy went mental. All those images happening at once made no sense."

Saint-Crispen shook his head slowly. "I don't know who's going to do it, Harry, but someone's going to *off* the prez. That much was clear to me. They're going to punch his ticket."

"Someone's going to assassinate Walker?"

Saint-Crispen moved from the shelves to the doorway. Turning the latch with a quick click, he stepped into the hall. "Yeah. Don't you understand English? Walker's going to be nailed, man. And soon. Plus there's one slambang of a nuke-out involved. World War Two Plus Uno."

"Nuclear war," Harry mumbled, following Saint-Crispen out of the room. How did the jumper figure into all of this? And how did Pratt fit in with the jumper?

"Nuclear something," the Saint continued. "Whatever it is isn't going to be very healthy. Ergo, I'm not going to get involved in it."

The two men found a stairway leading to the first floor. "You're already involved," Harry sighed.

"What do you mean?"

"Whoever it was that killed Flowers got a very good look at us. Eventually, someone is going to figure out who we are."

"Someone being the Prez's future assassins?"

"Could be."

The two men nodded to the guard as they left the hospital.

"Goddamn it! You've done it to me again," Saint-Crispen whispered. "The essence of my successful position in society lies in keeping a very low profile, man."

"I'm sorry."

"You're sorry?" the Saint exclaimed. "I'm going to be put on a professional hit man's pick-to-click list and you're just sorry?"

"Well," Harry theorized. "Maybe we're overreacting. Maybe you're interpreting what you peeped incorrectly. Did you actually see the President die in this vision?"

"No."

"And you didn't actually see a nuclear war take place."

"Not really."

"Okay. Then all we really have is some sort of disaster, a group of suicides and the President being surrounded by a mob of folks without faces. They could be snippets of ideas Flowers had come up with on different occasions. They could be caused by the stroke as opposed to being the cause *of* the stroke—or breakdown. That's an objective view. Your interpretation, being subjective, could be way off base."

"Uh-uh. I could *feel* what was going on," the Saint insisted. "It's hard to describe it to a layman, but I could sense it. I didn't have to have it spelled out for me in large type."

"Fine. Then, if your interpretation is correct, we're in big trouble."

"Then again," Saint-Crispen continued. "I could have totally misread the peeper's signal. You know, misinterpreted the old cerebral shorthand. I could be dead wrong, right?"

The two men walked over to a monobus stand. "C'mon," Harry said wearily. "I'll buy you dinner at Mecoy's."

Saint-Crispen was horrified. "You've got to be kidding. You're going to get me executed, cut down in my prime, and you offer me dinner in that dive? Hell, the busboys there wear flea collars!"

A bus pulled in and the two men climbed onboard. "You're exaggerating." The vehicle lurched along a single track.

"Am not," Saint-Crispen said, staring out the window.

"Are too," Harry replied, wondering how easy it would be for a gunman with a scope rifle to pick them off before the next stop. He briefly considered what it would be like to die that way without knowing the reason why.

II

"Society is a hospital of incurables."
Ralph Waldo Emerson

1

The monobus sputtered to a stop across the street from Harry's apartment building. Harry tumbled out the back door, a victim of another night without much sleep. He noted that the city's bus service was actually improving. He was arriving home only an hour later than he had intended. He glanced at his watch. It was after two A.M.

He had stopped at Bill Pratt's hotel en route only to find that Bill had checked out that afternoon. The room had been reoccupied by evening. Bill had paid for the room in cash. There was no forwarding address or credit card tab to trace. Harry had left the hotel wondering exactly what it was that could have frightened Pratt out of not only a job but a city as well. They had seen just about everything during the war. At least Harry thought they had.

Porter hesitated in front of the entranceway to the building, allowing the bus to clatter off behind him. He slowly approached the doorway, peering through its glass facade at the lobby within. Luck seemed to be on his side. An elevator sat, door opened, in the rear of the vestibule. At least he wouldn't have to wait for a car. He mentally gauged the amount of time it would take him to sprint from the entranceway to the elevator. This run for freedom was actually a daily ceremony, spurred on by Harry's intense desire to avoid the edifice's owner-landlord, Dr. Jorge. Dr. Jorge: the ageless, tireless, omnipresent one.

Since Harry's building had fewer than 200 units, it did not fall under New York State's rent-stabilization laws. In short, that meant that its landlord could (and, more often than not, would) raise the rent of its tenants sky-high at the end of each lease. Apartment leases these days were generally monthly affairs with the newer, luxury habs actually offering *weekly* stays of execution.

Harry theorized that Jorge would have offered him an hourly lease if he thought he could get away with it. Harry's problems with his landlord began shortly after his return to Earth from the American space habitat, *Island One*. He had penned a fulsome story detailing the corruption that permeated the colony. The article garnered him a lot of unnecessary public acclaim but not too much necessary cash—a fact which seemed to elude Jorge.

Suspecting that Harry was wallowing in riches, Jorge had whittled his lease time from six months to three months to one month. "Vat's a leetle cash to you," Jorge would chuckle knowingly at the renewal of each four-week contract, upping the rent with each ceremonious signing. Harry knew what a little cash meant to him. A lot.

He also knew that it meant very little to Jorge, taking into account the fact that Jorge owned and operated a chic psychiatric spa on the building's three uppermost floors. The spa offered a smorgasbord of deeply profound delights to wealthy whackos, ranging from nude Freudian analysis and primal therapy to dominance and submission group sessions. On weekends, old Ingmar Bergman and Woody Allen films were screened for free as part of an ongoing Remedial Guilt retrospective.

Jorge loved to corner Harry at every possible opportunity and wheedle more money out of him. Harry, in turn, loved to avoid such encounters as much as humanly possible. Hence, the daily sprint.

Harry eased open the front door, disregarding the lateness of the hour, and peered to the left and the right. He caught a glimpse of himself in the hallway mirror. He looked tired as hell. He needed a shave and his nose sported a lovely blue lump on its tip from its impromptu buss with the flat of the suicide's shoe. Harry squinted his eyes. The elevator door was still open. Lady luck was still in his corner. He took a deep breath and conjuring up the last remaining strength in his tired legs, quickly jogged across the thickly carpeted lobby.

Nearly laughing out loud with glee, he made it through the area unmolested. Jumping over an ashtray, he vaulted into the awaiting elevator. Once inside, he was confronted by the white-haired, diminutive, and ever-smiling Dr. Jorge.

"Meester Porter," the United European Psychological Institution's gift to humanity chortled. "An unexpected pleasure to be meetink you dis late."

Harry leaned against the wall and heaved a sigh. He should have known, really. In his building, there was *always* a five-minute wait for an elevator. Damn. He wished that Jorge had installed those clear, cylindrical jobs. He would have spotted him and taken the back stairway.

"Why, Dr. Jorge," he drawled. "What an unparalleled delight."

"Working late, eh?" Jorge winked knowingly. "Overtime pay, I suppose." He twisted his wrinkled features into a caricature of mirth. If Moses had seen Jorge's face, there would have been another commandment.

Harry pushed the button for the fourth floor. "Oh sure," he smiled. "I should be able to get that yacht I've been saving for."

"Yes?"

"Sure. Of course, I might not be able to fit the soap in the tub at the same time, but one has to make sacrifices."

"Yah. Yah. Yah," the man agreed. "Speaking of vich. Your lease is up at de end of dis monk."

"This monk, eh?" Harry said, holding his smile. "Time flies when you're having fun."

"Of course, I vill be raiskink your rent just a vee bit."

"How much of a vee?"

"Shall ve say 40%?"

Harry reminded himself that it was impossible to play the human jawbone like a cymbal and stifled his initial reaction. There was nothing he could do. Apartments were as plentiful as dodos in all of the boroughs except for the high crime districts. There, the landlords used pistols to separate you from your money. Somehow, that struck Harry as being a more honest approach. The elevator came to a stop. "Well, much as I'd love to chat with you, doc, here's my stop."

"You von't forget the extra money?"

"I guarantee you that I'll be thinking about it all night," Harry said, his smile beginning to slide. "Dreaming about it for several nights to come, probably."

"Vell," Jorge smiled as Harry alighted from the car. "Have a goot evening and remember the words of William Lowndes: 'Take care of the pence, and the poundz vill take care of demselves!'"

Harry waited until the door had almost closed on the old gentleman before offering: "And don't forget Emerson who said: 'Without a rich heart, wealth is an ugly beggar.'"

Harry watched the old man's face drop into stoic prune position as the door shimmied shut. "Gotcha, you greedy bastard."

He walked up to his door and placed his palm in the metal hand print beneath the doorknob. "Come in, Harry," Machine said, the door to his abode opening simultaneously.

"Darling, are the drinks ready? I've had a terrible day at the office." Harry tossed his suit jacket onto the floor, his sarcastic lilt aimed just as much at himself as it was at his home computer system.

"There is a certain mocking tonality in your voice that suggests agitation," Machine replied. "Perhaps it's best if you avoid consuming alcoholic beverages at this point. We both realize that you have a very human tendency to become somewhat morose after imbibing while in such an emotionally volatile state. It is totally counterproductive and quite—"

"There's a scrap metal drive taking place next week," Harry smiled, walking up to the bar/counter in his small kitchen. "Want to be part of it?"

"Will that be tequila? Straight up?" Machine intoned from the kitchen extension speaker.

"Uh-huh." As much as Harry hated to admit it, he was almost fond of his computer unit. He had shared a somewhat solitary existence with the electronic baby-sitter for nearly three years. Their meeting was the result of a fairly dire chain of events.

After watching a murder suspect deep fry his face off with a laser pistol not five feet from where Porter stood, Harry had retreated into a well-earned nervous breakdown. His job was on the skids. His wife was in the process of running off with the physical and mental equivalent of an oak tree. Harry found himself in a somewhat fragile state.

Once released from the hospital, Harry had returned to his apartment. His doctors had thought it best that Porter not be allowed to stew in his own misanthropic juices, however, so they had installed a home computer system that transformed his domicile into a fully automated abode, ruled by an ever-present female voice. The voice routine was an effort to induce Harry into relaxing and treating the computer as a fellow human.

Harry hadn't been fooled, however, and, out of sheer malice, had dubbed his machine "Machine," a moniker that served as a constant reminder that this highly sophisticated hunk of printed circuitry was no substitute for flesh and blood. Still, at two in the morning, with his body aching and his eyes fluttering with the need of an extended sleep period, it was nice to have some *thing* around to talk to.

A plastic container filled with liquor slid out from Machine's kitchen wall dispenser. "Here's listening to you," Harry said, gulping it down. He walked into the living room. "How about a bit of music? Mozart: Concerto in F Major for Three Pianos, K. 242."

Machine noted the request. "Are you sure you wouldn't prefer the Concerto in E-Flat for Two Pianos, K. 365? It's the more popular of the two pieces."

"Since when have I cared about popularity?"

"Valid point."

Harry sat in the living room before his wall-sized viewing screen. The rumblings of Mozart's concerto soon filled the room. Machine, of course, was right. The piece was generally considered highly conventional, but at its initial performance, Mozart decided to give the audience a thrill and improvise a full sonata at the piano. Feisty sonofabitch.

Now, why had Harry remembered all that?

Harry fostered a deep admiration for the composer, a uniquely obsessed fellow who didn't achieve true recognition until after his death. When Porter was tired and a bit drunk, as was now the case, he enjoyed comparing himself to every buffalo of an individual he had ever vaguely admired. Men out of step with the times.

Listening to Mozart gave him the necessary shot of adrenalin needed to get through the night. More importantly, it also annoyed the holy hell out of his upstairs neighbor, Lance Willis, a male dancer at a gay tranx bar who apparently only boogied with partners the size of major asteroids till the wee hours of the morning on weekends. Since weekends were slow news periods and, thus, Harry's only real chance to sleep, Willis' cacophonous concept of the *Kamasutra* proved somewhat annoying.

Although Harry secretly plotted to get back at his noisy neighbor by substituting Whacky Glue for his Vaseline, playing Mozart loudly on a weekday evening was good enough. By the "Adagio," Willis would be pounding on the floor. By the "Rondo: Tempo di Menuetto," he would be weeping openly into his phone, promising Harry that he would take it easy on the weekend if Porter would only lower the goddamned music.

Harry would eventually acquiesce, of course, but not until he had succeeded in driving the fellow around the bend, tactfully pointing out that it could be a lot worse. Porter could always listen to Wagner.

Harry had Machine pour out a second drink before he played back his phone messages on the wallscreen. Hooking up his videophone's deck with the unit, he summoned up a parade of oversized faces on the screen. One Bible salesman. One telephone survey-taker who wanted to know the amount of fresh produce in the house. Fascinating stuff. Harry fast-forwarded the tape, looking for any familiar visages.

A darkness overwhelmed the screen.

He slowed the tape down. Aha. That would be Anne: the love of his life, the wrecker of his dreams. A wonderful woman, really, just a bit confused. The way Caligula had been confused. The sole supporter of half the psychiatrists in the tri-state area, she periodically phoned him, covering up the camera on her side so no picture would be transmitted. Harry hadn't seen his ex-wife in two years. He did, however, hear from her every few months, her disembodied voice descending from the video screen like the vengeful god of the Old Testament. Usually she wanted more alimony, constantly suspecting that he was secretly increasing his salary without informing her. He wondered if she and Dr. Jorge collaborated.

"Harry," the darkness intoned. "The least you could do is be home occasionally when I call. I need more money. The checks you send me aren't big enough to keep a mouse in cheese for a week."

"Sentimental fool," Harry winked at the void. "I'm fine, thanks. How about you?"

"Raoul—"

"The mighty oak..."

"—is attending holistic dentistry classes and we could use more money. Tuition is high. I do my best, Harry—"

"You make twice as much as I do..."

"—but we really need the cash. Once Raoul is settled..."

"The way he settled into hair dressing before he nearly decapitated that overstuffed matron, or house painting or—"

"I'll be waiting for your reply."

Harry stuck his tongue out at the screen. "Reply given."

He sank into the chair. "Let's hear it for romanticism." There was a shrill beep as the next video message appeared. The anxious face of Douglas Libby, ever-sweating source for down-and-out newsmen filled the wall. Libby, a thin, wan fellow, who always looked guilty of some indescribably heinous deed, was determined to get as much information into his two-minute taping as possible. His speech pattern was closely akin to machine gun fire.

"Harry. Listen. I think I might have a juicy one for you. Exposé. I've been nosing around the nuke plant at Fountain Point. Just routine stuff. Nothing big. But tonight, on the highway, this old guy, Tap Hammill, strange name, right? Well, this guy's a drifter. A hobo. You know. Anyhow, tonight, this old geek is hitching a ride up north and he's run over by this electric van. Pow. Couple of witnesses in another car couldn't believe it. I mean, the guys, two guys in the van, musta saw the old duffer and just mowed him down anyhow. Pow. Now the witnesses, this couple neckin' with the lights off on the shoulder, I mean, the car lights out and the car's on the shoulder of the road, don't think that the guys in the van noticed them.

"Catch this, though. It was a Fountain Point van. Yellow nuke insignia and everything. I pull up, just by happenchance, innocent like, right after the accident and slip the kids some cash not to mention the connection between the van and the Point to the cops. Girl's a real looker. Tits? I wanna tellya. Anyhow, I figure this could make a good exclusive for some lucky reporter.

"But, catch this! Bigger news. I look at the body and it's covered with yellow paint. It was like the insignia came off the van on impact. Like it was just painted on. Okay. So why drive around with a wet insignia, right? Very mysterious. I'm on my way to dig up some dirt. I'll call back and we can deal. This one could be bigger than your space hab scam. Always thought you should have copped the big prize on that one. See ya, pal."

The screen went dead. Harry flicked off the unit. Libby was slippery as hell, but at least he had a sense of adventure, of excitement. "See ya," Porter repeated.

The doorbell chimed.

Porter slid to his feet. Upstairs neighbor? Hired assassin? At this late hour, he didn't really care. Mozart's "Adagio" began as Harry walked towards the door. The pounding on the ceiling began before he was halfway across the room. That eliminated the geek upstairs. He squinted into the door's peepscreen. Outside, Jessica West stood uneasily in the pale

light of the portal. Harry swung the door open with a tired
smile. "Up past your bedtime aren't you, sprout?"

A petite brunette with light blue bangs and equally azure
eyes sauntered into the apartment wearing a clinging bath-
robe. "I've worn out six baby-sitters tonight. I thought I'd try
you."

Jessica West was Harry's next door tenant. An attractive,
intelligent woman in her mid-twenties, West worked as a
publicist for a major holographic feature company. She enjoyed
baiting Harry with sexual innuendos almost as much as he
enjoyed being baited. Porter, in turn, poked fun at the
ten-year difference in their ages and the few light years
difference in their life-styles. Harry professed to be tired and
worn out. Jessica assured him that she carried around a
portable power pack for just such conditions.

The faulty spark plug in the entire mechanization was the
presence of Jessica's live-in beau, Peter Hayden, one of the
country's leading environmental crusaders and staunch
antinuclear activists. A tall, good-looking young fellow quite a
few years Harry's junior, he was brash, incredibly sober,
idealistic, and dashing. Harry loathed him.

"Well, sit yourself down and have a cup of hot chocolate,"
Harry said. "That'll put you to sleep."

"Hot chocolate keeps me up."

"Not the way I make it."

"It won't make a difference."

"I use vodka."

"Maybe I'll just take a sleeping pill."

"Good idea," Harry strolled into the kitchen and emerged
with a third round for himself. Jessica sat on the couch and
crossed her legs, allowing her robe to slip open above knee
level. The pounding on the ceiling continued. "What the hell
is that?"

"One-legged tap dancer lives upstairs," Harry said, sitting
next to her. "Tragic, really. But at least he keeps practicing.
Drink?"

Jessica bit her lower lip. "No. I can't stay long. I just got a
little restless, pacing up and down the living room by myself."

Harry leaped to his feet. "Want to pace in tandem? I ran
the four-minute throw rug in last year's finals."

Jessica allowed a distracted smile to materialize on her lips before returning to skin gnawing. "What would I do without you?"

"Pine away, probably. But will you love me when I'm old and gray."

"You *are* old and gray."

It was obvious to Harry that Jessica was in low spirits this evening. It was Porter's turn to play father confessor again. How awfully wholesome it was. He didn't mind, really. It gave him a chance to exercise his rusty social etiquette. Besides, they were good friends. They didn't see each other often, which, in turn, made them better friends. She also had great legs.

"Hey," he said, placing one hand on hers and guessing the cause of her concern. "Don't worry about him, okay? He'll be home soon enough. It's tough jousting windmills these days. The hours are awful."

Jessica sighed, stretching her legs before her. Harry nearly dropped his drink. "You're telling me. The Non-Nuclear Futurists are taking up more and more of his time these days."

"Maybe they'll adopt him and make it legal."

The woman stifled a laugh. "I wish they would. At least I'd know where I stand. At this point, I feel like excess baggage. Peter and I have been together over a year but lately—" She shifted her gaze to her left knee. She scratched it absent-mindedly. It was one of the few times Porter wished he was a human hand.

"I don't know how much longer I can exist like this. I'm just not that political, I suppose. I mean, I respect what he's doing. I support what he's doing. I think he's one hundred percent right. But—"

"You'd like to live your life present tense as well as worry about future tense."

Jessica's face brightened perceptibly. "Exactly! Is that wrong of me?"

"No," he replied, giving her hand a squeeze. "Not at all. I'd venture to say that ninety percent of the world's population allows their lives to slip away from them when they're not looking. Very few people concentrate on the 'now' part of life. They're usually all caught up in 'tomorrow' or 'yesterday.' But it's the 'now' that's the most important. It's no sin to recognize that."

Jessica burst out laughing. "You're really something."

Porter's face twitched slightly, growing a pale shade of pink. "Yeah, but what?"

Abruptly, Jessica asked. "What's your ex-wife like?"

"Anything she can get her hands on," he said, standing. Pulling Jessica off the couch, he paraded her to the front door. "Services are over, young lady. It's time for this prophet to collapse. Don't worry about young Peter. He's a big boy. If you feel that strongly about how he spends his time, talk it over with him. You two can find some solution."

Jessica paused outside the door. "Yes, I know Uncle Harry, we're young and in love." The woman squeezed Porter's hand and, impetuously, kissed him full on the lips before running next door. "Thanks, again."

Harry stood, befuddled, in the doorway, his lips tingling. "Anytime," he wished. A strange sensation swept through him. Closing the door behind him, he raised the forefinger of his left hand to his lower lip. Was it pleasure he felt? The thrill of expectation? He shrugged his shoulders. Whatever. It was better than getting kicked in the nose in public.

"Lights out," Harry called to the apartment.

Machine obeyed and the lights in the living quarters dimmed. Harry turned on the videophone answering machine and stumbled into the bedroom. Mozart's "Rondo: Tempor di Menuetto" echoed through the house.

The phone began to ring.

2

Douglas Libby had seen too much. The damndest thing was that he wasn't even sure what he had seen. He ran down the corridors of the Fountain Point Nuclear facility clad in his janitor's uniform, his thin legs pumping furiously. There was no way he could save himself. He realized that. His last act would be one of revenge. He'd phone Harry Porter and tip him off about what he saw.

A former aerospace engineer who had found himself being phased out of the National Aeronautics and Space Administration a few years back, Libby had discovered a way to turn a profit from his loss by selling all the less-savory details about the space program he had accumulated to the video boys. It was the first time he had acted as a paid "source." He had quite enjoyed it.

Soon, he had the practice down to a science. He began scanning the newsat and video items regularly, looking for trends that showed signs of future development. He would then embark on a chameleonesque life-style that would allow him to do the necessary investigative work. Over the months, he had developed a steady list of customers who paid well for his services. Porter didn't pay top dollar, but he was dependable. He was someone you could count on when times were lean.

A few months back, Libby had noticed an increase in the number of antinuclear demonstrations being held in the area. Talk about nuclear safety regulations and security standards was becoming common in New York. The Fountain Point power plant was the focal point for much of the chatter. Motoring northward from Manhattan and taking modest lodgings in the city of Fountain Point, Doug had managed to ensnare a job as a member of the custodial engineering squad at the plant.

Libby ran frantically to a stairwell, nearly diving down half a flight of stairs to a catwalk. Everything had gone smoothly until tonight. His standard procedure was to arrive for duty and then spend half the night pumping the two security guards on the night shift, Jim Bennings and Wally Gudling, for information about the plant. They aired their gripes and he listened. Tonight, he figured they might know something about the death of the hitchhiker. Tonight something had gone wrong.

He had gone to their station.

They hadn't been there.

Libby paused on the catwalk. Breathing hard, he placed his hands on his knees and inhaled. He stifled a cough. Cigarettes. He could hear the footsteps somewhere behind him. He had to find a phone. Fast. Darting off onto a side path, he trotted down another level of metal stairs.

When he had walked into the security station, he had found it totally deserted. Bennings' cigar still rested in its ashtray, burning. A cup of coffee sat next to the console manned nightly by Gudling. Libby had placed his long fingers around the surface of the plastic cup. The coffee was still hot. A video magazine was still whirring through a desk viewscreen next to the house public address system. Everything in the office was in perfect order—if one totally discounted the fact that its two occupants were conspicuously missing in action.

At that point, Libby had reasoned that the station, for whatever reason, was not too healthy a place to be caught in. He had backed toward the door. As he did so, he spotted a red blotch, no bigger than a Mother Jones dollar piece, two feet to the left of the door. He had extended a trembling forefinger downward and ran it through the puddle. He had then held his finger to his face.

Blood.

Libby had left his janitor's equipment outside the door. He phoned another security station for help. Two guards from the outside team had arrived within minutes. Libby led them to the empty station.

When they arrived, Libby found himself in a very real nightmare. Gudling and Bennings were sitting inside, as cool as could be. Libby had been speechless. He listened helplessly as the outside guards retold his tale to the amused pair. Gudling and Bennings had insisted they had been there all along. They alluded to the fact that Libby had drug problems and should be removed from the premises and put under medical observation—immediately.

That's when Libby had bolted. He had seen something alien in Bennings' eyes, a flicker of cunning that had never shown itself before.

Libby ran, skidding, down a well-lit corridor. A phone was perched at the opposite end of the hall. He sent his feet crashing into the hard surface of the floor, propelling himself at breakneck speed toward the instrument. Dropping in a dollar, he snatched the receiver off the hook and dialed Porter's number. The journalist's face appeared on the viewscreen. "Hello. You've reached the home of Harry Porter. I'm not at home right now but don't feel too badly about that. I'm probably having a miserable time no matter where I am. Please leave your name, time of phone call, message, and phone number when you see the starter's pistol. If you're my ex-wife, the check is in the mail. Bye."

A starter's pistol went off in Libby's face. Harry had always prided himself in his warped sense of humor. Libby quickly spilled his guts, attempting to regurgitate every detail he could in a two-minute time span. He was still talking when he saw Benning's reflection in the glossy surface of the viewscreen. He felt the needle plunge into his back. He lost consciousness almost immediately, falling backward into a pair of strong, male arms.

Within moments, a siren echoed throughout the corridors of the Fountain Point nuclear facility. Douglas Libby was taken to the Fountain Point Hospital psychiatric ward. The two outside guards made their way back to their posts.

Jim Bennings and Wally Gudling resumed overseeing the security of New York state's biggest atomic power plant.

"My readout shows that he made two phone calls," Bennings remarked casually, scanning a small screen on his console. "One to security station A-One. The other to an outside number."

"I'm way ahead of you," Gudling smiled, writing something down in his private log. "Way ahead of you. I've already tracked down the sap's name and address."

"Yeah?" Bennings said, impressed.

"Yup," Gudling replied, dropping the small pad into his jacket pocket. "It'll wait until tomorrow."

3

The young suicide's body struck the pavement with a sickening thud. Bones cracked. A fierce onrush of breath and a low moan shattered the stillness of the night. Bill Pratt opened his mouth to scream. Nothing emerged but air. Harry Porter fluttered his eyelids, awakening from a deep but troubled sleep. His body covered with sweat, he sat up in bed. Suicides. Assassins. Screams of terror. Such was the stuff that dreams were made of.

"It's nine o' clock, Harry, wake up," Machine intoned.

"I'm up," Harry muttered, struggling out of bed. "And, for the record, I didn't request a wake up call." His hands were shaking.

"True," the computer began, "but scanning your message units from yesterday, I—"

"You're pretty damned nosey for an artificial intelligence. Are you sure there isn't some human curiosity working its way into your cogs?"

"*Mister* Porter, I assure you that I am functioning as efficiently now as I was at the time of my installation thirty-four months ago. If you will consult your warranty..."

Harry grinned as he loped into the kitchen. "Don't blow a fuse. How about some liquid Vitamin C?"

A plastic container of orange liquid slid out onto the counter. Harry gulped it down eagerly. He placed the vial back on the counter, nearly gagging. "My God! This is JUICE! What are you trying to do, kill me?"

"You requested liquid Vitamin C, which I assumed—"

"Spike it, goddamn it! You know how I feel about healthy things."

A second vial appeared. Harry savored it, drinking it slowly and allowing himself to both calm himself and prepare himself for another eighteen-hour bout with insanity. "Any big news?"

"Locally, the Reverend Ashley Kapps' appearance at New Madison Square Garden broke all attendance records last evening. One million humans attended the ceremony. Another five hundred thousand were turned away."

"Where are the Druids when we need a really fun religion?" Harry ruminated aloud.

"Would you mind explaining the logical connection between my statement and your response?" Machine asked.

"Yes, I would," Harry growled, stepping into the bathroom for a fast shower. "The human mind is a mysterious phenomenon, my dear Machine. To explain the metaphysical quirkiness that exists between the old synapses would be impossible. However, that very quirkiness is why humans are invited to cocktail parties and computers aren't."

Harry stepped from the shower stall and stood under the dryer. "Not that you'd enjoy making chitchat or, in your case, chipchat, with the sort of creatures that show up at those gatherings. No, your intelligence, handcrafted though it may be, is much too lofty to waste on mere banter. Today, for instance, you can play Watson to my very confused interpretation of Holmes."

"I fail to comprehend . . ."

"You can help me straighten some things out." He slipped on a pair of trousers. "See if you can follow this. I have a friend who is missing. He disappeared yesterday morning."

"Evidence of foul play?"

"None. He checked out of his hotel and walked off his job. There's nothing mysterious about it except that he was frightened out of his wits twenty-four hours ago, made a date to tell me his life story, and then flew the coop. What course of action would you most logically pursue?"

"Since there is nothing really extraordinary about this human's erratic behavior pattern, I would suggest waiting until he contacts you a second time before acting."

"I was afraid you'd say that." Harry was mindful that the word "hunch" had no meaning to a computer. "Okay. Hypothetical question: What would you do if you found evidence that there was a plot against the life of the President of the United States?"

"I would inform the proper authorities immediately."

"Logical answer. How do you think those authorities would react if you informed them that you discovered the plot in another person's nightmare?"

Machine considered the point. "Do they possess good senses of humor?"

"Right," Harry nodded. "No one would take me seriously, would they? Logical supposition?"

"Logical."

"Then there's no use in my going into the other details of the nightmare, either," Porter muttered. He grabbed a shirt from his closet. "I'd like you to do some legwork, pardon the expression, for me today to see if we can find the basis in reality for this bad dream. You can hook up to the library computer's newsdata center and run a few checks."

"As you wish."

"I'd like a list of all the young people in this country who've jumped to their deaths within the last ten months. Once you compile that data, do a cross-correlation of their backgrounds and do up a sublist of any and all similar biographical traits."

"An elementary procedure."

"That's my line." Porter's brow furrowed, recalling the Saint's terrified expression after peeping the parapsych. "Then, assemble a list of any recent news stories concerning any major public figures who've either criticized or threatened the President of the United States before the media."

Machine pondered that request. "Harry, that could take days."

"Don't editorialize," Harry answered. "Major figures. Concentrate on major figures. People with money, resources, power at their command. People who could conceivably launch a large-scale assault on the government."

Harry returned to the kitchen. "Hey, there wasn't anything in the news today about a murder at NYU Medical Center was there?"

"Negative."

"Interesting," Harry muttered. A shrill beep resounded through the apartment. Harry glanced around for the source. The beep stopped. Harry ordered coffee. The beeping resumed. "Is that the microchip version of gas?" he queried.

"Your efforts at sarcasm grow more feeble by the hour," Machine informed him. "The source of that shrill intonation is your communicator, a device that you left in the lining of your coat last night. Your coat is at the side of the chair directly in front of the video screen."

Harry stalked into the living room. "I knew that. Who the hell could be beeping me at this hour? My story should have run in today's first edition. Jesus. Five hours sleep. I get tossed out of bed at nine in the morning after only..."

Harry picked up his suit coat and turned it upside down. He shook it once. He shook it twice. On the third try, a small bulge at the bottom of the coat finally tumbled up and out of the torn lining near the inside pocket. The communicator bounced on the carpeted living room floor with a thump. Porter picked up the small unit. "Yeah? What?"

"Porter—where the hell are you?"

"I'm home," Harry said, recognizing the hard-boiled personality of Leonard Golden, his long-suffering editor and mentor. "Where did you think I'd be?"

"I was hoping you would be at the Swank Club with me and our new publisher Perry DeWitt—just as I requested yesterday when I left what I thought was a rather succinct message on your idiotic phone machine. Breakfast at nine-thirty at the Swank Club. Be there promptly. Words to that effect. We are still communicating in English these days, aren't we. You're not in the vanguard of some strange Esperanto movement?"

Harry swallowed hard. "New publisher? Jeez. I didn't get the message, Lenny. Jeez. I'll be right down. Are you sure you left a message?"

"Get your ass down here, Harry."

"Right. Awww, Jeezus god." Harry clicked off the communicator and struggled into his jacket. "Why the heck didn't you tell me about this appointment?" Harry yelled at the ceiling.

"I tried this morning, if you recall, but you introduced an alternate line of conversation and—"

"And you let me ramble on, eh?"

"You pay the electric bills."

"And you complain about my sarcasm? How in blazes did I miss that message, anyhow?" He tucked the communicator into his jacket's inside pocket. Instinctively, the rectangular piece of equipment dove into the hole in the lining of the clothing and dropped like a rock to the bottom of the coat.

"Fast forward," Machine replied.

"Huh?"

"You fast-forwarded your message tapes last night."

Harry headed for the door. "You can be replaced by a dog."

"Recorder," Machine said patiently.

"Right." Harry scooped his miniature voice-activated tape recorder from a bookshelf and jammed it into his pants pocket. He ran out of his apartment and caught the first elevator to the lobby. Glancing at his watch while trotting towards the exit, he bumped into the wizened Dr. Jorge. "Guess what I haf?" the little man smiled.

It had to be bad news. "I give up, Dr. Jorge, what?"

"This veek's fuel pass-along!"

Harry's wallet seemed to shudder in his back pocket. "That's the second one in two weeks! It's almost summer!"

"The price of oil is always goink up!" the doctor declared, toddling away.

"Right." It wasn't until Harry reached the sidewalk outside that he remembered that his building was solar powered. The streets outside were crowded with pedestrians, all either pounding or riding the pavements to work. Traffic was at a standstill. Harry approached a bleary-eyed traffic cop, an acne-scarred bean pole of a woman in a blue tunic.

"What's going on?" he asked.

"Gridlock," she said sweetly.

"What's causing it?"

"A lot of cars."

Harry's mouth dropped open. "You're kidding me."

"Uh-uh," the woman replied earnestly. "Trucks and buses, too."

"I would never have guessed." With visions of his editor and publisher fuming over burnt eggs, Harry set off for the Swank Club on foot. "Have a nice day," the cop called.

"Right." Plunging into the slow-moving herd of pedestrians, Harry managed to negotiate his position from the upper East Side to midtown in a scant seventy-five minutes. As most people filed into their places of employment, Harry dashed into the Swank Club, a massage parlor/restaurant where the food was served by nude employees of the customers' sexual preference. Not the kind of a place to take Verna and the kids for a burger.

Despite his reputation as a hardened world traveler, Porter was caught off guard when the hostess, bereft of all material possessions, greeted him at the door. "May I help you?"

Harry gawked at the woman. She was tall, well rounded, and apparently designed on the same day as the Alps. He readied a wicked double entendre for a reply but found his mouth stammering "I'm here to—see sumbuddy" instead.

"We all are," the woman smiled, giggling. Her burst of laughter sent her breasts swaying from side to side.

Harry began to sweat. "Uh, no. I mean, I'm here to meet a friend of mine. Leonard Golden. He's with another man."

"Perhaps you'd like one of our male escorts to show you to his table, then."

"No!" Harry blurted. "A woman would be great. I mean, you'll do. I mean." Harry snapped his mouth shut and marched off. "Never mind. I'll find them myself."

He entered the main dining area, a dimly lit room designed like an ancient Roman bathhouse. In the center of the room, being attended to by a slim blond couple, male and female, Leonard Golden and Perry DeWitt sat in animated conversation. DeWitt's side of the chat was decidedly more animated than Golden's.

Golden spotted Harry immediately. Since his face wasn't contorted in blind rage, Harry figured that he had popped a tranc or two after their conversation.

Better living through science.

Harry stepped quickly to their table. Golden, dressed in his finest suit, still looked like an emaciated walrus. An old-time newspaper hound who has sparred continuously with both economics and public apathy for over two decades, he gave the impression of being a thoroughly beaten individual. Under his crusty, tired exterior was an equally crusty and exhausted interior. He always looked like whatever he was doing was painful and wherever he was physically located was the place he'd like to be least. Golden ran a hand over his alabaster moustache. "Ah, Harry," he said with control, "I was just singing your praises to Mr. DeWitt."

Perry DeWitt arose from the table, brushing aside his male waiter a bit too casually for Harry's liking. He was a middle-aged fellow whose once-trim body had settled around his belt. Apparently conscious of his receding red hairline, he wore a paisley cowboy hat indoors to conceal it. The problem with this solution was the man's habit of pushing the hat back on his head, thus revealing a large wad of skin highlighted by a larger absence of hair. He resembled a snake oil salesman at a Wild West show. Harry caught a glimpse of DeWitt's boots as the fellow stood. They had armadillo heads on the toes.

"Pleased to meet you, Mister Porter," DeWitt grinned. "I've been a big fan of yours for years and years and years—"

"Since you were in swaddling clothes, no doubt." Harry extended a hand. DeWitt clasped it. The publisher's paw felt like a day-old carp.

The threesome exchanged microscopic banter, so banal it didn't ever aspire to small talk status. After several minutes of mundanity, Golden glanced furtively at Harry.

"Mr. DeWitt bought the paper last week, Harry. He has some ideas about how we can improve it." Every muscle in Golden's face seemed to be heading toward his chin. Still, he managed a faint smile.

Harry forced an equally responsive grin. He had been through this before. Whenever some monied moron took over the newspaper for whatever brief period of time the novelty lasted, they introduced some idiotic editorial guidelines that would temporarily cripple the NTH's style. Subtly, however, the newspaper would slide back into its old patterns, so slowly and devilishly that the publisher was usually the last to notice—if he or she noticed at all. It was a fairly exasperating exercise in that quite a bit of time was wasted before normalcy was restored.

DeWitt grinned across the table at Harry. Harry sized him up. The guy was so dull he couldn't even entertain a doubt. "Yes sirree, Harry. I think I've come up with a formula that will take this paper to new heights, turn it right around, give it a shot with the masses, make it a real threat to the video news."

Porter grinned back. The guy was obviously rubber room material. It was the "yes sirree" that tipped him off.

"And do you know what the key ingredient to my formula is?" DeWitt beamed.

"Yeast?" Harry asked innocently.

"No," DeWitt semi-laughed, "But something just as 'up!'"

"I give up."

"Happy news!!!"

Harry's head almost took leave of his neck. "Happy news," he repeated, visions of rubber Bozo noses dancing in his head.

"Why, sure," DeWitt continued. "One of the reasons I believe a lot of people are depressed today is that they encounter so much bad news. I mean, let's face it, if you look at the world the wrong way, everything seems to be on the downswing."

"But if you look at the world the right way?" Harry ventured, dreading the inevitable rejoinder.

"You got it, good buddy," DeWitt said, grabbing Porter by the wrist across the table. "If you look at the world the right way, then everything seems to be just filled with hope. Down home in Missouri, my daddy, the senator—"

"Not Senator Chuck DeWitt," Harry exclaimed, "Electric Chair Chuck?"

"A smear campaign," DeWitt continued, "Daddy was a real optimistic sort of guy. He felt, and I feel, that the function of good journalism rests in its being perceived as sort of a neon sign lighting the way for man and womankind. I think that every story we run in our paper should help inspire people everywhere to look forward to the future, to think 'up' and to smile."

Harry winced and glanced at Golden. His editor was quietly popping pills in blissful despair. Harry was clearly on his own at this breakfast. "Uh, Mr. DeWitt, don't you think this formula calls for us to slant the news a bit?"

"Of course it does," DeWitt beamed, pleased at Harry's immediate grasp of the panacea. "Our aim is to make people happy, to give them something to live for. Once the word circulates that we're spreading the good news, more people will want to read our newspaper. And the more people who buy our paper, the more advertising we get. And the more advertising we get, the more money we make!"

"Which causes our publisher to look forward to the future and smile," Harry smirked.

"Right! Exactly!" DeWitt said, missing Porter's sarcasm. (Perhaps Machine had been right.) "We give people a dream and they give us their cash. We all go home happier at the end of a day. Sounds neat, doesn't it?"

"Incredibly tidy," Harry agreed.

"And you, being our most celebrated reporter, will lead us into the realm of good news, banner held high." DeWitt turned to Golden. "He's just the man, isn't he, Leonard?"

Golden nearly spit the pills out of his mouth, startled at being drawn so unexpectedly into the conversation. He cleared his throat in a Herculean effort. "Oh, decidedly so. If there's one thing I always say about Harry Porter it's that"—Golden stared glumly at Harry—"he's great with banners."

DeWitt turned his attention back to Harry. Golden tongued a pill out of his cheek and swallowed, apparently hoping for instant coma. "That's the ticket," DeWitt chortled. "Now, Harry, what stories do you have tucked up your sleeve?"

"None right now, but I do have a communicator stuck in my lining."

"No, no, no," DeWitt smiled, his humor beginning to fade. "What stories are you working on, ha, ha."

Harry decided he had nothing to lose. "I'm looking into a possible plot to kill the President, the cause behind the current suicide epidemic and the disappearance of a prominent medical researcher. Ha. Ha."

DeWitt's face began to harden.

"Oh yeah," Harry continued. "I have a source up at Fountain Point who could link some staffers with a vehicular homicide charge."

DeWitt raised his right hand and brought it crashing down on the table. "Wrong!"

"I don't have a source up at Fountain Point who...?"

"You haven't been listening to me, Harry. Happy news. Upbeat endings. Visions of a better tomorrow. We're hope merchants, Harry, not doomsayers."

"I'm a reporter, Mr. DeWitt, not a greeting card writer."

DeWitt's smile went rodent. "You're a print journalist, are you not?"

"You know I am."

"And we're the last newspaper in America, are we not?"

"Mostly through default."

DeWitt produced a pocket computer pad from his vest and began diddling with the buttons. "And, if you should lose your job right now, it would be a small financial disaster for you, wouldn't it? Just look at all these bills. Escalating rent. Hospital costs still outstanding from your extended stay of a few years back. Alimony. Home computer upkeep. Hell, just to insure you, this newspaper has to spend a small fortune because of your mental history, Harry. If you don't produce for us, you can only be considered a liability."

Harry's face reddened. His eyes would have burned holes through DeWitt's prissy head had he the proper laser attachments. He probably would have felt a lot less angry if DeWitt didn't persist in referring to him as "Harry" through all this nonsense. The pretense of friendship irked him almost as much as the publisher's idea of journalism.

"So," DeWitt continued, "considering the expenses you encounter in your day-to-day life and the paper's investment in you on a day-to-day basis, it seems wise that we continue to maintain a mutually beneficial working agreement, don't you think?"

"You're the boss." This month, anyhow.

"Fine," DeWitt purred. "As of today, I want you to forget all those silly cases. I'm giving you our first official news assignment."

Harry gritted his teeth. "Can't wait."

"We're going to do an in-depth profile of the Reverend Ashley Kapps, one of the greatest generators of hope in this country today."

Harry imagined DeWitt being flattened by a truck. It didn't help.

DeWitt patted him on the hand. "Now, what do you think of that?"

Harry wisely refrained from comment. Not being independently wealthy often led to compromises.

DeWitt did not withdraw his hand. "And, as our star reporter, the assignment belongs to you." He grinned into Porter's stoic visage. "What's the matter, Harry? You don't seem excited."

Harry shrugged and slid his hand from beneath the slimy appendage. "I guess I just have great self-control."

He pushed his chair away from the table. Walking out of the club in a blind rage, he took no notice of either the nude males or females skipping from table to table. He now realized what moved ordinary people to acts of extraordinary violence.

4

Harry grabbed the Lexington Avenue tramway and crawled up the East Side, homeward bound. At Seventy-seventh and Lexington, he spotted a crowd gathering around what, for Porter, was becoming more and more common a sight. A blood-soaked body lay, embedded, on the crushed hood of an electric car. Foreign sports model. Harry jumped off the tram as it stammered along its track.

He trotted over to the burgeoning group of onlookers. Taking his recorder out of his pocket, he clipped the penlike device to his lapel and approached a young woman of approximately twenty years of age. The woman was under the influence of a substance that was obviously quite effective.

"Did you see it happen?" he asked her.

"Did I?" she marveled, her eyelids remaining at half-mast. She shook her head violently from side to side, sending her close-cropped brown hair into small ripples of shudders. "Unfuckingbelievable, man. He looked so graceful coming down. Hit the car like a fucking rock, though. Unbelievable. Whammo. Like a fucking rock."

"Right," Harry swallowed, unsuccessfully avoiding the sight of the crumpled body on the car. The kid couldn't have been much over thirteen. His face was half gone. Harry had a sinus headache. A bad one. "Did he say anything before he jumped?"

"Did he ever," the girl smirked. "Made a goddamn speech."

"What did he say?"

The girl shrugged and began walking casually away. "The usual riff. You know, the world stinks. We're all bummed out. Then, splat! Like a fucking rock. Godda go. Can't be late for my lunch date. I only have an hour off."

Porter watched the girl slide onto a moving sidewalk with an amazing amount of grace, considering. He decided to walk the rest of the way home. The sirens were invading the air already. He glanced at his foot and saw a small vial of nasal spray on the concrete. The girl had probably dropped it. He picked up the plastic container and dropped it in his pocket.

If he couldn't change the world through his reporting, at least he would be able to clear his sinuses.

After a short walk, Porter entered his building. He didn't bother to check for Jorge's presence. Taking the elevator to the fourth floor without incident, he padded down the hallway and approached his apartment.

The door was open.

It should not have been.

Pausing near the portal, he slipped the recorder off his lapel and curled his left hand around it. If he had to take a swing at anyone, any bit of extra clout wouldn't hurt. He clenched his fist at his side. The recorder certainly was lightweight. If only he carried something a bit more substantial on him in his day-to-day activities—like a bowling ball.

"Machine?" Harry whispered, slipping into the apartment.

"Harry?" the computer answered. "Is that you? Harry, I can't see you in the living room. Are you there?"

Harry stood at the entrance to the living room, glancing nervously about. The place seemed empty. It had been ransacked. He walked to the center of the room. In the right-hand corner was Machine's camera eye. The way the unit was programmed, as soon as Harry left the apartment, the camera immediately began its automatic surveillance phase: swinging back and forth in its swivel perch, scanning the area. As soon as Harry's hand fit into the hand-print lock on the door signaling his return, however, the camera was programmed to cease scanning and focus its attention on the center of the room, its view distracted from the doorway.

The camera was now stationary.

"I seem to see the problem," Harry said, reaching up towards the lens and removing a three-dimensional photograph from in front of it.

"Harry," Machine said. "We've been robbed."

Porter stared at the apartment. His filing cabinet had been emptied. Old-fashioned typed documents as well as taped files were strewn about like confetti.

"I didn't see anyone," the computer stressed. "Yet, I'm not malfunctioning."

"Professional job," Porter commented. "Whoever tiptoed in here used their brains. Did they harm you?"

"Hardly," Machine stated. "Although, for whatever reason, I did not actually *see* the perpetrators, I *sensed* their unwelcome presence. I activated the burglar lights. Apparently, they were frightened off before they could do substantial damage."

"Poor bastards. That light show would panic an acid freak. Did you alert the police?"

"I was just making contact when you entered."

"Cancel the call."

"But—"

"I don't need a ballet of flat feet messing things up any more than they are already. We'll chalk this one up to experience." Harry walked slowly to the doorway. "This makes no sense," he thought aloud. "I can see how they got to you, but I don't understand why. If our guest or guests strolled along this wall," he said, inching along the wall leading from the door to the camera, "and you were already in a fixed position, you wouldn't see them. They could sneak up behind you and take a picture of the room from approximately the same viewpoint as your lens. Did you lose vision for a few seconds this afternoon?"

"As a matter of fact, yes. I attributed that to a minor fluctuation in the current. We have had problems since the solar panels were installed on the roof."

"More than likely they masked your lens for three to five seconds, just enough time for them to attach this picture, a three-dimensional shot of the room, to a bracket in front of your eye. With you focusing on this photo, they could have driven a tank through here and all you would have seen was the empty room."

"But that doesn't account for their getting into the apartment in the first place."

"I have no explanation for that, my dear device," Porter said returning to the door. He stared at the hand shaped imprint on its surface. "This hand lock is supposed to be impossible to break open. It's designed to respond to my print only, actually patterned to fit every little swirl and wrinkle in my palm and fingers."

He pressed his hand into the indentation. It fit securely. No one had tampered with the lock. Removing his hand, he found it damp. Whoever broke in had very sweaty palms. He slammed the door behind him. "Ah, well. No harm done, I suppose. Actually, I'm flattered by the attention. This proves I'm onto something. Now if only I knew what."

He reentered the living room. "Did you get me those lists I asked for?"

"Of course. I rationalized that you'd want to see them as soon as you arrive. They're on the kitchen cabinet along with liquid refreshments."

"Machine, there are times when you are a truly wonderous addition to this household."

"Mr. Porter, a common wrench would be a wonderous addition to this household."

"All right, so it's not the Taj Mahal." Harry walked into the kitchen. The drink was on the counter. The printouts were not. "Machine. You're sure the lists were on the counter?"

"Affirmative."

"Well, now we know what our guests were after. How fast can you get me duplicates?"

"Three minutes." Harry waited as Machine reassembled the material. Soon, a duplicate set of printouts were on the counter. Harry took the papers and his drink into the living room where he sprawled across the couch in front of the video unit. Somewhere in those lists had to be the key to the peeper's dream. Somewhere in those lists was the reality behind that nightmare of death, destruction, and political chaos. Absentmindedly pushing a small button on the armchair console, he played back his phone messages.

A sultry redhead appeared on the screen in a low-cut gown. After breathing for several endless seconds, she licked her lips and cooed into the camera. "Harry. This is Sybille DeVille—"

"The holographic porn star!" Harry gasped.

"You might remember me as Sally Ratchet, the UPI secretary you took to the Shuttle Anniversary Party five years ago."

"Holy Jeez?" Harry yelled at the tape. "Little Sally? How you've—grown!"

"I'm in town, Harry, and I'd like to pick up where we left off. You were a married man, then, Harry. I understood your reluctance. I was cherry. Now, we're both free."

Harry gawked at the screen. Or at least both reasonable.

"So, if you'd like to get it on for new times' sake, give me a jinglejangle and we'll let it all dangle."

Sybille's number appeared on the screen. Harry freeze-framed it, leaving it emblazoned on his wall. He was a sucker for poetry. Grabbing his phone, he quickly dialed the number and turned to face the phone lens, mounted on the wall in front of the receiver. DeVille's face appeared on the viewscreen. "Hi. This is Sybille DeVille. I'm not at home right now—"

Damn.

—"but you can leave a message when you hear me moan...if you're man enough."

A close-up of Sybille's lips filled the receiver. Moist. They parted. A low, sensuous utterance slithered out and enveloped Harry's ears.

Porter stared blankly at the camera, blinking several times before he could summon any words. "Sally? Sybille? It's me, Harry Porter. I'd love to get up to see you, I mean come over to see you. I saw your last holo, *Blazing Firehouse*. Very visual, uh. You have my number. I hope to hear from you soon. Uh. Glad to see you got out of the secretarial pool. Bye."

Harry hung up, flustered. Little Sally Ratchet. Puberty must have hit her hard. Harry returned to his messages.

The flushed face of Douglas Libby appeared on the screen. "Harry. It's Libby. Look. There's something strange going on up here at the plant. Maybe it's connected with the accident, maybe not. But there were two very important security guards missing from their post a couple of minutes ago, blood on the floor and everything. I called in another security squad, and we found the first two back in their station. They swore they'd been there all along. Look. I'll call you as soon as I can. If anything happens..."

The tape abruptly ended. Frowning slightly, Porter took a small computer pad from an adjacent table. He pulled Libby's hotel number from the source's file. He dialed it. A mousey-looking front desk jockey informed him that Mr. Libby had not returned to his room as of yet and that he might try again later on in the afternoon. He alluded to the fact that Libby often strolled in late after a night of, the mousey fellow colored slightly, carousing. Porter dialed Fountain Point. Libby had checked out at the end of his shift.

Overtime, Harry theorized, hitting the fast forward button once again. The ever-smiling face of Perry DeWitt filled the screen. "Great news, Harry. I've set up an in-person interview with you and the Reverend Ashley Kapps for this afternoon at three. He's delighted we're so interested in his cause. He'll be waiting for you at his office at 666 5th Avenue. He has the top fifteen floors."

Harry took note of the address and was thankful that he was not affected by Satanism. He glanced at his watch. He swore to himself, tossing the suicide/enemy lists onto the floor. He wouldn't even have time to take a shower.

He retrieved the readouts and shoved them into his filing cabinet. "Machine," he ordered, "guard these as if your existence depended on it—which it does. Someone is very interested in what I'm up to these days."

Whatever it was that Saint-Crispen saw must have some foundation in those readouts. At least, someone else besides Harry thought so.

Harry slipped into his jacket. "Keep your camera scanning when I leave. That's a direct order. Full ninety degrees. If there's a mouse in this room after I've gone, I want a record of it. I'll be back in a few hours. I'm off to see the wizard."

"Recorder?"

"Have it, mother."

5

Porter sat dejectedly in the opulent waiting room belonging to the Reverend Ashley Kapps. The place was large, at least thirty feet by thirty feet and decorated in a neo-NASA motif. Shots of deep space were blown up to mural size, segueing into small clusters of photographs of Kapps' faithful: the congregation of the Church of the Ancient Astronauts. Time was when Harry Porter would have gotten depressed at the prospect of being surrounded by this outerworldly malarky. These days, however, he tried to be philosophical about it all. It was part of his job. It paid the rent. It was a hell of a lot better than working for some stuffed shirt in a badly air-conditioned office or huddling around some home computer system conducting electronic business.

In spite of the pressures DeWitt would put on him, he'd still manage to salvage some sort of sense of accomplishment about it all. Hell, at least he was writing. He sat across from the direly perky receptionist with doelike eyes and a blond crew cut. He hadn't been reduced to mugging in front of a video unit to get by. He took some small amount of satisfaction from that.

He leaned forward in the form-fitting chair. It was the kind of seat found on contemporary NASA spacecraft. He gazed at the video magazines scattered on the table before him.

Field and Stream: TROUT: OUR ENDANGERED FRIEND

Wall Street Today: SPACE INDUSTRIALISM—BOOM OR BUST?

Harry fingered a third mini-disc. *News Today:* THE REVEREND ASHLEY KAPPS AT NEW MADISON SQUARE GARDEN.

They had certainly cranked this one out quickly. Harry tried to conceal a smirk as he popped the small disc into the player. He put on his headset and watched with morbid fascination as the contemporary religious event unfolded before his eyes.

He longed for a drink as he watched the blue jump-suited preacher ascend the massive stage of the Garden. Kapps had appeared out of nowhere less than a year ago and, during that short duration of time, become a bona fide cult figure. A spacey revivalist with an uncanny knack for stating the obvious via a litany of clichés, he had amassed a small fortune by simply telling people what they wanted to hear.

The masses, those stalwart citizens who gulped down their tranquilizers and stared at their television screens with astonishing regularity were, in Kapps' opinion, really descendents of the gods: alien Ancient Astronauts who had spawned on a pyramid or some other exotic hot spot and left their offspring the Earth to diddle with hundreds of thousands of years ago. Harry surmised that it was the cosmic equivalent of leaving your kid the keys to the family car.

As a result of humanity's stature as only child of the gods, Kapps could state unequivocably that happiness was just around the corner—or at least a light year or so away. The world itself might be nasty but the children of Kapps' Astronauts were A-OK. So okay, in fact, that some of the old space codgers themselves were heading back to Earth to give them a quick boost in the morale area.

And, if the faithful believed in this hopeful message and paid the reverend substantial sums of good old American greenbacks, Kapps would personally intercede with his divine bosses and spare his chosen flock the painful flames of intergalactic perdition earned by humanity for generally wreaking havoc on the planet in their less godlike moments. Kapps did not score high points in originality, but he was a master of repackaging.

After a song and a dance by the bosomy Kappettes ("The all-singing, all-dancing Angelic Choir!"), the Reverend on the video screen launched into a standard doom and despair sermon, not to subtly pointing out that he and he alone was the only real source of leadership in the world today. When and if the old cosmic shit hit the rotary blades, he was the only guy in town with a spiritual scooper. The throngs went wild.

Harry stared at the video projected face of the preacher. A tall, bearded man with close-cropped facial hair and rainbow-colored glasses, Kapps looked like an updated Biblical character who had opted for a layover in Vegas instead of the Sinai. His religious aura seemed derived from one part Bible thumping and two parts method acting. He was a professional antihero and a damned good one.

He had successfully stirred a swatch of an apathetic public into a state of movement. At this point, Harry wasn't sure whether this was a plus or a minus. He didn't totally disdain the reverend's science-fiction, snake-oil pitch. He simply felt that there were a lot more important topics for the public to rally around. Solar energy. Conservation. Space exploration. Overpopulation. The cure for the common hangover.

Harry watched the screen. Kapps called for the traditional procession of the walking wounded to make its way toward him. And that they did—limping, waddling and crawling up the center aisle of the Garden. "Come unto me, O Children of the Spacefaring Gods," Kapps intoned, a southern drawl magnificently woven into his hype. The faithful ascended the stairway to the stage on turbo chairs, aerofloat crutches and short-circuiting bionic legs.

Harry rubbed his eyes as a crutch-encased follower hovered humbly some four inches above the stage floor. His Tale? A tram accident had crippled him for life. Kapps' cure? The reverend lifted his eyes to the ceiling (and the overhead cameras) and shouted: "Fathers! Your humble Earthling descendent, Ashley Kapps, beseeches you to take pity on poor brother—poor brother—Say, I didn't catch your name."

"Norbert Peets," the fellow replied.

"On brother Norman—"

"Norbert—"

"Peets. He believes in me. He believes in the Ancient Astronauts. And through this belief, we hope to tap the mothership of your generosity and benevolence." Kapps faced his flock. "By their power, brother Peets, I say unto you, toss off your floaters and descend!"

Harry began rooting around the desk for the *Field and*

Stream disc during the predictable finale to this turgid drama:
the cripple alighting ever so gracefully on the stage and
tramping around the beaming man of the spandex.

Harry flipped off the video unit and yanked out the disc.
He was about to learn about his endangered friend the trout
when a faint voice echoed above him. He pulled his ear-
phones off and stared up at the Reverend Ashley Kapps in the
flesh. In person, Kapps seemed a lot less hellfire and brimstone. Clad in a loose-fitting tunic and slacks, he peered
down at Harry, hands clasped behind his back."

"Doesn't impress you, huh?" he asked.

Harry, uncomfortable at being caught in the editorial act,
tried to flub his way out of the situation. "Well, I've never
been too religious. Atheistic, really. It's nice, but I don't get
many holidays."

"No need to apologize," Kapps said. "It's a pretty rough
scene to deal with cold. Wasn't one of my best nights, either.
The acoustics in that hall are murder. Come inside and we
can talk."

Porter was genuinely taken off guard by the preacher's
candid attitude. At less than Concorde volume, Kapps' southern accent wasn't all that threatening or haughty. It was
downright friendly, in fact. Kapps led Harry into his inner
sanctum, a veritable media warehouse filled with sophisticated video equipment, tape libraries and an occasional bound
book or two. Three-dimensional murals depicting both
spacescapes and Kapps administering to his faithful graced
the walls. Kapps took a seat behind his large, semicircular
desk; a rounded, control-panel-shaped piece of furniture that
resembled a prop from a vintage science-fiction extravaganza.

Harry sat in the NASA chair before the desk.

"So," Kapps began, "you're here to do a penetrating study
of my work, eh, Mr. Porter?"

"Looks that way," Harry said, noncommitally. He couldn't
be sure, but behind the reverend's rainbow glasses he thought
he caught a glimmer of humor.

"Frankly, Harry. May I call you Harry? I was surprised to
find that a man with your investigative crime reporting
background would be interested in our little operation."

"No more than I was."

A smile broke across Kapps' face. "I was hoping that was
the case," he beamed. "I didn't think you were a believer or
even remotely interested in our cause. I prefer your skepti-

cism, however, to a journalistic angle connected with some of your past endeavors."

Harry chuckled lowly. "Afraid I was here to look for bodies or bogus checks?"

"Damned straight I was," Kapps answered. "Look, to be honest with you, I believe in what I'm doing. A lot of people don't. For every follower I have, I must also have ten detractors. People accuse me of being phony, and some will stop at nothing to prove their point. You're very vulnerable when you're in a position such as mine. You have to actively disprove every wild accusation tossed your way, or else you're held suspect by the press and, in turn, the people.

"It's the religious reactionaries I fear most. They detest what I do. Hell, I admit I have to exaggerate what I'm into once I'm on that stage. People expect ceremony in their religion. The Church of the Ancient Astronauts may be a relatively new organization but it's still got to appeal to the timeworn religious needs of the masses. They want a religion that is bigger than their everyday problems, that is majestic without being condescending."

"And on stage, you play up to that need?" Harry nodded. "The hellfire and brimstone act?"

Kapps drummed his fingers slowly on his desk top. "It's not so much of an act as it is a means of communication. If I got up on that stage and sat, casually, the way I am with you right now, and said to the people: 'I genuinely believe I have a way to save your souls'; two hundred thousand people would shrug their shoulders and say 'sure you have, buddy.'

"They wouldn't believe me, Harry, and do you know why? Because I would be speaking to them as one human being to another. Now, that may well work within the confines of this office, but if you put one human in front of two hundred thousand others, you'll soon find out that this line of intimate communication just doesn't cut it. It can't. The one human, thus, has to assume a stance that is equal to or greater than the presence of his two hundred thousand peers out there."

"Okay. Your stage act is a slight sham. How about your message?"

"The real thing," Kapps stated, leaning forward in his chair, rainbow glasses glistening. "In the beginning, I only half believed what I was saying. But when I saw the effect my words had on people, I became my own greatest convert. I genuinely believe that I'm providing a service, Harry. I'm offering people hope, but more than that, I'm offering them a way to believe in themselves: a way to see themselves as being something more than mere cogs in a vast sociological machine. My flock sees itself as being special, spiritual. I truly believe that what I'm offering people is vital to the future survival of this country, of this world for that matter."

Porter found himself leaning forward in his chair as well, involuntarily mesmerized by the low-keyed power of the charismatic leader. One on one, Kapps resembled neither ogre nor charlatan. He was merely a man obsessed with a vision, a vision that may or may not have been valid. That, however, was not up to Harry to decide. Porter's concentration was broken by the beeper on his communicator. "Excuse me," he muttered. "Duty calls."

He fished into his jacket in search of the device. "This will only take a minute," he mumbled, taking off his coat. He turned the piece of apparel upside down and shook it once, twice, three times. The communicator glided along the interior lining and out the tear next to the inside pocket. It hit the floor and rolled across the room. "I usually prefer using a phone," Harry grunted as he retrieved the squealing piece of machinery. "Porter, here."

"Harry, it's Leonard. Look, I wouldn't bother you but a friend of yours, a Dr. Cade, just called. He asked if you could meet him at Mecoy's. It's about whatever it was you were talking about last night."

That narrows it down to about sixteen subjects, Porter thought. "Thanks, Lenny. I'll call him in a couple of minutes."

"What did you think of DeWitt?" Golden sighed over the small speaker, his mind, apparently, still chemically altered. "A flaming idiot, isn't he?"

"Uh, Lenny, I'd rather not say right now." Harry cleared his throat, hoping that his own vocal sounds would camouflage Golden's monologue. He shot a nervous glance at Kapps. The minister still sat placidly behind his desk, hands folded before his chin as if in prayer.

"I don't know where these guys get their money," Golden continued. "It's not like they're intelligent or anything like that."

Porter surmised that Lenny must have swallowed a few uppers after breakfast to counteract the tranquilizers. If allowed, he would now swing into a one-man show of dire lengths. "Right," he snapped. "Gotta go. See you later."

Harry slipped back into his jacket and replaced the communicator in his torn lining. "Sorry about that. Politics."

Kapps shrugged, commiserating with his guest. "Tell you what, Harry. I know that you were coerced into this assignment, and I know that you're itching to meet your doctor friend. I used to do a bit of writing myself, and I know that old habits are hard to break. Why don't we make a deal."

Porter gave Kapps a fish-eyed look. The reverend, noticing it, eased into a gentle laugh. "Nothing that will impune your journalistic integrity. Why don't you follow up on your call, and we'll meet again tomorrow at, let's say, three o'clock. I'll tell you the sordid story of my life and take you on a tour of our facilities here."

Suspicious by nature, Porter waited for the bottom line of the deal. When he realized one was not in the offing, he found himself grinning like a schoolboy. "Tomorrow sounds just fine to me, Reverend. I appreciate your consideration. I really do."

Harry stood. Kapps, doing likewise, extended a firm hand. "The name is Ashley, Harry. Who knows? You might wind up writing a story that you'll truly enjoy. We're a pretty interesting group once you get to know us." He glanced at the ceiling. "And our chairmen of the board could probably help you in future assignments as well—if they approve of your copy."

Harry couldn't shake off his smile, despite his mental efforts. Kapps was a genuinely likeable individual. "I do the best I can," Harry replied while walking towards the door, "but I can always use all the help I can get."

"Well, beyond this story, if ever I can offer you any assistance—the church has some really fine research facilities: libraries and the like."

Kapps opened the door and led Harry back into the waiting room. "Why thanks, Ashley. I just might take you up on that."

"Until tomorrow," Kapps said before returning to his office.

Porter found himself waiting for the elevator feeling tremendously elated. He was filled with the warmth he usually associated with two shots on an empty stomach. He was exhilarated by the ease and good will generated by Kapps' demeanor. A sudden thought crossed his mind. Had he just actually had a religious experience? An epiphany?

He smiled at the receptionist as the elevator doors slid

open. No. It was probably just a reaction at running across a genuinely open individual during a time period of turmoil and posturing. He entered the elevator and jammed the lobby button. The car shimmied down for some twenty floors. It slowed down at the eighteenth level to pick up another passenger.

The door slithered open. Harry, paying only casual attention to the activity outside, glanced up in time to see a tall, gaunt figure aim a laser pistol at his head. Acting instinctively, he dived across the elevator as the gun released a pinprick of a beam through the air. He heard the back wall of the car sizzle under the heat of impact as he slammed into the side of the car with a crunch.

He hurled himself across the elevator a second time as another beam sliced through the air. He kicked the "door close" button with his foot as he rebounded off the floor and tumbled across the car again. A third blast missed his left ear by less than an inch, causing the hair on his short sideburn to crinkle.

The door shut and the elevator continued on its downward path. Harry stumbled to his feet. Either that gunman was trained at the Lighthouse Institute and was an incredibly crummy shot or someone was trying to frighten the holy hell out of him. If the latter was the intention, someone had succeeded magnificently. Porter's knees were shaking as he emerged from the elevator and faced the crowded lobby. He paused outside the car and dusted off his pants and jacket. As he did so, he heard an ominous rattling sound from within his coat. He felt the lining gingerly. It jingled when he touched it. Damn it. That was the fifth communicator he'd totaled in as many weeks.

6

Porter sat in the back of the taxi and shivered. Outside the window, the grit-encased corridors of Manhattan slid by. Eroded by time and architectural whims, the city now lacked any sense of personality, any semblance of soul. Its citizenry was in an equal state of decay, with faces as blank as the buildings.

Harry turned his attention to his hands clenched on his

knees. Someone had just come damned close to putting a premature –30– on his life story. He smelled of charred hair. His head was pounding. He couldn't breathe. Crossing his legs within the confines of the small electric runabout, he sent the contents of his jacket pocket tumbling onto the back seat. Three bus tokens and the container of nasal spray rolled onto the floor.

Harry repocketed the tokens and took three quick hits of the nasal spray. His sinuses were killing him. Bad choice of words, that.

This life-style was beginning to get to him, in spite of his efforts to keep his spirits constantly afloat. He closed his eyes and, for no reason, envisioned Anne as she had been when he had last seen her. Slender, smiling with a forced air of gaiety. She had known she was leaving him all along. He had not. He recalled the marathon bouts of wall staring late into the empty evenings.

He shuddered, his mind suddenly reconstructing a scene in an abandoned apartment at roughly the same time period. A small nervous man, a murderer, confessing all before turning a laser pistol on himself for Harry's benefit. He wanted Harry to have an exclusive. Porter, showered with gore, collapsed in a heap on the floor. Endless hospital corridors had followed. Muted whispers. Parapsych therapy.

He repocketed the nasal spray. Somehow, he had survived the breakdown and collapse of his life. He was a survivor. Period. Sometimes he ruminated over the possibility of life offering him a slightly more loftier goal than merely getting through the day in one piece. Most of the time, however, he contented himself with feeling borderline alienated but thoroughly above it all.

He pressed his hands against his knees.

Boy, was he feeling sorry for himself today.

He opened his eyes as the cab slowed down in front of the battered facade of Mecoy's. "You're not actually goin' in that dump, are ya?" the cabbie asked, amazed.

"I'm from the historical society," Harry said, searching for his wallet.

"That'll be eighteen-fifty."

"You're kidding me. We went only ten blocks."

"When was the last time you were in a cab, buddy?"

"This morning."

"Fares have gone up since then. Eighteen-fifty."

Harry pulled two tens from his pocket. "Here. Keep the change."

"Gee, thanks, mister. Now I can finish law school."

Porter struggled out of the cab. "As cabbies go," he said, "I wish you would." Jumping over the creaking pedway, he strolled into the murky bar. He squinted his eyes and made out the figures of Andrew Cade and Mitzi Smythe-Lewis in the center of the room.

"Have a seat, Porter," Cade said with a flourish. "I have mysterious tales to spin for your benefit."

Mitzi didn't bother to look at Harry. She made a small hissing noise either with her nose or mouth. Porter took it to be either an editorial comment or asthma. "What are you drinking, Porter?" Cade inquired.

"Nothing right now," Porter said, still feeling as jumpy as a kangaroo.

"Do my ears deceive me?" Cade said. "Harry Porter passing up a drink? Perhaps you didn't understand me. I'll buy. I'm a professional. I have cash."

"Nothing right now," Porter repeated.

"Mind if I check your pulse?" Cade reached across the table. Porter pulled his arm away.

"Look, Andy," he snapped. "Somebody almost zapped me in an elevator just now. I'm not in the mood for a drink."

"Landlord problems?" Cade smirked.

"Be serious, Andy. I realize that, over the years, I've bored you with detailed accounts of my problems, but this time, I have no idea who is after me or why."

Cade pursed his lips. "Are you nosing around any hot leads."

Harry realized that Cade was already feeling the effects of a few drinks. He relaxed somewhat. "Not officially," he replied. He briefly recounted the events of the past twenty-four hours, revealing the contents of the peeper's dream but scrupulously avoiding any mention of the hospital killing. If Cade had any knowledge of Flowers' demise, he didn't betray that fact. "So," Porter concluded, "if this shoot 'em out was connected to anything I'm looking into, it could be about our peeper, about Pratt, the suicides, the President, Fountain Point, or maybe even Ashley Kapps."

"Or D—none of the above," Cade muttered.

Porter turned and faced the woman. "By the way, Mitzi, I apologize about insulting Rev. Kapps. He's quite an interesting guy after all."

"Yesterday's news," she shrugged, still not lifting her gaze from the drink. "I'm into Seagullism now."

Harry shook his head in bewilderment. "I'm sure you are."

Cade was struck by a sudden thought. "Perhaps your new publisher has taken out a contract on you. Judging from his background, I can't imagine him looking forward to working with you."

"How did you know we had a new publisher?" Harry asked.

"Don't you even read your own paper?" Cade said, pulling out an edition of the HTN. "DEWITT PURCHASES HERALD-TIMES-NEWS: UPBEAT NEWS ON THE WAY. Rather catchy headline, wouldn't you say? He's quite the philosopher, this Mr. DeWitt. Would you care to hear some of the choicest morsels of cerebration offered herein?"

Harry brushed the paper aside. "No thanks. I had them delivered to me personally this morning."

"Well, cheer up, Porter. You do worry me when you're not overtly obnoxious. The reason I called you here was to fill you in on Pratt. He's a friend of yours you say? Odd fellow. Knowing how you simply adore mysteries, relish every iota of perplexing information, I've brought you the second installment in our continuing story of doctors Pratt and Weiner, our elusive staff members."

"You've heard from Bill?" Harry blinked.

"More than that," Cade replied. "They both showed up today at the center, acting very cool. Very calmly they cleared their newly renovated offices out. Then, without uttering a word to me, Andrew Cade, the benevolent head of the center who was giving—that was *giving*—them everything necessary for their research, they walked out the door. They dropped their letters of resignation on the reception desk as they beat a hasty exit. I stood there, in the hall, like a complete idiot. Not a word did they say. Not a farewell. Nothing."

"Strange," Porter murmured. "First Bill worries about being followed. Then, he disappears. Then, he shows up again just to take off?" Harry gnawed on his lower lip. "It doesn't wash. Why would he take a new position at the center only to leave it?"

"You tell me."

"Maybe he's left to go into hiding," Harry offered, immediately dismissing the thought. "No. If he was in trouble, he'd let me know." Harry drummed his fingers on the table. "Unless he was in so much danger that—but what danger could he be in? He's a syntheskin researcher, right? If he leaves his job, there shouldn't be a big fuss. Syntheskin's been around for years. You can always find replacements for Bill and Weiner."

"For a supposed man of the world, Porter, you are incredibly uninformed. In the world of medicine, when a discovery is made, no one has the luxury of throwing up their hands and saying 'finished.' No, we must all sit back and say 'Now, how can we improve it.'

"We are, in a sense, on a constant treadmill. Rethinking. Redoing. Granted, syntheskin goes back to the late 1970s. Dr. John Burke of the Shriner's Hospital in Boston and Professor Ionnis Yanas of Massachusetts Institute of Technology experimented for four long years on animals in their development of the world's first artificial skin. It wasn't totally synthetic back then, of course. It was fashioned from collagen, a fibular substance that's the supporting structure of all biological systems. It didn't look like real skin, either, rather grayish, I believe. It was, however, a start.

"Through the years, Porter, their ideas have been improved upon, refined. We now have totally synthetic skin. Living tissue grown in medical laboratories. But, my dear journalism major, the research is ever ongoing. These two men, Pratt and Weiner, were spearheading an entirely new area of research when they so abruptly departed. Retraining someone to follow in their illustrious footsteps will be a mammoth task."

"Then all this *really* makes no sense," Porter stated. "Bill's a dedicated guy. Gung-ho. It's just part of his personality. He's the kind of guy who doesn't look funny saluting the flag. He wouldn't throw in the towel."

"Perhaps he got a better offer from the private sector," Cade shrugged.

"No. He's loyal."

"He's also gone," Cade said. "His resignation is on my desk. That doesn't say much for his sense of loyalty, does it?"

A beeper shattered the silence.

Harry instinctively went for his lining. The jingling of smashed circuitry, however, reminded him of his electronic isolation. Cade deftly reached into his vest pocket and removed a communicator. "Cade, here."

"Bronson, sir. We need you at the center. Unidentified male; third and second degree; sixty percent of his body. The burns are at least an hour old. He's in shock. He actually walked in here."

"Christ," Cade hissed into the transmitter. "Prep him. I'm on my way." Cade leaped to his feet. "Want a feature story, Porter? You can view the practical applications of syntheskin yourself."

"Sure," Harry said, trotting after Cade. "I love upbeat stories."

"I'll call you later," Cade shouted at the woman from the doorway.

Mitzi continued to stare at her drink.

Avoiding the layers of people undulating through the pedway-laden city, Cade and Porter ran through the streets to the Burn Center. "How bad?" Harry puffed.

"Beyond bad, if what Bronson said is accurate." Cade easily outdistanced Harry and spoke over his shoulder. "Burns on sixty percent of his body. We'd be faced with quite a challenge if the burns were merely secondary. Secondary burns destroy the top layers of skin and can cause permanent scarring. But second *and* third degree. This is a touch-and-go situation. Third-degree burns destroy all the layers of skin. Skin burned to that extent is dead and useless. It practically invites bacteria to breed there.

"But more than just the victim's skin is affected by burns. The metabolism goes haywire; the body's biochemical defenders rush to combat the invasion of bacteria. Vital fluids pour into the area around the burn, draining and damaging other parts of the body. Every minute counts."

Cade and Porter dashed to the center. Cade suited up immediately. Porter took his place behind a glass wall panel overlooking the operating room. Harry saw Cade emerge in a white jump suit and sterile mask, accompanied by a small army of similarly garbed colleagues. The room was well lit by overhead lighting and filled with a series of oddly shaped opaque tanks, about four feet high. In one of the tanks, two doctors fondled a large, darkened, shriveled object. Harry had to look twice before he realized it was a human being.

He leaned forward on the glass, his knees giving, slightly, under the weight of the discovery.

"Are you all right?"

He turned and faced a small, black-haired nurse. "I guess," he says. "I've never seen anything like this before."

The woman's face assumed a thoughtful, almost meditative

look. "I've been here five years and it still upsets me," she said. "Eleanor Holmes."

"Harry Porter."

"The journalist?"

"Yeah. I'm a friend of Dr. Cade's. I was with him when he got the call. Do you think that poor sonofabitch in there will make it?"

Holmes gazed through the glass. "Hard to tell. Cade's good."

Harry detected more than a note of mere admiration in her voice. He watched the patient being bathed in a trough-shaped tub.

During the bathing procedure, a bevy of consoles were wheeled next to the tub. When activated, they provided a series of ongoing, computerized readouts. During this seemingly benign procedure, Cade moved across the room swiftly, causing Harry to nearly jump. The doctor dashed to the patient and inserted a tube down the charred body's throat.

"What's going on?" Harry asked.

"They're bathing the patient to keep the swelling down," Holmes said. "In this case, however, much of the skin has already ballooned, so the two doctors on the right are making small incisions to let out the fluid. The instruments to the left of the tub are sonar devices. The sound waves allow the doctors to probe the depths of the burned tissue to find out the extent of the damage."

A howling emerged from the tube and echoed eerily through the glass partition. The hair on the back of Porter's neck quivered. "They're removing the loose skin on the victim's body," the nurse continued. "It's a terribly painful procedure. But that pain is a good sign. It means that some of the burns are only second degree. On a third-degree burn you feel no pain whatsoever. Even your pain receptors have been destroyed."

"Why the tube down the throat?"

"Smoke inhalation most likely," Holmes said. "The throat can swell so much that a patient can smother. The tube makes breathing easier."

Harry watched as i-v units were attached to the writhing figure. "He's being fed Lactate Ringer's solution. It will replace the lost fluid in his body. He'll be fed that for twenty-four hours. It helps combat shock."

Fascinated yet repulsed at the same time, Harry stared as

the doctors fluttered around the patient—picking, prodding, bathing. Hands moved with the delicate swiftness of hummingbirds, removing shards of dead flesh, flesh that but a short time ago had been as warm and vibrant as Harry's was now. Two technicians wheeled in a stretcher bed that had, suspended above it at the end of a firm plastic pole, a transluscent domed top. The doctors gently lifted the patient and placed him atop the bed.

Harry pointed to the dome. "What?"

"Thermal shield. One of the biggest risks to a burn victim is heat loss. A burned body can easily become chilled even at stifling temperatures. If a thermal shield doesn't provide enough heat, we attach heating coils. Brace yourself."

Harry had no time to ask why. With most of the doctors holding the patient as firmly as possible without exerting excessive force, the patient was sprayed with a glittering substance. His screeches of pain cut through Porter's mind like a laser through an apple. "What the hell are they doing to him?" he demanded.

"White lightning," Holmes answered. "It's a liquified antibacterial dressing. Destroys all pathological germs. It feels like its nickname implies."

Porter wiped his eyes with his hands. They burned like hot coals. "So I gathered. How many times do you people go this procedure a week?"

Holmes shrugged. "Depends. We can repeat this routine a dozen times a day. Tenant fires mostly. Arson. The older, smaller buildings stand in the way of the bigger, more productive ones. Kids get hurt, mostly. Nearly four million people a year are burned in this country, half of them are children. Nearly a million of them are bad enough to require this sort of treatment. What can I say?"

Porter stared at Holmes, trying to find some trace of vulnerability in her face. She was a beautiful young woman, yet her face was hard. In a strange way, she resembled Cade. She had the same cold, almost haughty swirls of lines on her skin: designs that purposely distanced her from feeling. Here, in her environment, she dealt with life and death on a moment-to-moment basis. With such near-godlike responsibilities, how could anyone return to mere mortal status at the end of each day, each shift? Porter looked at the woman and then at the sweating face of Andrew Cade still visible on the other side of the glass pane. A whole new side of Cade's personality had appeared under the lights of the operating room. How solitary he seemed.

"What happens now?" Harry asked. "If the victim survives?"

"The dead tissue is removed with laser scalpels," she replied routinely. "That allows for minimum blood loss. Once the charred skin is removed, the exposed muscles and fat must be covered as quickly as possible."

"Syntheskin."

"Uh-huh. It's wrapped around the burned areas in large sheets. For smaller burns, we can actually spray the newer, experimental stuff on. Healing is slow but, with syntheskin, there is a minimal amount of scarring."

Harry gawked at the writhing human being rolled out of the room on the stretcher. As the patient passed Cade, he suddenly grabbed the doctor's hand and held it close, even though the act must have sent bolts of pain throughout his entire body. Cade bent over the man's face. The patient continued holding Cade's hand until the grasp was broken by a second member of the medical team.

"That must be the most painful experience in the whole god-damned world," Porter muttered. "Primitive, awesome pain—"

He turned around to discover Holmes gone. Alone in the visitor's area, he watched the patient disappear in the shadows leading out of the operating room.

At that point, Cade walked into the glass-encased cubicle. His face was white and covered with sweat. His gray-green eyes stared wildly at the empty operating room. "Horrible," he whispered. "Horrible."

"The burns?"

"More than that, much more than that, Porter," Cade said, collapsing in a chair with a deeply felt sigh. His eyes remained open wide. "That man in there was set afire. There was a combustible fluid poured over his entire chest. God knows if he can fight off the infection."

Cade blinked his eyes in disbelief. "And on the way out, the man, or what is left of him, grabbed my arm and pulled me toward him. I stared into his eyes. I recognized him. He recognized me. He whispered my name. Mumbled he was 'free.'"

Dr. Andrew Cade abruptly got to his feet, his lips quivering. "Goddamn it, Porter. I can't be sure of this as yet. There's no way to confirm this. But as far as I can ascertain, that poor bastard being wheeled down the hallway into intensive care is Doctor William Pratt!"

III

"Instinct is the nose of the mind."
Mme. Delphine de Girardin

1

Leonard Golden sat, a tranquil expression on his face, surrounded by data readouts. A vast, rounded desk stood before him, not an inch of its surface visible to the naked eye thanks to a covering of computer-generated, printed debris. Behind him, four deservedly underpaid HTN employees fiddled with their keyboards, abridging and correcting computerized copy being culled from the paper's flagging offices throughout the country.

Porter stood in the doorway, drunk and depressed. He was tired. He was confused. He was angry. He stared at the old man. Leonard seemed to be more than merely disheveled today. He had a strange, almost mystical sense about him: the aura a terminally ill patient exudes when he's made peace with his fate. Golden, of course, was no where near death. He was as healthy as a horse, albeit a slightly frustrated one. Life extension drugs and artificial nutrient enhancers had boosted the average age of the average citizen greatly—whether that boost was desired or not.

Like a shell-shocked walrus surrounded by a futuristic zoo, Golden gaped at the mounds of paper before him. His eyes, however, were clearly focused on something else. Past achievements? Ancient glories? His first days as a reporter? The waitresses at the Swank Club? Porter could only wonder. Clearing his throat loud enough to summon Golden home from his revelry, he strode on a rather strange angle into the tiny HTN office, one of three suites leased by the paper in a desperate bid to remain headquartered in New York.

Golden immediately fashioned a false smile on his face. "Harry! How's it going. How's my star reporter feeling? How's that Kapps piece going? Whaddaya say?"

Harry perched himself precariously on a windowsill close to Golden's desk. "Not tonight, Lenny, okay?"

"Okay." Golden began to frown. Harry held up the remains of a tiny rectangular talisman, effectively warding off his editor's abrupt change in temperament. "Relax, Lenny. I didn't come here to harrass you, just to pick up a new communicator..."

"How many is that this month?" Golden sighed, both impressed and appalled while doing some mental budgeting.

"I haven't hit two digits yet," Harry said. "By the way, about that Kapps piece—"

Golden held up a gnarled hand. "It's an assignment, Harry. I can't do anything about it—"

"I know that, Lenny. I know that your hands are tied. I know that you think DeWitt is an ass. So do I. I also realize you can't do anything to frighten him off at this point without endangering the paper."

Someone at one of the terminal screens barely subdued a giggle.

"But," Harry continued, his face reddening, "for the record, the Kapps story is a waste of time. It's fluff. Like a good boy who wants to pay his rent, I'll do it. But I'm not going to give up those story leads I mentioned over breakfast this morning."

Golden's mouth began to twitch. "Harry, I can't give you the go-ahead on any of that."

"Officially, no," Porter said. "But as my mentor, you could at least give me your blessing."

Golden reached into the top drawer of his desk and tossed a new communicator at Harry. "Uh-uh. Against corporate policy."

Harry jumped to his feet. "I'm onto something here, goddamn it. A friend of mine is lying in a hospital near death because of it!"

Golden began to take an interest. "Who."

"That missing doctor I mentioned. Look. He called me and told me he was being followed. He was afraid of being killed. He described the guy tailing him. A few hours later, the guy he described commits suicide. A peeper checks into this kid's mind before the big dive and never checks out. The kid is thinking good thoughts about a Presidential assassination and nuclear war."

"Maybe the kid read a lot of *TV Guide*."

"Then, I get a phone call from Doug Libby yesterday—"

Golden gazed placidly at the ceiling. "A veritable storehouse of reliable information, that Libby."

"Nobody's perfect," Harry fumed. "Okay. I know it all

sounds crazy, and I know I can't connect all the dots right now, but there *is* something going on. I have a bad feeling about all this, Lenny. Have I ever been wrong about my hunches?"

"Constantly," Golden said, perusing a readout before him. "I can't believe this headline. 'STIFF OPPOSITION EXPECTED TO ORBITING FUNERAL PLAN.' My god! What kind of staff do they have in Los Angeles?"

He refocused his eyes on Porter. "Look. I'm sorry about your friend. You've picked up your communicator. You have your assignment. You have your work. You've also had quite a bit to drink as far as I can smell."

"Someone tried to kill me, today!" Porter declared.

"Nice try," Golden responded. "Good delivery—properly impassioned. I'd give it a seventy-five percent."

Harry leaned on Golden's desk, placing his palms flat on two quivering wads of paper. "I'm serious, damn it. Someone tried to blast me when I was leaving Kapps' place. My apartment was also broken into. Professional job. They took two lists I was working up on both the suicide and the assassin angles."

"You always save the most exciting things for last," Golden answered. "You have a real future in video, my son. Now, please. Just pick up your typewriter and go."

Harry lifted his hands from the desk, sending the papers fluttering to the floor. "What typewriter?"

"*Your* typewriter. Who else still uses one of those cumbersome contraptions. The repairman dropped it off less than an hour ago. At least I think it was a repairman. The shape your machine's in, it could have been a talent scout from the Smithsonian. He said you weren't at home, and he didn't want to leave it with the doorman. I told him to just stick it in the mail room. I didn't want anyone walking into these offices and seeing that antique in here. It's bad enough we're considered old hat as a form of communication, but using equipment that Cro-Magnons would consider extinct—"

"Leonard," Harry interrupted, "my typewriter is at home."

"Then whose—" Golden shot Harry a quizzical expression.

Both men turned their attention to the doorway. Simultaneously, a blast from the next room sent a hot whirlwind rushing into the cubicle. Porter was thrown onto Golden's desk. The elderly editor's chair flew backward into the computer consoles. A maelstrom of paper and debris danced through the air as a flash of light cast shadows on the ceiling. A chunk of something solid tore into Porter's flesh just above his right eye. He tried to throw himself on the prone form of Golden to protect the editor from any additional shrapnel but found himself slipping in the opposite direction. In a last-ditch effort to shield the old journalist, he pulled the round table forward, onto its side.

Golden and the console operators huddled behind the desk. Harry, sitting on the opposite side, serenely faced the doorway. He muttered a quick prayer to the god of misplaced bravado and a second to whatever deity would prevent him from getting hit, straight on, by a further concussion. He watched the smoke ooze through the door, still half expecting to be torn apart by succeeding blasts.

After a few of life's longer moments, he got to his feet. "You guys okay?" he asked, peeking over the tilted desk.

Golden scrambled off the floor. "Jesus!" He gaped at the singed paper scattered around him. "There goes the early edition."

Porter wiped a trickle of blood from his forehead.

Golden took out a handkerchief and tossed it to Harry. "You'll do anything to prove a point, won't you?"

"I don't have any choice in the matter now, Lenny." Harry said. "I have to get them before they get me."

"I know, I know," the old man grumbled, his eyes sparkling with the thought of a world-shaking story in his midst. "And while you're at it, why not find out why they're out to get you—and who is out to get you. I'd like a beginning, a middle and an end in the story."

Harry flashed a grin at Golden. He suddenly felt invigorated. Almost sober. "I'll get you a story you won't believe," he said pumping Golden's hand.

"Please don't do that. Besides, I didn't give you an assignment." Golden was cautious. "Don't jump the gun. As far as I'm concerned, you're working on the Kapps feature. Period."

"Right," Harry said, rushing for the battered doorway.

"And Harry," Golden called. "Be careful, will you? Two inches to the left and you would have lost an eye just now."

"Yeah," Porter replied, "but two inches to the right and it would have missed me completely."

Porter disappeared from the doorway in a literal puff of smoke. Golden turned to his staffers. "Would one of you be so kind as to call the fire department and, perhaps, the

police? We might have a story here that someone might want
to read in our newspaper."

Golden straightened his desk with a great effort. He placed
his chair upright and began picking up the pieces of paper up
off the floor. Porter stuck his head in the doorway. "Uh,
Lenny," he hesitated. "I hate to bother you again but..."

Golden stared at Porter. The journalist's outstretched hand
contained a pile of gray-colored fragments. Harry managed a
sheepish smile. "You wouldn't have an extra communicator
lying around, would you?"

2

The fact that someone was trying to kill him didn't frighten
Harry as much as it should have. In an almost perverse way,
the death threats justified his existence. If someone was
trying to stop him, then he must be doing something that was
worthwhile.

He sat solemnly in his living room, gazing at the dormant
video screen, a cup of Machine-brewed coffee in his hand.
The moist stench of a New York spring night crawled in
through the open window. Porter remembered the scene at
the Burn Center earlier in the day. The howls of pain that
emanated from the thing that may have been Bill Pratt. Cade
had promised to keep Harry posted of any change in the
anonymous burn victim's condition. The phone hadn't squawked
in over an hour.

Porter was confused. The most annoying facet of his current predicament was not knowing why someone was determined to do him in. Was it because of his interest in the
suicides? Because of the holocaust-assassination connection
discovered by the peeper? Because of the peeper himself? All
of the aforementioned? None? All that he knew for certain
was that he had inadvertently stumbled onto something very
important. Now he had to accomplish two tasks. Find out
exactly what it was he had discovered. Stay alive while doing
it.

A sudden thought occurred to him. He dialed the New
York University hospital. A pretty night nurse answered. He
asked for a report on the condition of Dr. Hardy Flowers. He

was told that the doctor had checked out last night, transferred to a private nursing facility. Harry thanked the nurse and hung up. Flowers had checked out, all right. Now why would a cold-blooded murder in a city hospital be covered up?

Harry allowed himself the pleasure of one, brief, philosphical smirk. Interesting how a series of rapid-fire stimuli could energize him. His job had become his life. What an exciting guy he had turned out to be. At the age of thirty-six, the sole relationship in his life that was successful was one carried on with his automated home unit, a touching partnership between a boy and his cog.

Harry took a sip of coffee. "Rustoleum, 2001 A.D.," he carped. "A vintage year."

Despite the coffee's bitterness, he needed to stay awake a little while longer this evening. He had to amass a good deal of knowledge as quickly as possible. His life depended upon it and, if the peeper's vision were accurate, so did the lives of countless innocent people—not to mention the life of the President of the United States.

Harry's eyes pounded. Headache. Fatigue. He could barely focus them on the stack of printouts next to him.

Harry placed the coffee cup on the table next to the sofa. "Machine. What do you have for me on our suicides?"

"Without exception," Machine began, "all the suicides were teenagers; some two hundred in number. Ninety percent were between the ages of sixteen and twenty. Sixty percent were male. All came from respectably middle-class but troubled homes. Divorced parents. Communications problems within the family unit. None of the victims had criminal records."

"Just a bunch of all-American kids leaving their families in search of what? Security? Hope?"

"That is an area for speculation, Harry. I'm not programmed to indulge. May I continue?"

"Be my guest."

"Geographically speaking, the children came from a wide variety of areas, although seventy-five percent of the victims were from major metropolises or outlying suburbs—with the vicinities of St. Louis, Detroit, Chicago, Atlanta, Los Angeles, Boston, and New York accounting for the bulks. Of the remaining twenty-five percent, available information indicates that they were leaving their rural domiciles and plotting a course for a major city when last heard from."

"Interesting."

"More curious still is the fact that one hundred percent of the victims disappeared from public view for a period of approximately three months before making their last public appearance. All communication with family and friends ceased some ninety days before death."

"How about their speeches. Did they all make declarations of some sort before leaping?"

"Difficult to ascertain. Of the news reports available detailing the events leading up to the suicides, it appears that there is tangible evidence in favor of that hypothesis. It should be noted, however, that the combined news reports of these events are factually sketchy at best. At present, there are written or video reports on ninety percent of the suicides with only thirty percent detailing the events leading up to that act. Of that thirty percent, however, ninety percent recount the children uttering a credo of disillusionment before their deaths."

"Similarly worded, I bet."

"Correct."

"It would appear that someone is trying to turn a large segment of the youth population into teenaged lemmings."

"There does appear to be evidence of some sort of ceremonial preparation, yes."

"A teenage suicide squad?"

"Conjecture."

"Do a little more sniffing, will you, Machine? See if you can get beyond the standard news reports. Most of the major satellite services pick up the regional Police Blotter report. Little items that they stick on the screen between epics of earthquakes and rapes. See if any of our kids show up in any way, shape, or form. Vagrancy. Boosting. Whatever. Any infraction that might not be obvious enough to make it into a suicide feature. If the newsats can't help you, snoop around the police library. Just be nice."

"As you wish."

"What do you have on that Presidential hate list, prominent figures who have publicly stated that they loathe old Sonny boy?"

"That list," Machine answered, "is immense. Since President Walker assumed office, nearly eight years ago, there has been, according to the combined sat services, an average of thirty public outcries of one sort or another against his various policies per day. In addition, there have been fifty-five death threats phoned in to the Federal Bureau of Investigation since the beginning of the year, two aborted shooting attempts this month, and one hundred forty-seven cases of trespassers found on the White House grounds during the past calendar year."

"Must be his cologne," Porter surmised. "Still, there has to be a winner's circle, right? Consistent critics."

"If one totally eliminates any and all foreign dignitaries and powers, combined satellite services have narrowed it down to six."

"Now we're getting somewhere."

"Heading the list is Victor Carmichael."

"The solar engineer?"

"Correct. As one of the pioneering solar engineers who has consistently advocated practical application of solar power, Carmichael was publicly ridiculed by the President for his concept of solar-powered private transport. It is believed that Detroit's electric car lobby was behind the President's statement, a fact that Carmichael has stressed in public time and time again. He has openly called the President a madman and a leech."

"Colorful."

"To say the very least. His public outrage concerning President Walker's policies is rivaled only by Malcolm Robbins'."

"The TV host?"

"The controversial TV host. Robbins' anti-administration remarks very nearly cost him his position on the airwaves after the President's press secretary started a smear campaign, founded solely on innuendo, concerning Robbins' sexual preferences."

"A TV personality as a potential assassin. That's progress. I remember when the people behind the guns were weirdos who said 'Mr. Potato made me do it.'"

"There is also Jerry Lucas, NASA's young Administrator of Space Exploration. His career was nearly crippled as a result of the space habitat, *Island One*, being abandoned. Furthermore, NASA's space program budget was severely trimmed as a result of the incident."

"The guy must love me as well. I'm the one who exposed the mess."

"As a matter of fact, he speaks of you almost as frequently as he does Walker."

"Remind me not to invite him to my next dinner party."

"Ruth E. Tobruck, a giant of the automotive world reputed to have underworld connections, is also one of Walker's detractors. Her company, Chrysalis Motors, was nearly financially ruined when, after investing heavily in solar developments, Walker publicly endorsed electric vehicles."

"Walker certainly has a lot of friends."

"Also connected to Walker's energy policies is the wrath displayed by Peter Hayden: an environmentalist and member of the Nonnuclear Futurists. He has constantly attacked the President's pronuclear stance. His main argument is that a major accident at a nuclear power plant could effectively eradicate up to six percent of the nation's population."

"Peter as an assassin? I doubt it. The guy's too much of an intellectual. He's more interested in banning privately owned firearms than in using them."

"The last on the list is one Dr. Andrew Cade, an acquaintance of yours, I believe. As the head of the nation's most respected and progressive medical burn treatment center, he has chastised the President severely for cutting federal aid to troubled inner-city hospitals. He has gone on public record as saying that Walker's existence is a threat to the health and welfare of every poor and elderly citizen in the United States."

"Andy always did have a way with words," Harry remarked casually. "Well, I suppose we can eliminate Peter and Andy from our hit list. Andy is too dedicated to saving human lives to take one and Hayden is just too nonviolent."

"Humans have, on occasion, been known to take one life in order to save many," Machine stated.

"What were you saying about 'conjecture?'"

"I do not deal in conjecture. I was simply reiterating an established fact prevalent in human societies throughout the ages."

"Right." Harry made a face at the camera in his living room. "Think I'll turn in. That coffee didn't do much for my nervous system."

"It was decaffeinated."

Harry stood before the lens. "Who the hell told you to feed me decaffeinated coffee! No wonder it tasted like acrylic paint."

"Harry, you are just as aware as I that your doctor suggested—"

"Suggested!" Porter yelled. "He suggested. He didn't order! God! You would have loved Anne! Sonata No. 11 in A Major, K 331!" Obediently, Machine brought forth the sounds of Mozart. Harry stalked into the bedroom.

"You're forgetting your messages," Machine pointed out.

"You're forgetting I'm tired," Harry snarled. "The messages can wait. A condemned man deserves his rest."

Harry pulled his shirt off and gazed at himself in the full-length mirror next to his bed. He still hadn't joined the building's health spa. His muscles had all the tone of a week-old cadaver.

His scrutiny was interrupted by the door chime. He gritted his teeth, pulled the shirt back on and marched towards the door.

He approached the front door cautiously. If there were someone out there waiting for him, the person could snap a laser through the metal paneling quite easily after hearing a telltale sound from within the apartment.

Harry crept up to the door and silently activated the peepscreen. Jessica West stood, shivering, outside. Clad in slacks and with a towel barely covering her torso, she pressed on the buzzer. She glanced nervously down the hall. Her lip was cut, her nose bloodied. Her left eye was swollen. Harry swung open the door and pulled her inside.

"Christonnacrutch," he had time to exclaim before she wrapped her arms around him.

"Just hold me," she wheezed.

"What the hell happened to you?" Harry gasped.

Her body was trembling. Her blood-caked lips shuddered. She wouldn't cry. "The worm turned up tonight—in a big way." She pushed herself away from Porter. "Peter came home this evening. He was cold, aloof. He wouldn't answer any of my questions. He treated me like a stranger. We argued. When I tried to leave the apartment, he told me I couldn't until he said so. I told him what he could do with those kinds of rules. He pushed me onto the couch and just started punching at me. I didn't know what to do, Harry. He went wild."

Her mouth formed an oval. She began rasping for air. "It's all right, now," Harry said, putting an arm around her back and leading her to the sofa. "Just sit here. You're safe, now. It's all right."

"He just kept on hitting me. It was like he really hated me for being home when he walked in. He tore at my clothes. I don't know what he would have done if the phone hadn't stopped him."

"The phone rang and you slipped out," Harry deduced.

"He was totally different on the phone. He calmed down immediately. He was very businesslike."

"Could you see who was calling him."

"No," she said, calming, her face a portrait of concentration. "The screen was blanked out. I could see that by the way the phone was positioned. When I realized that Peter would be on the phone for a while, I ran over here."

"Good move."

"I'm furious with him," Jessica growled. "The nerve." She grabbed Harry by the arm. "Why don't you go back there and give him some of his own medicine, Harry. See how he feels being at the receiving end."

"Violence never solved anything, Jessica."

A small sneer appeared on her cracked lips. "You're not much of a man."

"The feeling's mutual." He watched the woman battle both anger and shock, her eyes flickering wildly. He walked to his phone. "Who are you calling," Jessica asked.

"The police."

"No," she yelled. "I couldn't do that to Peter!"

"Look what Peter's done to you."

"Well," she said, her lips quivering. "He's changed! Maybe he's under pressure. Maybe he's ill. Please, Harry. No police. Think what it would do to his career."

Harry stared at the phone. He stared at the woman. Machine must have been having a field day analyzing the logic in this little scene. He decided against using the phone for the time being. "All right," he said. "But, for the record, I think you're crazy. Now, come into the bedroom and grab a pair of pajamas. Then we'll have a look at that eye—followed by a look at your nose and your lip."

"I must look a mess," she said, hobbling into the bedroom.

"I've seen you looking better," he said, taking her by the hand. He reached into a circular closet and pulled out a chromotropic sleep suit. "Here," he said. "Untouched by human hands."

"Harry, this is a woman's sleepsuit."

"It was a present."

"For whom?" she said, holding the pajamas close to her chest. The sleepsuit turned a bright red.

"Someone who didn't like presents."

"Hey!" Jessica exclaimed, noticing the suit's evolving hues. "This fabric—it—"

"It changes color according to your mood or body temperature," he shrugged. "So control your passion or your most innermost, twisted desires will be mine to savor forever."

Harry left the bedroom, closing the door behind him. Jessica's weak laughter could be heard from within. "You're a real lifesaver, Harry."

"Everyone has to have a hobby," he replied, feeling slightly flustered as he walked back into the living room. He pulled out his nasal spray and took two deep hits in an attempt to stave off another headache. Jessica's laughter had touched an exposed nerve deep within the recesses of his memory. It was nice to hear a woman's voice in the house again. His lower lip trembled ever so slightly.

Suddenly he felt so empty.

3

The morning sun filtered through the gray haze successfully after a half-hour's battle. Sparrows, nestled on the block's lone, sickly tree, brought forth a few random chirps before fluttering down to street level in search of discarded candy wrappers. Harry watched the dawning of the new day from his living room window. He hadn't slept well on the sofa, awakening at six instead of nine.

Jessica believed she was safe in his home. Ironic. Nobody was safe in Harry's home at the moment, not Jessica, not Harry. How could he tell her that someone was attempting to kill him and that he was currently acting like a magnet for trouble. Worse yet, what could he do with her? Turn her loose and have her genius boyfriend play "Flight of the Bumblebee" on her head with his knuckles?

Best not to say anything just yet, he concluded, walking into the kitchen. What she didn't know, he hoped, wouldn't hurt her. "Some liquid Vitamin C, if you please."

A vial slid out onto the counter. Harry took a sip, spitting it out immediately. "Christ! There's enough booze in this to kill a cow! Just give me some juice, willya? You want to see my liver explode or something?"

A second glass appeared on the countertop. "Most inconsistent," Machine noted.

As Harry guzzled his juice, the door to his bedroom opened. Jessica West emerged wearing one of Harry's shirts. She seemed radiant despite the discoloration of her eye. "Good morning," she yawned. "You're an early riser."

"I never miss an episode of *Modern Farmer.* Coffee?"

"Yes, please. I suppose I should get ready for work. I'll pick up some clothes at the apartment."

Harry cleared off a paper-strewn kitchen stool for the woman, placing a cup before her. "Wrong. Call in sick today. You can stay here until you're sure that Peter has left the apartment. Gather some clothes and move in here for a day or so until all this blows over." If it blows over, he added for his own benefit.

"Oh, I couldn't impose, Harry." Her cheeks colored, making her even more attractive.

"No imposition. You give my shirts new artistic meaning. How about some breakfast."

"Only if I make it."

"Nothing doing. Machine here is a culinary whiz. Now, what'll it be?"

"Eggs?"

"Eggs," Harry repeated. "Eggs. Of course. Eggs." He had totally forgotten that some people actually consumed solid food for breakfast. "How are we fixed for eggs, Machine?"

"We are not."

Harry lifted his coat from a nearby chair. "Well, then, it's about time we were. I'll just run 'round the corner and pick up a few things at the grocery. It's about time I did the week's shopping anyway, wouldn't you say, Machine?"

"The last time you did 'the week's shopping' was July sixth, approximately ten mon—"

"I'll be right back," Harry interrupted, heading for the door with a stage wink. "Machine is such a kidder."

"Harry. It's not necessary. Coffee is fine."

"Nonsense," he said, backing out of the apartment. "Breakfast will arrive anon!"

He closed the door behind him. Anon? Jesus. He hasn't experienced this sort of giddiness since, well, since quite a long time ago. His mouth seemed to be moving independently of his brain. That could be a dangerous habit to lapse into. He pushed the button at the elevator, accidentally catching a glimpse of himself in the mirrored wall. God! He hadn't even remembered to shave. He looked like a well-dressed Bowery bum—and not that well dressed either, noting a bright coffee stain on his shirt.

He took the elevator to the ground floor, hesitating in the car until he was sure that Dr. Jorge wasn't on patrol. Not spotting the elderly miser, he quickly strode through the hall and out the front door, rounding the corner and entering Victor's Deli.

Victor, a tired old man with puffy eyes, gaped at Harry. "Whatsa matter," he asked from behind the button-encased counter. "You run outta booze this early?"

"I need some food."

Victor clutched his heart for effect. "God strike me dead. How long you been livin' next door? Four years? Five. This is the first time you've come in here for food. Let me call the TV stations."

"Don't get wise, Victor. I can go elsewhere, you know."

"Not dressed like that you can't," Victor grinned. "You'd better put some soda water on that stain fast. You know what they say, the longer it stays, the further it stains."

"Eggs," Porter declared. "You have any eggs?"

Victor scanned the dials and buttons before him. "Sure. What process you want?"

"Fresh eggs."

"Someone die and leave you money?"

"Never mind the cost," Harry said. Using that as a guide-line, Victor quickly sold Harry a dozen eggs, three fresh mangoes, two grapefruit, a quart of milk, a loaf of pumper-nickel (unseeded), and a jar of jelly for, roughly, the equiva-lent of four days of employment.

Harry took the sack and left the store. He had gotten three steps down the block when a pair of hands appeared from a darkened doorway. He was grabbed by the shoulders and yanked into the shadowy threshold. Harry hugged the gro-cery bag without thinking. Nobody was going to steal his breakfast, goddamn it.

He shook one arm free of his attacker and was pulling it back to strike when he was confronted by the panic-stricken face of Marion Saint-Crispen. "Damn it!" Harry shouted. "You almost made me drop my eggs!"

"Drop your eggs?" the Saint almost howled. "Drop your eggs? I'm almost poppin' my cookies because of you, and you're worrying about eggs? Well, listen up, buddy. The way things are coming down around here, someone's gonna scramble your eggs permanently. And I'm not going to hang around to fit onto that menu!"

"Calm down, Saint-Crispen. Let's take it from the top."

"Oh sure. Calm down. Mr. Cool here unleashes a regular Odin's box of horrors, and he tells me to calm down."

"That's Pandora's box."

"I don't care who owns it, we opened it. And we've got problems."

"Such as . . ."

"The peeper who got himself iced the other night right before our noses—"

"Flowers—"

"I didn't even send a card."

"The guy's name was Flowers, Saint."

"Oh. Right. Well, he wasn't an ordinary peeper. Oh, no. Harry Porter couldn't ask old Saint-Crispen to take the lid off just an ordinary peeper's skullplate. Uh-uh. Our little peeper was employed by the Federal Bureau of Investigation. Harry had to get his old pal involved in the icing of a fed. A *fed* for Chrissakes! Harry, in my line of work, being witness to a fed's murder is considered a high health risk. There's no future in that sort of activity."

Harry frowned. "All right. He was employed by the government. That's a point in our favor."

"Good?" Saint-Crispen was incredulous. "Are you thinking of suing your brains for nonsupport or something?"

"Look. Flowers showing up on the roof means that he was there on official business. Which, in turn, means someone else suspects that this suicide epidemic is more than mere mass psychosis. That also explains why his murder was hushed up. He's officially listed as checked out at the hospital."

"Word on the street is that we're going to be checked out ourselves if we don't watch our buns, Harry-boy." Saint-Crispen grabbed Harry by the coat, glancing down at Porter's shirt. "Man, that's a nasty stain. You oughtta wash that right away. The longer it stays—"

"Relax, Saint-Crispen. They're after me. Not you. Just stay put. Adopt a business-as-usual pose, and nobody will suspect you."

"Right. Just stay put and nobody will suspect me. They won't suspect me because I'll have frost on my nose. No one suspects a dead man of anything. They're totally above suspicion."

"Get to the point, Marion."

"Money. I want money."

"How much."

"Five hundred."

"One hundred."

"Three hundred and I won't go singing to the feds."

Harry shot the Saint an angry look. "There's no percentage in that for you."

"Oh yeah? If I turn state's evidence in a possible murder riff, I can walk away from it and leave you as the only official witness to a very nasty case of out-patient processing."

"You're fuller of beans than a bad burrito," Harry said, pulling three bills out of his hip pocket. "I'll give you the money if you do some legwork for it."

"Just give me the bread."

Porter held the bills in front of the Saint's sweat-drenched stubble. "First we talk. Then, I pay."

"Sure—sure."

"You know Ruth Tobruck?"

"Sure, who doesn't. The broad's family tree can be traced back to Sicily in the 1700s."

"She's Scandinavian."

"Okay. Her adopted family tree, Mr. Literal."

"I want you to go over to her New York offices and do a little nosing around. I'll toss in an extra fifty dollars for expenses. Talk to a clerk. A mail boy. Anybody. Find out just how seriously she dislikes the President."

"You want me to get fed to the kicking machine? Asking questions like that around Tobruck is bad news."

"If you get me what I want, I'll toss in an extra twenty-five dollars."

"Fifty."

"Fine."

A frown crossed Saint-Crispen's face. "Damn."

"What's the matter?"

"Just now I could have asked for seventy-five dollars, couldn't I?"

Harry handed Saint-Crispen three hundred fifty dollars and patted him on the shoulder. "You could have asked me for one hundred dollars and I would have given it to you."

Harry turned around and walked away, leaving the Saint dumbfounded in the doorway. "That's a lie, Harry Porter! You're just trying to ruin my blood pressure!"

"Maybe even one hundred twenty-five," Harry smiled over his shoulder.

"It won't work!" Saint-Crispen bellowed. You're just putting me on. I won't get upset. DO YOU HEAR ME, GOD-DAMN IT?!" He jumped onto the pedway moving in the opposite direction from Harry. "One hundred twenty-five dollars. Jesus Christ!"

Porter walked back into his apartment building and dashed through the lobby. He was nearly at the elevator when Dr. Jorge shouted at him from behind. "Mr. Porter!"

Harry smiled at the tiny man as the elevator door shut out his presence. "Whatever it is, Dr. Jorge, I don't have time for it now."

The door closed and Harry headed for the fourth floor. Dr. Jorge approached the elevator bay, shrugging his shoulders. "Your bag is leaking, Mr. Porter" he said to the elevator door.

Harry walked into his apartment, his coffee stain partially obliterated by the yolk of an egg. He rushed into the kitchen, depositing the bag on the counter. "Damn."

Jessica entered the kitchen fully dressed, laughing as she began unpacking the groceries. "Your shirt looks like a smorgasbord."

"I won't tell you what it feels like. You and Machine can flip for chef's duty. I'm getting out of this thing." He walked into the living room, sucking in his stomach while removing his shirt. At all costs he wanted to make a good impression. After all, he wasn't *that* much older than Jessica. His eyes bulging but his stomach trim, he sat, bare-chested, in front of the television screen and replayed the previous evening's messages.

The pockmarked face of his young cousin Leroy appeared on the screen. "Hey, Harry. You know how they only allow you one call? Well, this is it!"

Harry made a mental note to talk to his Aunt Christie about that kid.

Following Leroy, a close-up of moist, fulsome lips materialized. The camera slowly pulled back to reveal the abundant figure of Sybille DeVille. She was curled on a form-fitting sofa in a sheer swath of cloth that left absolutely nothing to the imagination—which was just as well, considering Porter's lack of imagination these days. "Sorry to find you out again tiger," she cooed into the unit. Harry's stomach popped forward with a sudden exhalation of breath. "I'm all alone tonight and I thought you might want to come over..." She patted a pillow next to her thigh. "Here."

If eyeballs could sweat, Porter's would have been veritable shower nozzles watching DeVille lean forward. The gown slid off her shoulders, revealing the breasts that a nation of raincoat-wearing holograph fans had come to know and grope after in darkened theaters. "Hope we can connect next time pet."

Harry squinted at the screen in disbelief for several seconds after DeVille's departure.

"Are your messages always that hot?" Jessica asked, walking into the room.

Harry quickly inhaled, sending his stomach into an advanced macho position once more. "Uh, no. Not really. She's an old friend."

"She didn't look that old to me."

"Excuse me, I have to get another shirt." Harry trotted into the bedroom.

"Hurry before your eggs get cold," Jessica said, returning to the kitchen. "Although I suppose you could just hold onto them and watch that tape again if you wanted them reheated."

"An old friend, visiting," Harry said, returning in a clean shirt. He sat down at the counter and ogled a sumptuous meal. It was the first time he'd encountered food in his kitchen that hadn't been boiled, dethawed, or processed in years. He stuck his fork into the pillowed scrambled eggs and wedged a piece of bacon onto the end of its prongs as well. "Looks delicious."

The face of Leonard Golden appeared on the video screen in the next room. "Sorry you're not at home, Harry," Golden said. "A couple of things. Your appointment with Kapps has been moved up to noon. And I thought you'd like to know. They found Doug Libby tonight in a ditch near Fountain Point. Heroin overdose. He'd been dead for over twenty hours. I never took him for a junkie, too much energy. Odd bird. Call me when you have the time. I'm sorry."

Harry replaced the fork on his plate.

"Harry?" Jessica asked. "Who's Libby?"

Porter remembered Libby's nervous face on the viewscreen the day before. He should have tried harder to get in touch with him. He should have gone all out to track him down. He shouldn't have forgotten about him. What if Libby had stumbled onto an important lead? What if Libby had died because of something Harry had instigated? What if . . ."

Porter pushed the plate away. "I'm not hungry anymore."

"Most inconsistent," Machine remarked.

4

Reverend Ashley Kapps leaned forward in his chair and gazed into the haggard face of Harry Porter. "I appreciate your skepticism, Harry. I realize that in these troubled times the concept of a faith healer is, at best, a tentative one but, believe me, I'm no sham. I actually do have the gift."

Porter attempted to bring himself into the conversation, the death of Doug Libby still nagging him, the fate of Bill Pratt still a mystery. "I'm not here to believe or disbelieve you, Reverend Kapps—"

"Ashley."

"I'm just here to get a story. I need background information, point of view, that sort of thing."

"Well," Kapps said, scratching his close-cropped beard. "Why don't I just run through the biographical spiel from the beginning. If there are any questions, just stop me as I ramble."

The easygoing tone of the preacher caused Harry to relax slightly. "Sure."

Kapps slid back into his chair. He clasped his hands before him earnestly. Still a young man, Kapps had the unsettling habit of crinkling his facial features for effect—reducing the eyes behind the glasses to slits, his mouth to a bowed line, his face to a study of either intense thought or internal injury. This exaggerated expression may have worked on stage, but within the confines of a small room, it struck Harry as being overly theatrical. Still, he sensed that the man of the cloth was acting naturally, his physical nuances were neither planned nor contrived.

The reverend ran through most of the facts Harry had picked up from Kapps' biographical readout. From a broken home, the son of a New York senator and a New Jersey alcoholic, Kapps had been a fat, acne-infested child. He kept to himself, retreating into a world of books. Science fiction novels, mostly.

"I devoured them," Kapps intoned. "Lived vicariously through them. I was John Carter sprinting across Mars. I was professor Challenger delving into lost worlds. I was Doc Savage, flexing muscles of bronze. But more than merely experiencing a sense of heroics missing from my life, through these books I was able to get a taste of what the future could or should be like for people such as myself—people blessed with inventive minds but less than captivating features.

"Science fiction seemed to me to be a literature of unparalleled ideas. Every concept under the sun could find its way into its pages. I read and read, meeting and corresponding with other fans through various science-fiction conventions. I discovered that most of my young peers were also dreamers, idealists, and, most interestingly, social or physical misfits.

"As I grew older, I shed some weight. My acne, along with my French lessons, disappeared with the end of high school. I attended college and, while in school, began writing."

"Science fiction?"

"Yes," Kapps smiled. "My first novel, *Family of the Gods* was, to my surprise, accepted by both the first publishing house I submitted it to and the public at large. Basically, it dealt with an all-American family who discovered that the human race was directly descended from a species of humanoid aliens, ancient astronauts who visited this world during its formative years.

"I wrote a series of six books dealing with the subject: *House, Temple, Reunion, Picnic,* and *Vacation of the Gods*. The thoughts came easily to me. The public response grew increasingly positive with each new book. Then, it occurred to me that I wasn't really writing novels."

"You weren't?" Harry answered, remembering several prominent literary critics who had alluded to that very fact when the books were first published.

"No. I was spreading the word of the *real* ancient astronauts. Unbeknownst to me, I had been chosen as their vessel on Earth—their tool, their communicative device. The novels I had written had actually been dictated to me by these alien beings in an effort to spread their message. They came up with the ideas, and I took them down."

"Intergalactic steno," Porter mused.

"Of a kind, yes. It was all part of a plan to make known the origins of the human race before the second coming of the astronauts. When the astronauts return, they will mate with humans, Harry. There will be a wonderful intermingling of species: one mortal, one immortal. A whole new strain of life will be spawned. That race will, in turn, be taken to populate yet another planet—a veritable Eden. But before this historic coupling takes place, Harry, Earth's population must be elevated both mentally and spiritually."

"And that's where you come in."

"Exactly. Once this plan was clearly revealed to me, in the guise of a twenty-four hour dream, I realized that my writing days were over. It was now time for me to take the word of the ancient astronauts directly to the people. The masses needed a leader to elevate them, a catalyst. I had to be that man. And, as crazy as this sounds, no sooner had I made my first public speech than I was bestowed with remarkable healing powers, powers I had never experienced before."

Kapps raised a wiry hand and held it a foot in front of his multicolored glasses. "These hands—hands that once fondled the pages of every Fu Manchu novel ever written—can now heal the sick and repair twisted bones." He slammed his hand down on the top of the desk. "Far out, huh? I have the powers of the old gods at my fingertips, Harry, given to me by the new gods."

Kapps tilted his head slightly to one side and raised his lenses skyward. "And how am I rewarded for my efforts?"

Monetarily, Harry thought.

"By love, certainly. But also by hate. I am hated, Harry. Despised by those who condemn me for even suggesting that the old ones or my new gifts exist. Now, I ask you, Harry, is that any way to treat someone who is only out to spread the word of the new gospel?"

Harry let his shoulders rise and fall. "My landlord and my ex-wife hate me, and I pay them most of my salary."

Kapps returned his gaze to Harry, a mirthful hue in his glasses. "Sorry. I was getting pompous, wasn't I? It's difficult to remain down to earth, no pun intended, when speaking about all this. I'm not a spiritual man by nature, so this is still all very new to me. But it really upsets me to hear my cures dismissed as magic tricks, my cured brethren labeled stooges and psychosomatic cranks, and my followers called brainwashed zombies. And me? I'm supposedly the devil incarnate."

He stood from behind his desk. "Let me show you some of the evil I've concocted during the course of a single year."

Kapps escorted Harry out of the office and into the waiting room. An elevator door opened immediately. The pair stepped in and were sent hurtling up to the building's penthouse. When the doors opened, Harry was faced with a massive loft space filled with jump-suited young people. They all bustled around video units, splicing machines, and tape consoles.

"This is just a small taste of my depravity," Kapps said mockingly. "Everyone in this room is a volunteer: people who have joined the church because they believe in the second coming of the gods. This is where we put out our home video magazine. It's a weekly and we have a circulation of over one million. Our members pass it out for free. We *do* accept any and all donations, however. But just look at the faces of these young people. Don't they look like they're enjoying their work, that they're getting a sense of accomplishment from what they're doing?"

Harry looked around the room. It was true. The kids all seemed incredibly earnest but content.

Kapps placed Harry on an escalator leading downward. "Most of these kids were really messed up when they joined the church. They were social outcasts. Misfits. Products of broken homes. Kids hooked on pills, alcohol, self-hatred, and defeat. Here, within the confines of the church, they meet people with the same background who have found a sense of hope in our religion and turned their lives around. The flame of hope can spread like wildfire, Harry.

"Today, we have millions of happy members. They're not zombies, as you can see. They're not fad followers or drones. They're dedicated, talented people who willingly devote their time and talents to a common benevolent cause, spreading spiritual awareness and hope to citizens of a society which dismissed optimism as a viable pursuit years ago."

Harry followed silently as Kapps displayed four more floors of productive teenagers—youths producing jump suits, books, T-shirts, and assorted memorabilia. The profits all went back into the church to continue the operation.

"In this building alone," Kapps said, "we have four floors of small apartments, dorms, for our members. They are paid small salaries, spending money really. We provide food and housing. They have the option to stay or leave as they wish. If they stay, however, they are guaranteed a home for as long as they want it and a peer group with mutual goals."

"Sounds like the army," Harry replied.

"Nothing that drastic," Kapps commented. "We're not a group of religious zealots, and we're not out to make a profit. During the past twelve months, we've established fifteen shelters in major cities designed for the homeless and needy, ten drug clinics, and twenty-seven Ancient Astronaut ranches— halfway houses where new recruits are gradually taught self-discipline and self-respect."

"Training camps."

"Harry," Kapps said, slightly exasperated. "Why do you persist in viewing all this in fascistic terminology? You just can't take a kid out of a broken home and toss him into a loving atmosphere. He'd be suspicious, even resentful. You have to gradually teach him that he's cared about. You have to lead him to the point where he cares about himself. Once he trusts himself, he'll trust others. Once he loves himself, he'll love others.

"The ranchers give the new recruits several months to do just that, to be eased out of an uncaring world into a totally loving one. We also have top-notch educational facilities."

After a brief tour of the dorm facilities, Kapps led Harry back to his office. Porter eased himself into a chair. "Sounds to me like you're an expert on troubled kids."

Kapps shrugged. "Takes one to know one."

Porter remained silent. Finally, he said, "I'm working on a story about troubled kids, Reverend. I was wondering—"

"If I could help you? Certainly. How." Kapps replied.

"I'm not sure, yet," Harry said. "But if I could come up with similarities of speech patterns or biographical details, could you try to come up with personality profiles of different kids?"

Kapps scratched his beard. "It wouldn't be all that scientif-ic," he ventured. "But I think I could conjure up something that was in the ballpark."

"Great," Harry said.

"But I'll only help you on one condition," Kapps advised.

Harry rolled his eyes heavenward. "What."

"That you give the church the benefit of the doubt in terms of it being the beginning of a new movement towards a workable, perfect society—as perfect as this secular world can tolerate anyhow."

Harry nodded affirmatively.

"Tell you what," Kapps beamed. "For our next interview, why don't I take you to our upstate ranch. 'You'll see our members working in a relaxed, rural setting. We can compare notes on your troubled kids when we're up there as well."

"A trip to the country might do me good," Harry hedged.

Kapps leaned back in his chair. His rainbow-colored glasses sent prisms of light dancing onto the ceiling. "A perfect way to cleanse both the soul and the mind."

Harry watched the reverend glisten. "You can dry-clean my soul," he answered, "but I'd prefer my mind to remain dirty."

5

By the time Harry arrived on the scene, the body had already been sprayed with a form-fitting bag and been carted off in an ambulance. All that remained was the blood-spattered alleyway, a few stragglers, a television camera and a laser-light outline of where a young girl had landed, arms and legs akimbo.

Porter huddled next to Saint-Crispen in a small vestibule. His head was splitting. He reached into his pocket for his nasal spray. He had left it at home. "I'm walking along the street," the Saint chattered, his forehead still moist. "It was the strangest feeling. You know me, Harry-boy, see no evil, hear no evil, the whole bit. Live and let live is my motto. All of a sudden, I have this feeling that people are staring at me. I flip out, considering my line of work and all."

Harry started to shiver. A light acid rain began to fall outside the doorway. He jammed his hands into his pants pockets. He really had to start listening to the weather reports more. He was freezing his recorder off.

"So, I turn around," Saint-Crispen continued, "and sure enough, all these people are eyeballing me. I check out their orbs, though. They're looking above me. Lord knows what made me look up but I did. There was this chick, see? Babbling like a looney on this ledge. Before I could even give a listen to what she was saying, she steps off the ledge and heads straight for the haircut area of yours truly."

Saint-Crispen paused, taking in a deep breath of air, apparently to underscore the full severity of the girl's action in regards to his future tonsorial status. "So, I jumped out of the way and into this here hall. See? You can see where I chipped off some plaster."

He picked up a small stone and tossed it at an overturned garbage can outside, sending two stray cats scurrying. "I hate cats. Anyhow, since I'm the closest thing to this little darling when she lands, I'm the first one to reach her, you know. I was trying to help her as much as I could. I went through her pockets for some ID."

"And cash," Harry said. Porter sneezed.

"You don't look so hot, Harry-boy," Saint-Crispen said.

"Sinuses."

Saint-Crispen fumbled in his pocket and pulled out a container of nasal spray. "Here. Keep it. I never touch the stuff. It was in the hallway here."

Harry took the spray and inhaled four times. His headache seemed to fade.

"Anyhow," Saint-Crispen said. "I found this..." he produced a torn piece of newsprint from his pocket. Porter took the paper scrap and scrutinized the headline. "President Planning New York Trip."

Saint-Crispen noted the intense look on Harry's face. He nodded vigorously. "That's right, Harry-boy. This little chippie had an itinerary on her of the Prez' stops in the Apple. That tallies with what we figured was going on with the swan divers, don't it?"

"It certainly backs up what you saw in the peeper's vision."

"But better than that," the Saint said, "it'll give us some weight to get the feds in on our side, right? As it is now, Harry, we're primo targets for somebody because of being mixed up in all this. But if we have some real evidence of some sort of conspiracy, the feds will have to come in on our side, right?"

Harry stuck the paper in his pocket. "I'll do the best I can. Anyone see you palm this?"

"Give me some credit for finesse."

"Did she have any ID?"

"Nope."

"Cash?"

"Three tram tokens."

Porter stuck his hand deep into his right pocket, both to warm it up and deal with a more practical matter. "How much do I owe you?"

Saint-Crispen feigned surprise. "Harry. I'm disappointed in you, man. How long we go back? An eternity or two? To think that you would even consider the idea that I'd hit you up for some bread just for turning up this small, but very important, scrap of information."

Harry stared at the Saint. The con man's face, framed by his outmoded Afro, was a study in innocence. "Okay," Harry sighed. "What do you know that I don't and, in all likelihood, I should if I want to stay healthy?"

Saint-Crispen shifted his body from side to side. "Nothing. Honest. Why is it whenever I try to do you a favor, you always think I'm up to no good? I'm hurt, Harry. I truly am."

Porter disregarded Saint-Crispen's protestations. "If there wasn't any cash on the jumper and you're not charging me—" He nearly swallowed his tongue. "Are you scamming anyone at Ruth Tobruck's office?"

"Nope. Absolutely not. Never would even enter my mind. Honest," the Saint babbled.

"Marion," Porter said, sliding his hand out of his pocket and grabbing the Saint's right shoulder firmly. "If you're screwing around down there and anyone catches onto you, you're going to find out exactly how many places a human leg can be broken simultaneously. Those people don't fool around."

"Aww, Harry," the Saint shrugged. "I'm only selling a little real estate. I've been hanging around the office posing as an insurance rep. I started jawing with a couple of guys and one thing led to another—"

"Give it back."

"Huh?"

"Their money. Bank checks made out to cash, right? The Ticonderoga Realty Company selling acres of farmland in Florida?"

"Montana."

"Give it back, Saint, or you'll wind up walking around bearing a marked resemblance to a harmonica poster boy— every other tooth will be removed."

"It wasn't *that* much," Saint-Crispen protested.

"Then you won't mind losing it."

"If I do, I'll have to charge you for today's transaction."

"If you even consider that," Porter replied, not smiling. "I'll take care of your dental work before anyone at Tobruck's even thinks of it."

Saint-Crispen left the protective covering of the hallway and stalked off. "All right. All right. Some friend you are. Here I am, putting my ass on the line, doing all your legwork, and I'm starving for it. My mother in the hospital, still waiting for that operation, and you deny me the means to give her peace of mind."

"Your mother's had peace of mind for ten years," Harry called after him. "She died when you were in stir, remember?"

"That was my foster mother," the Saint shot back.

"Just keep it clean."

A sudden wave of sadness enveloped Harry. Maybe it was the weather. Maybe it was the day-glo outline of the girl's twisted body. Porter waited until the crowd had thinned and the video teams left the area before he stepped out into the rain. The fewer people who saw him drenched the better. He still had some sense of dignity. He double-timed it through the rain-soaked alley. Things were beginning to fall together, although in random order.

The peeper's concept of an assassination plot seemed more feasible with each suicide. But what were the connecting factors involved? There were too many loose ends. How did Pratt figure in with the suicide two days ago? What was it that Libby saw at Fountain Point? And World War III? Harry didn't even want to think about that.

As the drizzle soaked through his clothing, he stepped out onto Ninth Avenue. A sudden gust of wind caused him to shiver. His right knee suddenly locked. Harry cursed as his leg stiffened. Lapsing into a limp, he made his way back toward his apartment. Traffic was snarled. There wasn't a bus or a tram in sight. Cabs, of course, had disappeared with the first sign of bad weather.

He'd begin checking into that possible assassin list the first thing in the morning. Surely, one of those men would know something about any possible organized effort against Walker. Even a rumor would do. He strongly doubted any of them were actively involved themselves. Jesus. He needed sleep.

As he dragged himself up Ninth Avenue, past the tranx bars and six-tiered pleasure domes, he noticed a sleek private vehicle following him at a discreet distance. Coincidence? He decided to postpone panic for as long as possible. He made a quick turn onto Forty-fifth Street. The long black sedan did likewise. Harry was about to make for the nearest doorway when the vehicle accelerated and pulled up alongside him without a sound.

Porter glanced nervously into the car. A uniformed driver was at the wheel. In the back seat sat the rotund figure of Malcolm Robbins, television commentator and acknowledged misanthrope. Robbins affixed his baleful stare on Porter. "Harry, if you continue gimping around in the rain like this, you will catch double pneumonia at the very least. Please allow me to give you a lift to wherever it is you're headed."

Harry offered a soggy smile. His interrogation of possible plotters would commence ahead of schedule. The popeyed talk show host slid over in the back seat, giving Porter ample room to sit and drip. "Shall I turn on the blowers?"

"No," Harry chattered. "I'm fine. Really. How are you, Malcolm?"

"Unappreciated as usual," the corpulent man huffed in his strange delivery. "But overpaid." Robbins paused for a moment. I always thought you should have won the Pulitzer for that space station story, by the way. A very strong piece of work considering it was done entirely in the print medium. Ironic coupling in that piece: a progressive space science story done in an antiquated communicative motif."

"I'll take that as a compliment," Harry said. "Was I supposed to?"

Robbins emitted a hissing noise that Harry assumed to be a chuckle. "By all means. You didn't win, though, did you, poor egg? A piece of video reporting took the prize that year."

"Video writing," Harry grimaced, "not reporting."

"Ah yes," Robbins acknowledged. "I seem to recall it now." He aimed his soft-boiled eyes out the window, in seeming search of history. "What was it, that one again?"

"A feminine hygiene commercial," Porter said, realizing he was coming up with the punch line. "The judges thought it was very well done: informative, succinctly written, visually stunning."

"Unappreciated as well, you are."

Harry had begun massaging his right knee. Robbins shot him an inquisitive glance. "War wound," Porter stated. "Acts up in damp weather."

"Ahh," Robbins commiserated. Actually, it was a remarkably well-aimed kick by a sixty-year-old woman picket that had chipped Harry's kneecap over a year ago. Story on cryogenics that hadn't exactly panned out.

"What brings you out on such a bleak day?" Porter asked.

"The same topic as you, Harry. Suicide."

"Really."

The talk show host shook his head slowly in an affirmative motion. "Yes. I'm planning a concept show on contemporary suicides. Victims. Methods. Etcetera."

"Nice angle," Harry shrugged. "Not many of the video boys have really explored that."

"No one has," Robbins winked. "Have you noticed any similarities between some of our more youthful victims of late? Similarity in terms of method, for instance."

"As a matter of fact, I have," Harry said.

"I was afraid of that," Robbins sniffed.

"Relax, Malcolm. I'm not officially working on any suicide story."

"So, unofficially you're risking pneumonia? You really should invest in a private vehicle, you know."

"Who can afford one on a print newsman's salary?"

"Then make the jump to video," Robbins said, suddenly animated. "I can put in a few good words for you at the station. You'd be a natural. I can see that. The character type. Reassuring uncle. Definitely not the pretty boy pansy."

"I like what I do, Malcolm."

"What do you like? Putting up with buses that don't run, cabs that strike, shoes that wear out in horrible weather like this? You can't be serious."

Porter glanced at his shoes and noticed they were badly scuffed and coming apart at the seams nearest the toes. "I'm serious. Now, if we're going to debate my professional values for the rest of this ride, you can let me out here."

"I wouldn't dream of it," Robbins said, hissing again. "Your company is very enjoyable, Harry. Very enjoyable. Where shall we proceed?"

"East Ninety-second, off Madison."

"So be it."

Harry rubbed his hands in a vain attempt to return some semblance of warmth to his fingertips. "How's the national political scene striking you these days?"

"Below the belt, as usual," Robbins said, licking his lips in a gesture of distaste. "Walker is an absolute menace. But that, of course, is not big news. It's more of a way of life at this point in time. There are three things that one can be sure of in America: death, taxes, and the idiocy of our President. My God! The man's a threat to Darwinism."

"Dislike him, eh?"

"My dear Harry, anyone with a brain of a gnat or more dislikes the man. Hates the man. Unfortunately, the populace in general hasn't exactly been scoring overwhelmingly well on day-to-day intelligence tests. Hence, they seem quite content with this man's ineptness."

"Maybe not content," Harry offered. "Maybe resigned."

"Possibly. Possibly," Robbins nodded. "However, I detect an ulterior motive to your chattiness regarding our beloved leader."

Porter offered a sick little smile. His penchant for misleadingly snappy patter was growing less effective with each subsequent attempt.

Robbins continued: "You are the second person today to sniff around concerning my dislike for our leader."

"Really?"

"Yes," Robbins nodded. "Back at the suicide site, a fellow came up to me and started chatting shamelessly. 'I watch all your broadcasts. I agree with you one hundred percent on all your positions. Why, I hate the President almost as much as you do.' Honestly, Harry, the fellow was dressed *so* casually and was *so* magnificently ingratiating, I could only assume one thing."

"A fed."

"Only the federal fellows are so consistently awful in covering their tracks. Something's in the wind, I suppose. Another Presidential assassination in the offing?"

Harry should have been surprised that Robbins took the entire affair in such a cavalier manner but somehow wasn't. "I'm not sure," he said, choosing his words carefully. "It's possible. I think there's something big going on, Malcolm. I'm trying to find out who is behind it and why."

"Well," Robbins shrugged, folding his chubby arms around his rippling middle. "I would very much like to help you. As a team, I believe we could work wonders. You handling the print medium on one day and me providing penetrating video coverage the next. The quick one-two media punch. I would very much enjoy that—however—"

He placed his two hands palms up before him. "I have nothing to offer you. I average about four obvious federal

once-overs a year. Whenever the boys in D.C. get an inkling
that someone with a bit of backing is gunning for Walker, they
sniff around my office thinking that I must have some link to
an organized, radical underground. I'm flattered, of course.
I'm five foot two inches tall, of Hungarian descent, have thin
hair, high blood pressure and at least eighty pounds more
than I should have. It's nice to be thought of as a personable
threat.

"Unfortunately, I know nothing, as usual. And, as an
assassin, I would be a washout. I simply don't have the height
for it. To make matters even more confusing for the assassin
stalkers, I believe that ninety-five percent of this country, if
given the opportunity, would take a shot at the old boy. He's
a positively awful leader. But Vice President Reeves! That's a
different story. A leader. A former military man. He has
charisma and vision."

"I didn't mean to suggest that you were personally involved," Porter injected.

"Not to worry, Harry old dove. It's quite all right. Really.
I'm honored to be involved, in any small way, with a chink in
the administration's armor."

"You said you're investigated *quarterly* by the feds?" Harry
repeated.

"At least," the man replied impishly. "There is a small but
star-studded group of us who are usually targeted: Ruth
Tobruck, Jerry Lucas, Victor Carmichael—"

"Peter Hayden and Andrew Cade," Harry finished.

"You have been doing your homework," Robbins smiled
admiringly. "We would make a spectacular team."

"So you six are the FBI's best bets."

"They seem to think so. The list grows or shrinks according
to the seasons, but we're the core."

"You don't seem to take your status too seriously," Porter
commented.

"None of us do. Perhaps even the federal gentlemen are
just going through the motions. As a crime reporter, Harry,
does it really strike you as feasible that somebody as much in
the public eye as any of us would actually back a plot to kill
the President of the United States? Think of the risk involved. We may dream of it, yes, pray for it, maybe—but
actually get involved? Highly unlikely. It would reduce our
personal incomes to nil."

"If you were caught doing it—" Harry pointed out.

"If we were caught doing it," Robbins repeated wistfully. Of course! There is always the wonderfully optimistic thought that one of us could pull it off and not be found out! A splendid notion but very nearly impossible. If one of us did manage to succeed, I do believe we'd blow our cover by bragging about our accomplishment to everyone we came in contact with."

The car pulled up outside Harry's apartment building. The rotund figure pointed to the drizzle outside the car window. "Here you are, Harry. We must get together again, soon. You have absolutely brightened my day. Just envisioning such a nefarious deed will keep me chuckling for weeks. Months perhaps. Ah, the arrival of hope can take the damndest of forms."

Harry shook hands with the eccentric personality and stepped out of the car. "By the way," Robbins added, "if you'd like, I'll call the rest of the half dozen and ask them to cooperate with you fully. It will save you a lot of time and make things easier for you. Many of them demand references before being grilled."

"References?" Harry said, the rain once again beginning to soak through his jacket.

"Yes indeed. With my help, instead of having to slither around in the rain outside their doorways, you can just call them up and make an appointment to badger them. I'm sure they will find your methods as enjoyable as I have."

"Thanks, Malcolm. Whatever you think is best."

"Excellent." Robbins executed a quick wave as his electric car pulled silently away from the curbside. Harry stood in the rain, glancing inside his building for the figure of Dr. Jorge. He sighed to himself while trudging through the lobby. This investigation wasn't turning out as discreetly as he had planned.

"References?"

6

Porter dripped through the hallway towards the door, elated. Inadvertently, Robbins had justified Porter's involvement with this entire affair. If federal agents were sniffing around a Presidential assassination lead, Harry was onto something.

And if Harry was onto something, there was tangible proof that the peeper's dream dealt in future facts.

Since the government was already investigating, Harry felt that there was no reason he shouldn't have access to whatever information had turned up officially. Perhaps the feds could unknowingly explain just how Bill Pratt was involved in this mess, or Doug Libby. At least, that was Harry's feeling as he walked into his apartment.

"Jessica," he called, entering the home.

"She grew bored within the confines of this cubicle," Machine informed him, "and went to her place of employment."

Porter shrugged.

"She also said that she was considering taking a vacation, flying to her uncle's cottage in England..."

Harry's face dropped.

"...and she would be pleased if you would accompany her."

Porter's spirits perked up immediately. Funny how emotions could short-circuit the brain. Sitting at his viewphone, he dialed the local FBI branch. A very ordinary-looking fellow appeared on the screen with a nearly visible chip on his shoulder the size of a major calamity. The fellow stared at the phone for nearly thirty seconds before he even attempted to speak. Harry figured the guy had a testimonial plaque from Simon Legree at home somewhere. "Federal Bureau of Investigation," the receptionist snapped. "State your business."

Nice touch of etiquette. "Agent Bronkowski, please."

"Who's calling."

"Harry Porter, *Herald-Times-News*. Friend of small children and animals."

The agent's face clouded before disappearing from view, replaced by a tape of the American flag fluttering in the breeze. "God Bless America" was cranked out by a rather listless orchestra. The second stanza was cut short by the intrusion of the tough, chiseled features of Dennis Bronkowski, a New York based operative. Porter figured Bronkowski had been an ordinary, nice-enough guy years ago. Porter also believed the story of Chicken Little.

"You calling me can only mean trouble," Bronkowski said, his lips the only part of his face that moved. "What do you want?"

"Nice to see you, too, Denny. How's the wife and kids?"

"Wife's divorced. Kids are wild. Life is tough. What's up?"

"I think we're digging around identical pig sties, Den."

"Farming isn't our area. Is that it?"

"Is Presidential assassination your turf?"

Bronkowski didn't flinch. Porter was amazed how much he resembled Mount Rushmore. He couldn't figure out which head, though. "You know it is. If you have any information about an alleged plot, you are required by law to inform us of same. If you're prying, I'll see you around."

"Look, Bronk," Harry said. "I know that you guys are checking out potential murderers. We both hit on the same guy today, Malcolm Robbins. He was quite flattered by the attention. Look, I just thought we'd compare notes, that's all."

"There are no notes to compare," Bronkowski stated flatly. "Assassination rumors surface every day. We're always checking something out. It's no big deal."

"This investigation is different."

"How?"

"It dovetails with this suicide epidemic and the possibility of World War III." Jeez. He wished he hadn't said that.

"How?"

Porter glared at the phone, his face reddening. "I'm not sure."

"Then how do you know this supposed plot exists?"

"A peeper discovered it."

"And he told you about it?"

"Not exactly. I talked a friend of mine into peeping the peeper. He saw it in the guy's head."

"And the peeper didn't know you were prying."

"Let's not play games, Bronk. The peeper was sedated at the time. My friend and I got to him right before someone took him out of the game. The peeper in question, by the way, was one of your boys: Dr. Hardy Flowers. Recently deceased."

If Bronkowski was startled by Porter's revelation, he didn't show it. Then again, with Bronkowski's rough facial terrain, it would have been hard to tell if he was experiencing orgasm let alone mild surprise. "No one named Flowers works for me."

"Not now he doesn't," Harry said. "He's fertilizing daisies somewhere."

"I'd know about it."

"I'm sure you do."

"Are you through, Porter?"

"No I'm not, Dennis. You have to level with me on this one. One friend of mine is dead and another is close to it right now. They were trying to get information to me. One of them, at least, can be connected directly with all this."

"How's the wife and kids, Harry."

"Divorced and unborn! Bronkowski!" Harry was shouting at the small screen when it went blank. He slammed down the phone. He was onto something all right. He knew it. Now if only he could come up with those niggling little details involved: like who, what, where, when and why?

No wonder those suckers always wound up in the front of journalism textbooks. You just can't have a story without them.

The baleful sighs of sirens cut short his thought. Something was happening nearby. Harry opened his living room window and stuck his head outside. He was met, full face, by a gust of warm, acrid air. A crowd was gathering down the block. He dashed out of his apartment and made for the elevator. He limped out into the street within a matter of minutes. The rain had stopped.

At Ninety-second and Park, a young girl teetered on a small windowsill outside a fifth floor apartment window. Apparently, the girl had just stepped out onto the ledge. A crowd was only just forming and a single squad car was on the scene. Sirens in the distance heralded the arrival of at least one more black and white and, probably, an ambulance from Mt. Sinai. Harry eyed the young woman. She was blond, brown-eyed. Fifteen years of age. She seemed totally calm. The girl surveyed the street below her. She sniffed three times and wiped a trickle of fluid from her nose with the back of her left hand.

Harry theorized that, if this suicide was part of the pattern, he still had a precious few moments to intercede. The girl had not started her oration as of yet. If her soliloquy ran according to schedule, she'd speak for a good ninety seconds or more.

A small, electric pickup truck, its open backside empty, idled at an intersection light. Its driver, a long-haired lout, stood outside the vehicle, ogling the girl. Sneaking into the passenger's side of the truck, Harry slid behind the wheel and tossed the stick into drive. The truck lurched forward. The startled driver turned around to see Harry speed away.

"Police business!" Harry waved. "Be back in a jiff!" He hoped.

Porter leaned on the horn of the van, sending pedestrians scattering for the safety of the moving sidewalks. Making a sharp turn onto Lexington, Harry spotted his target: a furniture store. Backing over the moving sidewalk in front of the small shop, he plunged the rear of the truck through the building's plate glass facade. An alarm went off as the shards of glass cut through the air. "Police business!" Harry yelled as he dived through the broken window.

He ran around the back of the vehicle. He took two inflated mattresses from an all-zebra bedroom display and tossed them onto the back of the vehicle. "Hey!" screamed a very unhappy store manager.

Harry scrambled back into the truck, pulling away from the utterly destroyed front of the store. "Bill the precinct!" he yelled. "Police business!"

Porter sped around the block and back onto Park Avenue. The girl was still on the ledge a block away. The police had erected a barricade across the avenue, however, effectively blocking Harry's path. Harry stared at the girl. She was speaking, wiping her nose. From his vantage point, he couldn't hear just how far along she was in her swan song. He caught an almost imperceptible quivering in her knees. She was readying herself for the leap.

Harry gunned the motor. The electric van silently sliced through the plastic barricades, producing a stark, crunching sound as well as equally harsh epithets from the cops who were forced to dive sideways for safety.

Porter hastily pulled the truck up onto the moving sidewalk, frantically angling the back of the van to cover the proposed point of impact. Beneath the truck's wheels, the anguished cries of machinery being pulverized echoed as the moving sidewalk slowed down to a painful halt. Porter had no time to back the truck into a better position. The girl jumped unexpectedly.

She jumped wide.

"Shit." Harry held his breath and threw the truck into reverse. The truck jerked backwards some six feet. A wire mesh trash container was reduced to wire mash under the left rear wheel. The girl's body sailed like a knife to street level.

She hit the back of the truck with an explosion of air, landing flat on her back. Her body completely deflated the first mattress. An explosion of air rocked the cab of the truck. The jumper came to rest on the second mattress before slipping onto the sidewalk.

Harry tumbled out of the cab, reaching the girl's body before the ambulance attendants. The victim, her light skin without blemish, stared vacantly into his eyes. "The worst of all worlds—" she muttered. "Need a leader... sacrifice too great."

The crowd burst into a round of spontaneous applause when it realized that the girl had just been saved as the result of a rescue attempt that rivaled the best holographic entertainment currently being shown in first-run holo parlors. Harry motioned the two white-suited attendants over. "Can you take her to NYU instead of Lennox?"

"Mt. Sinai's closest," one said.

"Dr. Andrew Cade at NYU has dealt with these kids before," he lied. "Maybe if she's not hurt too badly?"

"Well," the attendant hedged.

Harry slipped him a twenty.

The white jump-suited figure examined the girl quickly. "Possible broken leg. Bruises. No signs of internal injury. All right. It's NYU."

"Great," Harry said, climbing into the back of the ambulance with the girl. "I'm coming too."

"Next of kin?"

"Innocent bystander, let's go."

The ambulance pulled away with Harry at the rear window. He watched a gaggle of frazzled men in blue run up to the scene. The truck sat on the now dormant pedway. The cab was tilted downward, it's front wheels in a pothole of their own making. The truck's driver pointing wildly at the policemen, the ambulance, the sidewalk, and the van. Harry wasn't sure, but he thought he saw the manager of the furniture store jog through the debris as well, hands waving spasmodically. Porter leaned against the back door and watched the girl shimmy on the stretcher.

The way he figured it, the safest place for him to be right about now was in the back of this ambulance.

Dr. Andrew Cade stared at the last computer readout on the ever-changing data sheet. "She's fine, physically," he said, glancing at the young woman in the hospital bed. "Not a broken bone. Not even the slightest signs of a concussion. Porter, you amaze me." He regarded the journalist with a mixture of awe and amusement. "Despite the fact that you are one of the most unathletic, uncoordinated individuals I have ever encountered, you do manage to accomplish the most mind-boggling of deeds. You have undoubtedly just saved this woman's life. How? What is your secret? Prayer? A strict diet?"

"Positive thinking," Harry smiled. "Besides, I was quite a good driver before I had my license revoked."

"How long ago?"

"Six years. Seven maybe."

The girl stirred in her sedated sleep. "World...needs leader...no...sacrifice...great...."

"She's been mumbling that sort of stuff since she landed," Porter said. "Drugs?"

"Were that only the case," Cade said, gravely. "There are no traces of any type of alien chemical substance in her body. In fact, the girl, prior to her fall, must have represented the ideal American specimen of adolescence. Skin tone perfect. Muscles well exercised. Superteen. All we're getting now is intense activity in her brain waves. She's thinking up a storm."

"Could she have been brainwashed?"

"A crude term, Porter, beneath you, really." Cade said. "But yes, one could assume from her fairly limited conversational skills, at this point, that she was coached to some degree."

Cade's face sagged under the weight of pressure or pressures unknown.

"What's up, Andy?"

"I'm sorry to have to hit you with this now, Porter," Cade answered slowly, "in light of this young woman's condition. It's about yesterday's burn victim."

"It was Bill?"

"Yes, I'm afraid it was."

"Was." Porter realized that both he and Cade were speaking of Pratt past tense. Porter without thinking, Cade with the knowledge of a hospital administrator. "He didn't pull through?"

"I'm afraid there was no stopping the infection," the doctor sighed. "He went into shock. We tried, Porter. We really tried."

Harry leaned against a wall, his head reeling. His eyes throbbed. He wanted to lash out and strike something.

Anything. "How did he get here, Andy? Who could have done this to him? His whole life was devoted to saving lives. He wouldn't even carry a gun during the war."

"We don't have any answers, Harry. All we have are questions."

"And his own field of science couldn't save him," Harry muttered. "Ironic. But who the hell would want to murder a medical technician?"

"Researcher," Cade corrected softly.

Porter slowly pushed himself away from the wall. "It's more than ironic, his death. It's illogical. Bill's appearance here as a patient doesn't coincide with his showing up yesterday and resigning, does it?"

Cade pursed his lips. His sloped eyebrows nearly met over his nose. "Frankly, the sequence of events does leave me a bit puzzled."

"You called me as soon as he walked off, didn't you?"

"Yes. I left word with your editor..."

"Who called me at Kapps..." Porter began to pace within the confines of the jumper's room. "He shows up and resigns. Forty-five minutes or so later, he's admitted to this center covered with burns. Your men figure that those burns are at least an hour old. If Bill quit at, let's say, three-thirty and then was admitted at four-thirty P.M. as a patient...."

Cade consulted his chart. "Four twenty-five."

"Then something's definitely out of whack with the time sequence, isn't it? According to your boys, Bill would have already been burned at the time of his resignation. What's the margin for error on estimating the time of the accident?"

"With today's computerized skin layer scans, five minutes at the most. And that is highly unlikely."

"So, unless Bill was exuding flames while he was bidding you a fond farewell, something is wrong here. Very, very wrong."

"The computer could be off, of course," Cade announced, as if he was trying to convince himself.

"Let's assume that it wasn't," Porter answered. "We're then faced with an impossible situation."

"Indeed," Cade conceded. "One that I really don't want to consider."

Porter pressed his lips together, forming a thin white line. "You were visited by a bogus Bill Pratt."

"Impossible."

"Is it?" Harry continued. "Let me try this out on you. Bill and Weiner arrive in New York. Bill thinks he's being followed. I tell him that he's just experiencing big city paranoia because I'm such a highly sensitive and perceptive soul—" Harry cursed himself silently, recalling the conversation. If only he had taken Bill more seriously. "They both show up one fine day at this institution only to disappear. Twenty-four hours later they reappear in order to resign. We assume that they're leaving of their own choice. But suppose they're doing no such thing? Suppose they were abducted from the center on the first day because of their research."

"The world of cloak and dagger just doesn't fit in with our day-to-day operation, Porter," Cade said. "You're stretching it."

"Maybe. But common sense tells you that Bill couldn't quit at the same time he was being badly burned. Those facts aren't being stretched." Harry stopped pacing. "What kind of developments were Bill and Weiner working on?"

"Some new form of syntheskin application. I'm not sure of the details myself and, since their notes are gone, it may be months or years before their research can be duplicated."

"Suppose they were kidnapped for their knowledge in the field."

"And then—eliminated once the knowledge was gleaned?"

"Yes," Harry nodded slowly. "Eliminated. But whoever it was who tried to kill them both didn't figure on Bill Pratt's will to live. You would have loved working with him, Andy. The guy had a heart as big as a house. And guts? It took real nerve to be a medic on the mainland during the Chinese war. This guy made it all look easy. Okay. Our thugs burn Bill badly after they kidnap him. They think he's dead. But he's not. Something in the back of his mind tells him he can't quit just yet. He has to get back here to the hospital. He has to let you know what's going on. How he got here and from where? I don't know, but I swear to God I'll find out."

Porter formed a fist with his left hand. "He gets here, badly burned. That means only one thing; the Pratt who showed up to quit was not Bill but someone altered to *look* like Bill."

"Via syntheskin?" Cade said. "That's ridiculous."

"Let's pretend it isn't. Do you realize what this technique could mean to organized crime? A quick change of identity after every transaction?"

"As much as I think your theory is utter hogwash, Cade said, agitated, "I have notified the local authorities. The Federal Bureau of Investigation has sent a man over to check into the angle that, perhaps, commercial conglomerates are involved."

"Have you met the agent yet?"

"No."

"Is his name Dennis Bronkowski?"

"Sounds like the man. How did you guess?"

"Reporters are all clairvoyant," Porter said, accompanying Cade to the door.

Harry swung the door open. Bronkowski had two of his burlier agents with him. They stood like three Olympians, shoulder to shoulder. Each agent had a wing span of what Harry took to be eight feet. They were dressed in somber, blue, three-pieced suits. Tradition, he reasoned. Next to the FBI men a shorter, more disheveled fellow stood, bouncing on the soles of his feet. The shorter man's face turned a bright crimson when he spotted Harry.

"If you know everything, Porter," Cade whispered, "the presence here of Lieutenant Groux will come as no surprise." Cade grinned at the policeman. "I believe you wanted to chat with Mr. Porter, Lieutenant?"

"Damned straight!" Groux snapped.

"Hello, George," Harry smiled as the short arm of the law approached him in the best of bulldog styles. "How's the blood pressure."

"You've certainly taken care of that today!" the lieutenant blustered, his face almost radiating heat. "I have a little business with you."

"Really?"

"Really! Let's talk Porter!"

"About what?"

"About impersonating a police officer, about driving without a license, about the destruction of private property, about grand theft auto, about the destruction of public property, about a moving sidewalk that isn't moving any more, about..."

Harry backed away from the soon-to-be frothing officer, bumping shoulders with the grinning Dr. Cade. "Hey, Andy, tell him that I saved a girl's life and he can't arrest me."

Cade shook his head in mock dismay at Groux. "He saved a young woman's life, Lieutenant. You really can't arrest him."

"There, you see," Harry said.

"I can't?" Groux said, dumbfounded.

"Think of the negative publicity involved," Harry shrugged. "Gee, George. It would be awfully bad for morale in this city. It would make the department seem awfully mean, too."

Groux's bulldog jaw flopped open and shut as if to speak. Instead, an exasperated woosh of air and a gutteral "Je-eezuschristgodalmighty" noise emerged. He spun on his heels and left the five men behind.

Bronkowski took Dr. Cade by the arm and politely but firmly led him into a nearby office. Harry attempted to follow, his route abruptly blocked by Bronkowski's two companions. Harry stared over their shoulders at the retreating twosome. He muttered a hasty "excuse me" and tried to squeeze his way past the two FBI men. He found himself rebounding off their immobile chests.

"Hey!" Harry called after Bronkowski. "What do you feed these guys, steel?"

"It's not the food costs," Bronkowski smirked. "It's the rabies shots."

"Mind if I sit in on the meeting?" Harry asked Bronkowski's back.

"Very much so," the agent replied, standing in the doorway of the office.

"Damn it!" Porter yelled. "This is a fine way to treat a hero!"

"Life's been hell since they took away ticker-tape parades, Porter," the agent said, closing the door behind him.

Harry loped from the hospital. He was angry. He was pained. Whatever Bronkowski and Cade discussed would have to do with Bill's death. Harry owed Bill on that count. He'd find out who was responsible. If humanly possible, he'd make sure that they paid in full.

To hell with the President and the rest of the world. Porter had let a friend down, perhaps even contributed to his death. He had a hell of a score to settle. Worse yet, he was running out of time. He didn't know exactly why, but he instinctively felt that if he didn't discover all the puzzle pieces very quickly, he'd never get the chance again.

Stepping out into the street, he squinted into the hazy sun. Out of the corner of his eye, he saw a private vehicle jump the tram track and veer, dizzily, through two-way traffic. The electric car was heading his way. Harry turned around and walked towards the hospital park. When the electric car showed no sign of either slowing down or altering its course, Harry broke out into a run.

The car jumped the curb and, flying over the pedway, silently sliced through the grassy enclosure. Strollers were sent scattering. Porter sprinted through the park, zigzagging through bushes and park benches. The car pursued him relentlessly. Spotting a source of possible salvation, Harry aimed himself towards a large, ornate statue of three astronaut medics standing in the middle of an open field.

He didn't have too much choice about choosing his haven. He couldn't rely on the small benches for cover. The car certainly couldn't scale a statue. In order to reach the manmade sanctuary, however, Harry had to abandon all cover and dash out into the open.

Forcing his legs to pound harder, he darted for the statue. The car followed him, slowly accelerating. Although the electric vehicle made no noise whatsoever, Harry could feel its presence behind him. "Don't look back. Just watch the statue." The three gigantic astronauts stood twenty yards away. "Don't look back. Just watch the statue." Harry's legs strained against the pain. He could almost feel the grille of the auto slashing into his ankles, pulling his body beneath its spinning tires. "Don't look back. Just watch the statue." Porter tipped his body forward in an attempt to increase his momentum. Ten yards more. His chest began to ache from the consistent lack of breath. "Don't look bac—" He glanced quickly over his shoulder. The car was almost upon him. "I shouldn't have looked back." Feeling no need to retain his grip on solid ground, Harry allowed his body to soar into space.

As he leapt, the car swerved behind him, brushing against his right foot. Porter's body cut a line parallel to the grassy knoll, sailing through the air for over six feet before slamming into the outstretched hand of one of the astronauts. He clasped the hand. He swung one foot onto the elbow and shinnied up to the shoulder. A pain erupted in his chest. He might have broken a rib on that one.

The electric car smashed into the side of the concrete edifice, tearing one of its plastic doors off in the process. Remarkably, the vehicle continued on its mad drive, skidding towards an exit at the opposite side of the park. A crowd of passersby began trotting towards the statue. The car disappeared from view. Two nurses reached the statue before the army of the curious.

Harry, slightly dazed and definitely out of breath, slowly climbed down from the astronaut's shoulder. "You get a really nice view of the park from here," he coughed at the nurses.

IV

"There are two kinds of weakness:
that which breaks and that which bends."
James Russell Lowell

1

"Assassinate the President?" Jerry Lucas smiled over the videophone. "What a wonderful idea." The long-haired NASA official's perpetual smirk momentarily faded. "I don't mean to give you the wrong impression, Porter. I wouldn't actually advocate such an event, but, then again, it would be in the public's best interest, wouldn't it? I mean, Walker's hurt the U.S. space program almost as much as you have. No mean feat."

"I only reported what happened on Island," Harry said. "I didn't invent the facts."

"No one ever said you did," Lucas replied, the smirk reappearing. "But, quite coincidentally, *Island's* woes led to Harry Porter's fame, didn't they, and fortune? You became a regular celeb, didn't you. Gone the way of all flash?"

"Who was that lady I saw you with last night?" Harry asked.

"I don't get it," Lucas countered.

"I thought that as long as I was playing straight man, you might want to work that one into your act." Harry grimaced at the phone. "Look. I'm not calling you up to fence. I'm in no condition for sports, verbal or physical. I've got two taped ribs, a couple of dead friends, and an army of thugs to contend with. I think someone is trying to off Walker.

"I'm asking your help. I need information. I'm not saying that Walker is a good or bad leader. I don't really care. The world is in a bad way, Lucas. But it could get worse. You're a critic of the present administration. You're young. You're involved in politics. You may have access to rumors, anything."

"Ohh. I get it. You want to know who'd be interested in taking out Walker?" Lucas laughed.

"Right."

"Well here's a tip, scoop. Check the white pages of your phone book. Potential assassins are found listed under the letters A through Z. Have fun."

The phone viewscreen abruptly faded to black. Harry tossed the phone back into its cradle. That guy would throw a drowning man both ends of a rope. Massaging his head slowly, Harry spun his chair in a semicircle. "Minuet No. 1 from K. 601," he requested.

Mozart entered Harry's life. So did a furious pounding at his door. "Now what?" he muttered. Clutching his left side, he hobbled to the door. Porter glanced through the peepscreen. He was greeted by the sight of the furious Adam's apple of Ruth Tobruck and the panicked eyes of Saint-Crispen. "Great, just great," he said, flinging the door open. "Here for happy hour?" Harry smiled as Tobruck stormed past him, dragging Saint-Crispen by the collar.

Tobruck, a tall, bleached-blond woman with a horselike face, deep-set blue eyes, and a skyscraper forehead, was built like an Amazon: the kind of woman who'd be safe from advances if she cooked while nude in a lumber camp. She tossed the Saint onto the carpeting with a flick of her massive wrist. "You want to ask me questions, Porter? *You* ask me questions. Face-to-face."

And man-to-man, Porter thought. "If it's not happy hour, could it be dinnertime?"

"You don't send me yo-yo's like this!" she raged, pointing a chunky forefinger at Saint-Crispen. "Trying to snoop around and all the time stealing money from my guys!"

"I still have some eggs left if you'd like an early breakfast," Harry continued.

Ruth Tobruck grabbed Harry by the lapels. She raised him within inches of her face. Harry swallowed hard, not knowing what the next part of his body to break would be. The woman smelled of cheap perfume and sweat. Porter could feel her breath on his forehead. For once, he was thankful that his sinuses were screwy. His nose was even with her mouth. He gaped at her. She had the kind of map only Rand McNally could love. She shook Harry like a rag doll.

"You have a few screws loose upstairs or something?" she growled. "Am I getting through to you or am I not? You want your shell cracked permanently? Now, what do you want with me?"

Harry grinned at the woman. "Lady, if you don't get your hands off me, your childbearing years will be prematurely ended."

Tobruck glanced down. Harry's knee was already in direct line with her pelvic area. "Okay. Okay. I tend to overreact. It's hereditary."

Tobruck released Porter and collapsed on the couch with a sigh. "It's the coffee, too. I drink a lot of coffee. The doctor tells me I gotta quit. A lady with my job and the pressures. All the time on the go. But I love my work, you know? I like meeting people, working with people. I like communicating, you know? So, you want to communicate something to me? Let's communicate, Porter. What the hell do you want from my life?"

"Someone's trying to kill the President," Harry said, sitting across from Tobruck and above the whimpering form of the Saint. "Is it you?"

A smile appeared, lopsided, on Tobruck's thick lips. "You're a funny guy, Porter. You got balls. I bet you're a union man. Guild. Hey, I admit it. I hate the President, you know. But me? Kill him? Hell, that's un-American. Worse yet, it would make things too easy for him. I prefer watching the guy squirm under public scrutiny. Give him another term, and the people are going to lynch the sucker. I don't have to use any clout to eliminate him. He's doing just fine all by himself. His way is just a little more roundabout. It's one of the pluses of the democratic system."

Harry nodded.

The woman placed a large hand on her knee. "I wish I could help you, Porter. You've always been fair to the working man. But I haven't heard a whisper about anything serious. Just the usual grumbling."

"Well, I appreciate your coming over, Ms. Tobruck," Harry said.

Tobruck smiled. "See. We've communicated. We've gotten all our problems solved save one." She stared angrily at Saint-Crispen. "This sonofabitch has caused me undue grief, Porter. Your little messenger boy has gotten himself into some big trouble. He filched quite a bit of cash from my men. Five grand, I figure."

"Saint-Crispen!" Harry said, exasperated. "I warned you."

The curly-haired man on the floor whined. "I didn't filch any money."

"The hell you didn't," Tobruck said, her face beginning to twitch.

"Didn't!" Saint-Crispen insisted. "A few guys at your office may have invested a few dollars here and there in some casual real estate speculations I was involved in—but that's not filching. There's always a risk involved in speculative transactions like that."

"You're going to find out how much risk," Tobruck said, the veins on her high forehead suddenly blossoming.

Harry slid down in his chair. "Where's the money, Marion?"

"It's gone," Saint-Crispen offered, timidly.

"Gone?" Tobruck bellowed. "Gone? You spent it already? You just stole it this morning! In six hours you pissed away five grand?"

"I didn't spend it," Saint-Crispen said, haughtily getting to his feet. "I reinvested it. You know, you make a little dough, you put it back out onto the street. It's like the stock market. You keep it circulating. You build up a real cash flow."

"If you don't get that money back to my boys by tomorrow," Tobruck said, standing silently and moving towards Saint-Crispen, "the only commodity that's going to be flowing around here will be your bodily fluids."

Saint-Crispen backed himself against the oversized video screen. "Harry! Tell her I'm good for it. Tell her about the time I made you a fortune in real estate."

"If I told her that my nose would grow," Porter replied.

Tobruck advanced on Saint-Crispen. The Saint slid down the wallscreen, assuming a defensive fetal position on the floor. Burying his head in his hands, he emitted a high, powerful wail. Harry couldn't believe the sheer cowardice of the man.

His embarrassment suddenly exploded into pain, however, as the sonic sound evolved into a cerebral siren. The Saint's fear slashed Harry's insides apart. Porter grabbed his head, as if trying to contain its churning contents. He tumbled onto the carpeting.

"Shit" he hissed. A trickle of blood slithered from his right nostril.

The Saint, still huddled against the screen, continued his fearful noise. Tobruck froze. Her body quivered within her pants suit. For no apparent reason, her form shot backwards across the room, slamming into the front door and shattering the fragile peepscreen.

"Saint-Crispen," Harry barked, wiping his nose. "Knock it off! Knock it off!"

The Saint slowly raised his head. "Huh?" he blinked. "What?"

Harry struggled to an upright position, dabbing his nose. He glanced around to see Tobruck climb up the side of the door. "You okay?"

"I'll take the loss, okay?" Tobruck said, opening the door. "Just keep this goon away from me." She paused at the doorway. "Unless, of course, he'd like to work on my security team—at the office. We sometimes encounter representatives of various rival organizations whose manners are reprehensible." Tobruck smiled slightly. "Yes, that idea appeals to me." She nodded towards the Saint. "If you're interested, give me a call, punk."

Harry walked over to Saint-Crispen and straightened the crouching man. "Remind me to have a long talk with you about your telepathic endeavors."

"Well, she was going to hurt me!"

"She wouldn't have done anything to you with me here," Harry scoffed. "Besides, she would have hurt you a lot less than you did her."

"Damn it," Saint-Crispen moaned. "Now see what you've done to me? I thought I had that problem licked. I never should have peeked into that peeper. Here I've been popping tranx, keeping a lid on this shit for ten years, trying to act like a goddamned freak. I do you a favor and what happens? I'm being tailed by thugs, by the law and, now, to top it all off, I'm having my seizures again. You've ruined my life, Harry! Ruined it! I'll never be a normal human being again!"

Harry led the Saint to the sofa. "You never were. Now, sit down, Marion."

"I'll never know the joys of smelling flowers in the rain. Never be able to settle down with a wife and kids, a home in the suburbs, a lawn astronaut, a kidney-shaped pool, a social security card . . ."

"Knock it off, Marion. The closest you've come to having a wife and kid is when you were pinched in that black market baby scam. You even got that screwed up."

"It could've happened to anybody," the Saint pouted.

"Right," Harry nodded, retrieving two shots out of the kitchen. "There are plenty of black kids named Chang running around the city."

"You ever try picking up a kid in the dark? Between their blankets and the diapers and stuff they're practically invisible."

Harry handed the Saint the shot. "We're in trouble, Marion."

"Big news."

"No. I mean real trouble. That friend of mine, Bill ·Pratt, the guy I told you was being tailed by our first·jumper? He's dead."

"Like in deceased?"

"Yup. Someone tried to nail me too, today. Sent a hit-and-run driver after me."

Saint-Crispen gulped down his drink. "Right now you don't seem the best person in the world to be around in terms of personal safety, Harry-boy. This has nothing to do with my great affection for you, bud, but I've been thinking about taking a vacation anyhow so, until the heat is off, adios."

Saint-Crispen practically jogged towards the door. "If you find out who's trying to do you in, let me know. Write me a letter or something."

Harry watched the door slam shut. "I'm still amazed at this fragile flower we call friendship," he smirked.

"Semantics has always been a subjective science," Machine noted.

2

"I can't help you, Harry," Leonard Golden said, sitting at the back of Mecoy's. The full moon attempted to shine through the establishment's smoked glass window, apparently decided against it, and retreated behind a dark cloud. "I'm getting a lot of pressure. A lot. Pressure about your story on Kapps not being handed in on time. Pressure about our mailroom being sent into low orbit."

·He placed a hand on his forehead. "Little things like that."

"I realize that, Lenny," ,Porter countered, massaging his eyelids. "I'm getting pressured, too. I've had one friend murdered, a source found dead, and an apartment ransacked. I've stumbled across an assassination plot no one will acknowledge, and there's somebody out there who'd like to see me become an endangered species to boot. I've been shot at, run down, and blown up. I'm not too pleased about it. I'm sorry about dragging my heels on the Kapps piece, but staying alive right now is top priority in this reporter's notebook. Maybe if you ran some interference for me with DeWitt?"

"No can do," Golden frowned. He reached into his pocket and produced two tranquilizers. He washed them down with bourbon. "Never mix, never worry," Harry commented.

"Save the snappy patter for your big story," Golden said, making a sour face. "You think the feds are mixed up in all this?"

"I know so. Why else cover up that peeper's murder? If Cade hadn't clued me in about Bill Pratt's death, I get the uneasy feeling that the government would have put the lid on that, too. I just can't figure out why. I can't see how all the pieces fit."

"Maybe they don't," Golden shrugged, his eyes fluttering.

Harry pushed his eyelids down with his thumb. He shouldn't harrass his editor any further than necessary. The old guy obviously had his own problems. The beeper on his communicator went off.

He removed his coat from the back of his chair and shook the device out of the lining. "Porter here."

"Harry," came a metallic feminine voice. "It's your automated home computer unit."

"What's up, Machine?" He was irritated that his computer would track him down during his alleged leisure hours.

"I was casually scanning the newsat reports for any possible information pertaining to your investigation, and I encountered a story filed only minutes ago."

"Okay. Shoot."

"I beg your pardon."

"Shoot!"

"Mr. Porter, I was programmed at the behest of a medical facility to, essentially, behave in a nonviolent manner; bearing that fact in mind—"

"It's a colloquialism. What happened?"

"Someone has just tried, unsuccessfully, to kill the President of the United States."

Harry's mouth tightened. "How?"

"A fairly haphazard maneuver. A small rocket device armed with laser weaponry was set off at Dulles Airport by person or persons unknown. It was tracked before it could reach its destination and was neutralized by Air Force beams."

"The target?"

"The White House, of course. Very primitive engineering, apparently."

"Maybe it was meant to be," Harry said slowly.

"I fail to see the logic behind a shoddy construc—"

"A warning," Porter theorized. "Perhaps it was meant as a warning, designed to show Walker that whoever is cooking up this plot means business. The next time around, they won't be bluffing. And there will be a next time around, Machine, you can bet on it..."

"Games of chance are of no interest to—"

Leonard Golden surged to life, albeit briefly. "Here's your chance, Harry," he sputtered. "No one will pay attention to you locally, right?"

"Right."

"Well, now here's your chance to go national. With the Oval Office in a state of shock right now, it might not be a bad time to bring up this other plot! If they have any sense, they'll listen!"

Harry nodded. Since when had anyone in Washington any sense? He held the communicator to his lips. "Machine, can you get me patched into the White House switchboard? I want to speak to the Vice-President. David Reeves. Can you arrange that? Have the call transferred to the wall phone here. You know the number."

"By heart. However, it may be difficult to arrange an appointment, even by phone, with the Vice-President at this late hour, especially in light of these recent developments."

"Tell him who I am. He knows who I work for. Mention the fact that I have information concerning the assassination attempt."

"Do you?"

"Just dial the phone. I'll stand by here."

Harry walked to the bar's pay phone and waited in silence. As he had hoped, the phone finally rang. He picked up the receiver and the handsome young face of Vice-President David Reeves stared directly into his. "What is it, Mr. Porter? Your unit said that you have information concerning today's assassination attempt..."

"Not exactly, Mr. Vice-President," Harry smiled. "I knew the attempt was coming, though. I just didn't know what form it would take."

Reeves did not bother to hide his skepticism, his male model's face wearing a fairly snide expression. "And how, may I ask, did you deduce that there would be an attempt on President Walker's life?"

"Ask the FBI," Harry replied sweetly. "I reported it all to them and they ignored me. Look, there's going to be a second attempt. Soon. Within days, probably. It may be connected to the threat of a nuclear war as well."

"A nuclear war?" Reeves asked. His voice didn't betray a mere note of derision. It was an entire symphony wafting over the receiver. "Come on, now."

"I know it sounds outlandish, but there is a plot against Walker that somehow involves nuclear warfare. It was all part of this peeper's dream."

"Dream?"

"Right. This peeper picked up the thoughts of a teenaged suicide before the kid leaped. He saw evidence of a conspiracy against Walker carried out by a nameless army. The attempt would, in turn, dovetail with World War III."

"Mr. Porter," Reeves said politely. "The area I see in the background. Is that a bar?"

"Why, yes, it is, sir," Harry replied.

"And have you been drinking?"

"No more than usual," Porter replied, insulted.

"Allow me to suggest, as tactfully as possible, that you abstain from alcohol the next time you have the impudence to call the White House about dreams of unknown armies and nuclear wars. A clear head might save you a few dollars the next time around. You'll forgive me if I disengage myself from this informal chat, Mr. Porter, but I have some very real problems to deal with, as will you—should you persist in making these crank calls. The FBI takes a very dim view of this sort of practice. Pleasant dreams, Mr. Porter."

The screen went blank. Harry slammed the phone down. What more proof did they need, a Presidential cadaver?

He stalked back to the table. "Hey, Lenny, you've got to help me with this one. Not even the Vice-President will..."

At the table, Golden sat, hands clasped on his stomach, fast asleep. Even in slumber, his face looked tense, worried. Harry turned his back on the old man and headed for the door. "Pleasant dreams, Lenny," he whispered, meaning it.

3

Machine's assessment of the assassination had been accurate. The attempt really amounted to nothing more than low comedy. At best, it was a crude publicity stunt for an organization calling itself the American Freedomaires—a heretofore unknown mob which claimed responsibility for the misguided missile after parroting a few choice phrases condemning the ineffectual leadership and economic policies of the President to a local television station. They threatened another such event. Maybe next time, they'd use slingshots.

Vice-President Reeves had, in true heroic fashion, held the fort down amiably. Appearing four times in three hours before the television cameras to emphasize that the Administration would not be intimidated by such deranged behavior, he stressed that the President was preparing a tough antiterrorist bill to take before the Congress soon. The President himself, oddly enough, never appeared on camera, which led Harry to deduce that Walker was either out somewhere juicing it up or looking for a large desk to hide under.

By the time Harry had filed his wire service paste-up story, left the newspaper office, and headed home, it was quite late, and he was quite tired of hearing about the aborted attempt. Emerging from his building's elevator on the fourth floor, he immediately heard a woman scream.

It was coming from a stairwell at the far end of the hall. He ran towards the door, the woman still screaming, pleading with her attacker, on the other side. His body went cold as he realized he knew the voice.

It was Jessica West.

He hastened his pace. He hit the door with his shoulder, the pain searing through his patched ribs. The door didn't budge. Grabbing it by the doorknob, he swung it open. In the stairwell, a seemingly mad Peter Hayden crouched, his hands around the neck of his fiancée, Jessica. Harry jumped at Hayden's hands, involuntarily wondering whether he would have ever resorted to such dementia had he remained married.

"C'mon, Peter," Harry said, trying to pry the youth's fingers loose. "That's not the way to settle an argument. The law tends to frown on it."

Harry assumed his best Father Confessor tones. Hayden, a tall angular boy with a farm boy's sandy hair, appeared to be either drugged or completely deranged. Either way, Porter reasoned that a soothing voice would have more of a positive effect than a quick punch to the throat, especially with such an intellectual, preppy type whose strength lay in reason as opposed to martial arts. Hayden, apparently, did not view things that way; ignoring Porter's pleas, he tightened his grip around Jessica's throat.

Harry grew alarmed. The kid's grasp was too firm for your basic bookworm. "C'mon Peter. Smarten up."

Hayden relaxed his grasp momentarily and gazed at Harry. His boyish face was twisted, pale, distorted with rage. His eyes seemed to possess a luminescence of alien intensity. Releasing the whimpering woman, Hayden struck out at Harry. The back of his hand caught Porter on the side of the head, sending the startled journalist cartwheeling down half a flight of stairs. Harry stretched his arms out before him in an attempt to break the fall. His palms jammed into a rubber-tipped stair, causing his body to jackknife. Landing flat on his back, he took a quick biological inventory, carefully assessing whether any vital parts had exited his body during his impromptu display of athletic grace.

He was about to crawl to his feet when Hayden let loose with a shrill yell and darted down the stairwell. He whirled his foot down toward's Harry's head. Porter barely had time to avoid the blow, rolling his body flat into a wall. He heard a short grunt of pain as Hayden's heel smashed into the concrete floor. That evened up the score in terms of bum knees, anyway, Harry thought as he tottered into a standing position.

"Didn't they teach you that violence begets violence in any of your philosophy courses," Harry asked, ducking a sharp left hook sent barreling at his chin.

"Cut a lot of classes, huh?" Harry huffed, leaping to the other side of the stairwell.

Against his better judgment, Harry attempted to defend himself, pawing the air with his right fist. As he did so, two jabs from Hayden's right hit him square in the stomach. His ribs seemed to explode. He immediately doubled over both from pain and surprise. Hayden formed a fist with his left hand and raised it high above his head, the intention, obviously, to shorten the back of Porter's skull by several inches. Impressed with what a college education had done for this kid, Porter decided to rely on his street sense. Acting intuitively, he flopped onto his side. Hayden's fist whooshed harmlessly through the air, the momentum sending the gangly youth tumbling headfirst into the wall.

Harry regained his balance as Hayden's head struck the wall with a resounding thud. Acting fairly unheroic, Porter latched onto the irate suitor's face. If he couldn't pummel him to the ground, perhaps he could pull him onto the floor and kick the holy hell out of him. He dug his fingers into the boy's cheeks. Much to his horror, his hands slid downward, taking off large slivers of skin as they did so. Porter hesitated, a chill sweeping his body. Hayden, his face torn but not bleeding, pushed Harry away. Looking almost as shocked as Harry, the boy leaped past Porter and hopfrogged down the stairwell.

Harry stood, wobbling, on the stairway. He stared, baffled, at the tiny wads of flesh on his fingertips. "How do you feel?"

The woman, holding her bruised throat, nodded dumbly. "Could be better."

Harry pulled her out of the stairwell and into the hallway. "I told you to stay in the goddamned apartment," he said.

He paused before his door, placing his hand in the print lock. "Open the door, Machine. Fast." Harry shoved Jessica into a chair and rushed into the kitchen. Taking a small jar and a knife, he carefully removed the slime from his fingertips with the edge of the blade and scraped it along the rim of the jar. He then ran to the phone and began punching buttons like crazy.

"This is Andrew Cade," the taped message at the other end of the line declared.

Porter waited for the tone. "Cade, call me as soon as you get in. I have something here that will interest you."

Harry slammed the phone down and took the stunned woman by the hand. "Why the hell did you leave the apartment? You could have been killed! Jesus! You have some taste for picking boyfriends, you know?"

"He tried to..." she said, her eyes blinking.

"Yeah," Harry nodded.

A hoarse, sobbing noise erupted from deep within Jessica West. She didn't cry. She just sat there, sobbing.

There were three things that broke down Porter's flippant facade. A woman's sobbing placed first, second, and third in that category. "It'll be all right," he said, leading her into the bedroom. "Try to get a little rest. Think about your trip to England. Uncle's cottage, eh? Sounds nice. Great, in fact."

The woman sat on the edge of Harry's bed. "I don't want to alone."

Porter was perplexed, not at all sure of her meaning. He sat next to her. The two of them reacted to each other naturally, instinctively. They eased themselves into the folds

of the bedsheets, still fully clothed. They held each other as if
their lives depended on it. As their eyelids grew heavy, it
occurred to Harry that, perhaps, that was indeed the case.
The man and woman drifted into sleep, their arms still
entwined, protecting each other from the nameless fears that
haunted their waking hours.

Porter was awakened by the vague hint of daylight stream-
ing into the bedroom window to the tune of an incessant door
chime. He felt like he had only just closed his eyes. He
slowly disengaged himself from Jessica. She murmured something and, brushing a strand of blue hair from her eyelid,
turned on her side. Harry quietly got to his feet and stared at
the woman asleep in his bed. Despite all the confusion and
the danger, his heart felt strangely elated. His arms, however,
felt nothing, having gone numb from resting beneath her
body for hours.

The doorbell chimed.

Porter stumbled into the living room, closing the bedroom
door behind him. "I'm coming," he whispered to the door.
"Keep it down to a roar, willya?"

He tried gazing through the fragmented peepscreen. He
got a good look of his fragmented reflection. He opened the
door. Perry DeWitt, in all his pink-cheeked glory, lounged
outside. "My God!" he exclaimed, the apples falling from his
cheeks. "Did you sleep in those clothes."

"Yes, as a matter of fact," Harry said. "My jammies were at
the laundry. What brings you here so early—or at all, for that
matter."

"Didn't you get my message?" DeWitt said, stepping
cautiously into the room. Whatever Harry had, he was visibly
worried about contracting it. Porter pointed to the sofa in
front of the wallscreen. DeWitt obediently sat down. "Coffee?"

"Please."

"Machine, two of your muckraker specials." He padded
over to the video screen. "I forgot to check my messages last
night. What earth-shattering pronouncement did I miss."

"Well," DeWitt began, a cup of coffee sliding up to his side
on a small, automated service tray. "Since you were progressing
so slowly on the Kapps story on your own, I decided to
contact the reverend myself."

"Great," Harry smirked, fiddling with the playback switch
on the message machine. "Nothing like a show of support for
your guys in the field."

"And I arranged for a quick trip up to his country farm this morning. He's going to show us all around the place." He pointed to a small camera hanging around his neck. "Since I'm also a photographer—"

"A regular renaissance man—"

"I thought I'd take a few snaps to run with your piece."

"I don't suppose it ever occurred to you that I might have other plans for this morning," Harry jammed the playback button with his left thumb.

"I don't suppose it ever occurred to you that it's I who signs your checks every week."

"Bet you finished first in your debating class, too."

Harry fast forwarded the message unit. He zipped through DeWitt's prerecorded spiel, transforming the eternally effervescent publisher into a singsonging, high-pitched spasmatic. Harry glanced at DeWitt, the latter horrified at watching himself on the big screen looking like an auctioneer on speed.

DeWitt's eyes nearly exploded when the next message appeared. The screen was filled with a spread-eagled shot of a woman's clitoris. A beautifully manicured female hand slid its way up the left leg, perching precariously above the tuft of hair surrounding what, Harry assumed, was Sybille DeVille's calling card. The accelerated movement of the tape sent the sensuous fingertip careening around the porn star's pelvis, her voice an unintelligible squeal.

"What kind of people do you associate with, Porter?!" DeWitt howled in disgust.

Harry pushed the off button. "Probably an ad for a new massage parlor or something. Junk calls."

Porter walked to a small living room closet. He activated a clothes carousel within. A series of drab suits slid by. Well worn. Nearly all the jackets had identical tears in the inside lining. "Do I have time to shave?"

"You might try showering as well," DeWitt said through chapped lips, still staring at the offensive video screen.

Harry accomplished both tasks in a matter of minutes, opening a large slice on his neck as he angled his razor recklessly. By the time he emerged, his new suit of clothing was just as rumpled as the one he had slept in. It was quite a knack, perpetuating a consistently trod-upon look. It was an art form Harry had unintentionally cultivated over the years.

"You look like week-old kitty litter," DeWitt shuddered.

"I practice. Ready to go?"

DeWitt, still eyeing the video screen with utter contempt, headed for the door. Harry tossed his communicator directly into the lining of his jacket, eliminating the middleman. He pocketed his tiny recorder. "Machine," he said on the way out, "Keep an eye on Jessica and make sure that someone gets up here to replace the peepscreen, okay?"

"Affirmative."

Harry closed the door behind him. "Any chance we'll be home by lunchtime?" he asked DeWitt. "Somebody's trying to kill me, and I thought I'd see if I could find out who and why."

His publisher pushed the elevator button. "Oh, très droll, Porter. You realize that you're approaching this excursion with the entirely wrong attitude. Rather than worrying about the amount of time we might spend up there, you should be concentrating on the amount of information we might amass while we're visiting the compound."

"Right," Harry nodded. "How much do you think we can amass before lunchtime. Enough?"

"You're trying my patience," DeWitt whispered.

"Want to try some of mine?" Harry smiled. "It's only fair."

"Cretin."

"Orthodox." The elevator door opened. Inside stood a lone passenger: Dr. Jorge. "Meeeester Porter," the landlord bubbled, his face a maze of suddenly uplifted lines. "Just the fellow I vas vanting to zee."

Harry stepped into the car, resigned to his fate.

4

Porter hated traveling on the mag-lev underground tube systems, especially for periods of time lasting over two minutes. It wasn't that he was claustrophobic. His was not an unnatural, unwarranted reaction. His was a genuine fear that, one fine day, the entire magnetized tunnel structure would collapse with him inside, an innocent, skeptical victim.

Riding to Mount Pleasant, New York, took four minutes which, in Porter's estimation, was about three and a half minutes too many to spend in the company of Perry DeWitt. The publisher's vocabulary was small, but the turnover was terrific. He talked incessantly, a veritable treasure chest of blind optimism. On the tram leading to the tube and on the tube itself he repeatedly stressed the fact that he was a die-hard futurist. A freethinking individual who was willing to take any new idea and clasp it eagerly to his bosom.

By the time the two men emerged from the Mount Pleasant tubeway stop, Harry would have enjoyed visiting a veteran's hospital. Honest pain would have been a welcome relief from DeWitt's mindless prattle. Taking the lift to street level, Harry caught his first glimpse of Mount Pleasant. For once, he was appreciative of the literal quality of a geographic name. Mount Pleasant was a panorama of ecological delights. On one side of the small station stretched vast expanses of green, unblemished hills; on the other stood a smaller area of woodlands and man-made lakes. The place looked like a "best of" collection of Sierra Club posters.

Harry found himself enjoying the view despite the endless waves of "oohs" and "aahs" churned out by his traveling companion. Before DeWitt had the chance to work his reactions up to inundation level, they were interrupted by the approaching figure of Ashley Kapps. Clad in his pale blue jump suit and with the sunlight striking his rainbow glasses dramatically, Kapps looked like a vision borrowed from an updated New Testament, a bearded fellow who could probably jog across deep space as well as the ocean of your choice.

Kapps slowed his pace and glanced quickly from DeWitt to Porter, flashing what Harry assumed to be a conspiratorial "I'm on your side" grimace Porter's way. Porter was beginning to see the three dimensionality behind Kapps' multicolored lenses and was enjoying it immensely. The preacher seemed to be as street wise as he was spiritual, which was, Harry supposed, the main source of his charismatic appeal. He might be just the man to help Harry out in tracking down the causes of the teenage suicides. Kapps had done a lot of living in his four decades or so. His viewpoint might be a distinct plus.

"Why Reverend Kapps," DeWitt oozed, "a delight, a total delight."

Kapps offered a hand. "Mr. DeWitt. A pleasure."

"You know Mr. Porter, already don't you?" DeWitt said, adding sarcastically, "I believe you've spent a few minutes together."

Harry pulled a sour face. Kapps suppressed a smile. "Actually, we've spent a couple of afternoons discussing the world's problems and their philosophical implications, haven't we, Harry?"

"Afternoons?" Harry deadpanned. "Days."

"Really?" DeWitt's confidence was shaken.

"Didn't want to brag about it," Harry whispered.

The three men walked from the station to Kapps' electric van. "The compound is a five-minute drive from here," he said. "This area is more of a tourist trap, filled with a constantly changing parade of hikers, picnickers, whatever. We prefer seclusion for a couple of reasons. It affords us the privacy to reach our more troubled guests. It also gives them fewer physical distractions to worry about. There isn't a major city within twenty miles of our ranch, which is just fine by us. We're surrounded by nothing but sky and land. Our way of life calls for a relaxed and informal study of nature as well as a reawakening of our appreciation of her gifts."

Kapps started the van and eased the car onto a small service road. "We deliberately built the school grounds in the midst of a wooded area so as not to spoil the overview of the area for the hikers who use the tubeway station. You can't spot it from here although we're only five or six miles away."

"An ecologically positive attitude," DeWitt chortled. "Man cooperating with the environment, feeding off natures's spirituality while increasing the spirituality of his fellow man."

"Woman, too, I bet," Harry added.

Within minutes, the van approached a series of large geodesic domes. The site of the encampment nestled in the woodlands was truly phantasmagoric. Towered over by ageless trees and mounds of sloping grass, the domes glistened in the sunlight like great, earthbound jewels, the sun's rays sparking a myriad of cascading reflections. It dazzled Porter's eyes and mind simultaneously. He couldn't decide whether what he was experiencing was a religious rebirth or a newfound reverence for architectural design. The domes' continual radiance was almost hypnotizing.

The van pulled up before the smallest of the six domes present. A gaggle of jump-suited youths passed by the vehicle, oblivious to the visitors. One or two nodded a greeting at Kapps, but it was the type of casual acknowledgement more attuned to a low-keyed college campus than a coven of alleged religious fanatics. DeWitt, naturally, was spellbound by everything in sight, including two or three lean young men in snug jump suits. Harry, however, keeping in mind the church's critics, carefully noted every detail of the compound, watching for any obsessive sign that could add extra zest to his interview piece. The more he saw of the ranch, however, the more impressed he was with the practical positivism of the place.

"Although we are a religious organization," Kapps said, leading the men into the first dome, "we care for the secular needs of our members as well. Essentially, this is a university— an institute for the expansion of the mind and the soul. This building is one of two classroom units we have here. As you can see, the members of the church are quite eager to learn, even the ones who initially came to us seeking a way *out* of society."

Illuminated by the multicolored sunbeams, the interior of the city-block-long dome resembled a gaily lit space habitat. The jump-suited students, smiles on their faces, moved from small rectangular classroom to classroom, video texts and computerpads were tucked under their arms. Despite the high gloss sheen, the domed institution reminded Harry of the pamphlets he had ogled with envy when he was of college age. Booklets depicting the flawless, happy life-styles espoused by students of such bastions of learning as Harvard, Yale, and Notre Dame—campuses wherein every male student had a co-ed on his arm and all skin was free of pimples. The Church of the Ancient Astronauts' compound seemed a mere twenty-first century variation of a traditional, twentieth-century ideal. Blue jump suits had replaced corduroy blazers.

Kapps answered DeWitt's unceasing stream of questions amiably enough. "This is positively inspirational," the publisher repeated. "The deification of the human spirit."

"That may be a slight overstatement," Kapps gently pointed out. "We don't deify the human spirit. We just give it a quick patch-up job and restore it to its original shape. It's not at all easy for people to retain their self-esteem, their dignity, their sense of optimism in a society such as ours. Harry, being on the street day after day covering news events, can tell you that.

"America has lost its heroes. We are asked to choose between two puppets every four years and then told to feel proud of the fact that we have exercised our god-given right to pick the lesser of two evils. On a national and global level, we are faced with dishonesty, opportunism, and a blatant disregard for spiritual needs on a daily basis. What we try to do here is rekindle optimism. Not blind optimism, mind you, but a sincere and realistic belief that, through the efforts of individuals banded together in a common cause, positive change can come about. The key to saving man's spirit lies in reaching his mind."

"Inspirational," DeWitt rejoined. "Positively inspirational."

"We try," Kapps said, a trace of sarcasm entering his voice. He led the two visitors on a brief tour of the compound's two dormitories, the offices/chapel dome, and the science and technology dome. "We try to keep up with the latest developments in all areas of knowledge," he explained, "from computerized life-monitoring systems housed in our hospital to three-dimensional video transmissions in our closed-circuit TV studios. We feel its important for our students, as direct descendants of the ancient astronauts, to have fundamental knowledge in as many fields of endeavor as possible. When the ancient ones return for their second coming, we'll be ready to go out into space and populate new worlds with a breed of superhumans—super, not in a physical sense, but in an intellectual, emotional, and philosophical one."

"Stirring, to say the very least," DeWitt gushed.

Walking through the sea of smiling young faces, Harry was struck by the difference between these content adolescents and the troubled youths he had been colliding with over the past few months—the desperate, disenfranchised kids who saw suicide as their only salvation. Since he was quite sure that he wouldn't be able to shake DeWitt at all during this trip, he decided to ask Kapps for help in front of his publisher and hope for the best.

"Ashley," he said, casually, "lately we've been noticing a lot of youthful suicides throughout the country."

Kapps was visibly relieved to be robbed of his tour guide duties. "A tragedy," he nodded. "A waste of gods know how many years of future positive endeavor."

"Well, I've been toying with the idea that these kids were programmed somehow..."

"Porter, please," DeWitt began.

"They seem to be part of some bizarre downer cult," Harry continued. "They haven't been drugged, as far as I can tell. In fact, that's about the only factual bit of evidence I have. But their behavioral patterns prior to death seem almost identical. Is it possible to program kids to lose all hope *without* the use of drugs. I mean, here, you seem to do just the opposite through positivism and encouragement. Could there be a flip side of the coin?"

"Porter, why must you be such a pessimist?" DeWitt whined.

"Harry has a valid question," Kapps countered. "And an interesting theory. Yes, it is possible to induce hysteria, depression, obedience, and even suicide on a mass scale. As an ex-writer myself, I had the need to research this phenomenon for some of my early short stories. If you investigate this angle, you'll find that, during the twentieth century, the world—especially this country—was fascinated with depressing cults of one sort or another. Many of these groups chose religious trappings to hide their motivations, most of them dealing with money and power.

"The mental attitudes hammered into the followers of cult leaders, from small-scale figures like Charles Manson to major names such as Jim Jones, resulted in mass blood letting. And what were the twentieth-century's Nazis if not blind followers of a genetic philosophy nurtured by Adolf Hitler?

"On less ominous levels, Satanic cults as well as strange, fascistic Christian groups often got into violent clashes with local citizens uninvolved with their religious beliefs during the last century. The zealots had convinced themselves, through a repeated reaffirmation of their faith, that they were the only citizens of this country to know the *one* true way to live.

"To a lesser extent, disciples of the Reverend Moon, a self-proclaimed Korean prophet, and followers of Krishna were often accused of being zombies—mindless drones who had been programmed to obey their leader's wishes largely through a program of sensory deprivation and suggestion. There was some truth to be found in these charges. Physical conditioning can result in the virtual loss of one's free will.

"These practices aren't prevalent today," Kapps concluded, "but, then again, in today's drug-laden world, they really aren't necessary. People can become zombies in the privacy of their own homes, now, and fall under the spell of their almighty home entertainment units. They'll watch *this* show or buy *that* product all because someone got to them while they were susceptible. It's all the same principle."

Kapps emitted a soft sigh. "It's a shame to prey on people

in such a manner, Harry. All people want is a daddy to follow.
A leader. Throughout history, people have followed the most
flamboyant characters around. Sometimes those leaders have
represented good, sometimes..." He shrugged his shoulders.

"So we *could* have a cultist at work here," Harry theorized
aloud.

"It's possible," Kapps said, "but unlikely, unless his following is really small. You would have seen some outward
manifestations of his group by now—if this suicide leader was
really strong. Luckily, the forces of good seem to be growing
faster than any possible evil counterpart. Look at our church.
Despair can be conquered, Harry, if one is up for the battle."

Kapps flashed Harry a searching look. Porter retreated
immediately. "I licked despair years ago," he said. "It's angst
I'm up against now."

Kapps smiled and allowed Porter and DeWitt to sit in on a
philosophy course detailing the works of the twenty-first
century Bronx existential writers. Since there were only two,
the lecture was short. Porter couldn't keep his mind on the
professor anyhow. Kapps had, in a roundabout way, given
credence to Harry's theory that a suicide squadron existed in
this country.

Now, all Harry had to find out was where they were and
what they were after.

By the time Kapps drove the pair back to the tubeway
station, DeWitt had gotten all the information he needed to
become a member and enough snapshots to fill a small world
atlas. Harry had gotten a beesting on the back of his right
hand.

"It was a sincerely invigorating experience," De Witt announced, pumping Kapps' hand while Harry pondered what an
insincerely invigorating experience might have added up to.

"Thank you, Mr. DeWitt. I trust your snapshots will do as
much justice to our movement as Harry's prose undoubtedly
will."

"I'll try to be inspirational," Harry smiled.

"By the way," Kapps said. "If there's any way I can help
you with that suicide angle you're pursuing—"

"On his own time, I hope," DeWitt said between clenched
teeth.

"Give me a call," Kapps went on. "I might be able to dig
up a few books or videos on cults and old-fashioned brain-
washing techniques. Most public libraries don't stock up on

that stuff anymore and, gods know, we have enough special-ized material in ours to start a major quirk center. In order for us to know all the 'do's' of rehabilitation, we have to be aware of all the 'don'ts' as well. I'm always at the office."

"I'll probably take you up on that," Harry said, stepping into the elevator leading down to the tube.

"What a wonderful day," DeWitt giggled as the lift spiraled downward. "I can't wait to join that church. I look so nice in blue. A wonderful day. Wonderful. Wouldn't you say it was a wonderful day, Harry?"

"Yeah," Harry replied, looking at his watch. "We'll be home by lunch."

5

The lobby to Harry's building was swarming with police. Harry plowed his way through the blue-suited mob and made it to the elevator, instinctively knowing that whatever trouble existed in the building had to center around his apartment. If that was the case, it also had to be centered around Jessica West. He emerged from the lift on the fourth floor and was met by the ever-crimson faced Lieutenant Groux. "Well, well," the jowly policeman said with ill-concealed cynicism. "If it isn't our roving reporter. You do get yourself in the strangest of situations, don't you?"

"What happened here?"

"Not much." The lieutenant's air was casual. "We were notified about a disturbance in an apartment on this level. It turned out to be your apartment. By the time we got here, your place had been tossed and your landlord"—he punched a button on his computer clipboard—"Dr. Wilhelm Jorge shot during the burglary."

"Hurt badly?" Harry asked, thinking only of Jessica.

"Nah. Caught a short blast in the leg. Old coot wants to bill you for the medical charges, though."

Harry smiled vacantly, thinking of the old man still clinging to his greed as he was carted off in the ambulance. The two men walked briskly to Harry's door. The door was in perfect condition. There were no visible signs of forced entry. The interior of the apartment, however, was a shambles. Books and video cartridges were scattered about. Drawers had been emptied. The plush couch in the living room had been slit open, its stuffing spread out onto the rug.

"Looks like a remedial burglary class' field trip," Porter cracked.

"Any idea what they were after?"

Harry considered the question. "Not really."

"Know who they might have been."

"Not exactly."

"How not exactly?"

"What would you think if I told you that the people who did this are part of a conspiracy to kill the President."

"I'd think you were reading too many of your own stories."

"I figured as much. No, I don't know who did this."

"Can't figure out how they got in," Groux said, pointing towards the door. "You have one of those print-lock jobs. Supposed to be foolproof."

"Maybe these guys weren't fools," Harry said, walking into the bedroom. Every piece of clothing had been removed from the closet and thrown onto the floor. "Where's the woman?" Harry asked.

Two plainclothesmen rummaged through the bathroom.

"What woman?" Groux asked.

"Jessica West. My neighbor. She was sleeping here when I left this morning."

"No one was here when we arrived, except for your landlord. How did you spell her name?"

"I *still* spell it W-E-S-T," Harry said, moving into the kitchen. The vial containing the scrapings off the door was gone. The knife used to scrape the substance off Harry's fingertips, however, remained in the sink. He snatched a small plastic bag from a drawer and dropped the knife inside. He then stuck the knife into the drawer and closed it quickly.

"Anything missing?" Groux asked.

"I won't know until after I've cleaned this place up," Harry said, absentmindedly. "That could take years."

"About the girl," Groux asked. "What do you know about her."

"Attractive. Brown hair, blue streaks. Five five. Blue eyes. Mid-twenties. She works for a motion picture studio, holographic division, as a publicist. I don't know which studio. Her boyfriend is Peter Hayden, the antinuker. They had a run-in yesterday. He decided to use her face for a handball court. I let her stay the night here."

"Friendly relationship?" Groux sneered.

"Totally platonic," Harry snapped, adding a casual "war wound" for effect.

"Gee, sorry," Groux said, stumbling over this new aspect of Harry's personality. "I didn't realize..."

"Don't mention it," Harry nodded. "Look, I'd appreciate being left alone for a while. Are your boys just about finished here?"

"How about it guys?" Groux yelled.

The two plainclothesmen shambled into the living room. "No prints. Nothing. Can't figure it."

"They could have worn gloves," Harry said.

"Oh, yeah," one cop agreed. "That could be it."

"We'll be in touch, Porter," Groux said, walking to the door. "If we get any leads on the girl's whereabouts or any tips on the break-in..."

Harry escorted the three cops to the door. "I'd appreciate hearing about it."

"Sorry about the wise remarks," Groux sputtered. "War can be a heavy duty trip."

Harry shut the door slowly. "Yeah, well. There's always the hope of a transplant."

The police gone, Harry reentered the living room. "Machine? You all right?"

"Affirmative."

"Did you tell the police anything?"

"Negative. No one saw fit to interrogate me."

"Thank God for city-supervised IQ exams," Harry sighed. "Okay. What happened. From the top."

"It's all very confusing," Machine began. "Shortly after you left, I contacted Dr. Jorge's terminal and had it arrange for a repair force to be sent to this apartment to tend to the peepscreen. One-half hour later, I heard three voices outside the door. One was that of your landlord, Dr. Jorge. He argued with the other two voices, also male, about letting them into your apartment. He hadn't seen any proper ID backing up their claims to be repairmen. The altercation lasted several minutes. Apparently one of them brandished a firearm. Dr. Jorge retreated, judging from the footsteps. A blast was fired. I understand, from what the police said later, that he was hit in the lower portion of the left leg. He fell to the ground and began yelling in a foreign language. I believe he crawled to the elevator.

"At that point, I contacted the police terminal, outlining the events as I had heard them. I then felt the pressure of a hand on the printlock. Much to my surprise, it was your hand. The door opened without incident."

Harry opened the door and inspected the lock. It was moist. He closed the door and returned to the room. "Go ahead."

"Once inside, these two intruders, both Caucasian males, began tearing the room apart. I decided to assume a low profile in order to conceal my presence from them. I reasoned that, if they knew they were being spied upon, they might take measures to permanently terminate my existence."

"They didn't notice your camera system?"

"Apparently not," Machine answered. "It struck me as a rather odd combination of intellectual and practical skills on the part of the intruders. On the one hand, they possessed the ability and dexterity to open a supposedly unopenable security lock, yet they did not have the presence of mind to investigate the possibility of any further security systems. A parodoxical situation to say the very least. I attributed their rashness to their lack of years."

"They were young."

"Barely post-pubescent. One of them had a fairly bad case of acne. They searched the area in a rather haphazard manner. The noise awoke your house guest, Miss West. One of the youths grabbed her. The two argued about whether they should terminate her on the premises or not. They eventually decided against the idea, choosing to consult with superior or superiors unnamed. They stunned her with a rodlike appliance."

"A tranxstic," Harry nodded.

"Pardon?"

"First cousin to a stun gun. It's used for tranquilizing larger animals being treated by veterinarians. Cows, horses, whatever."

"One of the men dragged her out of the apartment while the other continued his search. He entered the kitchen, noticed the container you left last night, and took it with him before leaving. The police arrived moments later, having experienced a minor contact delay en route to the scene."

"Contact delay?"

"Their vehicle made unexpected contact with another while crossing an intersection."

"Great," Harry muttered, heading for the door. "Get in touch with Cade or his unit. I'm on my way over to the center. Have Cade on call with a lab on standby when I arrive. Then, call this building's super installation and see if you can get someone over here to put this mess back together again. Monitor my phone messages. If anyone you feel is important calls, contact me either by communicator or phone."

"Anything else?"

"Yeah," Harry said. "I don't know what's going to happen next in here or who might show up. Watch your ass."

Harry snatched the knife from the kitchen drawer and slipped it into the lining of his coat. He slammed the front door after him. The silence of the apartment was broken by the sound of Porter's tape-recorded voice greeting an incoming call. A video transmission entered the phone unit. A gigantic mammary gland, well oiled, commanded the rectangular screen. "Harry, honey! I just can't believe it! You must be the busiest man in all of Manhattan!"

A ruby-tipped finger appeared, tracing small circles around the breast's lubricated nipple. "Can't you make a little time for me . . . with me? Call me Harrykins."

The screen faded to black.

Machine theorized that this was not the type of call Harry Porter would consider important enough for it to note.

6

Harry Porter slouched in the dimly lit phone booth. His eyes burned. His teeth ached from the constant grinding activity he had been practicing for the past hour. The hospital corridor outside reeked of disinfectant and death. "Look, Saint-Crispen," he growled into the receiver, "it could save both our skins!"

The face in the viewscreen remained dubious. "I don't see it that way," the Saint said. "If I use my sources to track down info for you, I'm putting my backside right out in the open, if you catch my drift. Since I am very attached to my backside, it being part of a whole set of things I've grown accustomed to having on me at all times, I don't see any pluses in my risking its existence for you."

"Saint-Crispen," Harry sighed. "The most I can do to your ass is kick it. The people we're messing around with can feed it to the fishies at the bottom of the Hudson."

"On the other hand," Saint-Crispen continued, "we *have* been friends for a lot of years so I guess it wouldn't be too much of a bother for me to put out a few feeler's for old time's sake."

"You're a saint, Marion."

"Yeah. It's on my card."

Harry left the booth and walked down the hallway to Cade's laboratory. Cade was sitting behind a viewscreen staring at the readouts appearing in brilliant blue. His gaunt facial features seemed more emaciated than usual.

"Well?" Harry asked.

"It's syntheskin all right," Cade answered. "Where did you find it."

"All over my goddamned house! This particular snippet came from the face of my next door neighbor who decided to take a short tap dancing lesson on me and his girlfriend last night. There was also a thin covering of it on my door print lock. Coincidentally, my apartment has been broken into the two times this stuff showed up on my door. The way I figure it, the syntheskin was put on my lock somehow. That would make a mold of my own handprint, my print being part of the metallic surface of the lock itself. Any hand inserted over the skin and pressed against the lock's grooves would, then, in the lock's computerized little head, become my hand: an organic specimen complete with my telltale squiggles and swirls and scars."

Cade ran a hand through his longish mien, his beak nose flaring at the nostrils. "Damn," he muttered. "I was afraid something like this would happen."

"I figured as much," Harry remarked. "You and Bronkowski were jawing about this yesterday, right?"

"Yes, we were indeed discussing almost just such a situation in hypothetical terms. Today, however, our hypothetical crimes seem to have become operable transgressions."

"And you didn't see fit to include me in any of your hypothesizing."

"There was really no need for you to know, Porter. What Bronkowski and I discussed was hospital business. It concerned Dr. Pratt, Dr. Weiner, their work, and possible problems concerning crime."

"Don't con me, Andy. You should have told me. We're friends."

"We're also professionals, Porter. You are a journalist. I am a physician. I cannot have possible scandals linked to this hospital because of our friendship. I tell you things. You print things. Bad press is something I don't need right now."

"I wouldn't have run with it," Porter frowned. "You could have trusted me. As a result of your pigheadedness, my pompous old pal, an innocent woman may be injured right now." Or worse.

"If it makes you feel any better," Cade said, his face stiff from chagrin or something that just made his face stiff, "I admit that I may have erred in my judgment."

"Maybe it makes you feel better. Not me. I think you'd better fill me in on everything right now."

"Perhaps I should," Cade said, shaking his head slowly from side to side. "But you must believe me. I don't know much more than you do at this point. When Pratt and Weiner disappeared that first day, they were in the process of setting up one of our labs for their needs. They were set to continue with a series of experiments they had begun, dealing with a new, quick-drying formula for syntheskin: synthetic flesh that could be applied as quickly and effortlessly as the cosmetic makeup used in contemporary films and holographs. It was designed especially for very critical burn victims, victims whose chances for recovery are hampered by the amount of dead flesh present and the slowness of healing. This new skin would speed up the healing process through an entirely new form of application.

"A membrane-thin layer of it would be sprayed onto the burned area: a face, a leg, torso, whatever. After a few seconds, this skin could be painlessly peeled off, effectively capturing the outline of the part of the body that needed to be repaired, capturing the exact dimensions of the area.

"Doctors could then take this outline and fashion a mold of thicker, more resilient syntheskin. This mold could then be applied to the burned area in one, less-painful procedure. The new face, the new hand, the new arm would fit exactly onto the charred portion of the body. There would be no need for the patchwork procedure we're reduced to now.

"All we'd have to do would be minor cosmetic surgery after

the fact—supplying the proper facial characteristics, distinguishing birthmarks, whatever the patient saw fit. This new process would allow healing in approximately one fourth the amount of time the present operation takes."

Harry whistled through his teeth. "Bill was pretty modest about his skills. He didn't let onto me at all about this."

"You can understand why," Cade said. "This discovery, when it's successfully tested, will send waves through the medical community."

"Somebody's already using it to make waves," Harry said, "and in the global community."

"Why do I get the feeling we have now entered the realm of Harry Porter's speculative fiction?"

"Give a listen." Porter began to pace the room. "If Bill and Weiner were abducted on their first day here and tortured in some way, they could have revealed all their trade secrets to our omnipresent thug element, assuming that the thugs had medical men under their thumb who'd know what to do with the information." He stopped in midpace. "Now, with the information sketched out, Bill and Weiner have almost outlived their usefulness. Almost, but not quite. Their own faces could have been used as models for real, live, syntheskin face masks."

"That's possible," Cade acknowledged. "Thus making the two men who came back to resign . . ."

"Bogus technicians."

"Researchers, Porter. The word is researchers. Technicians can be the people who plug things in, and yes, it does seem likely that the two men were phonies and that Weiner has met with a similar fate as Dr. Pratt."

"Taking that one step further," Harry said. "With the two phonies snatching all of Bill's formal notes, this medical miracle is now in the hands of someone who will no doubt use it for very bizarre and, more than likely, illegal activities. Within a day or two there could be an army of pseudo-citizens walking the streets committing whatever crimes they want."

Harry snapped his fingers, remembering the peeper's dream. "It all fits—to a point. Bill mumbles 'I'm free.' Of course he was free. He was free of his captors—faceless captors!" Harry stared meaningfully at Cade.

"Porter," Cade said ominously. "I don't know what you're talking about. "But, since I smell a rather acrid odor emanating from your direction, could it be that those sundry devices above your eyelids are attaching even more dire overtones to this already ill-omened incident?"

"If you just said what I thought you did, yes," Harry nodded. "The peeper on the roof's dream is becoming reality. Peter Hayden was an antinuclear activist, right? If that wasn't Peter Hayden I fought with yesterday, it means that someone has gone to a lot of trouble to replace him. To what end, you might ask?"

"Or, I might not," Cade injected.

"Now, while I admit that these connections are very tentative, don't laugh at me until I'm done. The peeper who was murdered was a fed. His vision concerned the assassination of the President, a nuclear holocaust and an army of faceless individuals. Now, Hayden *is* connected with the nuclear industry, even if it's in the role of a professional gadfly. And the faceless army, right about now, seems to me to be quite a nice mental metaphor for a group of people who can change their identity at will. People who use this new type of syntheskin for a chameleon effect.

"So, we have a powerful antinuclear radical replaced by a conspirator and an army of untraceable assassins running around loose. Now, if we can somehow work in the suicide squad and the President into all this, we're home free." He hoped. For everyone's sake, mostly Jessica's.

Cade's face sagged perceptibly. "I'm not laughing at all, Porter. Your ideas strike me as being less mirth inducing than usual today."

Harry backed out of the lab. "I'm sure we're both going to sit back and laugh about all this in a few days."

"I hope so. I'll contact your federal friend and let him know about your findings."

"No," Harry cautioned. "Hold off on that for about an hour or two. I don't want Bronkowski's men clunking around this while Jessica's still missing. Let me nose around on my own, okay?"

"Against all schools of logic," Cade said, returning his gaze to the datascreen, "I will agree to your wishes."

"I'll be back within an hour, providing our faceless men don't catch up with me." Harry smirked on his way out the door. "When I show up, you'd better be ready to pinch my nose to make sure it's me and not my double. If it comes off in your hand, you're in trouble."

"If it comes off in my hand," Cade smiled thinly. "It will be a distinct improvement."

7

Swirls of damp night air enveloped the two figures huddled in the doorway. On the streets of lower Manhattan, slime-spattered figures passed the two by, preferring to sidle up to private vehicles stopped at red lights or passengers on slow-moving pedways. They asked for handouts. If refused, they threatened.

Porter's teeth chattered as the moisture made its way beneath his skin. His nose made a whistling sound, air moving through only one nostril. He slipped his nasal spray from his coat and inhaled four times deeply. The spray began to unclog his blocked passage. He felt particularly downtrodden. He couldn't understand why.

Saint-Crispen nestled against the steel door, his eyes casually but carefully noting every move the street people made as they staggered by. There was always the chance of unexpected violence erupting in this district.

"I have news, Harry-boy," Saint-Crispen announced, his words producing white tufts of breath in the air. "All of it bad."

"Let me guess," Harry shifted his weight from foot to foot in a vain attempt to ward off the chill. This was supposed to be spring, damn it. "Nobody knows who broke into my place and took Jessica."

"As far as anyone down here knows, you were done in by phantoms."

"No leads at all."

"I tried, man. I even got Tedesco to let me use his computer console. Big Joe has a line on all the action in the tri-state area, major and minor. His filing system makes the NYPD's mug files look like an abridged edition of a short story. He's got everyone who's anyone in his machine. I fed it the m.o. Got nothing. We cross-referenced the procedure with bungled capers. Again, zip. Kidnapping. Baby faces. No matter what variations we tossed into this thing we got the same result back. Zilch. Whoever pulled this off was a first timer, Harry."

Porter took another hit of nose spray. He leaned against the doorway and stuck his hands down into his pockets. His thumbnail got caught on his pocket recorder, and he broke the corner off while wiggling it free. Saint-Crispen was upbeat about it all. "Hey, what's the matter, Harry. You should be overjoyed, man. Dancing in the streets! Look, if those guys were non-pro, that means the heat's off us, buddy-boy. There's no mob link. We can relax a little. Unwind. Hey, how about a drink to cheer you up? I'll even buy. We'll drown our sorrows."

"Give me a break, will you, Marion?" Harry shot back. "Can't you think about anyone but yourself?"

"I was thinking about you, too. The heat's off both of us."

"We can relax. Fine. What about Jessica? If her kidnappers aren't pros, if they're real bush leaguers, it's going to be ten times as hard to track them down because they won't be operating in any set pattern. They'll also be prone to panicking easily, to make dumb mistakes, to hurt her or . . ."

Suddenly Porter felt totally miserable. The intensity of his hurt shook him. His lack of perception had cost at least one friend his life, probably two. And now, Jessica was in danger. The full weight of his guilt hit him with the force of a brick to the forehead. He sat down on the single step outside the doorway. "C'mon, Harry," Saint-Crispen said, extending a hand. "You're going to catch a cold that way."

"Damn it!" Harry said hoarsely. "Damn it. Why is it that everything I touch turns to shit?"

Saint-Crispen withdrew his hand, warily. "You can't blame yourself, man. Maybe it was her zeroid boyfriend or someone like that. He sounded like a real nut case."

"She was in my apartment, though. It was my house she was hiding in. She got in the way of people who were breaking into my apartment, not hers."

"A coincidence."

"Some coincidence. It happened because of me, Marion. Because of who I am and what I do. Look at me! I'm thirty-six years old and I'm sitting on a step in the middle of the goddamned Bowery in the middle of the night! For what? Damned if I know!"

"You're working on a story, man. That's your gig."

"I'm always working on a story, Saint. For a couple of dollars a week and an apartment that I probably won't be able to afford next week. . . . What do I have to show for ten years of working on stories? Nothing, that's what."

"You're exaggerating, Harry-boy. You've got, uh, you've got a great machine there at home. Smart as a whip. And personality? That unit's in a class by itself."

"What a marvelous summation of a life-style," Harry smirked. "I have a computer that's smart. Well, who the fuck has a computer that's dumb? Let's face it. I've screwed up royally. I've put my precious life-style above everything and everyone, and now, someone totally innocent may die because of it."

"A fluke," Saint-Crispen insisted. "Think of all the good you've done, man. All the facts and stuff you've given the public!"

"Facts that the public has ignored, Marion. And while I was out digging up those facts, the world, my world, just zipped right by me. Phhhffft. In a matter of seconds it seems. Annie's gone. She won't even talk to me in a sentence that doesn't have an exclamation point on it, anymore."

"Hey, plenty of marriages go down the old toilet, Harry-boy. Just think of all the friends you've got."

"Right. Friends who are married, raising kids and leading normal lives. I fit in real well in that setup. I show up to visit alone and everyone acts nervous. It's like I'm a member of the leper of the month club or something."

"Will you cut it out, Harry? You're scaring the shit out of me! You drunk? You've got plenty of old cronies still around."

"Like who?"

"Alice Garrett."

"Married and moved to Texas."

"Jeannie Sarlin."

"Became a Krishna."

"Tommy Lee Thompson."

"Killed last year. Open manhole."

Saint-Crispen sat down on the step next to Harry. "Jesus. Now you've got *me* depressed."

The two sat in the mist. "Sometimes you just have to do the best you can, Harry-boy," Saint-Crispen finally offered. "A lot of people can't even manage that. Besides, you don't have it so rough. *I'm* your friend."

Harry stared at his shoes. He wiped a trickle of fluid from his left nostril. His lips began to quiver, gradually forming a shy grin. "Screw it. You're right. I appreciate your friendship, Saint. I suppose we're two of a kind."

"Except that I'm more popular," Saint-Crispen answered, standing.

"In police lineups, maybe," Harry said, straightening. "What did you find out about Peter Hayden?"

"What everyone else has. Don't you read your own paper?"

"I've been busy. Why would Hayden be in the paper?"

"He's all over the front page, man. He and three of his antinuke nuts took over the Fountain Point plant this afternoon. Two guards shot dead. He and his pals have barricaded themselves in the central control area. They can play funny games from there."

Harry's face was ashen. "Demands?"

"Not yet."

Harry stepped out into the street, narrowly avoiding a bum. "It's all happening, Saint-Crispen. We were just interpreting Flowers' vision the wrong way. The nuclear scene. We assumed it was World War III. It could have meant the sabotaging of a nuclear facility as well."

Harry quickly filled in the details of the preceding twenty-four hours to the Saint. "And if that's not the real Hayden up there at the Point," he concluded, "it's one of Flowers' faceless army!"

"I knew I should have moved to Detroit," the Saint muttered. "Now what?"

"I don't know," Harry said. "I could try warning the President again. No. We still can't *prove* anything. And everyone I've mentioned this to so far has figured that I'm up for a quick return voyage to the laughing academy."

Harry slapped his hand on a nearby lamppost, sending a metallic ring echoing through the damp street. "Hell. We're in the middle of an organized attempt to overthrow the American government. Do you realize that? Someone has meticulously constructed a three-pronged attack, and we're the only ones who are aware of it. And who the hell is going to believe us? We can't even connect the President to it, as yet. We don't even know how all the pieces fit!"

"Maybe it's time we had that drink, eh? Does that sound like a good idea to you yet?"

"And Jessie is somewhere in the middle of it all!"

"Oh yeah. Jessie. We wouldn't want to have a drink with

old Jessie still being in the middle of it all, would we? Not even a small one, I bet," the Saint muttered, trailing down the street after Harry.

"There has to be something we can do, though. Come on, Saint, use your head. Help me out." Harry stopped abruptly in the middle of the street. Saint-Crispen nearly slammed into Porter's back. "That's it!" Harry exclaimed. "You can use your head!"

"As well as the next guy, I guess," Saint-Crispen said, modestly. "I'm no Einstein, but I can cook up a scam that will fool most marks."

"No. No. Your head. Your brain. Your PSI abilities!"

"You're a real kidder, Harry-boy."

"Who am I kidding?"

"You're kidding yourself if you think I'm going to try that shit again. Do you realize what you've done to me already? If I get upset, I start bending forks! It's a horrible condition to be in. As of now, I'm downplaying that side of me."

"But you can do it expertly! You peeped Flowers, didn't you?"

"Yeah, and earned the nickname 'the human javelin.'"

"But this time it would be a lot easier. It's a little girl I want you to peep."

"What girl?"

"The girl I saved. The jumper. She's still under sedation at the hospital. She's our only clue to this whole setup. If the suicides have knowledge of this plot and take that knowledge to the grave with them, then this young lady, being very much alive, must still have all the facts resting safely in her noggin."

"I'm not peeping another cerebral stewpot."

"The girl will be a snap. Trust me."

"The peeper was supposed to be a snap, too. Reading him was like diving headfirst into *Shock Theater* reruns. How do I know this kid isn't as spazzed out?"

"She's just a girl, Marion. A little girl."

"A little girl who tried to splatter herself in public—a real normal kid."

"Will you do it?" Harry asked.

"I'm not sure," Saint-Crispen hedged. "How much you offering?"

"Nothing. I'm tapped out."

"I'm sure." Saint-Crispen began to walk away.

"Come on, Marion," Harry said pitifully. "For old time's sake. You're all I've got. Annie's gone. And Jeannie. And . . ."

"Spare me the roll call," Saint-Crispen hissed, stepping onto the rolling pedway. "I know when I've been conned. Let's go."

Harry jumped on the sidewalk behind his friend, flashing a smile. After a half block of uptown trav ling, his smile faded as he felt the sole of his left shoe tear off.

8

The hospital corridor, like all hospital corridors, was sterile and serene. The overhead lighting was harsh and yellow. The people in its glare were reduced to jaundiced portraits of worry and concern. Harry sat in the inflated couch outside Jane Doe's room, his eyes closed. Bits and pieces of the recent past meshed with his present, all to the accompanying tune formed by the constant prattle of the hospital loud-speaker system.

Harry opened his eyes and stared vacantly at the wall across from him. He was mentally and physically depleted. He was running in circles. He knew it. He was attempting to thwart a disaster in the making that, sometimes, he didn't even believe existed. He focused his attention on a small chink in the spray-painted wall. Barely noticeable, this irreg-ularity was made all the more interesting because of its totally bland surrounding. He mulled over that fact for a moment, considering the possible philosophical import inherent there-in. Deciding he'd only give himself a headache by stretching the point, he turned his gaze thoughtfully to his knuckles.

Much to his astonishment, he found his hands to be shaking worse than an alky's. Maybe DeWitt was right. Maybe he should just concentrate on the lighter side of life. If there wasn't a lighter side to concentrate on, maybe it would be better for all concerned if he fabricated one. Hell, he could leave the withering newspaper world with a clear conscience if he wanted to. It was the captain who was supposed to go down with the ship, not the deckhands.

A nurse in a wonderfully short tunic walked by, her legs made all the more noticeable by a pair of candy-striped tights. He barely glanced at her. He wondered if he'd ever see Jessica alive again. He examined that thought. Was he really concerned about her or was it merely academic. Did he have the capacity to care for her? Was he upset only because she was abducted from *his* home? Was it just a blow to his pride? After all, someone had invaded the privacy of *his* home, upsetting the contents—Jessica included.

Realistically, he hardly knew the woman. She was just the kid who lived next door, literally. Still, her brief appearance in his life had certainly been welcome. She had had a lot of spirit. She had trusted him, and he had felt protective of her.

An orderly nearly tripped over his extended legs. Harry snapped back to present tense. Damn. He had gotten that headache anyway. Andrew Cade stepped out of the hospital room and sat next to Harry. "You look like hell."

"Imagine how I *feel*."

Cade glanced at the floor, his brows arched inquisitively. "What happened to your shoe?"

Harry took in the sight of limp sole dangling from his left foot. "I bite my nails. What's going on in there?"

"Nothing, unfortunately," Cade said. "Your acquaintance may be a very powerful telepath but he certainly isn't very well trained. He blew out three lightbulbs trying to hone in on the girl."

Harry shrugged. "Neatness was never the Saint's forte."

"The Saint, eh?" Cade mused. "He's certainly going to need divine guidance to peep our Jane Doe. Whoever has programmed her has patched up all possible cerebral chinks. She's impervious to any of our drug treatments or hypnotherapy sessions. We even had one of our staff peepers try to communicate with her."

"Any luck?"

"We wouldn't be sitting here staring at your shoes if anything had happened, Porter. The frustrating aspect about all this is that the girl *must* be alert under that facade; her brain waves show that. During her waking hours, all she does is chant, repeating that nonsense about no sacrifice being too great."

"A one-woman political rally."

Cade crossed his arms and arched his head back suddenly. Staring at the ceiling, he breathed deeply and heaved a wistful sigh. "You know, Porter. Sometimes I think back to the old days before we met. Life was so placid then. So ordinary.

I would come into work, do my job, and go home. I got such an extraordinary sense of accomplishment from the little tasks I performed: life-saving surgery, skin grafts, those silly kinds of medical things. With the advent of our friendship, however, I have found myself surrounded by intrigue, insanity, and utter confusion. I'm tired during every waking hour and unable to sleep at night. You've wreaked havoc with the very fabric of my being, Porter."

"You're a lot more interesting at parties now, aren't you?"

Saint-Crispen exited the room, shaking his tousled head. "Man, that chick might as well be sealed up in concrete from the neck up."

Harry got to his feet, offering Saint-Crispen his seat. "Nothing?"

"Nada," Saint-Crispen said, slumping into the soft piece of furniture. "It's like diving into a rubber wall. I've been bouncing off her brain so much that my eyeballs could lead a sing-along. She's a regular Alamo above the eyes."

"The Mexicans took the Alamo," Harry pointed out.

"Yeah," the Saint nodded. "Maybe if I had a taco or something. I'm starving. What time is it, anyway? Two in the morning?"

"Go back inside and try again," Harry answered.

"Give me a break, Harry. This is a freebie and I'm starving."

Harry was about to reply when Cade stood. "He's been in there for nearly an hour, Porter. Our peeper lasted only twenty minutes before he threw up his hands in disgust. Why don't you let him relax for a while, regenerate his strength." He turned to Saint-Crispen. "Our cafeteria is still open, Mr. Saint. Why not have an early breakfast. My treat."

"You're talking my lingo, doctor," Saint-Crispen said, scrambling off the chair. "Coming Harry?"

"Nah," Harry said, returning to the couch. "You two go. I'll catch you later."

Porter began his careful scrutiny of the wall across the hall once again. Somehow, he realized, the key to all this had to be locked in that girl's mind. Her memory had to be tapped. The floodgates had to be opened. But how? Two young male nurses walked by. Harry made a vague mental note that one of them wore a handlebar moustache, the likes of which hadn't been seen since the funeral of Cosmo Nordiska—the tight-rope walker of the interspace circus who had been prone to sneezing fits at the most inopportune moments.

A doctor strolled past. Harry glanced at the fellow's blinking visage and filed the fact that the white-smocked fellow seemed familiar. That wasn't noteworthy in itself considering the amount of time Harry had spent at this hospital over the past few days. The doctor entered Jane Doe's room with a computer-clip under his arm. Must be time for the half-hourly check, Harry surmised.

He crossed his feet, flopping his severed shoe sole casually against the tip of his right foot. He attempted a genuine stab at self-pity but was too preoccupied to summon up anything more than mild indigestion. Something in the back of his mind was whirring around, sending out a faint but distinct alarm. A chill rippled through his body as the doctor's face reappeared in his mind. The heavy-lidded eyes. The spasmodic blinking. That face didn't belong to one of NYU's staffers. It belonged to the thug who murdered the peeper, Flowers.

Harry jumped out of the chair and ran into the girl's room. The doctor had already tossed the clipboard onto a nearby chair and had withdrawn a laser pistol from his pants pocket.

The pistol was not yet raised. Surprised by Porter's breathless entrance, the assassin hesitated for a millisecond. It was all the time Porter needed. Pleading with his leg muscles to hold up, he dropped into a crouch and dived, headfirst across the room. Hands outstretched, he grabbed the killer around the hips and pulled him onto the floor.

The assassin, although wiry, proved more than a suitable match for Harry. Quickly rolling himself atop the reporter, he lashed out furiously with his left fist, landing a solid blow to Porter's chin. With his right hand, he grabbed the barrel of the gun and was about to send the butt slamming down onto Harry's forehead when a well-aimed knee to the small of the back caused him to arch his body violently backward in a sudden spasm of pain.

Harry slammed the palm of his hand under the man's chin, snapping the murderer's head back even further. He thought he heard teeth crack. The blow sent the man in white rolling backward, costing him the possession of his weapon. The small handgun glided across the floor, coming to rest next to the wall closest to the door. Paying no attention to the killer's movements, Harry crawled on all fours to the spot where the pistol rested. He fully expected to be tackled from behind by the maniac and was surprised when he managed to scoop up the gun unaccosted.

Spinning around on his knees, he faced the girl's bed and saw why he had been allowed to go free. Poised above the catatonic patient was the blinking man, a knife drawn. Harry trained the gun on the phony physician and tilted himself back onto the balls of his feet. Standing slowly, he kept the gun pointed at the killer's chest. "Don't try it, friend," he whispered nervously.

The intruder blinked four times in rapid succession. He glanced quickly in Harry's direction before focusing his attention entirely on the girl. Harry moved forward softly. "You, of all people know what one of these toys can do at close range. Now, why don't you just put that knife down on the table and move away from the bed. Slowly."

The man in white showed no sign of having heard Porter's instructions. He clutched the knife with a sense of purpose that was awesome. Harry continued his leisurely advance. "I'm warning you, friend. I know how to use one of these things."

He really didn't, although he'd often been at the receiving end of such usage.

"And I wouldn't think twice about fast-frying you where you stand."

He'd have nightmares for months.

The heavy-lidded man nodded casually before erupting into a strange, fish-eyed expression. Cocking his head quickly to one side in an innocent, childlike manner, he quickly raised the knife above the girl's throat. Harry had no time for consideration. He squeezed the trigger. A bright red flash of light blinded his eye momentarily. He went numb as the assassin staggered backward into the opposite wall. His eyes tearing from both the light and the enormity of his deed, Harry watched, dumbstruck, as the small hole in the intruder's chest spewed forth a shower of blood and steaming chunks of matter. The white smock grew crimson.

His nose filled with the aroma of charred flesh, his knees buckling, Harry tottered back into the closed door, the gun still attached to his hand, his hand hanging limply at his side. The intruder's arms and legs thrashed about in brief seizures. Small, gurgling sounds hissed from deep within his throat.

Harry hugged the wall. The woman patient slowly regained

consciousness, her bedsheet splattered with red. "The world needs a leader . . . no sacrifice too great," she began to chant, oblivious to the events around her.

Harry dropped the gun to the floor. He was grateful he hadn't eaten that evening.

9

"And you have no idea why this guy was determined to off the kid?" Lieutenant Groux said, flopping his lips open and shut for deliberate effect.

"I told you," Harry replied, hugging a chair in Cade's office. "It has something to do with the peeper's dream."

"Ah yes," Groux smiled, pacing around Harry's chair. "That all important dream. The dream wherein World War III, zombies, and dead presidents cavort."

He pushed his face close to Harry's. He looked like the first husband of a widow. "That dream is a positive legend downtown, Porter. It rates right up there with the Bermuda Triangle, the Lost Continent of Atlantis, and the Balanced Budget."

"Give it a rest, Groux," Harry said, rubbing his eyelids with his right thumb and forefinger. "Dick Tracy was bumped out of the funnies years ago. So was his square-jawed approach. I personally don't give a shit whether you believe me or not. You know that the syntheskin stuff has been stolen, and you know that Pratt showed up badly burned. I just killed a man in there, and I'm not real crazy about that fact. My stomach is growling. My knees are knocking. My head is pounding. So, you'll forgive me if I don't want to play cat and mouse with you, okay? I've just told you everything I know, from the first suicide to the last murder. If you don't believe me, just ask Bronkowski about the blinky creep. The guy took out one of his local men, a peeper named Flowers. The originator of your favorite nightmare, by the way. Go ahead. Ask him about it."

Groux stared at Bronkowski who, in turn, sat passively in the corner. Cade, stretched behind his desk, surveyed the entire scene with a sense of intellectual disdain.

"Feel free to jump right in whenever you see fit, Bronk," Harry said. "I love three-part harmony."

"Don't get wise, Porter," Groux advised. "I can lock you up for manslaughter right now."

"Try it and see if it sticks."

Groux snored through his nose and began circling Harry's chair once again. "So, you insist that the only possible reason that this bogus doc might have had in wanting this girl dead rests in your cockamamie dream theory, eh?" Groux folded his arms and stood, rocking back and forth on his feet, before Harry. "Well, pardon me for laughing, pal, but I don't buy it. I don't go for any of it."

"Who's surprised?" Harry smirked. "The only way you'll broaden your mind is to put it under a train."

Cade's phone rang. He picked it up immediately and spoke to a subdued orderly on the other end. A strange smile appeared on his face. "Thank you," he concluded, the recipient of a brief monologue, too brisk to be overheard. Standing in all his aristocratic glory, Dr. Andrew Cade stared from Groux to Bronkowski knowingly. In a tone of total superiority, he announced: "Gentlemen, you may be interested in knowing that our friends at the atomic power plant have made their demands. If the President of the United States isn't delivered into their hands by six o'clock this evening, they will sabotage the plant—effectively contaminating most of New York, Connecticut, and New Jersey."

Groux stood there dumbfounded.

Harry hissed a terse "sshit."

Bronkowski was on his feet immediately. "Did they say they'd harm the President?"

"On the contrary," Cade replied, his hawklike features crinkled in obvious amusement at the law officers' chagrin. "They say they only want a chance to state their grievances concerning the ecological condition of spaceship Earth to the President in person. But, under the circumstances, I believe Mr. Porter's funny theories might be regarded with more, shall we say, solemnity?"

Groux was on his way out the door. "Doesn't mean a damned thing. Coincidence."

Bronkowski followed Groux. Harry put out a restraining hand, clasping the FBI man by the elbow. "What do we do now, J. Edgar?"

"*We* do what we have to do, Porter," Bronkowski snarled. "But you do nothing. You stay out of it altogether. Is that clear?"

The FBI agent shook off Harry's paw and stormed out of the room, slamming the door behind him. "Thanks, Andy," Harry said.

"Don't thank me," Cade said, walking to his liquor cabinet. "Thank Peter Hayden or whoever it is up there making demands. Drink?"

"I could take a whole bottle intravenously right about now. I'm still shaking." He slumped down in a chair. "Jesus."

"Want to talk about it?"

"No. If I talk about it, I'll start thinking about it. And if I start thinking about it, I won't be able to keep the drink down. Hell. Andy, it happened so quickly."

"Every aspect of the human experience happens quickly, Porter," Cade said, pouring out a glass of bourbon. "And, for the most part, they happen unexpectedly. A hospital environment seems to underscore that fact. You were presented with an either/or situation: the girl's life or the killer's. Under the circumstances, I believe you made the right choice, no matter how distasteful it strikes you." He handed Harry the glass. "Will this do?"

"Gasoline would do." He downed the drink immediately. "The dream is becoming solid, Andy. Flowers' vision is materializing before our eyes. The thing that worries me most, though, is the identity of the original dreamer. It's a frightening thought to imagine one person, or one organization or one power behind this plot. It's so well planned . . . it borders on insanity!"

Porter rested his chin on his palm. "Who would benefit from the President's death most? Who'd go out of their way to kill Walker?" He raised his head. "Reeves! He'd be the biggest winner if Walker was offed."

"The Vice-President murdering his own Commander in Chief."

"Sure. It makes sense. The constitutional amendment of '08 made it legal for a President to run for a third term again. Reeves has been called a potentially wonderful leader, a real old-fashioned hero. Yet, he'll be saddled with Walker again this fall. He can't rebel without fragmenting his party, and he can't jump parties without looking like a turncoat, either."

"An entertaining thought, Porter, but a bit farfetched."

"Maybe it's a foreign power, then. A country you wouldn't ordinarily suspect. How about Canada? They've been having problems about fishing in territorial waters, right? With Walker out of the way..."

"Porter—nobody kills for fish!"

"Captain Ahab did!"

"Porter, you are dense and quite myopic. You have an entire list of potential assassins to consider," Cade raised his glass in a toast. "Of which I am proudly a member."

"Hell," Harry said, twitching his lip into a near-snarl. "It could be anybody. If only we could make some inroads with that girl."

"We're doing our best. Your friend is back in there with her now."

Harry banged his glass down on Cade's desk. Cade examined the finish disapprovingly. "Why didn't I think of this before!" Harry exclaimed. "Kapps!"

"You think *Kapps* is behind all this?" Cade said, surprised.

"No, no. I think Kapps is just the man to help us, though. He's an expert on kids: their likes, dislikes, dreams, nightmares. He's quite a guy."

"I thought you considered him a charlatan."

"A guy can change his mind, can't he? When I first met you, I thought you were a stuffed shirt."

"I *am* a stuffed shirt," Cade replied stiffly. "And I'd appreciate it if you remembered that fact."

"Just proves what a great judge of character I am," Porter said, tugging Cade out of his office. "I met with Kapps a few times. He's all right, pretty down to earth for a space age messiah."

"Please don't belabor the point," Cade frowned, reaching for his coat. "Where are we going at six in the morning?"

"To Kapps' office. They have a living quarters there, too, Kapps told me he's always reachable there. He's quite an expert on programming. If anyone can give us a line on what's keeping Jane Doe in the ozones, it's the reverend."

The two men exited the hospital in the early morning light. Hailing a cab, they puttered to midtown, alighting at 666 5th Avenue. Entering the building's massive lobby, they signed in under the sleepy scrutiny of a uniformed guard and entered the elevator.

The car stopped on the 122nd floor. Harry stepped into the darkened waiting room. The receptionist's desk was deserted.

Harry walked over to the desk and flicked on a lamp. "Nobody home."

He walked into Kapps' office. A lone newsticker provided sound. The place was deserted. "Wonder what time they set up shop?"

"Probably at some incredibly self-indulgent, bourgeois hour," Cade replied icily, sitting down on the couch in front of the video magazines, "like nine A.M."

"Let's try the other floors," Harry suggested, stepping back into the elevator.

Harry programmed the car to stop at five more of Kapps' fifteen floors. The elevator slid to a smooth halt on each level, but the doors did not open. "All the floors must be closed," Harry said.

"I don't see why they shouldn't be," Cade sighed. "Most business offices would be shuttered at this hour."

"Yeah. But this isn't exactly a business. Suppose I was some lost soul seeking solace. I show up here after closing time and have to wait until nine the next morning to receive sanctuary? Nah."

He poked the buttons once again. The elevator stopped at each floor, but the door remained shut. "I don't like this," Harry said.

"Nor do I. I get motion sickness very easily."

Harry brought the car back to the reception area. "There's something fishy here," Harry said, walking through the waiting room.

"Please, Porter, spare me the hard-boiled detectivisms. The image does not fit someone with a ruined shoe."

"If this was a business office, and I walked out of the elevator," Harry said, "there would be some sort of partition here, wouldn't there? Plexiglass or some sort of transparent wall that would keep me from just walking in here and rifling through the offices? I mean, if I was a thief, I could just walk away with everything in this place, Kapps is too worldly a man to be so lax in his security."

"He's also a religious man."

"Jesus, I hope nothing's happened to him," Harry said, sitting at the receptionist's desk. "Half the people I've come in contact with during the past three days are either dead or missing."

"Or exhausted," Cade added.

"Maybe the phone will work." Harry dialed the main

number of the church. A young, blond face formed on the viewscreen. "Hello. You have reached The Church of the Ancient Astronauts. None of us spacefarers are at home right now..."

"Come on, Porter," Cade admonished, arising from the chair. "We can come back after nine or you can just call the man at a decent hour. For god's sake, don't just sit there gaping at the blasted phone!"

"But to close down a church?"

"It's done all the time, Porter," Cade remarked, stepping inside the elevator and pushing the lobby button. "St. Patrick's Cathedral and mall have been locking up shop at sundown for decades. The threat of hooliganism is too great."

Porter trotted into the car. "But Kapps is such a progressive thinker."

"Maybe today is a progressive religious holiday."

Cade and Porter walked through the lobby and out of the building. "Something's happened to him, Andy, I can feel it," Harry said.

The pair took the pedway back to Harry's apartment. Porter did not resist, having already sacrificed his left shoe. "Machine will make you a cup of coffee while I change," Harry said, walking into his apartment and heading towards the bedroom shoe tree.

Machine dutifully prepared two cups of coffee as Harry changed shoes. "Any important messages?" he called to the ceiling.

"Negative," Machine replied. "A few personal calls. Nothing of any relevance. One interesting note, however, concerning my ongoing investigation into the background of the youthful suicides. With each successive compu-scan I instituted, less and less information was offered on public record. It would appear that the data being made available to the public access computer system on these subjects is dwindling."

"Interesting." Harry walked into the kitchen and took the two cups. Someone was systematically removing biographical information on the suicide victims from public scrutiny. "Federal boys, you think?" Harry muttered aloud.

Machine understood the fragmented connection.

"A logical assumption."

"Which, in turn, means that they're onto this mess as well. Yet, they won't admit it." Harry handed one cup to Cade. "Well, I guess that's it for us. Dead-ended in suicideville."

"Not exactly," Machine added.

"I thought that the information we need has been syphoned away."

"It has," Machine acknowledged. "But when I first noticed this occurrence and computed the most likely place the data was going, I quickly contacted the main computer system of the NYPD. I hypothesized that the federal officials would not see fit to readily contact the local law enforcement bureaus and share their plans. I believe that was a correct assumption in that, according to the police computer, the information is still retrievable from its storage center. It is considered official police business, however, and not made available to the public. Through some negotiating, I believe I have arranged a way to actually obtain some, if not all, of the information you seek on the suicides."

"How?"

"Simple. Last month you were involved in a story dealing with underground crime—"

"That's underworld—"

"Semantics. Underworld crime and the influence it exerted over certain games of chance in the New York metropolitan area. The police would very much like to examine your source material. In essence, they want the name of the human contact who spied on the operation and then revealed the facts to you in order to facilitate your composing the story."

Cade was puzzled. "Aren't journalists supposed to protect their sources?"

Harry grinned wide. "Sure we are. But my source doesn't need too much protection right now. Benny Mardonis. As soon as the piece was published, he was turned into fish fodder by the local family members."

"I beg your pardon?" Cade said, arching an eyebrow.

"He was given cement track shoes and asked to run the minute mile at the bottom of the Hudson by a bunch of geeks with no necks."

"Oh . . ." Cade said, swallowing a gulp of hot coffee. "I wasn't aware people did that sort of thing anymore."

"Old habits die hard." Harry looked at the camera in the corner of the living room. "So you'll give the police computer the name of my source who, at this stage of the game, is one hundred percent past tense and useless."

"A fact the police computer does not realize at present,"

Machine stated, "the identity of your informant still being a mystery. I have suggested a small exchange of information: the trivial biographical readouts of the suicide victims for a human interest story you're planning for the very valuable identity of a master informant who can aid an investigation currently being carried out by the NYPD. I believe the system will get the human clearance necessary to complete the transaction."

Harry walked into the kitchen and collapsed in laughter on the countertop. "I don't believe it! Machine! You're running an honest-to-god con. I probably have the only computer in the entire country that can be called devious!"

"There is nothing dishonest about the transaction," Machine injected. "I have merely concealed one small bit of information from the opposing system, which, after all, pertains to the unknown commodity it is bargaining for. It appears to me that I have constructed an exchange in a most correct and beneficial manner."

"You've pulled off an excellent scam," Harry smiled at the lens. "I'm proud of you."

The system hesitated. "Thank you, Harry," it finally replied. "I'm pleased that it meets with your approval."

Harry pushed himself away from the counter and pointed to the door. "Let's go, Andy. Finish your coffee, and we'll head back to your hospital. Maybe our peeper tom has gotten a reading on Jane Doe. We don't have too much time before Walker has to give his answer to the terrorists."

Cade and Harry headed for the door. Harry paused at the threshold. "Machine, contact me as soon as you get the information on those kids. Maybe we can track down their depression to one source."

Harry shut the door. The video screen came to life once more. An ample-bosomed Sybille DeVille lounged in a tub filled with multicolored bubbles. "Harry!" she called out. "I don't believe it! It's seven-thirty in the goddamned morning! Where are you?"

Machine lowered the volume on the phone recorder. It was the double-jointed female again, it noted. Not a call to bother Harry Porter about.

10

There are certain fears that are palpable—tactile dreads
that remain crouched in the recesses of the adult human
mind simply awaiting the chance to leap forward and dredge
up the shapeless terrors of childhood. Harry Porter was well
aware of these fears, having collided with them many times
over the years. He had a profound respect for them. They
weren't mere shadows of traumas past, psychological echoes.
They were real emotional warning bells fortelling catastro-
phes firmly rooted in the present.

As Harry walked into the hospital entrance with Andrew
Cade, a sudden prickling sensation swept through his body in
a single, ominous shiver. Something horrible was about to
take place. He felt it lurking at the end of the corridor—
formless, yet as three-dimensional and solid as the nurses and
orderlies patrolling the hall.

Without a word of explanation to his companion, he ran
towards Jane Doe's room, surmising that the trouble was
centered there. Cade must have sensed it as well. He followed
Porter silently, a look of concern on his face.

They had not jogged half the corridor when they heard
the screaming.

Harry quickened his pace, his bad knee clicking every time
his left foot pounded, flat, onto the floor. Skidding around a
corner, he saw the source of the disturbance. Jane Doe was
standing outside her room. She was pressed tightly against
the wall. Her arms were outstretched, palms downward. She
resembled the classic concept of the criminal flattened against
the prison wall in a vain attempt to elude the blazing stare of
the searchlight.

Across the corridor, not ten feet away, Marion Saint-Crispen
swayed helplessly. Pitiful and puppetlike, he rocked, loose-
limbed and oblivious to his surroundings. He had apparently
made mental contact with his patient, unleashing whatever
mental reserves were housed in her twisted young mind.

"Telekinesis is an inexact science," Harry recalled a doctor
whispering over his own hospital bed three years ago. They

had given him a sedative after his breakdown and assumed he was totally under while they discussed his fate. His metabolism going wild from stress, however, had allowed him to successfully cling to consciousness. A doctor and a parapsych had argued over the use of PSI art on him.

The doctor had lost the argument, adding, as if for Harry's benefit, "for God's sake be careful. All one has to do is accidentally tap a hidden current, an unconscious pocket of unchartered mental power and all hell could break loose. I know. I've seen it happen."

Harry shook his head suddenly, dismissing his past with a shudder. He stared at the Saint's eyes, rolled back into their sockets. He cursed himself for forcing his resourceful friend into this horrible state.

The girl's mouth twisted into a sneer. Her soft, brown eyes seemed to harden and bulge from their sockets. White flecks were spattered on her dry, cracked lips. Harry made a move forward. The girl turned and faced him. He felt a sudden jolt slap him in his forehead with the power of a fist. He flew backward onto the floor. The girl returned her gaze to the Saint. Marion slowly, almost inaudibly, began to whimper. His eyes slowly slid back down into their proper position. He stared back at the girl, his face taking on a look of both terror and anger. His convulsed movements slowed. Presently, they ceased. He stood, granitelike, across from the girl.

As soon as Jane Doe's gaze locked into Saint Crispen's, her body seemed to relax totally. Her arms lowered to her side. She emitted a childish, innocent giggle. All tension dissolved from her face. She was suddenly transformed into a gay, carefree sixteen year old. She took three steps forward and stood, inculpable, in the middle of the hall.

Her appearance changed again so rapidly that Harry had difficulty assimilating the scene. Jane Doe continued to laugh softly, naturally. Without any provocation, however, blood suddenly spurted from her nose. It dribbled from her ears. It oozed from her mouth. Her eyes rolled back. Her head tilted backward, and a rasping noise burst forth from her throat. The laughter ceased. She collapsed on the floor. As she hit the surface, Marion Saint-Crispen let out an agonized yell and slid down the surface of the wall.

Harry jumped up and ran to the Saint's aid. Cade, who had remained frozen behind Harry, darted to the bleeding young woman.

"Are you all right?" Porter asked, pulling the Saint up into sitting position.

"The little bitch almost deep fried my eyes!" Saint-Crispen sputtered. "She's some tough cookie."

"What happened?"

"I'll be damned if I know. I'm peeping her like crazy and getting a blank slate. So, I decided to take a breather, you know? Go outside and have a smoke. I figured maybe I'd get myself included in that little card game going on in the chow hall kitchen." He cut himself short. "Uh, I didn't actually see the card game, you understand. I swear, I've been in that room since you split. I just heard about the game, that's all. I never actually walked down there to confirm the rumor or anything."

"Saint-Crispen!"

"Oh yeah. So, I'm sitting outside Sleeping Beauty's castle here when suddenly I feel this hand on my shoulder. I figure maybe it's Bett—this nurse I had run into before. Not in the cafeteria card game, by the way. Then it strikes me that this hand is a little clammy, ice cube city. I turned around and there was our little pal, just staring at me. It was horrible, Harry-boy. A braver man would have split and run."

"But you didn't?"

"No way. Besides, who could break her grip, man? That girl has muscles in her fingers. So, I'm staring at this little kid when all of a sudden, her face pulls a quick-change act. Harry, she looked like everyone's worst nightmare. She's drooling and snorting and actually growling. *Growling!* Can you imagine how spooky it is to see a sixteen-year-old chick doing a *Call of the Wild* number six inches from your face? I try to shake her off, but before I can get two steps out of the chair, she's slammed me up against the wall. She more than just physically threw me there, she put me there with her head. The thought suddenly occurred to me that I had peeped a little too deeply on this one, let the funny bunny out of the basket, you dig?"

"You hit a power source."

"Maybe. It was almost as if there was a trap in there, just waiting for someone to poke around. I'm not sure whether I hit into a power source or an antipower source, you know? Like a deflective shield or something. Still, she had to have some sort of oomph to keep this shield intact for so long. I figure that maybe she's a latent, like me. Maybe I reactivated her skills by peeping her the way Flowers rejuvenated mine."

Saint-Crispen licked his lips. "Now, I must confess. At this point, I'm scared shitless. All I need in my present nervous condition (with my mother ill and all) is to get involved in a wrestling match with some growling girl. I figure I'll try to reason with her. I send out some cooling vibes. Visions of little wildflowers, babbling brooks, puppy dogs. Greeting card shit. No dice, man. She floors me with a major whammy. Pow! I'm up against the wall. So, I then say to myself, 'no more mister nice guy.' I try to peep her but good, find out what's behind all the foaming. While I'm in there, I thought I'd also check out whether there was any extra stuff that you could use."

"I'm touched," Harry said. He was.

"Anyhow, I keep on getting this one fuzzy picture. Bubbles on a lawn. Makes no sense to me. She's foaming and growling and I'm getting bubbles. I try to fine tune her. Nothing. Get the same reception over and over again. It was worse than rerun season. I see that I'm not making any progress and I try to backpedal. Only I can't. She's got me locked in there. I can't get out of her head. Only here's the weird part. It's not her that's holding me in there."

"I don't get you."

"I can't figure it, either. But there are dozens of head trips going on in there doing distinct numbers. You know how a parashrink cures his patient by giving him a new set of happy reference points? You get depressed after the cure, and bingo, you automatically flash on this happy buzz point that your peeper has planted?"

"But that doesn't always work, right?" Harry pointed out from experience. "Sometimes the original psychological make-up of the patient is strong enough to resist reprogramming."

"Right. But, you figure, if you get someone like Bambi over there to participate in a peeper show, more than likely she could be programmed. She's young and pliable, right? Well, dig this, she can't be tampered with. She had at least a couple of dozen mondo depresso trains of behavior going on in there, strong enough to cancel any good vibes sent in. Her brain is a tangle of short circuits, man. She's a real zombie.

"I discover that little fact, and whammo, I'm out cold. I mean, I don't remember a thing after that. I got so scared, I think I started to cry. After that? I'm on the floor here; she's on the floor there, and you're standing over me."

Harry pressed a hand on Saint-Crispen's shoulder. "During the time period you peeped those suicidal tendencies, Marion, you freed her from their influence. For a split second, she became a normal kid again. And then..."

Saint-Crispen turned and saw the bleeding girl for the first time. "Jesus H. Christ!" he said, horrified. "What happened to her?"

"I'm not sure."

"I didn't do that, did I? Oh, sweet Jesus. She was just a baby."

Cade slowly walked over to Harry and the Saint. "She's dead," he said softly. "I won't know for sure until after the autopsy, but I assume it's heart failure."

"I killed a little girl," Saint-Crispen muttered. "I'm a murderer."

Harry shook his head negatively. "I don't think so. You found a whole set of Pavlovian references within her mind, right?"

"Uh-huh."

"When those behavior patterns had run their destructive course, what would their ultimate conclusion be?"

"Suicide?" Saint-Crispen guessed.

"I'm pretty sure of it," Harry responded. "That would explain all the teenage swan divers. Countless kids programmed to pursue a self-destructive act, coached in some school of self-loathing. When we saved our Jane Doe from jumping, we didn't pull her out of the suicidal abyss. We merely postponed the inevitable conclusion of her program. I think her body just completed the act, punctuated the sentence."

"It wasn't my fault, then?" Saint-Crispen asked hopefully.

"It's doubtful," Cade interrupted.

"If anything," Harry said, "your temporarily relieving her of her mental burden gave her the last peace of mind she experienced in her lifetime."

The Saint exhaled slowly, the guilt almost visibly expelled from his body. "Man, I could use a hit of tranx."

"I bet you could," Harry remarked, "but we have a lot of work cut out for us in the next few hours."

"Now what?" Saint-Crispen moaned. "I did my bit. I didn't see anything at all in there that would help you. Now, I'd like to get onto more interesting things—like sleep, for instance."

"Wouldn't we all," Harry smiled. "But we still don't know how the peeper's dream connects the suicides with the death of the President or what's going on at Fountain Point. We still don't even know *who's* behind it. It could be anybody. From the Vice-President to..."

"Reeves!" the Saint suddenly exclaimed. "That makes sense to me. Power corrupts and all that!"

"I'm not sure it's Reeves," Harry said, patiently.

"He *did* ignore your warning," Cade replied.

"So did ninety percent of the Manhattan phone directory." Harry bit his lower lip. "We still don't have a single name or organization to pin this on."

"We seem to have an army of potential killers, though," Cade added.

"That's it!" Saint-Crispen declared. "It's the U.S. Army that's behind it. I mean, that sort of revolutionary shit happens every day in Brazil and Spain and all those South American beaneries, right? Makes a lot of sense to me."

"You are a walking contradiction of terms, Mr. Saint-Crispen," Cade said, shaking his head sadly. "To think that such unlimited PSI processes inhabit that small and apparently vacant space above your eyes..."

"I'm up for some coffee," Harry muttered, walking away from the scene. His two companions followed as the attendants lifted the girl's battered body onto a stretcher.

11

The television newscaster was appropriately grim yet suave. Sitting before an ever-changing relief map holo of the world at large, he stared meaningfully at the audience on the other side of the camera lens and told them, in gripping tones, of the latest developments in the Fountain Point Power Plant story. Flanked by Cade and Saint-Crispen in the hospital cafeteria, Harry sat, sullenly, before the wall-sized video unit.

He'd always wondered why television newscasters never seemed to sweat. There they were in front of millions of people, under hot lights, and in confined quarters. Yet, they always seemed unflappable on the air. They never sweat. Maybe they wore rubber makeup that jammed all possible exits of moisture. Maybe they caulked their pores the way homeowners did windows.

Harry nursed a cold cup of coffee as the newscaster met Porter's gaze with fierce intensity. "We repeat, the President of the United States has agreed to meet with the terrorists— even though it means risking his life in the process. In a statement read by Vice-President David Reeves, President Aaron Sonny Walker let it be known that although he realized the jeopardy he was putting himself in on a personal level, he was willing to make any and all sacrifices necessary to keep the three great states of Connecticut, New York, and New Jersey contamination free. For a further report, we now switch to Tessie Bohle live from Washington."

The stern face of the square-jawed, middle-aged newsman faded from view, replaced by the prettier, but equally passionate, visage of a small brunette woman who, wearing a short-short haircut, gave the impression of being a rather overly earnest pixie. "Thank you, Chad. Here in Washington, the mood is grim but hopeful. Everyone of both political parties realizes the chance that the President is taking but agrees with President Walker wholeheartedly on his assessment of the situation. If the terrorists live up to their promises once their demands are met, then Sonny Walker's act of good faith will save the tri-state area from a nuclear calamity unparalleled in this nation's history. A few minutes ago we chatted with Vice-President David Reeves about the explosive situation."

The screen fluttered slightly. Presently, the serious pixie was seen debating the cleft chin of the Vice-President. Tessie Bohle gazed upwards into Reeves' totally calm Adam's apple. "You agree with the President's decision, Vice-President Reeves?"

The former war hero thought a moment before answering. "Yes."

"It never occurred to the Oval Office to ignore the terrorists' demands?"

"No."

"What would you say the mood in Washington is right now?"

"I haven't the vaguest idea."

"Would you say the mood is grim?"

"Yes, I suppose you could say the mood is grim."

"Yet hopeful?"

"Well, yes."

The screen fluttered a second time and Tessie Bohle returned to the screen solo for yet another meaningful close-up. "So, there you have it, Chad. It's official. The mood in Washington is grim yet hopeful. Back to you."

Chad Nelson, America's favorite newsman, resumed his position on the wall unit, sheltered safely behind his desk. "Thank you, Tessie, for that incisive observation. We will continue to cover the President's trip to Fountain Point throughout the day, preempting regularly scheduled programming. Should the crisis extend into this evening, tonight's installments of *Celebrity Embarrassments* and *Those Insane Americans!* will be seen in their entirety following the conclusion of the Fountain Point incident.

"Although the mood in Washington is grim yet hopeful, there is always the chance that the terrorists will not live up to their promise and will attempt to send a deadly nuclear cloud floating over the states of Connecticut, New York, and New Jersey, no matter what. Evacuation procedures have already begun in certain areas of those states. Panic was reported in Trenton and Danbury, rioting and looting in Newark and Buffalo. Oddly enough, however, New York City seems to be taking this potential cataclysm in stride. For a close-up report of just how New York is reacting to the Terror at Fountain Point, we've got our own Baskin Florescu in the streets. Baskin?"

A pencil-thin, continental type, sporting slicked back hair and an anemic moustache smiled at the camera. He was standing outside of Times Square, laser lights and holographic billboards convulsing behind him. "Yes, Chad, New Yorkers are remaining amazingly calm in the face of this possible disaster. For the past ten hours, since the terrorists first made their demands, there has been no rioting, no looting, no panic, and, surprisingly enough, no rush to flee the city. Why? Well, we asked several New Yorkers to explain their sense of serenity to our Action People Cameras."

The prerecorded face of a toothless hag, carrying a spandex bag, gaped at the camera. "What terrorists?" she asked.

"The terrorists at the nuclear power plant at Fountain Point," Florescu explained.

"Where?"

"Fountain Point."

"Never been."

"It's upstate, ma'am."

"Mus' be nice."

"It's very nice."

The hag squinted an eye and zeroed in on the reporter. "Well, if it's so goddamn nice, why ain't you there, sonny? Why you still here in this cesspool uva city?"

The woman was removed from the screen, replaced by a flashy cab driver who just laughed at the newsman. "Nucleer clouds poisoning dis city? Mister, where have you bin? A nucleer cloud couldn't poison dis city enny more than it already is. Haw! Haw! Have you smelt the diar you been breedin' lately? Smells like gawbage! Day olt gawbage! Maybe I'd rather have it smellin' nucleer."

A perky blond art student, clad in a sheer jump suit, licked her lips before emitting a series of well-rounded giggles. "It's exciting. I'm not worried. I believe in the system. I believe in our government, in man's humanity to man. Besides, Daddy has a shuttlecraft on the patio airstrip. Anything happens, I'm in Miami."

An old man selling video magazines at Grand Central Tubeway stared impassively at the lens. "I'm not worried."

"No?"

"Nope."

"Why not?"

"Why should I be?"

"Because the terrorists might blow up the power station."

"They won't."

"They could send a radioactive cloud all over this area."

"Never happen."

"They could poison the air we breathe, the food we eat, the water we drink."

"No way."

"How can you be sure of that?"

The old man shrugged and leaned against his newsstand. "'Cause it ain't ever happened before—has it?" He flashed a triumphant smile.

Harry rubbed his eyes with the thumb and forefinger of his right hand. No wonder there wasn't any panic in the city. The problem wasn't immediate enough for anyone to pay attention to. A nation reared on instant playbacks and seventeen-minute plot lines had to have things spelled out for them.

"Be right back," he said, leaving the table. He still was in the dark concerning the connection between his suicide epidemic and the terrorists. Cade couldn't help him on that score. Neither could Saint-Crispen. Kapps was his last hope. Perhaps if Kapps could just come over and look at the girl's body, listen to what Saint-Crispen saw in the kid's mind. Examine the body for any telltale signs of bizarre programming that only an expert would notice. Perhaps Kapps could give them the clue they so desperately needed. They had less than eight hours in which to act. Eight hours before the imbecilic President of the United States strolled into what surely was a trap.

Harry dialed Kapps' church. He received the same prerecorded message he had earlier. He hung up the phone and returned to his chair.

Chad Nelson was finishing his report. "And so, tension mounts as the Terror at Fountain Point continues speeding towards its deadline. We'll be back again in twenty-seven minutes with an update. Until that time, we hope you enjoy the California intramural cheerleading finals. This is Chad Nelson taking his time to wish you a good time all the time."

"The guy's a regular physicist," Harry grimaced.

"Don't knock Chad Nelson," Saint-Crispen glowered. "You un-American or something?"

Harry made a sour face. Cade drummed his fingers on the table. "This is pointless. This is unbelievably pointless. We three are sitting here, witnesses to a fantastically heinous plot to destroy the country, and we can't lift a finger to prevent it. We can't even figure out how the plot works!"

"Or if there is a plot," Saint-Crispen said smugly. "I mean, I haven't seen anything that looks like a plot." He shot a meaningful glance at Cade. "All we have is Harry's word. And, frankly, Harry has been known to tipple a bit, if you catch my drift."

"You're going to catch my right in a minute," Harry muttered. "I'm sure the key to all this is lying right in front of us." He slammed his hand on the tabletop, sending a plastic utensil flying.

"That's a fork, not a key," Saint-Crispen commented.

"We've struck out, Andy," Harry said, jamming his nasal inhaler up his snout. He inhaled deeply, almost reveling in his despair. "We can't even count on Kapps. No one answers his phone. Something's happened over there. I know it. Kapps is a religious man, but he's secular, too. He wouldn't close down a multimillion dollar corporation just on a whim."

"Do you think he's met with foul play?" Cade asked.

"I'm not sure," Harry replied. "I just have a bad feeling about all this. There's something floating around in my head. Something I can't put my finger on but still bothers me. It's back there, hovering around."

"Maybe you inherited some of Jane Doe's bubbles," Saint-Crispen smirked. "Little bubbles in her head." He looked at the tabletop. "Sheeesh."

A strange look came over Porter's face, one of sick recognition. "The bubbles. Jesus." He pounded his fist on the table once. He would have done it a second time but the initial impact had hurt too much. "I must be the biggest sap in the world."

Cade glanced at Saint-Crispen before looking at Harry. "An acknowledged fact. Why the sudden soul-searching?"

"I've been suckered," Harry said. "We all have. Those bubbles, Saint. How many did you see?"

"I dunno," the Saint replied casually. "Half a dozen, maybe. Not a lot."

"Six?"

"Six. Half a dozen. Not a lot."

"Just normal bubbles?"

"Just plain old bubbles. Just sitting there."

"The bubbles weren't floating? They were resting on the ground?"

Saint-Crispen thought a moment. "Yes. No. They were on the grass. In the grass."

"Round bubbles on green grass."

"Yeah, well, they weren't round anymore, exactly. They were resting on the ground so they were sort of flat on the bottom."

Harry rolled his eyes towards the television screen. "The girl *did* give us the clue we needed. I just wasn't bright enough to notice."

Cade and the Saint stared at him uncomprehendingly. "Those bubbles you saw weren't bubbles," Harry stated. "They were geodesic domes. Six circular structures sprawled across green terrain."

"How can you be sure?" Cade asked.

"Because I spent the morning there yesterday. It's Kapps' retreat at Mount Pleasant."

"Kapps?" Cade repeated. "I can't believe you're connecting

him with that poor girl. Especially in light of the glowing portrait you've painted of him."

"Yeah," Harry snorted. "It must sound off the wall, but it makes some sense. Kapps is a great performer, the difference between his onstage and offstage persona is staggering. Hell, he even went out of his way to stress that fact to me. He could probably con anyone into believing his total innocence. But, it just occurred to me. One of his main philosophical spiels concerns the fact that the world is lacking in leadership. Maybe he thinks he's the leader that the world is waiting for. He's also good with kids. Maybe it sounds crazy, but there's a definite connection between his own credo and the nonsense that these kids have been spewing before they swan dive."

"That's a very tenuous connection," Cade replied.

"How else do you explain his absence from the city? He's up to something, in league with the Fountain Point mob. Christ. To think how he bragged about his expertise in programming."

"I can't accept that hypothesis, Porter," Cade answered. "There are too many loose ends. Loose? Positively disconnected. Kapps is an intelligent individual. Exactly how, do you suppose, does he think he will be able to assassinate the President in public, cripple the government with the entire world watching, and then, calmly, assume control of the country."

"There's only one way to find out," Harry answered. "We pay a visit to Kapps. We take a trip to Mount Pleasant."

"You can count me out," Saint-Crispen said. "I don't want to wind up spending the rest of my life in day-glo city."

"What are you talking about?" Harry asked.

"That Mount Pleasant place is just too near Fountain Point for this world traveler's comfort."

Porter and Cade exchanged startled looks.

"Out of the mouths of intellectual babes," Cade said, shaken.

"Look," Harry countered. "If we go up there and nothing is wrong, we can just say 'hi' and head back home. I'm doing a story on Kapps anyhow, so no one on the compound would be all that suspicious. But we have to go up there, Saint. It may be our last chance of finding Jessica alive and saving Walker's hide."

"For the record," Cade enunciated slowly. "I'm still not at all convinced. Most of the evidence you have amassed is entirely circumstantial."

"You're a sweetheart, Andy."

"I'm no such thing. I'm cold and calculating and misanthropic."

"Hey," Saint-Crispen injected. "As long as we're into the adjective game, I think you're pretty much of a snob."

"Who asked you, Marion." Harry's communicator began to beep. Lifting the side of his coat, he stuck his hand into the torn lining. He managed to locate the wailing device. Pulling it out, he also disinterred a handful of loose change that promptly cascaded onto the floor and rolled the entire length of the cafeteria. "There goes this week's salary," he smirked. "What is it?" He addressed the tiny communicator.

"Machine here," the diminutive device said in a parody of a female voice. "I've cross-referenced the material I obtained from the local police facility and have found one or two additional points common to all the suicide victims."

"Go on."

"They are all psychologically troubled: depressives, seekers of solitude, overtly neurotic."

"That description fits most teenagers."

"They all had problems relating to their peer group. They were highly susceptible to stronger, more mature personalities. Interestingly enough, they all expressed a fascination, at one time or another, with the Church of the Ancient Astronauts."

"Bingo," Harry said. "Thanks, Machine." He dropped the communicator back into his lining. He heard it click against the remainder of the coin graveyard at the bottom of his jacket. "I should have trusted my initial feelings about that guy. The first time I saw him on video I thought he was greasy enough to take a change in oil instead of a bath. But I let him con me!"

"Porter," Cade cautioned, "you still have no substantial proof. . . . Why not inform Lieutenant Groux of these new developments and see what . . ."

"Why bother," Harry said. "He'll only throw me out of his office."

"Proper procedure, Porter."

"All right," Harry said, leaving the table and heading for the phone booth. He didn't exactly know what he'd tell Groux if the lieutenant even bothered to take the call. Much to his surprise, Groux did appear on the viewscreen when summoned.

"What is it this time, hotshot?" Groux demanded.

Porter tried to pick and choose his words well. Should he tell the cop about the telltale bubbles in the girl jumper's memory or Kapps' abandoned headquarters or the location of Kapps' retreat or the man's expertise in programming.

"What is it, Porter?" Groux asked a second time.

"It's Kapps!" Porter blurted. "We figured out that the man behind the suicides and the nuclear terrorists upstate is Kapps!"

"You did, huh? Care to tell me how you reached that conclusion?"

"It's a long, involved story," Harry hedged.

"I bet it is," Groux announced. "Now listen, hotshot. I'm going to tell you this one more time. Stay out of all this. You're slowing us down. You're slowing the federal boys down. Every time you make one of your funny phone calls or come near us in any way, shape or form, you waste precious time. My time. The FBI's time. The phone company's time. You are the proverbial monkey wrench tossed into the smooth-running machinery. If I run into you one more time during the course of any of my investigations, I'll arrest you on the spot. I can keep you on ice for forty-eight hours without charging you, and I'll take advantage of that fact just to keep you out of my hair—what little there is left of it. I'll get you for jaywalking. I'll get you for loitering. I'll get you for standing in a no standing zone. But, rest assured, Porter, that I will get you for something."

"It's nice to know the system works."

"I hate you, Porter."

"You don't believe it's Kapps, huh?"

Harry hung up the phone and returned to his seat. "What was Groux's reaction?" Cade asked.

"Allergic," Harry answered. He placed his elbows on the tabletop and rested his chin on his hands. "I guess we're on our own."

"You spoke to Vice-President Reeves once," Cade suggested. "You can try again."

"For what? So I can tell my grandchildren that I was once hung up on by Washington's Who's Who? Nope. I'm going to take a little drive up to Mount Pleasant myself."

"When you use the word 'I,'" Cade frowned. "I assume that you're really groping for the pronoun 'we?'"

"Of course, you're invited," Harry said. "Both of you."

"Well you can count me out," Saint-Crispen said. "If that nuclear power plant goes, I want to be as far away from it as possible."

"Unless you own a private shuttle," Harry answered, "there's no way you'd be able to get out of the area fast enough on public transit or roadways. The place will be a mob scene. I also figure that death up there would be less painful than it would be down here. A lot quicker, that's for sure. People down here will have to wait for the cloud to hit and then, slowly, wilt under its radioactive power. There'd be panic. Violence. Up at the site itself, if worse came to worse...pffhht. All over within a matter of minutes."

Saint-Crispen pushed aside his coffee. "Well, it's a nice day for a drive anyhow."

Porter turned to Cade. "Andy, can we use your car?"

"I was waiting for that."

"Well, my car's at the shop," Harry explained.

"For the last ten years," the Saint chuckled.

"Do you want me to drive, too?" Cade asked, standing.

"Good idea," Harry responded. "I don't have a license."

The three men walked briskly to the hospital parking lot. "You know," Harry ruminated aloud, "you were wondering how a man like Kapps could kill the President in public and get away with it? Suppose that Kapps is behind this all. Using syntheskin, he's already replaced Pratt, Weiner, and Hayden with puppet doubles. Couldn't he do that with the President of the United States as well?"

"Who'd notice?" Saint-Crispen chortled.

That's what Porter was afraid of.

V

"Don't hit at all if it is honorably possible to avoid hitting; but *never* hit soft."

Theodore Roosevelt

1

A persistent pang throbbed in his upper right eyelid. Porter fished into his trouser pocket and produced the small flask of nasal spray. No, the headache was too great for the spray. He replaced the spray and groped around until he produced three small pain-killer capsules. He popped them into his mouth and bit down hard. The sour, gritty taste swept through his palate instantly. Harry sat in the back seat of the small auto, staring vacantly at the scenery outside. The city had given way to the suburbs, and now, the small rows of identical, prefabricated homes were slowly being replaced by ever-growing clusters of greenery. Cade's car was approaching what was left of New York state's countryside. Driving would take longer than the tube to Mount Pleasant, but, Harry reasoned, having a private vehicle at one's disposal was always an advantage in the event of a hasty exit.

Harry began massaging his eyes furiously. "Headache?" Cade asked, noting Harry's plight through the rearview mirror.

"Yeah," Porter answered. "Can't shake it. Nerves, probably. Does your dash computer have a vocal track?"

"It most certainly does," Cade answered. "Want some pain-killer?"

"Just took some. Doesn't really help. Could you activate your console, patch it into Machine?"

"Done," Cade said.

Harry leaned forward and spoke to the dash. "Machine, using world studies conducted on terrorists, what possible actions might saboteurs take in a nuclear facility?"

Out of the car's tiny speaker, Machine's voice emerged: "The predicted actions of terrorists in a nuclear facility are dependent upon the classification of the proposed terrorists, according to studies done by several large, nonprofit institutions."

"Exactly what are the classifications that have been developed for nuclear terrorists?"

"Categories are: hostile employees, personally motivated adversaries and psychotics, economically motivated adversaries, ideologically motivated adversaries, mass murderers, and professional arsonists."

"Has there ever been an incident where one of these ideological groups has damaged a nuclear facility to prove a point."

"Negative. Although a terrorist group in this category may seek to exploit the fear that could be generated by a ploy involving nuclear extortion, instigating a nuclear crime that could kill or harm hundreds of thousands of people would work against the group's aims. It might split the ranks of the terrorist organization, alienate its supporters and sympathizers, arouse public revulsion, and provoke severe repression."

"In other words, blowing up a nuclear facility would effectively wipe out the group's popularity as well as a slice of the public."

"Crudely worded but accurate."

Great, Harry thought, massaging his head. They were about to witness a first.

"Just what are you fishing for?" Cade asked.

"I want to see if anyone has come up with a possible scenerio for what's going on up at Fountain Point," Harry replied. "We're not sure who's in there, why or what they're after. If we can come up with a couple of possible answers, we may know what kind of people we will be running into at Kapps' camp. I'd like to have some sort of idea of what we're walking into before we actually stroll through the front door."

Harry was stymied. "Let's suppose that we're dealing with powermongers who want to use the facility for some sort of leverage. What sort of activities could they take to destroy the facility?"

Machine responded with ease. "There are eight obvious ways a terrorist group of any ideological background could disrupt service at a nuclear power facility: theft, diversion, sabotage, pseudo-diversion, kidnapping, standoff attacks, the disclosure of classified information, and the misuse of the facility."

"Sabotage," Harry repeated. "If they wanted to contaminate the area, could as few as four people do it from the control center?"

"Affirmative. Sabotage with radioactive release could be carried out easily once security was breached."

"But it's never been done in the past."

"Affirmative. During the last four decades of the twentieth century, several low-level sabotage attempts were made in nuclear facilities, mostly in North America, West Germany, and Spain. A total of fifty-seven bombings with meager results. In 1968, two hundred tons of nuclear ore were hijacked by Israeli commandos, and it is generally assumed that the same country's commando units damaged two nuclear reactors being built in France in 1974 for the country of Iraq. In 1981, a French-made nuclear installation in Iraq was nearly destroyed by Israeli air force members piloting American fighter planes.

"In the past twenty years, over one hundred fifty low-level nuclear sabotage attempts have been carried out. In addition, twenty incidents of kidnapping and one hundred fifty incidents of arson have been reported in nuclear facilities. The reason for the lack of impact of these actions and the relatively minor damage inflicted was the fact that, at no time, did the terrorists actually rupture any installation's security perimeters. All facts and descriptive phraseology copywrite, Associated Computerized News Network."

"So," Harry concluded, "someone could conceivably sabotage Fountain Point without the use of any explosives or large-scale devices if they gained access to the plant and had a working knowledge of the installation, which, I gather, is also available via Associated Computerized Blabbermouths. All they'd have to do is to pull a few plugs and let the system perk."

"Oversimplified, sarcastic, but generally true."

"Hey, Andy," Harry muttered, "how about saying good-bye to Ms. Chips up there and turning on some music. My headache has just gotten a lot worse."

Cade took a pain-killer with one hand, keeping his other on the steering wheel. "It seems to be spreading to the front of the car. Pain-killer?"

"What flavor?" Harry asked.

"Orange."

"Fine."

Saint-Crispen stared out the passenger seat's window. "Have any pineapple?"

"How's guava?"

"Fine." He grabbed two pills from the doctor's hand and placed them in his mouth, washing them down with bourbon from a flask found in the car's glove compartment. "Pulling a plug can nuke out three states," he whispered. "Sort of makes you humble, don't it? I mean, *I* can pull a plug. I wonder how many people they employ up there are clumsy."

Harry suddenly noticed the road. "Here, Andy. Pull over."

The electric car silently made its way to the side of the expressway. A small, three-dimensional sign hovered atop a post. "Mount Pleasant—Hikers Welcome." An animated hand with an outstretched forefinger pointed to a dirt road, branching off the main thoroughfare.

"I think we should go the rest of the way on foot," Porter stated.

"What the hell for?" Saint-Crispen nearly shouted. "There might be bears or worse in there!"

Harry stared at him.

"Just waiting to pounce!" the Saint added.

"If you don't hoof it, I'll pounce on the back of your lap," Harry said. "Look. This is a dirt road, Marion. If we take this car to the compound, it'll kick up enough of a dust tail to announce our arrival in the next state. If there is anything going on in there that's nasty, it would be swell if we had the element of surprise on our side."

Saint-Crispen was not convinced. "What about the bears?"

"Did you bring the dead fish, Andy?"

"Drat," Cade said, stepping out of the vehicle. "I left them in my office."

"Very funny," Saint-Crispen scowled. He kicked open the passenger door. "If anything happens to me, it'll be your fault. It'll be up to you two to support my infirmed mother— who's probably under the knife at this very moment. Here I am, the sole source of financial support."

"What happened to your brother Ralph—the Jesuit missionary?" Harry asked.

"Lions got him."

"Well, if you get eaten alive, at least you'll be carrying on in the family tradition."

Porter began the long walk on the dirt road. The further away from the highway the trio hiked, the thicker the shrubbery grew on the sides of the road. After a mile or so, Harry paused for a moment. "When we get near the compound, act as if you belong there. If anyone spots us, we're all working on my story."

"Is this place much further?" Saint-Crispen asked.

Harry motioned for Saint-Crispen to be quiet. The sounds

of rustling underbrush could be heard behind them. It was too steady to have been caused by human footsteps, approaching too quickly to have been anything but an electric vehicle of some sort. Abruptly, the sound stopped. Porter assumed it was either a routine patrol, a lost vacationer, or a tail. If it were a tail, the van had pulled onto the dirt road and would follow them discreetly until Porter and company had moved into an area of high vulnerability.

Harry continued to march, not at all enjoying the situation but helpless to change it. He hoped that he was wrong about Kapps. He cursed himself for walking headfirst into a trap should his suspicions be correct.

He caught a glimmer of movement before him. He had no time to react. Ten feet in front of the trio, six blue jump-suited figures trotted casually out into the road from the dense foliage. Each carried a laser rifle. Before the men could scramble for safety, a blue electric van pulled up behind them, disgorging another three armed members of the Church of the Ancient Astronauts.

Harry offered a weak smile to the religious group. "Hi boys and girls, out looking for converts?"

The leader of the group, a tall bespeckled girl with a single, blond pigtail cascading down her back did not smile. "Into the van, Mr. Porter. Your friends as well."

"It's such a nice day, couldn't we just walk?"

She raised her rifle to meet his eyes. "The van, Mr. Porter."

Harry shrugged his shoulders and turned around to face the small truck. "Then again, one of my friends here was just mentioning the fact that his legs were tired. A ride to the compound could be just what the doctor ordered."

Feeling that discretion was the source of valor, Porter climbed into the back of the van. Cade and Saint-Crispen meekly followed. The girl leaped in behind them. "If you would all sit in the corner—on the floor."

"Where do you think we are, honey, India?" Saint-Crispen complained. "This ain't some two-dollar haircut you're talking to. I mean, these threads cost, you know? Sitting on the floor will reduce their resale value to nil."

"Mr. Porter," the woman said, raising her rifle towards the Saint's head. "I think you're familiar with this type of weaponry. Would you please advise your companion that by following my suggestion, he would be prolonging his life span?"

Harry sat down on the floor of the van. "Saint-Crispen," he said. "What Joan of Arc has in her hand could turn you into a half a pound of ground round."

Saint-Crispen's lower lip formed a pout. He slowly crouched down to floor level. "You're going to get my cleaning bill, Harry-boy."

Harry stared at the rifle. "Better that than a hospital bill." He surveyed the truck's innards. "Nice van. Customize it yourselves?"

Four more armed guards entered the compartment and sat directly across from Porter. The door slid shut behind them, plunging the cramped quarters into near darkness. The windows had been coated with a deep blue tint, making vision nearly impossible.

"What were you saying about the element of surprise?" Cade hissed at Porter.

Harry crossed his legs slowly. "We were surprised, weren't we?"

The trio sat in silence as the van slowly rolled along the dirt road, picking up speed as it approached the compound.

Sitting in the van, being jostled with each passing bump, Harry tried to predict his fate. He and his friends could be killed instantly. That thought brought a slight twinge to the old intestinal track. He dismissed that conclusion as illogical, however. If Kapps wanted them dead, the jump-suited goon squad could have held a roadside barbecue. The trio could be tortured and killed, but that didn't make sense, either. Why would Kapps want to torture them when the reverend had all the answers? No, Kapps wanted them at the compound. Exactly why, Porter couldn't figure out.

Oddly enough, despite the rifles trained on his head, Harry was most concerned about Jessica West, an innocent in the midst of all this insanity. Harry hoped she was still alive. Perhaps, if Kapps was behind the kidnapping, he would prove to be more of a humanitarian than the faceless arch-fiend Harry had feared yesterday.

The truck decelerated, gliding to a smooth stop. Daylight poured into the back of the van as the door was pulled open. The four rifle-toting boys in blue jumped out of the compartment first, motioning with their gun barrels for the prisoners to do likewise. Harry was the first to alight from the van, which had pulled up in front of the main geodesic dome.

Standing before the building was a positively ebullient Ashley Kapps, his beard and moustache shaved off, his rainbow glasses firmly in place. "Why, Harry, I thought you'd never get here."

"We stopped for coffee," Harry said, being prodded forward by the woman with the gun and the braid. "What happened to the Jésus look? Is it pledge week here on the campus?"

Kapps stared vacantly over Harry's shoulder. "I see you've brought along some company."

"Now, where are my manners?" Harry replied, waving his companions forward and the woman's rifle barrel aside. "Dr. Ashley Kapps, this is Dr. Andrew Cade of the NYU Burn Center and Mr. Saint-Crispen of the School of Hard Knocks."

"That's not funny," the Saint muttered. "Glad to meet you, Rev. Nice digs you got here."

"The pleasure is mine," Kapps said, offering a hand. "It's not often that I meet a prestigious surgeon and a saint."

Saint-Crispen attached himself firmly to Kapps' grasp. "I have to tell you, Rev, I've been following your crusade closely for years now. I really dig what you're doing, helping out the troubled and the whackos and all that. I never believed for one minute all the stuff that Harry said you were up to. 'The Rev up to no good?' I said. 'That can't be true.' Those were my exact words, so help me God or the alien being of your choice. So, now that we understand each other, why don't you tell Yolanda to stop pointing her joystick at my backside. I'm with you one hundred percent. The way I figure it, you can always use a devoted follower such as myself. I mean, I'm a former cleric. I was going to be a priest, but I had to leave seminary school on account of my dear, sainted mother taking ill and all. My brother Leon, however, did have the calling and became a Dominican missionary. He was killed by elephants in Africa, rest his soul."

"I thought it was lions and his name was Ralph," Harry interrupted.

"That was my *other* brother, the Jesuit," Saint-Crispen snapped.

Kapps smiled beatifically at the Saint. "Incredibly loyal, isn't he," he said to Harry.

"If the price is right," Porter muttered into the rifle muzzle.

Kapps addressed the pig-tailed woman. "Take the good doctor and this jackal to room number twenty-seven. Mr. Porter will accompany me."

The woman made a wide arc with the gun barrel in the direction of the dome. "Wait a minute!" Saint-Crispen yelled. "Why does Harry get special treatment? I can tell you stories about him that would turn your glasses white!"

Cade shoved Saint-Crispen from behind. "Enough of your venomous verbiage. We are in enough trouble as it is."

"Excellently stated, doctor," Kapps said in a genteel tone. "I assure you that the accommodations in room twenty-seven will be to your liking. Mr. Porter will join you in a few minutes."

Kapps nodded to the woman. She raised her gun a second time. Cade and Saint-Crispen walked towards the entrance-way to the dome.

"I hope Ms. NRA doesn't have an itchy trigger finger," Harry muttered.

"Not at all," Kapps answered. "She's quite the cool one."

Harry noticed the four other armed guards were still standing outside the van, directly behind him. "I don't suppose you'd like to tell me what's going on here, Reverend Kapps."

"Ashley," the man of the cloth corrected. "And, in fact, I thought you already knew."

"I know a little. Suspect a lot."

"I haven't underestimated your mental facilities, then," Kapps cackled. "Excellent. I'm pleased that I decided to allow you to live. I'll explain everything to you, of course. But, first, would you like to see your friend Jessica?"

The knot in Porter's stomach concerning the woman slowly began to unravel. "She's unharmed?"

"Surely," Kapps replied. "Although how long she remains that way is totally up to you."

Kapps took Porter by the arm and waved the four guards away. He began to walk towards the dome housing the compound's laboratories and learning facilities. "Why is it," Harry ventured, "I have the feeling that this tour of your fairgrounds isn't going to be as much fun as my first."

"That's all your decision, Harry. As one civilized fellow to another, there's no reason why we can't work together on the rest of this exercise. I will, eventually, want my story to be told and you seem to be the ideal chronicler."

The two men approached the dome. "Tell you what. Before we drop in on Miss West, let me explain a little bit about what we're trying to do here."

Kapps guided Harry to a small bench outside the dome. The two men sat. Harry gazed straight ahead at the rolling hills and the ice-blue sky. A group of brooding thunderheads were making their way south from the Canadian border, heading for the unsuspecting sun.

"What we're about to accomplish, Harry," Kapps began, "marks the beginning of a complete cultural, political, and spiritual renaissance of this country."

"You're going to eliminate the President."

"Yes . . . and no," Kapps replied enigmatically. "Exactly how much have you deduced about my operation?"

Harry gnawed on his lower lip. Instinct told him that the time for bravado was long gone. He might as well take his chances with this maniac. "Truthfully," he began, "not all that much. I've connected you with the suicides and the power plant, but that's been a result of guesswork. As a matter of fact, I didn't even make those connections until a few hours ago."

"Don't feel too badly about that," Kapps consoled. "In truth, I've put a lot of time and planning into this operation. I've taken great pains to conceal my efforts from any suspicious parties. It's a great tribute to your deductive powers that you have progressed this far. I'm very happy to have you here with us, though. In fact, if you hadn't arrived in a half hour or so, I would have had the girl call you and plead hysterically with you to come up here and rescue her."

"I'm flattered," Harry shrugged. "Why the fuss?"

"I wanted you up here with me at the time of my victory, Harry. I respect the hell out of you. You've got a sense of professional pride and integrity. That doesn't surface too often these days. The way I see it, we're two of a kind. We're idealists. Romanticists. We want the best of all possible worlds. We do have our differences, however. You secretly dream about your Utopian worlds. I, on the other hand, have managed to amass enough resources to actually create one."

"How?"

"It's a long and involved story."

"I'm not going anywhere."

"Valid point," Kapps acknowledged. "Well, this entire affair began quite accidentally. I was leveling with you when I explained how this church evolved. I believe in all the precepts I mentioned previously. I started out in all this quite naïvely. But, as the church grew and the monetary contributions began to mushroom beyond my wildest reveries, I began to sense how eager people were for a new cause to follow, for a new way of life to be given to them. The people were in desperate need of a leader. In a small way, I fulfilled that need.

"Their political leader, that idiot Walker, was doing nothing to help them emotionally, economically, or politically. I seemed a natural stand-in. I started toying with the idea of what the consequences would be if I ran for the Oval Office this fall. I soon dismissed that thought, however, because of the many detractors I have. People are always skeptical of religious leaders of any kind. Putting one in the White House seemed highly unlikely."

Kapps clasped his hands together while Harry caught up with his foot dangling. "I put that idea on the back burner until I saw a small feature on the news explaining the progress NYU's Burn Center was making in scarless treatments. The report casually mentioned the new experiments being conducted around the country with syntheskin, how new faces could be molded for burn victims that could practically replace the original ones in terms of detail. Soon, they said, new developments would lead to even more fantastic breakthroughs. They didn't specifically state what breakthroughs they had in mind but, being an avid science-fiction fan from way back, I had no problem taking the report to its logical conclusion. If faces could presently be reconstructed *on* burn victims, couldn't further developments bring about a process where new faces could be built *for* them? Faces that could be made independently of the victim. After all, if you have to have a new face, why limit yourself to the one you started out with?

"I was imbued with divine inspiration, Harry. A vision from the Ancient Astronauts themselves. 'Ashley,' a voice whispered. 'Here's your chance, boy, go for it!'"

Harry peeked at the inspired speaker with the corner of his

eye. Kapps seemed to be in a trance. His face was flushed. His rainbow glasses sparkled in the sunlight. He was as happy as if he was in his right mind.

"By relying on the brilliance of contemporary scientific research," Kapps continued. "I could actually *become* the President of the United States—not by running for office but by literally *becoming* the President of the United States."

Kapps lapsed into a brief bout with tranquility, giving Harry time to assess the situation. "Using the real President as a model, you could make a mold of his face and then construct a syntheskin mask."

"Exactly," Kapps said, coming back to life. "The mask would eventually heal onto my own face and become my day-to-day exterior."

"Sounds simple," Harry remarked, "but more than a little risky. There are voice patterns involved, manners of movement, personal pieces of trivia—"

"Don't underestimate me, Harry," Kapps said, a trace of irritation filtering into his voice. "I made this decision nine months ago. Over that time, I have studied every physical nuance, every audio tick possessed by Walker. I have, in essence, learned how to become Walker physically and vocally. One of our lobbyists got himself appointed to a pet committee of Walker's in Washington and, by sucking up to the good ol' boy, managed to get him liquored about once a week for the past seven months. Walker has spilled his guts to our informant consistently. That information, in turn, has been relayed back to me on a weekly basis. Right now, I know all that there is to know about Sonny—on and off the record. By consulting newspaper and video files, I've memorized his public life-style completely."

"You were probably one of those kids who enjoyed homework, too," Harry sniffed.

"Point of fact, I cheated like hell. Anyhow, with my role being carefully researched and developed, I then went about setting the stage for my takeover. We positioned half-a-dozen church members in the burn center as orderlies. They monitored all developments. We knew who was doing what and when. Then, using the church as a base of operations, I fomented a fairly subtle but depressing atmosphere across the country."

"The suicides."

"A stroke of genius, don't you think? Using very basic

programming techniques, I created a suicide squadron. A league of lemmings conditioned for one act and one act alone—suicide in a public place. Our plan was simple: spread out these youngsters around the country, have them show up in heavily trafficked areas, make a speech stating their profound unhappiness with American society and the lack of leadership in particular, and then—kapow!"

"Kapow," Harry repeated, slightly giddy from Kapps' lack of emotion.

"The kids made an impression, both figuratively and literally, on the local scene. The nicest thing about their actions was the gradual buildup they caused media-wise. At first, they went practically ignored. Eventually, reporters such as yourself took this suicide trend and placed it firmly in the national spotlight, thus stressing the younger generation's total despondency over the current administration. And so, our little contribution to national malaise ticked off other currents of dissatisfaction, pushing them to the surface. This wave of disgust, of course, has put a lot of pressure on Walker."

"It never bothered you that hundreds of kids were dying for nothing?"

"Oh please, Harry," Kapps intoned. "Don't turn moralistic on me. They were soldiers. Pawns. They died for a cause, one of the greatest causes of all time. Besides, they were miserable and suicidal when they approached us. Once they embraced the faith, they embraced the concept of a cosmic afterlife as well. Who the hell knows where they wound up after exiting planet Earth? They're probably a lot better off rubbing elbows with the Ancient Astronauts right now than they were scrounging money from their rich parents."

Harry interrupted. "But how did you condition these kids? Through peeping or hypnosis or—"

"We used, uh, organic methods that I'll show you in just a bit. It's very important that you get this time sequence straight in your mind."

"Why?"

"To keep it clear for retelling, of course. Now," Kapps said, placing his hands on his lap. "At this point, the tone of the country was obviously attuned to our plan. We then implemented it further. We made a few strategic moves that would both get us into the Fountain Point power plant and into the world of syntheskin research. We kidnapped two of the leading researchers of the field from their NYU laboratories as soon as they arrived and, again, using our distinctive conditioning methods, extracted as much information as we could from them. That information, in turn, was passed onto some of our medical whizzes here. This church, by the way, also attracts the wealthy and the bored, the elitists and the intellectuals. A good thing, too.

"Using the information given to us, we duplicated the researchers' newfound methods of creating lifelike face masks. Taking their facial imprints as experimental prototypes, we transformed two of our church members into their doubles. We then sent the doubles back to the center, had them formally resign and clean out the researchers' filing cabinets. It all worked fabulously well. Since the researchers were new at the center, no one knew if this behavior jibed with their personalities or not and, so, didn't bother to question it."

"And the original researchers?" Harry asked, knowing the answer.

"They outlived their usefulness to the cause," Kapps shrugged. "They were terminated. We took them out to a field behind the tubeway station and our members used them for target practice. Ghoulish, perhaps but a unique exercise for our newer shootists."

Porter duly noted the fact that Kapps betrayed no knowledge of the fact that Pratt made it back to NYU "after" being terminated. Could he have stumbled into the tubeway in that condition? Harry clenched his teeth, recalling both the tenacity of his friend and, apparently, the callousness and apathy of the general public.

"Simultaneously," Kapps enthused. "We painted one of our vans in a manner to create a replica of the Fountain Point security runabouts. We then sent it up to the Point where we felt confident it would be allowed on the grounds with little or no problems."

"But you did have a problem," Harry blurted. "You hit a hitchhiker on the way up there. The paint on the front of the van smeared."

"Yes! Yes that's right!" Kapps shouted in both amazement and admiration. "We had to repaint the van's insignia en route. It set us back only a few hours, however, so I didn't feel it important enough to relate to you. My, Harry. You do keep your fingers in things, don't you?"

"And you'll notice I still have all ten left," Porter grunted.

"Once inside the facility, two of our people removed two night guards at the facility's power station. We syntheskinned their faces and put our two men in charge."

"But a janitor caught onto the scheme and you had him removed."

"With the original two guards," Kapps agreed. "You knew more about this operation than you let on, Harry. Admirable. Yes, I believe we'll work well together. So, now we have two guards inside the plant and the ability to create syntheskin doubles of whomever we desire. We picked up one Peter Hayden, did a mold of his face and created our own model. A model, by the way, which you almost ruined prematurely with your roughhousing."

"He started it," Harry muttered, beginning to genuinely loathe the man next to him.

"Ah yes, that was a little complication we hadn't foreseen. We assumed that the tiff we engineered would get his lady friend out of the picture and allow our Hayden to familiarize himself with the original's life-style in privacy, a crash course as it were. When the woman returned, however, and started all this whiney 'you don't seem like yourself' business, we tried to terminate her involvement in this affair. Your interference slowed down our efforts. Eventually, however, it all worked out for the best. We got the girl and the girl, in turn, got you here."

"You wanted me involved in all this?"

"Almost from the start," Kapps said. "I stress the word almost because, for a time, I debated whether to eliminate you or use you. It was quite a point of contention within the ranks of the church. After meeting you, however, I began thinking that your participation would be a distinct plus. I cannot stress how much respect I have for you as a chronicler of current events. It occurred to me that this marvelous plan of ours should be presented to the public some day. It must go into the history books. You are here to act as the eyes and ears of future generations of Americans, Harry."

Harry reflected on his position. He had risen from obscurity and was heading for oblivion. Horatio Alger would be damned proud.

"When we decided to actually enlist your aid," Kapps continued, "we tried to arrange our normal operations in such a manner as to constantly pique your interest. We felt it necessary to kill the peeper, Hardy Flowers, but we arranged it so it would be done before your eyes, our hospital staffers alerting us to your presence.

"That was clever of you, by the way, to try to peep the peeper and connect the suicides. You were the first, much to your credit, to attempt to find a physical or mental link between the various victims. Nice work. You were miles ahead of the authorities on that one."

"Let's hear it for me."

"Of course, some of the time you were in very real danger. The attempt on your life in the elevator, for instance, was real but sloppy. But, for the most part, we were just toying with you: the apartment break-ins, the car chases, etcetera, etcetera. We had to keep you interested. Once we had you hooked, and you began to investigate, we began escalating the violence naturally. You grew more frustrated and confused, and we drew closer to our goal. It was quite entertaining."

"I've always enjoyed show business," Harry smirked.

"You were wonderful. I hate television," Kapps answered.

"One question," Harry ventured. "The original Hayden."

"His role in our project ceased as soon as he was captured."

"And so did Hayden."

"Of course. Now, where was I?"

"You were telling me what a great little trooper I was," Harry said, sliding down on the bench.

"Ah, yes. You were wonderful. We had to lead you on without actually giving you any concrete evidence that you could share with the authorities. We nearly slipped up with Sally Weberman, the poor unfortunate you saved from her suicide. Fortunately, our directives did her in after you removed our assassin."

A chill ran through Kapps' body. "That was a little too close for comfort. It all fit into the master drama, however. With you doggedly on the trail, the stage was now set for our denouement! Our in-house Hayden and his crew attacked the Point. They succeeded, of course, thanks to our security teams inside. A few guards were shot for realism's sake. Our Hayden made his demands, threatening dire consequences. Those consequences, by the by, were never intended to be enacted. Only a madman would take out three states."

"Right," Harry nodded. He sighed, wondering how the hell he always wound up one-on-one with creeps with one-crack minds.

"With Hayden making his demands and the mood of the country a restless one, President Walker, had no choice but to agree to the meeting. It was either that or disgrace the entire country in the eyes of the world. Or, worse yet, lead to an unequaled physical disaster."

"What happens when the President arrives at the Point?"

"He'll be met by some of my people. We'll capture him and use his face for a mold to create the new, improved President—yours truly: the walking, talking, spittin' image of our woeful leader, ya'll."

Harry watched the sun disappear behind a mountain of storm clouds. "But, hell, Kapps. Why would you *want* to take Walker's place? He's a total cockup. The people of the country consider him a bad joke."

"Well, brother Porter, behold the transformed Sonny Walker," Kapps waved a hand in front of his face and stuck out his clean-shaven jaw in a tough-guy parody. "A straight-talking, right-thinking man of authority who is not afraid to use his power for the propagation of good. Tonight at the power plant, Sonny is going to overpower those terrorists almost single-handedly. Seizing a laser rifle, he'll mow the lot of them down, rescue the hostaged guards, and become a born-again hero in the eyes of the country.

"Not only that, but he'll publicly recant his willy-nilly ways—saying that it took a life-threatening crisis like this to make him realize how important it is for the American people to have a leader more interested in their welfare than his own, how crucial it is to maintain a sense of pride and self-esteem both individually and nationally. He will emerge rejuvenated. He will suddenly embody the strong, charismatic, and fearless characteristics that made the pioneers historical legends."

"The end," Harry said. "Pause for applause."

"Don't be sarcastic, Harry," Kapps said, standing. "I know you're a little appalled about all this, but once you look at it objectively, you'll realize how really clever it all is."

"Some people are still marveling over the Nazis," Harry noted.

"And that was nearly one hundred years ago!" Kapps chortled. "Sorry, Harry, I really can't allow you to rain on my crusade. Don't feel bad about not catching onto all this," he said, putting his arm around Harry's shoulder and leading him away from the bench. "The plot was so intricate and involved that it was impossible to spot. A work of genius, Harry. I mean, we're not introducing any new elements into the American system. Using sleight of hand, we're just substituting some new pieces into an old puzzle. It's like the old shell game, remember that?"

"Yeah," Harry said. "Three shells and one pea. You mix the shells around, and you ask the mark to pick out which shell houses the pea."

"But the mark never finds the pea," Kapps grinned, "thanks to sleight of hand. No matter what shell he picks, it's the wrong one. To prove your honesty, however, you pick up one of the remaining shells and, bless my soul, there's the pea. That's our game, Harry. With syntheskin, we have an endless amount of shells to slip under. And we'll never be discovered if we carefully plan our sleight of hand."

Kapps led Harry into the glittering domed ediface. "What happens if I say 'no' to your offer," he asked. "Suppose I refuse to be your historian because, let's say, I think that your plan smacks of anarchy and insanity?"

Kapps made a few tisk-tisking sounds with his tongue. "Well, in that case, I'd have to eliminate you from our game plan."

"No big loss," Porter smirked. "Besides, maybe I'd prefer not to be around to see the final chapter of this horror story."

"Yes," Kapps nodded sagely. "I didn't think your own death would gain us much leverage with you. That's precisely why we've kept the young lady alive. Some of our conditioning methods, if misused, are not very much fun to watch, Harry, especially if you are on intimate terms with the subject."

Kapps' face broke into a radiant smile. "And you, yourself, have provided us with a second and third act for our subplot: Dr. Cade and Mr. Saint-Crispen. We could conceivably stage a three-ringed conditioning circus for your personal edification!"

Harry glared at his feet as Kapps led him down a glistening corridor. "I never did like circuses."

2

The laboratory was small and quite unexceptional in appearance. It was dark. It was cheerless. A glass-enclosed booth, filled with electronic data collecting materials, both audio and video, and monitoring devices, took up one third of the space. The entire lab, booth included, could not have exceeded a thirty by thirty foot space. Outside the booth, in an area twice its size, stood a lone, egglike plastic shell. Some eight feet in height, it was opaque, black in color. Its section of the lab was illuminated by two strips of pale florescent lighting. The lights gave off a green glow. It made the egg look sick.

Harry stood inside the dimly lit control booth. "I don't understand. What's this setup for?"

"This is, Harry, simply one of the facilities used in our programming process. One of the main cogs used in the creation of the perfect machine, the perfect follower."

"Where's Jessica?" Harry asked, his gaze incapable of avoiding the egg-shaped thing.

"In the tank, of course," Kapps replied cheerfully. "Blissfully floating in a saline solution, hallucinating her little mind away."

"You have her jammed in a desensitization chamber?" Harry clenched his fists. "How long has she been in there?"

"On and off, for a day and a half," Kapps stated.

"Try not to overreact. It's harmless enough. It helps weaken her into a state of docility and allows us to circumvent the procedure of administering tranquilizers of any pharmaceutical nature. We in the church feel those types of drugs to be very unorganic."

Harry gnashed his teeth together until he swore he could feel sparks as his fillings collided. "So you keep her in that safe-deposit box instead."

"Relax, Harry. She's fine."

"I want to see her."

"Sure," Kapps walked to the control panel and passed a hand over a small glowing square. Immediately, a side of the oval tank became transparent. Inside the tank, her head barely above water level, Jessica West floated, naked. The interior of the tank glowed with an eerie, greenish hue, giving her body a bloated, cadaveresque sheen. Harry had to restrain himself from gently taking Kapps' head and smashing it into the glass retaining wall.

"Obedience in various areas is a necessity in the church. Basically, all members are put through a ten-day indoctrination period. We don't do too much to them, most of them being as spineless as chocolate eclairs. We save this particular room for the more, um, resilient members of the fold."

Kapps broke into an easy smile. "We avoid hard-core drugs for this type of conditioning, relying, instead, on methods calculated to naturally erode the resistance of the individual. Normally, we isolate all recruits for several days, depriving them of all outside stimuli. They are not allowed to eat, sleep, or defecate during their first forty-eight hours here. Afterwards, sleep is allowed at random hours and for varying lengths of time.

"There is no consistency to these rest patterns and, after a surprisingly short amount of time, we wear our members down. It confuses the holy hell out of them, not knowing when they're supposed to be on their feet or on their backs. At that point, one of our conditioners, usually a senior staff member, spends some time with the recruit, offering friendship and gradually rebuilding his or her emotional makeup to fit our purposes. Suggestions are made while the recruits are in this disoriented state. These suggestions are reemphasized repeatedly during the training period. Ten days and they are ours. From that point onward, they—"

"Do everything the *herd* way?" Harry offered.

"I do so enjoy humor," Kapps chuckled.

Harry attempted to divorce his intellect from the sight before him. "What about your peepers?" he asked. "Those suicides were programmed. Their mental resources were phenomenal. That ten-day program couldn't apply to them."

"Ah yes," Kapps chuckled. "We really threw you a curve there. We've never ever used a single peeper to get our kids to swan dive. We place a tremendous value on the human mind, Harry. So, why get an outsider to muck around with it when, actually, with a little coaching, an individual can do just fine on his or her own."

"I don't follow you."

"Harry, the brain has enough godsdamned chemical activity going on to almost drug itself into any behavioral state. That's a scientific fact. We just push the process along when we need drastic behavioral change."

Harry wasn't sure whether Kapps was babbling or not. Catching the gleam in the reverend's eye, he decided that Kapps was not. Somehow, that fact made him feel worse. "I was always rotten in science," he replied.

"The brain creates its own drugs, Harry," Kapps said,

tapping his own forehead with his left forefinger. "Every time little electrical impulses scurry along a nerve cell up here, they force each of its fibers to release a chemical known as a neurotransmitter. That's the stuff that allows the spark of an idea to pass from one brain cell to another. It transmits the message. Those chemicals, or drugs, regulate our personality. When there's just the right amount of everything, ideas zip around normally, and we're just fine. Knock 'em out of whack, and you have some real fun. Science has been aware of that fact for decades.

"Endorphin, for instance, is a pain-killer, an opiate that exists in the brain. A synthesized form of it is used to help schizophrenics. Enkephalin, another brain drug, when added to the mind in large doses can actually increase intelligence. There are all sorts of chemicals up there that can cause some interesting reactions: MSH, ACTH, LRH, vasopressin..."

Harry stared at Kapps. "Right," he managed to mutter.

"So," Kapps said. "Disrupt the amount of any neuro-transmitter, add or subtract too much or too little, and you can distort the thinking pattern in any way you like. If you alter the metabolism enough, you can have your subject just hallucinate away up there for a period of time lasting up to twenty days. He or she creates a hallucinogenic whirlwind. That, by the way, is what the unfortunate Dr. Flowers tapped into on the roof of that building. He didn't encounter another peeper or even a latent telepath. He merely unleashed the full fury of the human brain gone wild, its thought patterns repeating endlessly, like a tape loop."

Harry tightened his jaw, recalling the woman in the hospital writhing as her brain patterns eluded her control. "We took fairly submissive youths," Kapps shrugged, "and trained them here in both the conventional way and the slightly more creative manner. We fed them various synthetically produced neurotransmitters. You didn't find drugs in their systems because there were no alien drugs there, per se. They inhaled the fluid from spray bottles. We put large doses of the chemicals into vials that looked like commercial nasal spray products. We even manufactured our own labels to avoid suspicion. The kids were programmed to snort the stuff every day. We kept them way off balance, their prime directive being suicide on a given day of the month. Being the passive little lambs they were, they did as they were told. And, so, we created a small army of manic-depressives, wild-eyed, monomaniacal, superhallucinating, suicidal babies! Praise be the mothership."

Harry tapped his pants pocket. He still had a nearly full vial of the spray intact. Never could tell when the stuff would come in handy. Synthesized brain chemicals. That would explain why he became so goddamned depressed whenever he snorted the stuff.

Harry left the control booth and walked up to the tank. He pressed his face up to the transparent plastic surface. Jessica remained hovering inside. Had he not known she was alive, he would have assumed she was a long-dead specimen of humanity frozen forever in a cryogenic chamber. He stared at her pale, youthful skin, now wrinkled from repeated immersion and tinted with the unholy glow of the tank. Her lips were flecked with salt, her eyelids dry and cracked. On her head, wires for monitoring purposes wriggled under their tape tetherings. She looked like a high-tech Medusa.

Kapps passed his hand over the glowing square on the control board and Jessica disappeared from view. Harry slammed his hand into the side of the tank and stormed into the booth. "Get her out of there!"

Kapps held up a restraining hand. "Don't blow it, Harry. She may not look her best right now, but she's perfectly all right."

Harry hated feeling trapped. Logic told him that the best route to survival, for everyone, rested in his cooperating totally with the madman. His blood, pounding in his head like a pneumatic drill, ignored his intellect. "Get her out of there," he repeated evenly, his features hardening with each successive step towards the minister.

Kapps was unperturbed. Harry guessed he had marksmen hidden out of view. "Am I to consider this a cheerful offer to join our cause as historian?"

"Yes, damn it. Just get her out of the tank!"

Kapps took Harry by the arm and led him out of the lab. "In a little while, Harry."

"The deal was that she wouldn't be harmed if I cooperated. I've said I'd cooperate."

"And I promise you that she won't be harmed. I never said anything about turning her over to you immediately, did I? I'd lose my bargaining power very quickly that way and give you the opportunity to attempt lords know what kind of foolhardy stunt."

"You're a real shit, Ashley," Harry said, wrenching his arm away.

"A quality necessary for true success in this country," Kapps shrugged.

Harry quickened his pace, walking towards the exit ahead of the reverend. The two men stepped out into the fast-fading daylight. Swirls of violet clouds churned atop the nearby mountains.

"Looks like rain," Kapps breathed, leading Harry back to the central dome. "I love a good thunderstorm. It cheers me immensely. The power of it. The energy discernible in the very air itself. The all consuming loneliness of a stray bolt of lightning."

A gust of wind sent a chill through Harry's body. "And the thunder!" Kapps enthused. "The grandiloquent language of the thunder! I remember as a child being mortally afraid of that sound and being comforted by my grandmother. She'd see me cowering and she'd say, 'Ash'—she called me Ash— 'there's nothing to worry about when you hear that thunder. Do you know what thunder is?' And I'd say, 'No, Nanny. What is it?' And do you know what she'd say to me, Harry?"

"That thunder is the angels bowling in Heaven?" Harry deadpanned.

Kapps slowed his pace down, thoughtfully. "Why, no. She'd say, 'Thunder is just the sonic result of two different air masses, one cold and one hot, colliding high above the Earth's surface.' I didn't know what the hell she was talking about, but it sure calmed me down." He furrowed his brow. "The angels bowling: That's a good one. I must remember that."

He prodded Harry into the entrance of the main dome. "I do so enjoy humor," Kapps sighed.

3

"The man is crazy!" Saint-Crispen shouted. He paced the length of the claustrophobic room, hands flapping up and down at his sides either in an act of nervousness or a vain attempt at flight. "The guy is unreal! Unreal!" His forehead beaded with sweat, his already frizzy hair made even more wired by constant tugging, Saint-Crispen resembled a longtime resident of a rubber room.

Andrew Cade sat in a canvas chair in the corner of the room. He was silent. His thin lips were drawn into a very taut line. His arched eyebrows were fixed in a steeper angle than usual. "Genius," he whispered. "Demented—but genius."

"I would have popped him one, Harry," Saint-Crispen said. "Right in the old wazoo!"

"Sure you would have," Harry replied, nearly losing his control. "Fearless Saint. When they made you they broke the Jell-O mold, pal. What was that about when we pulled up here? You nearly threw yourself at Kapps' feet. What were you looking for? Canonization?"

"That was just a scam to buy time, man," Saint-Crispen said from under a twitching moustache. "I would have been your inside man. Your ace in the hole. I could have sprung us all. You didn't think I was saying all that stuff for real, did you?"

Porter sat on the floor opposite the room from Cade. The cubicle was cramped but comfortable. Several canvas director's chairs, a sink, a toilet, a table, and three inflated cots made up the contents. There were no windows. All light emanated from recessed tubes tucked into the top of the flat ceiling. In essence, they were housed in a small box constructed within the larger dome. The sound of rain could be heard falling outside.

"Are you feeling all right, Andy?" Harry asked. "You look a little pale."

Cade blinked his eyes, dragged away from his rumination. "Yes. Just overtired, I suppose. You say your friend was in good physical condition within the tank?"

"I have only Kapps' word on that," Harry said. "For all I know, he might still be feeding her those brain drugs. I know this sounds strange, but I think he was leveling with me. I still trust him in a way. He seems honest. Crazy, but honest."

"Yes," Cade acknowledged. "I would concur with that opinion. The man has obviously gone to extreme trouble to concoct this plan. He has managed to dabble in biochemistry, medicine, guerilla warfare—"

"A regular renaissance madman."

"But there's an amazing amount of organizational skill to be found in his madness."

"Hey," Saint-Crispen blurted. "I hate to break up this

testimonial to the rev, but I'd like to remind you both that this guy is not wrapped real tightly and will probably give us all the chance to buy the farm pronto unless we can cancel the sale."

Cade heaved a sigh and looked at Harry. "There is a definite art form in consistently speaking like that, I suppose."

Harry got to his feet. "The Saint does have a point. There's going to be a lot of activity around here in the next few hours, so if we're going to try to get out of here, now's the time. The first thing we have to do is figure out how to get Jessica out of that tank."

"Count me out of that caper," Saint-Crispen said. "I'm no hero."

"You're going to be a martyr to the cause if you don't can it," Harry snapped. He paced in silence for a moment, before beginning to think aloud. "In order for us to get over to the lab, it would be a good idea to get our hands on some of those cute little blue jump suits that seem to be in vogue here. It might help us blend in with the crowd, right? Right. So, I'm going to have to get us one. With a little luck, I'll parlay it into two more."

Harry walked towards the door. "If anyone is religious, this is the time for a quick prayer."

A peal of thunder echoed through the room.

"Guard?" Harry called. "Guard?"

The peepscreen to the door activated. The apathetic face of a young male, devoid of all personality, appeared. "What is it?"

"Hasn't Kapps gotten the word to you, yet?"

"The Reverend Kapps?"

"You have two Kappses here?"

"Uh, no," the young man answered, perplexed.

"Fine, then get me out of here."

"I can't do that," the youth replied firmly. "I have no authority."

"Well, open the door and I'll show you some authority."

"I'm not even supposed to communicate with—"

"Look," Harry barked. "Kapps has told me all about the moves you folks are putting on the President. The syntheskin. The power plant. The works—"

"He has?" the guard asked, flustered.

"Yup. He brought me here to document all the events. History is being written here right now, boy. Right within these walls as we speak. I'm here to let the future citizens of Earth know just how unselfish and grand the actions of the Church of the Ancient Astronaut's members were."

The door began to open slowly. Harry took out the vial of nasal spray and pumped six deep blasts of the stuff into the air a split second before the guard entered. A thick mist hung in the air before the door. The young boy placed his head right in the middle of it. He began sneezing immediately. Harry made a movement towards him. The quick-reflexed boy, pointed a rifle at him. "I was only going to offer you some nose spray," Harry said, hoping that Kapps, like most generals, kept most of his plans secret from the foot soldiers.

The guard continued to sneeze. "Well, maybe. Sure. Thanks."

The boy inhaled twice from the bottle. "I don't know what set that off. My allergies usually don't act up until the fall."

The boy's eyelids drooped as he handed the bottle back to Harry. "Thanks." He shook his head suddenly from side to side, as if warding off a bad thought. "You've been asked by the Reverend Kapps to write an account of our actions?"

"That's right," Harry grinned. "Now just come in here for a minute and let me start working. Maybe Kapps hasn't gotten the word to you yet about my having total access to this place. Fair enough. I understand how long it takes word to filter down from above..."

"Too long," the boy said sullenly. "Half of the time we don't even know what we're doing. It's not fair."

He'd gotten a good snort of that sniff, Harry realized. "Right. Well, I don't have too much time to waste. The President will be showing up at Fountain Point in about, about..."

"An hour. But will I get to go? Noooo. I have to stay here. For what?"

"Right. I have to use the time wisely. So get yourself comfortable, and I'll interview you for starts."

The guard's face colored slightly. "Me?" he hesitated as he stepped across the room. "I'm merely one of millions of followers devoted to Reverend Kapps and his cause. I'm not important—"

"Oh, but you are..."

"Yeah, damn it, I'm very important."

Harry offered a hand and gently pulled the guard into the center of the room. The young man clasped his laser rifle in his right hand while allowing himself to be led by the left.

"You and all your brothers and sisters," Harry cooed, "are like individual grains of sand. Meaningless in themselves, correct? But without those single grains, where would the deserts be?"

"Yeah, definitely, yeah," the guard said thoughtfully.

"Okay," Harry grinned. "That's settled. Let me get my recorder out of my jacket here." Harry reached inside his coat. He began to wiggle it around beneath the folds of the vestment. The guard watched, mesmerized. "It's about time somebody realized how important I am," he muttered, gazing at every movement below the coat.

When Harry saw that he had the boy's undivided attention, he smiled and said. "Question one. True or false: I like my front teeth."

"Huh?" the guard blinked.

Harry pulled his hand out from beneath his coat in the form of a fist. The boy swung at Harry, losing his balance and tumbling to his knees. The guard tried to lash out at Harry, landing a few punches on Porter's ankle. Harry raised his hands above his head and brought them down onto the back of the boy's head. The guard slammed face first into the floor. If the impact of Harry's fists didn't knock him out, the concussion caused by his forehead meeting the floor certainly did. The boy lay, awfully still, at Harry's feet. Porter shook his right hand angrily. He thought he had broken his thumb. He raised his hand before his eyes for inspection. It was swelling already. "I hate doing stuff like this," he mumbled, kicking the laser rifle out from under the guard and sending it spiraling across the floor.

Harry shut the door. The trio stripped the guard of his jump suit. Harry slipped it on over his slacks and shirt. Saint-Crispen jammed the boy's socks into the unconscious guard's mouth and tied his hands with the sleeves of Harry's jacket. Harry picked up the rifle and walked towards the door. "Be ready for a real punchfest when I get back," he smirked. "Two more jump suits coming up, the hard way."

Cade and Saint-Crispen waited in nervous anticipation for several long minutes. The Saint tugged at his hair. Cade wiped a trickle of perspiration from his upper lip. He flexed his hands slowly in front of his face, as if reviving physical attributes abandoned eons ago.

Harry's voice suddenly approached the doorway. "I didn't know what to do," he complained. "All three of them started fighting at once. I looked through the peepscreen, but they were out of range. I didn't want to open the door and go inside myself because it might have been a trap. I know how much importance the reverend attaches to their presence here."

"You were wise to notify us," a male's voice echoed. "New here, aren't you."

"Just in from Hollywood."

The door opened wide. Two guards, a man and a woman, strode into the room. Harry strolled in behind them. As the pair rushed in and were confronted by the sight of a naked man, hog-tied and with socks in his mouth, Harry snatched the gun from the confounded male guard. "Gotcha!" he said, shutting the door firmly behind him.

Saint-Crispen sprung at the unarmed man, hitting him midsection.

Cade leaped from his chair and grabbed the second guard from behind. Cocking his left fist back, he spun the church member around and was about to unleash a well-aimed punch when he realized the object of his fury was a female. The startled guard, a short-haired redhead, gaped at Cade's upraised hand. Instinctively, Cade lowered his fist and smiled sheepishly.

The girl snorted and flipped the butt of her rifle into Cade's chin. He staggered back against the wall. She raised her rifle to fire. Before her finger could locate the trigger, the butt of a second gun slammed into the back of her skull. The sound of cracking plastic echoed in the small room. The woman tumbled onto the floor, blood trickling from her scalp.

Harry, the butt of his gun reduced an inch or so in length, helped the doctor to his feet. "Good thing I'm not a gentleman," Harry grinned.

Saint-Crispen and the first guard continued to roll around on the floor. The two men were nearly exhausted. Harry and Cade stood, side-by-side, watching the wrestling match.

"We haven't got all day, Marion," Harry advised.

Saint-Crispen, for some inexplicable reason, shoved his fingers down the throat of the guard. "I'm doing my best, goddamn it."

The guard bit down on the Saint's hand. The Saint let out a yell. "Kill him, Harry! The guy's a real animal."

Porter walked over to the exhausted guard, picking him up by the nape of the neck. He stood the guard in front of him.

The fellow stared at him, mumbling. Trembling from fatigue, the guard made whining noises at Harry's face. Porter smiled and cocked his head to one side, commiserating with the guard's plight. The man realized what was to come and nodded slowly in a helpless but affirmative motion. Harry hit him once in the jaw with his left hand. The guard fell back, more in a swoon than in recoil.

Harry sucked his left thumb. "I'm sure I broke one this time."

The three men removed the jump suits. Cade and Saint-Crispen donned their disguises. Harry made sure the three real guards were securely bound and gagged before he opened the door a crack. "All right, fellow astronauts. Let's double-time it to the lab."

Lightning illuminated the percolating, plum-colored sky. Shafts of light whizzed above the trees, accompanied by deafening roars of thunder. Rain spiraled down from above, whipped into a confused frenzy by the heavy winds.

Three jump-suited figures trotted through the sheets of rain, the wind causing their bodies to shake as the water seeped through to their skin.

"Man, I'm gonna have to pop a lot of C's after this," Saint-Crispen chattered.

"The storm's to our advantage," Harry Porter whispered, spitting rainwater from his mouth. "Everyone seems to have been caught off guard by it."

Harry surmised that the rain had increased from a drizzle to a downpour within the past few minutes. Jump-suited denizens of the compound dashed around the domes, covering open-roofed vans and cars with plastic. Without much difficulty, the trio reached the dome housing the tank lab. Entering through the front portal, Harry cautiously led his two accomplices down an empty corridor.

"Keep your rifles ready," he advised. "If anyone sees us, act as if you belong here. If they look suspicious, you look indignant. If they go for their weapons, prevent it."

Harry jogged down the length of one hallway before turning down a second. "I'm pretty sure it's down here."

"Most encouraging wording," Cade muttered beneath his breath.

"This is it," Harry whispered, placing his hand on a door latch. He pushed the door inward slowly. He raised the rifle to his chest. The door swung inward, revealing a deserted control room. A cup of hot coffee sat on a tape console. "Inside," Harry hissed.

The three men ran past the booth and directly toward the egg-shaped tank. Harry puzzled over how to gain access.

Cade ran across the lab and located a small footstool. He returned and placed it next to the tank. Climbing to the highest rung, he braced himself against the tank's rounded surface and located an almost imperceptible latch on the uppermost section. Using his right hand, he pushed mightily and shoved the handle upward. He popped the top off the egg. "I'll need some help here," he said. "She's unconscious."

Harry balanced himself precariously on the top of the stool as well. The two men reached down into the tank. Each ensnaring one of Jessica's arms, they slowly pulled her out of the water. It was definitely not the best way to lift an unconscious person, Harry theorized. The leverage was in her favor. "Dead weight sure is heavy," he gasped.

"I realize that, thank you, Porter," Cade huffed. "We touched upon the wonders of gravity and the like just for the hell of it in college."

The two men struggled to maintain their grips, the saline solution making it difficult to keep Jessica's arms from slipping through their hands. Eventually, they managed to pull her upper torso over the opening in the egg. Harry motioned the doctor away. "I'll get her down."

Cade took his place at the base of the tank. Harry pulled Jessica out of the solution. He took her in his arms and swung her away from the tank. His knee wobbled, emitting a low snap. Nonetheless, Porter made his way down the five steps of the stool.

Harry carried Jessica to a cot located on the opposite side of the tank room, next to a shower stall. "I hesitate to mention this," Cade frowned, following Porter, "but we've neglected to come up with any clothing for Miss West."

Harry grabbed a towel from the shower stall and hastily dried off the still-unconscious woman. "Damn," he muttered. "I wish you had mentioned that when we were still in our cell. We could have popped another guard."

Jessica's eyes began to flutter. She stared blankly at Harry. "Jessica?" he whispered.

"Peter?"

Harry's mouth sagged downward, his face a parody of a sad-eyed harlequin. He felt like hell. Cade took the towel and finished drying the girl. "We don't have time for this, Porter."

Harry faltered, both embarrassed and hurt. Before he had time to reply, a terse "What the hell is going on in here?" brought him back to present tense. He spun around in time to see a jump-suited engineer stumble into the control room. The guard instinctively raised his rifle. Saint-Crispen brought forth a shrill "ssshhhiiiit!" and pressed his finger on the trigger of his weapon. A white slice of light shot across the room, missing the guard by a good four feet and burning a hole in the clear panel above the controls.

The guard darted out the door.

"Goddamn it," Harry yelled. "Why did you do that! Now he knows we're phonies."

"He would have killed us!"

"We could have talked our way out of it," Harry ran toward the door in a fast limp. "Now we've got to stop him before he finds any friends."

Harry dashed out of the laboratory, his left knee sending small pulsations of pain up and down his leg, his fists still throbbing from his recent stint as a pugilist. He stopped in the corridor, listening for footsteps. A roar of thunder shook the dome. A flash of lightning sent a wave of multicolored reflections shimmering onto the walls. Harry glanced to his right and caught a fleeting glimpse of a shadow heading down an adjoining corridor. He hobbled off in pursuit. Running the length of the hallway, he paused at a point where his path abruptly ended, branching off into two side corridors.

He bent over and massaged his leg. There was no way he was going to catch up with that guard. Consequently, there was no possible way he was going to be able to prevent an alarm from being sounded. For the first time, it occurred to him that there was no way all of them, any of them, were going to get out of the compound alive.

Harry returned his attention to the corridor. He saw two jump-suited figures walking his way. He suddenly smiled to himself, admiring his mental prowess. He limped towards the guard. "There's trouble in the lab!" he shouted. "Intruders are trying to kidnap the woman patient!"

The two guards, one male and one female, ran to Harry's aid. Harry, already limping, stressed his infirmity even further for their benefit. "I heard a noise. They jumped me. They thought they had knocked me out."

"Where's Rossington?" one guard asked. "He was at the booth."

"One of the intruders took a shot at him," Harry wheezed. "He missed. Rossington took off. When I tried to stop the guy with the gun from following him, a second let me have it from behind."

"There are only two of them?"

"That's all I could see," Porter answered.

The guards charged down the hall, rifles in hand. Harry jogged placidly behind. The woman guard saw the open laboratory door and, rifle raised, leaped inside. The man followed. The pair caught Cade and Saint-Crispen in the act of reviving Jessica. The dazed woman was sitting up, a towel wrapped around her quaking frame.

"Freeze," the woman ordered, leveling her rifle at them from the control booth.

The second guard swaggered toward the three prisoners. "Reverend Kapps doesn't like his guests to take advantage of his hospitality."

"Guess he'll really be pissed off at me," Harry said from the doorway. The two guards froze where they stood. Harry took one step inside the room. "Okay, boys and girls, let's all drop our weapons before somebody gets hurt."

The guard nearest Cade let his rifle fall to the floor. The woman at the booth hesitated. Harry walked up behind her and pressed the barrel of his rifle into her back. "I'm an eccentric," he said. "I have an aversion to violence—especially when it's directed at me. So, let it fall, hon."

The guard lowered her rifle onto the floor. "That's nice," Porter smiled. "Now let's kick our rifles all the way across the room to where the Reverend Kapps' guests are standing."

The guards did as they were told, which put Porter somewhat at ease. He would have hated to harm either one of them. "Now, turn around and face me," he said evenly.

"Who the hell are you, anyway?" the woman demanded.

"I'm here with the bus tour. Now, both of you, take off your suits."

The two guards eyed each other sheepishly but obeyed. Porter took in their naked forms. The woman was amply endowed, her physical attributes effectively hidden by her jump suit. The young man was muscular, his body the product of constant exercise and proper diet. Suddenly, Harry's stomach felt very cumbersome. He'd have to join that health spa soon.

He couldn't be sure if he was imagining it or not but Harry thought he caught elements of delight in the two guards' furtive glances at each other. "Okay," he continued. "I want both of you to walk over to that tank and climb inside."

"That tank is designed for only one subject!" the man exclaimed indignantly.

"Yes," the woman agreed. "We'll be killed in there!"

"Hardly," Harry said, pointing his rifle, "but you will get to know each other a lot better."

The two guards walked sullenly to the tank. "May I suggest that the young lady step down into the liquid first?" Harry said. The woman complied. "Now, the young man. Yes, you might as well face each other. You may be in there for quite a while and eye contact may help pass the time."

Harry smiled as the two guards snuggled close to each other in the tank. Tossing his rifle to Cade, Harry climbed up the footstool and slammed the lid of the tank shut. He loved happy endings. He walked over to the cot and gave Jessica a kiss on her forehead. She immediately convulsed, leaned over the side of the bed and vomited. Harry held her forehead as her body reacted against the day in the tank.

After a moment, she returned to her sitting position. "I like a guy who holds my hair when I throw up," she said, brushing her blue bangs back into place.

"Romantic fool," Harry smiled.

"I'm confused and wobbly, Harry," she stammered. "What's this all about?"

"I'll explain later," Harry answered. "Right now, we should take leave of this love nest posthaste. By now, there's a very pissed-off engineer rounding up a posse dedicated to frying our bacon." He retrieved his rifle from Cade. "Since I'd really enjoy not using this thing, I think you'd better jump into one of those jump suits right away."

"And then what?" Jessica asked, being handed a suit by Saint-Crispen.

"Then we run like hell," Porter replied.

Jessica donned the suit. The three men ran towards the exit. The woman trotted into a wall after four steps. "Sorry," she muttered as Harry returned and put an arm around her waist. "I'm still a little dizzy."

"Just lean on me," he said, realizing that he was now mouthing clichés that had gone out of style with such ancient delights as George Lucas films. He colored self-consciously. As much as he hated to admit it, he was getting some small amount of satisfaction in playing hero for her benefit. He was scared as hell and playacting helped. Besides, he knew it was only a front. As long as he kept that in mind, the acting wouldn't hurt. At least, he hoped not.

The four fugitives entered the hallway. Slowly, confidently, they strode down the hall, marching like guards en route to a patrol.

"When we get outside," Harry whispered, "calmly make for the nearest vehicle. Once we're behind the wheel, we will very naturally head for the dirt road. And once we're on the dirt road, we'll make for Cade's car like the devil himself was on our tail."

"It's safe to assume he will be," Cade remarked.

The imposters walked unmolested to the front door of the dome. Harry scanned the lobby of the building. It was deserted. A small twinge made itself known in the back of his mind. There was something about this situation that didn't ring true. Harry ignored the warning, chalking it up to his physical discomfort. Besides, there was no other way to go but forward.

The quartet dashed out of the dome, headfirst into a wall of rain. The storm had intensified, plunging the early evening into a pitch black panorama of shrieking wind and rolling thunder. Strangling fingers of lightning wrapped themselves around the landscape, squeezing the last sense of tranquility out of the earth. Porter felt a tremor pass through Jessica's body. The rain soaked down to his second layer of clothing. Soon, he'd feel it down to his skin. The rain pummeled his face so frantically, he couldn't see five feet in front of him. Each droplet stung like a stone pellet.

His feet plunged soddenly into the river of mud that had passed for solid ground a half hour before. The foursome hadn't trudged but twenty feet from the dome when they were struck by an unexpected, sustained burst of light. The night seemed to come alive with piercing, illuminated eyes. Harry dropped his weapon, shielding his eyes from the blaze. Squinting into the rain, he made out the source of the sudden illumination. Completely surrounding him, lined in a semicircle, was a fleet of electric vans, their headlights trained on the escaping prisoners.

"Please throw down your weapons," came a vaguely amused voice over a loudspeaker. "If you don't... we'll kill you."

"Toss them," Harry said, turning to Saint-Crispen and Cade. He felt both frustrated and foolish. "And don't panic. If we got this far once, we'll get even further a second time."

"How do you figure that, Einstein?" Saint-Crispen growled.

"Because we'll already have practiced." A sudden burst of wind drove a leaf into Harry's face. He tore it off savagely, cursing his stupidity and the senselessness of his escape plan.

Wearing a sky-blue pancho, Kapps slowly walked up to the four fugitives. He was laughing aloud. "Harry! You do astound me. You are a remarkable potpourri of contradictions. A man of intellect who resorts to animal instinct. A fellow who professes to abhor heroics yet resorts to the most clichéd of actions in vain displays of just that. You are most entertaining."

"I joust windmills at private parties, too," Porter grimaced. "Weddings, bar mitzvahs, the whole bit."

"Humor," Kapps bowed. "I love it."

He turned his gaze to Harry's companions. "Well, since everyone here is dressed up, I suppose that, as a good host, it's up to me to provide someplace to go. Well, we have a couple of vans just waiting to take you on our mystery outing. This way please."

Kapps led them to an awaiting van. Harry noticed it had a bright yellow nuclear insignia painted on the front. "We wouldn't be going to Fountain Point, by any chance?"

"Party pooper," Kapps laughed. "Yes, of course we are. It's time for the climax of our drama. The arrival of the old President, the creation of a new and improved one! Today, Sonny Walker will make his debut as a real heroic kind of guy. The kind of guy you'd enjoy going to a ball game with, Harry."

"I hate baseball."

"Too bad. I bet the President has box seats for the New Senators' home games."

"I live in New York."

"Try any more foolishness, and you'll die in New York as well," Kapps smiled, walking back into the darkness.

The guy was as stimulating as a subpoena, Harry thought as he was pushed toward the back of the van. He straightened his back momentarily. The rifle barrel poked him hard a second time. He spun around to face his original captor, the woman with the blond braid. "Look, Enigma Jean," he grumbled. "I'm not a track star, okay? I've been running laps all afternoon. I'm tired. I'm cranky. I'm not much of a gentleman, so I don't really care if I die trying to stuff that rifle barrel down your throat. One more poke should do it, ma'am."

Harry's outburst stunned himself almost as much as the blond guard. She backed away immediately. Kapps rode by in a second van, calling to the guard. "Take good care of Mr. Porter. He's to be our resident historian. He's had a trying day, so should you have to reprimand him . . . no external bruises."

Harry stepped into the back of the truck. Cade, Saint-Crispen and Jessica were shoved in behind him. The woman with the rifle entered last. The door slid shut and the five passengers were plunged into near darkness. Porter sat dejectedly in a corner. His three companions huddled across from him, their faces reflecting both their fear and hopelessness.

Porter tried to smile, envisioning what the two guards in the egg-shaped tank would do to pass the time in the ensuing hours.

A flash of lightning outside the van sent a small spot of light cascading onto the muzzle of the guard's laser rifle.

Porter's smile faded.

Heroism sure wasn't what it was cracked up to be.

4

The rain pounded on the roof of the van mercilessly. Its steady, staccato beat reverberated through the back of the vehicle, boldly mimicking the wild pounding of Porter's heart. The stone-faced woman with the solitary pigtail peered at her four captives sullenly. Her hands were firmly wrapped around her rifle.

"Just for conversation's sake," Harry asked, his body lurching with each jostling movement of the truck. "How do you plan on getting us inside the power plant?"

The woman stared at him menacingly.

"Hey, look," Harry said. "I'm a guest on this clambake, a working guest at that."

The woman seemed to consider that fact for a moment before replying. Her voice was husky and somewhat lyrical, not at all resembling the hard-nosed droning intonation he had expected. "The President of the United States is due to arrive at the facility within the half hour. Outside security at the plant has been increased tenfold. A ring of facility guards are positioned outside the area occupied by the terrorists. A constant stream of security personnel in vans such as this one have been filing onto the site for the past two hours.

"Several of the faithful were included in that caravan, replacing security men removed earlier. The guards who are posted at the outermost gate are also church members."

"So we'll just drive right through," Harry thought aloud.

"Exactly."

"You plot your secular activities pretty well for a religious outfit."

"We live in a secular society."

"I hadn't noticed." Harry slid out of his wet jump suit. The guard frowned. Harry slid back into his wet jump suit. If this woman didn't kill him with her rifle, she'd allow walking pneumonia to do the deed.

The rain smashed into the roof. Bursts of lightning shone through the front windshield. The thunder now seemed constant. Harry found himself avoiding the gaze of his three companions. A small smirk slithered across his lips. It was ironic, really. The biggest story he had ever tumbled onto and he'd never get the chance to report it.

The van slowed down but didn't come to a full stop. The driver said something that was obliterated by a sudden clap of thunder. Harry assumed they were passing through the entranceway to the plant.

The vehicle picked up speed once again. Harry and his accomplices slid across the floor as the vehicle swerved sharply. Driveway, probably, he guessed.

The van rolled to a halt. The two guards in the cab jumped out and slid the back door open. The woman with the braid trained her gun on the four prisoners from inside the truck. "Out."

The quartet stepped out of the van. They were inside a vast underground chamber. "Where the hell are we?" Harry asked.

"An underground garage beneath the control center," the woman replied. "You'll be staying down here for a little while. We have a locker room prepared for you. It's empty, of course, because of the considerable activity topside."

"Gee, I was hoping for some company," Harry smiled.

The woman motioned them forward with her rifle. "I'll be right outside the door." She began to strut forward. "Walk this way, please."

"Reminds me of an old joke," Harry said, gazing at the gun barrel.

"Porter, if you don't mind," Cade said glumly.

Harry shrugged and trudged through the garage. "Where are the rest of your playmates?" he asked as casually as possible with three weapons trained on his back.

"Topside, mingling with the personnel."

"In those blue jump suits, don't you think they'll be spotted?"

"They are no longer garbed in church vestments. We have created replicas of the military uniforms utilized at the plant. They changed en route."

"But you can stay in your civvies because you're down here guarding us?"

"Your grasp of the situation is commendable."

"I did well on my college boards, too."

Harry was pushed into a locker room. Cade, Saint-Crispen and West were likewise herded into the cubicle. The woman with the pigtail stood in the doorway behind them, regarding Porter with a look that could pass for compassion, pity, or disdain: the sort of look that an eight year old bestows on an earthworm before she carves it up into ten pieces to test its knack for survival. Harry wasn't too enthused about any of the possible interpretations.

"We'll be just outside your door," the woman stated. "Behave accordingly."

The guard slammed the door behind her, leaving the four people alone in the room. Harry sat down on a rounded bench. "Anyone for charades?"

"Porter," Cade spat. "How can you take all this so lightly? Have you considered the gravity of this situation?"

"Sure, I've considered it," Harry said. "Now consider the size of the hole that a laser rifle can cause at close range. It sort of makes you appreciate your present surroundings more."

Saint-Crispen crumpled in a heap next to a row of transparent lockers. He began to whine at low volume but high pitch. Harry felt a slap of pain above his eyes. "Marion! Knock it off with your worrying. You're giving me a migraine."

"I can't help it," the Saint declared. "I'm scared."

"So am I," Harry stated. "I don't know about you, but I have plans for the future. In order to make them work, I have to have a future. So don't give up just yet. We'll get out of this intact if we play it by ear."

"You're sure of that?" Jessica asked, slightly astounded.

"Would I lie?" Harry lied.

Marion erupted into a coughing fit.

The door to the locker room swung open and a cheerful Ashley Kapps strolled in. Wearing a three-piece suit, he looked every bit the high-powered business executive. He still wore his rainbow-colored glasses. "Ten minutes and counting!" he exclaimed. "I can't tell you all how exciting this is for me!"

"Don't try," Harry cautioned.

"Come on, now, Harry," Kapps said, still radiating good cheer. "You really shouldn't be moody about all this. After all, you and your friends are witnessing one of the most important events in contemporary history."

"Yeah," Harry acknowledged. "It's like the good old days, having a ringside seat at Hiroshima."

"Compared to the impact our little maneuver will have on the free world, Hiroshima will seem like a mere firecracker in the future history texts. We're going to change the shape of the world!"

"It won't be round anymore?"

Kapps managed to retain a thin smile. "Don't try to dampen my spirits, Harry. It won't work. That sort of role doesn't suit you. However, if you must persist in your attempts at obnoxious self-righteousness, I'll give you two minutes to recite the 'you'll never get away with this' monologue."

Harry stood next to the bench. "Actually, I had toyed with that phrase earlier on in the evening."

"Passé, though, isn't it?" Kapps grinned. "Besides, it doesn't really apply in this case. We will get away with it. At this moment, we are, in fact, getting away with this."

"Granted, but let's try this one on for size," Porter said. "Suppose you do actually succeed in this attempt and become President. So what? You're limited in terms of how much time you have to actually influence the world. A President can only serve three terms. Walker is finishing up his second this year. That gives you four-and-a-half years tops in the White House."

"That's just the beginning, Harry," Kapps laughed. "Use your imagination. With the application of syntheskin, I can restage this sort of routine any place in the world at any time. I can become almost anyone I want. All I have to worry about, really, is the height requirement. Weight I can alter. My face can be changed whenever I want. Granted, if I wanted to become, let's say, chancellor of West Germany, I'd have to brush up on my Berlitz tapes for a few months, but I could manage it. All future plots would merely require research, practice, and follow through."

Harry sagged down onto the bench.

"And besides," Kapps said enthusiastically. "If I really enjoy being President, I can always become my own successor. I'm about the same height as David Reeves. At the end of this term, Walker can die, leaving the reigns to Reeves. He, in turn, could become the party's next candidate. Another three terms could be mine for the asking. Heck. It could go on forever, as long as I picked vice-presidents of similar physical stature and managed to govern in a way that would inspire the populace!"

Harry was dumbfounded. Everything Kapps said was insane, of course, but had a nauseatingly truthful ring to it. Porter sighed. "You'll never get away with this, Kapps."

Kapps raised his hands in applause. "Well played."

"What do you have planned for the President once he arrives here?" Cade asked.

"Oh, I'm sure you'll appreciate the finesse involved in this, doctor," Kapps answered, beaming at the seated physician. "Walker will be sprayed with the skin immediately. We'll then make a quick mold. Within fifteen minutes of his arrival, Walker will be down here visiting with you, and I'll be donning my new face upstairs.

"I've already told you about Walker's sudden burst of heroism to come, correct? Well, I've decided to stage a truly magnificent shoot-out. The hostage personnel will be saved. Most of the terrorists, I believe there are half a dozen of them running around with our pseudo-Hayden at this point, will live. I'll pardon them at a later date once the world is enamored with my heroic attitude. I couldn't very well terminate such an effective commando squad when I might want to rely on them in the future, could I?

"There will be casualties, of course, but most will have their faces seared away during the laser battle."

"The President, the real President, being among them, no doubt," Cade said.

"No doubt. He'll be dressed in a guard's uniform with one of the IDs of the already terminated guards on him."

"Fingerprints," Harry exclaimed, leaping to his feet. "How will you duplicate the President's fingerprints."

"The same way he'll duplicate his face," Cade answered.

"Foolproof, wouldn't you say, doctor?" Kapps chortled.

"It would appear that way," Cade observed.

"What about us?" the Saint blurted.

"That depends on two things," Kapps shrugged. "The first rests solely on Harry's value to me as an historian. I could probably slip all four of you out as easily as I got you in. That would be no problem at all. The second variable, I'm afraid, rests more on whim than anything else. The further this drama develops, the less enchanted I am with your presence here. Nothing personal, you understand, I'm sure you're all very fine people.

"I admit that Harry is a very good journalist but, frankly, there are other journalists around. In the final analysis, everyone is expendable. Should my good humor dissipate by the conclusion of today's adventure, and if I have neither the time nor desire to pluck you out of the facility with my followers, you, too, will become facelees victims of this shoot-out. Lords know there are enough guard uniforms and IDs to go around."

"Your Ancient Astronauts probably wouldn't approve," Harry cautioned. "From what I gather, they weren't a bloodthirsty bunch."

"The lords work in mysterious ways," Kapps said, heading for the door. "There are countless ways to interpret scripture, especially my own. One man's god can be another man's devil."

Kapps walked out the door. The braided woman closed it behind them with an abrupt thud. Harry blinked three times. Sometimes it paid to be agnostic.

The Saint began to whine. This time, both Cade and Porter grabbed their foreheads. "Not now, Saint-Crispen," Harry ordered. "I told you we'd get out of here."

"How?" Saint-Crispen asked in a truly pitiful tone.

Harry stared at the wiry man with the frazzled hair, a pang of remorse gripping his chest. Forcing the overwhelming grasp of desperation out of his mind, he concentrated on coming up with a way to save both their morale and their skins. He slapped the side of his head slightly. It wasn't much of an idea, but it was better than a poke in the eye with a sharp stick.

"I think our spacefaring demigogue just gave us our answer. If we're dressed as guards, we can become those faceless victims he wants quite easily enough. If we're dressed as guards while we're still breathing, however, we can become part of the frantic mob scene upstairs just as easily. We won't be noticed heading for an exit during the commotion."

"Then let's suit up," Saint-Crispen said, scrambling towards a locker.

"Not yet," Harry advised. "Remember that the President himself is due to make an appearance down here soon. We don't want our blues band outside to catch us with our pants down, do we?"

"I wouldn't mind if the babe with the pigtail did," the Saint snorted, "if it was a mutual consent deal."

"You're a real class act," Harry smirked, admiring the Saint's one-track mind. If his plan worked, not only would the four of them be able to walk out of the Point alive, but the President, properly outfitted, would make the stroll to freedom as well. He let out a sigh of relief. Sometimes he liked himself quite a bit.

"Now," he told his friends, "just relax for a few minutes and think positively. Imagine all the wonderful things we'll do after we get out of here."

"Booze! Drugs! Sex!" Saint-Crispen began to chant.

5

It was with a profound sense of loss that Harry Porter watched the President of the United States stumble into the locker room. In a perverse sense, Sonny Walker fit in with his surroundings perfectly. The room itself was a holdover from the last century, a small, rectangular area, long outmoded. Metal lockers had been replaced with attractive, plastic ones, wooden benches by curved, polyurethane models. Yet the place still retained a bleak, stagnant atmosphere, amplified by the dim lighting provided by a series of dim florescent bulbs dangling from the ceiling. The room was dull and decidedly passé. So was Walker.

Walker was not a contemporary figure in any sense. A throwback to the backslapping, bribe-taking political days of yesteryear, he had been elected as a novelty item, really—a rustic tossed into the world of space shuttles, genetic engineering, high orbit industrialization and advanced robotics. The novelty soon wore off, however, and, for the past eight years, the insecure Walker had slowly eroded the nation's pride and confidence. The only reason he still held office rested in the fact that the only candidates concocted by the opposition party had all the warmth and appeal of a convicted child molester.

Walker stood in the doorway, the door latching firmly behind him. He had seemingly aged an eon since Harry saw him last on the video, four weeks prior. His face seemed drawn, as if there was something causing it to collapse from within. His eyes were heavily lined, either from lack of sleep or one crying jag too many. His silver hair was brushed back yet managed to spring out in wild tufts around his ears. His mouth was open, giving him an idiotic, slack-jawed appearance. He trembled at the sight of the room, temporarily ignoring its occupants. His green eyes darted aimlessly about, scrutinizing every shadow for some sign of danger.

So this was the Commander in Chief. Harry scrutinized the man in a detached manner. He had met only two Presidents in his lifetime: James Brugarner on his deathbed, and David Orwell shortly before the Pentagon sex scandal prematurely ended his political career. Both men, despite the obvious problems assailing them hourly, retained a certain amount of stature, dignity, and integrity until the end. But Walker?

Walker wore the expression of an alky faced with the unexpected rigors of drying out. Harry was deeply saddened at the sight of the direct cause of America's élan. He felt that pang that countless teenagers must have grappled with upon discovering that their most revered heroes were all too human after all: that half of the astronauts were woman-chasing louts, that the head of the FBI was into Chicano boys, that Major Moishe Wu-Sung, the hero of the Sino-Israeli War, managed to conduct his entire career while on hallucinogens.

Harry focused his attention elsewhere. Everyone in the room seemed visibly embarrassed by the President's appearance, including the irreverent Saint-Crispen. For some reason, the silence enveloping the room angered Porter.

"Where am I?" Walker suddenly exclaimed. "What's going on here?"

"This is a locker room," Harry explained patiently. "And this whole setup is a presidential assassination. Welcome aboard."

Walker suddenly turned his gaze on the speaker. "Porter!" he declared, mixing an obvious sense of relief at the sight of a familiar face with unbridled anger and resentment. "I should have known you'd be here. Wherever there's a mess, just look for Harry Porter!"

"If that axiom were true, I would have been a member of your cabinet for years," Harry answered.

"What the hell is all this, Porter?" the President demanded, his bravado giving way to stark fear somewhere between the subject and predicate of his sentence. "I demand an explanation!"

"Don't look at us," Porter shrugged. "We're all in the same boat which is, I might add, rife with leaks. Oh, let me introduce you to—"

Walker whirled around and faced the closed door. "Don't they realize what they're doing? Don't they realize who I am? What I am?"

"Yes to all of the above, especially the latter," Porter said. "Now, why don't you just sit down and be quiet."

"How dare you speak to the President of the United States that way?"

"Ex-President," Harry drawled, stretching his legs before him.

"What do you mean?"

Harry briefly outlined the situation. The President was too panicked to be impressed. "That's impossible. It will never work! No one can take my place!"

Porter noted Walker's sweat-encased forehead. Not unless they hire a mental deficient, he thought.

"You have to stop these men!" Walker declared. "I command you, as your Commander in Chief, to—to—"

Harry folded his arms in front of him and got to his feet.

He leaned against a locker. "Oh, come off it, Walker. We don't have time to play soldier right now. Our primary purpose at the moment is getting out of this alive. We can dispense with sapheaded revenge later. We have to work together if we're going to pull this off. Down here, you're not Commander-in-Chief, you're one of the captured. As a matter of fact," Harry added with a quirky grin, "you're not Chief of Staff upstairs, either."

"They can't do this to me! It's illegal!"

"A safe assumption."

"They'll never succeed with the scheme," Walker muttered, a dull flicker of what could pass for cunning appearing in his eyes. "There's an army out there beyond those gates, more FBI men than you've ever seen in your lifetime. They're all undercover, of course, but," he patted his wristwatch. "One signal from me and they'll be swarming all over this place. I can't be harmed with them out there. As long as they know I'm safe, they remain outside. The first sign that anything is going wrong in here and this place will look like an FBI reunion. There'll be good ol' boys all over the halls. A real turkey shoot."

"Interesting choice of words," Harry noted. "Look, Walker. Don't you understand? Your FBI buddies will never realize that you've been, uh, removed. There will be an exact double of you upstairs for all the world to see. He will become you in the eyes of the public."

"But I'm the President!" Walker bellowed, pacing the room. His three-piece suit became more and more rumpled as he staggered to and fro. "Millions of people respect me!"

"They'll respect you even more after today," Harry stated. "At least that's the plan. The bogus Walker will be a leader of men, a real two-fisted hero type."

Walker took two steps towards Harry, trembling. "And I'm not."

Porter remained silent.

Walker collapsed onto a bench, folding his hands between his legs and gnawing on his lower lip. "Oh, I know what you all think," he babbled. "You all assume that it's easy being President. It's a great job. Well, you're all wrong. There are . . . responsibilities involved that are frightening. I mean, I admit that I love the prestige of it all but if it hadn't been for Muffy-Bird, god rest her soul, I never would have gotten involved with this at all. I was really content hosting *Outlaw*

Theater on TV. I mean, I had a respectable career as an actor and a state senator. I didn't need this job, but Muffy-Bird convinced me. 'Sonny,' she said. 'You're a natural for the part.' I was still skeptical. 'Plus,' she said, 'the demand for your old movies will mushroom.'

"Since I own the syndication rights to all my old flicks, I figured, 'What the hey, Sonny. Why not give it a shot?' And I did. And I was elected. And do you know what? I hate the goddamned job. It scares the shit out of me. It always has. Nobody likes me anymore. They're all out to get me: my cabinet, my closest associates, hell, even that sissy-boy Reeves wants to get his licks in. It's awful. I get up for breakfast, and I'm afraid someone has poisoned my corn flakes. I go out for a quick shuttle flight, and I'm worried about my pilot being a KGB agent. I take a walk and look for laser barrels in the bushes. It's a hellish world."

"You could have resigned any time you wanted to," Harry replied.

"And give up the power?" Walker said, amazed. "Not on your life. I mean, I'm a respected individual now. The leader of the greatest country on the face of this here earth! I've managed, through following the polls and trusting my allies, to keep abreast of national trends. I believe I've handled all our various crises well."

"You've handled them all badly," Harry smirked.

"The hell I have!" Walker declared, his green eyes now tinged with red. "Look at the *Island One* fiasco. When I discovered that there was crime aboard, I shut down the whole space habitat, didn't I?"

"You sure did, crippling the U.S. space program and turning over a potential industrial gold mine to a foreign power and a private corporation."

"And what about those student riots in California? I nipped those in the bud, didn't I?"

"You got rid of the riots by getting rid of the rioters," Harry found himself sneering. "'If it takes a bloodbath, let's get it over with. No more appeasement.' Wasn't that the way you phrased it? How many kids died? Fifty? Sixty?"

"They were fascists!"

"At the time, you called them 'communists.'"

"Communists, fascists, they're all the same to me!"

Harry felt his teeth grinding together. "That's the problem, Walker. Everyone who doesn't agree with you, who doesn't think exactly like Sonny, automatically becomes an enemy and all your enemies look alike to you. You don't hear what they're saying, even if what they're saying is constructive. I mean, we're all sitting down here watching a complete lunatic take control of the government and, watching you, I find myself thinking that it might be an improvement. That scares me, Mr. President."

Walker lurched to his feet and staggered towards Porter. Harry remained seated. The sweating man in the three-piece suit swayed above him menacingly, like a washed-up pug taking on a young challenger and praying for an early decision. "That's treasonous talk, Porter! I'll have you jailed for that at the very least. If there's a death penalty that can be invoked, I'll see that it is. You and your kind, the press, the fourth estate, have done nothing but lie about me for the past seven-and-a-half years. You've distorted the truth! You've made me look like a buffoon. Well, it hasn't worked, Porter. The people still trust me! I know they still trust me! They still think of me as good ol' Ranger Sonny!"

Harry tried to ignore the panicking President. "You were never even nominated for an Oscar."

Walker nearly doubled over. "Treason! Treason!" he began to shout.

Harry let out an exasperated sigh. Leaving his bench, he calmly walked to the back of the locker room.

"Treason! Treason! Treason!" Walker continued to yammer. Abruptly, his raving ceased. Harry and his three companions turned in time to view Sonny Walker's face evolve into a portrait of bloodlessness before turning a bright violet hue. His body stiffened and toppled onto the ground. Cade ran to the stricken man. He loosened the President's tie.

Abruptly, Cade faced Harry, a look of vague consternation on his visage. "He's dead."

Harry walked slowly to where Walker was sprawled. "Are you sure?"

Cade's expression took on a sickly pallor. "Heart attack. Jesus Christ, Porter. Do you realize what you've just done with your verbal maneuvering? You've just killed the President of the United States!"

Harry emitted a low sigh and plopped down upon a bench. "Did you ever have one of those days?"

A sudden thought entered his head. He lunged for Walker's body. "At least his death won't be in vain. He tapped this

wristwatch when he mentioned contacting his FBI guard
dogs out there." Harry removed Walker's wristwatch. "There's
nothing stopping us from calling in the feds with this little
baby and heading off Kapps' action."

Porter held the watch in the palm of his left hand. "Shit! I
don't believe it."

"What's wrong?" Jessica asked.

"This idiot was wearing an ordinary watch!" he growled,
his face turning beet red. "This isn't a communicator at all."
He smashed the watch on the floor, sending pieces scattering
across the room. "Digital. No receiver. No transmitter.
Zippo."

"That guy wouldn't have lasted two minutes on his own in
my neighborhood," the Saint finally opined.

"Well, let's suit up," Harry muttered. "If we're going to get
out of here, we're going to have to do it without the benefit of
the FBI cavalry."

"Do you think he was lying about those agents beyond the
gate?" Cade asked.

"I doubt it," Harry said, jimmying a locker. "I don't think
he would have agreed to come here if there wasn't a pretty
heavy backup plan. I also think he was too thick to come up
with a lie as clever as that." The lock fell apart as Harry
prodded it with a small vibrating wire. Inside the locker,
several security suits were hung. "Okay. It's change of clothes
time again, kids. Let's see if we can make it out of here
before the real fireworks begin."

An explosion shook the building. A trickle of plaster dribbled from the ceiling. Harry tossed his blue jump suit into a
corner and donned the khaki-colored model worn by the
plant security team. "Showtime!" he muttered as a second
blast rocked the room. He walked towards the door.

The faint "wooshing" noises made by laser rifle fire could
be heard hissing through the maelstrom of sound above the
garage. Harry stood, poised at the door. He motioned his
three friends to one side of the room. With one, sudden
motion he yanked the door open, grabbed the female guard
by her pigtail, hauled her inside the room, and slammed the
door shut. Taken by surprise, the woman sailed backward
onto the floor without crying out. Harry snatched the rifle
from her as she flew past him.

He then stepped out into the hall, training the weapon on

the remaining two male guards. "Fling 'em or fry with 'em," he grinned.

The two young men dropped their guns immediately. At least Kapps had taught them the importance of logic. Harry pointed his rifle barrel at the locker room. "Inside."

Cade, Saint-Crispen, and West darted out of the room as Harry forced the young church members in. He pointed to the back of the cubicle. The three sullenly marched to that location. "Don't move," Porter smiled. "I want to forget you exactly as you are."

He slammed the door shut. Taking the laser rifle, he unleashed a well-aimed beam and struck the door latch. The latch wilted under the molten gaze of the gun, effectively sealing the door closed.

"That should cut down on their travel expenses for a little while," Harry cracked.

He handed a rifle to Cade while Saint-Crispen snatched a second from the floor. Cade stared at his weapon. "Do we have a plan as of yet," he casually inquired. "If so, I'd like to be privy to it before I start aiming this mechanism at any living creature."

"As a matter of fact," Harry answered, "as blindly optimistic as this may sound, I think we can rely on Walker's cowardice as a way out. Let's assume that he was telling the truth about the FBI contingent outside the gates. If the feds are out there, all we have to do is get in the van and ram the holy hell out of the entranceway. We reach the FBI and send in the troops, as it were."

"Simplistic," Cade stated.

"But sound," Harry nodded. "We even have a van at our disposal." He motioned to the abandoned vehicle they had arrived in.

"The only mitigating factor in all this, I assume," Cade injected, "is the fact that Kapps' men are probably in full control of the security system by now and will be watching, and aiming at I might add, any unplanned movements on the field."

Harry considered Cade's theory. "Right," he added. "So, in order to make sure that the van gets off the grounds safely, a second, diversionary tactic will have to be executed from within."

"Executed?" the Saint repeated sorrowfully.

"Figure of speech," Harry continued. "While the van is heading for the gate, we'll take out the plant's security room."

"And just how are we going to do that?" Jessica asked.

"Well," Harry said, confidently, "we have an expert at debilitation in our ranks."

"We do? Great!" Saint-Crispen beamed, his face brightening before assuming a mournful expression. "Oh no!" he shouted. "Not me! I'm a pacifist, not a commando. I won't even use an eggbeater at breakfast!"

"We don't have time to argue," Harry stated. "With your mental abilities, you can cream the guards upstairs before they know what's hitting them."

"I'm not doing it, Harry. I can't turn this stuff on and off like there's a faucet up there. And once it *is* on, I can't control the power. I won't do it."

"Would you rather die here?"

"Then, I won't do it for long. Just a little bit."

"Well," Cade said, vaguely amused. "Since you and Mr. Saint-Crispen are so attuned to each other, in a manner of speaking, may I volunteer to take the joyride outside?"

Harry looked at Cade's ashen face. There was something unnatural about it, a detached calmness that didn't jibe with the present circumstances. "Are you up to it, Andy?"

"If I can drive my own car through Manhattan daily, I feel quite qualified to drive a van through anything."

"I'll keep you company," Jessica offered.

"Out of the question," Cade snapped, his jaw tightening instantly. "I'm sorry," he quickly added, his voice softening. "It's a chauvinistic streak, I'm sure, but I honestly feel that you'll be safer with Harry and Mr. Saint-Crispen than with me. In here, dressed as security personnel, you'll have the option to blend in with the crowd should complications arise."

Jessica gave Cade a puzzled look. Porter reached out his hand, genuinely moved by the doctor's sense of chivalry. He suddenly realized how close they had grown. Cade, apparently sensing Porter's feelings, took the hand and squeezed it firmly. "No undue sentiment, Porter," he advised. "I do not consider this a particularly melancholy mission. I will simply avoid all ground fire and ram the gate. There is nothing wonderfully original or complicated about it. I'll see you after the hubbub subsides."

"Right," Harry nodded. "Just watch yourself, okay?"

"I'll be most judicious," Cade smiled thinly, leaving the trio behind. Straightening himself to his full stature, he marched to the van. Porter watched his friend pass through the shadows of the underground garage. Cade stepped up to the van. He paused for a moment. He ran both hands through his hair, pushing it straight back until it resembled the feathers of a great bird of prey. Furrowing his angled brows, he peered into the cab of the truck. The keys were still in the ignition. He climbed behind the wheel and rolled down the window on the driver's side.

Poking his head through the space, he called to Porter. "I'll give you exactly five minutes to prepare some disturbance upstairs. After that, I'm on my way."

"Piece of cake," Harry called, giving him an overly optimistic "thumb's up" sign. Harry pointed to a well-lit stairwell behind an open door. "I'm pretty sure the security center is on the top floor. We have a three-flight job ahead of us unless we can find an elevator."

He darted into the stairwell and began climbing rapidly, his knee clicking with every step. A sudden wave of fear swept through Porter as he reached the end of the first landing. Casually trying the first floor's exit door, he found it barred shut. What if the third floor's was as well? Porter glanced at his watch. In four minutes, Cade would exit the building. They had to distract the security team's attention in order for Cade to make it. Porter hissed a curse and continued climbing, with Saint-Crispen and West laboring behind.

The second landing had no exit door.

Porter was sweating. The sound of muffled voices echoed through the stairwell.

The third flight had a door. Porter came to rest in front of it. He grabbed the handle and pressed his shoulder against its surface, muttering a prayer to the patron saint of lost causes. The door budged. Harry slid into the hallway. The sound of laser fire emanated from somewhere nearby. Kapps' elaborate drama was unfolding.

The trio approached several stern-faced security guards who were running in the opposite direction. Harry effectively assumed a stoic, militaristic countenance and nodded in their direction. The guards grunted and jogged by.

After what seemed like hours of walking, Porter stopped in front of a clear plastic doorway. Inside a room, seven guards sat around what appeared to be an all-seeing video complex.

A wall of flickering monitors stood majestically above a bevy of button- and lever-littered consoles.

The guards placidly stared at the video screens. On the monitors, a casual fire fight was underway. The President of the United States and three commandos were charging through near-empty rooms, firing randomly at anyone foolish enough to move. Apparently, a few human sacrifices were being prodded into firing range for target practice. Kapps calmly gunned down an unarmed man. Every war needed its casualties, Harry reasoned. The events were, more than likely, being recorded so the video boys would have colorful evidence of the President's heroics for the evening news.

"All right, Saint-Crispen," Harry whispered, glancing at his watch. Two minutes left. "This must be the security room. You've got to neutralize it."

"I know that," the Saint replied, wide-eyed. His curly hair seemed serpentine, shaking as the result of the man's involuntary trembling. "Maybe we should rethink this, Harry. There are seven of them in there and only three of us."

"But none of them has your power."

The Saint began to ramble. "Yeah, well, about that power. I never did get the hang of it. I don't know if I can pull this off. I mean, I could probably peep one of them, but I'm not sure about any physical damage, I mean."

Harry checked his watch. Only a minute left. He silently motioned for Jessica to back off down the hall. "Saint-Crispen do you know what Kapps will do to us if we're caught up here? Do you know what will happen to us if we don't succeed?"

"Yeah," Saint-Crispen gnawed his moustache. "Sort of."

"Sort of?" Harry grimaced. "Marion, he's an expert in physical and mental conditioning, in torture. Do you think he'll kill us right away when he can get his jollies by watching us suffer? Let me tell you about some of the things I witnessed during the last war..."

"I wish you wouldn't," Saint-Crispen said. "I'll try my best but..."

"I've seen guys beg for death," Porter lied. "Plead, scream for hours. Simple laser routines. First, a finger is sliced off, slowly. The laser passes through the skin so slowly that it cauterizes the wound. The hand doesn't bleed, but the finger? The finger hits the floor. The pain is excruciating."

Basically, Porter was recounting a scene he had viewed in

the last James Bond movie, the sixty-ninth in the series. He was so good at the retelling, however, that he almost believed that he had actually witnessed it.

Saint-Crispen began to sweat. He was nearly pulling his moustache into his mouth, now; his lower lip worked feverishly. Harry felt a slight tingling sensation above his eyes. "Then another finger is cut," he went on, "and another, until all that's left is a stump; a stump reeking of seared flesh and charred hair..."

Saint-Crispen let out a sob, envisioning a similar fate for himself within a matter of minutes. "When they finish with the hands," Harry said cruelly, "they train a thin beam on each eye. The cornea is slowly burned out. The eye waters like crazy, the tears sizzling down the face. If one of the torture crew refuses to hold the prisoner's eyes open and the prisoner closes it instinctively, the beam cuts through the eyelid and—"

"No!" Saint-Crispen moaned. "Not my eyes!"

Harry felt a twinge of guilt for frightening his friend into a state of near-madness, but he needed results and fast. "Not my eyes!" Saint-Crispen screamed.

The guards inside the room turned around, catching a glimpse of the sobbing security man in the hallway. They flashed each other quizzical looks. Harry stared at his watch. Damn. Cade was already gone.

"Your eyes!" he goaded. "Your legs. Your body whittled away until you're nothing more than a screaming slab of a man, begging for death to come."

"NOOOOO!" Saint-Crispen bellowed. The door to the security room exploded open. Harry was thrown back against the wall, his head pounding, his nose bleeding. Leaping to his feet, he dived, headfirst, into Saint-Crispen's back, sending the screaming telepath tumbling into the security booth. The guards grabbed their guns. Saint-Crispen saw their movements and yelled "Keep away!"

Harry was hurled backward out of the room by the Saint's new wave of fear. The guns exploded in the guards' hands. The men slammed down onto their consoles. Blood poured from their noses.

The metal frames of the consoles twisted upward, curling like a strip of paper held under a match. Glass and plastic fragments took to the air as the wallscreens began to explode. The guards shivered on the floor, hands clawing their ears, their heads. Bleating like lambs, they clutched their faces, shredding the newly applied syntheskin covering. Saint-Crispen, shaking in the middle of the decomposing room, continued his mantra of terror.

Seeing the terrible transformation of the guards' faces, his ripples of mental terror increased in frequency and power. Harry watched, mesmerized, as the far side of the room simply collapsed in a heap. He suddenly remembered something the Saint had mentioned about a peeper gone wild. It was a warning about the full impact of their unleashed power. If Saint-Crispen's fear regenerated itself wave after wave after wave in an ever-increasing motion, not only would his friend destroy the entire booth and Porter's mind but he'd start to disintegrate the entire nuclear complex as well, setting off the core meltdown everyone had feared in the first place.

Porter, his nose now spurting clots of blood and tissue, ran into the room. Staggering blindly, he collared the Saint. The two men tumbled down onto the debris-laden floor. Harry shook Saint-Crispen into a state of consciousness. "Marion! Come out of it! It's all right!"

The Saint closed his mouth. He blinked his eyes four times, like a child coming out of a deep, restless sleep, awakened from a nightmare by the reassuring voice of a parent. "How did I do?" he asked feebly. "Did I wreck anything?"

"Did Vesuvius wreck Pompeii?"

"That good, huh?"

"Too good," Porter said, standing. "The monitors are all gone. We can't watch Cade from here."

"Sorry," Saint-Crispen said, sitting up and surveying the damage. "But if we can't watch him, no one else can, either, right? I mean, this is, was, spotter central, right?"

Harry reached out a hand and pulled the Saint to his feet. "Yeah," he smiled. "All Andy will have to worry about is ground fire." A frown suddenly appeared on his face. "The ground fire!" he exclaimed. "Listen! The fighting on this floor has stopped! If they're not fighting inside—"

"They're shooting up a storm outside," Saint-Crispen finished.

Jessica appeared in the doorway. "It looks like a small war went on in here."

"It's happening outside, now," Harry replied, scurrying towards the door. "Grab a rifle."

6

Andrew Cade knew he was a dead man as soon as he entered the truck. He sensed it before then, actually. He realized that time had run out as soon as he had entered Kapps' compound. He didn't fully comprehend why he reached that conclusion. Perhaps it was a by-product of his years in medicine. After facing death, battling death, twenty-four hours a day, seven days a week, for too many years, one couldn't help recognizing its presence.

Cade smiled grimly behind the steering wheel. Time was up and that was that. The realization didn't upset him nearly as much as it should have. His entire life, it seemed, had been a constant tussle with time: how to get it, what to do with it.

Once, time and Andrew Cade had been allies, participants in the perfect symbiotic relationship. He had been a young man, then, married to Joanna. He had his own practice. He was going to be something. Time spent at the office provided him with enough money to create the finest of times at home. He relished his time with his wife. He looked forward to the time he spent in medicine.

But then, the very fabric of time was wrenched away from his control. Bad times? Bad timing? He toyed with all the clichés in an effort to muddle his way through the parade of bleary-eyed hours, days, weeks after Joanna's death.

What had happened? A drug-crazed kid, a baby-faced being lurking in the body of an adult, behind the wheel of a car. A single turn, misjudged. The car was electric. Its motor made no sound. The car silently, lethally, had shot across a deserted street . . . a not quite deserted street. She had stood at the crosswalk, calmly waiting for the light that would never change in her lifetime. She had stood, not thirty yards away from the safety of her own front door. Cade often wondered if she had seen the car coming or if the experience had come as a total shock. Had she focused her final thoughts on the unchanging light? On the front door? Had she thought of him? Of what they would do to pass the time that evening? A quiet dinner at home? A holo show later, perhaps?

Cade found little solace in concocting a scenario wherein she had entertained good and comforting thoughts before encountering General Motors' deus ex machina. He tried to convince himself that the blow came unexpectedly, killing her instantly. He attempted to believe that her body landed peacefully and unmarred on the pavement.

He had clung tenaciously to these beliefs all throughout the boy's manslaughter trial and after the acquittal. He had ignored the police photos of the scene, splattered with crimson and plastic debris. He had shut the world out and faced the prospect of elongated, hollow time with an aloofness that was carefully nurtured in order to afford the most amount of protection for an indefinite period of. . . .

He began to notice that time was defying all its traditional classifications. Suddenly, moments stretched out well beyond their conventional spans. Days were transformed into vast, yawning crevices of inactivity and boredom.

Andrew Cade was alone and could not handle it.

Where lesser men would have cracked, would have cried, would have run whimpering into the arms or cushions of the nearest therapist, Cade created a time-consuming character. He was determined to conquer the inactivity, the loneliness, the gnawing despair.

He plunged headfirst into his work. He gave up his private practice. He attached himself to NYU and often sacrificed twelve to sixteen hours of each day to medicine. It was selflessness, his peers said admiringly. No. It was selfishness, a way to pass the time. He worked until he could work no more. Then he slept fitfully in order to begin the entire exhausting process again.

He cultivated but a few friendships with individuals as aimless as he; his bond with Porter was the strongest of them all. He sought to distort whatever free time he still was saddled with by paying homage to the bottle, by supplicating Dionysius and being rewarded with a stupor that brought back the past in a benign manner, without yanking him totally from the present. When he needed female companionship, the medical profession provided him with a large reserve of professional groupies.

He had filled his time, marked his time, as best he could. Now, time was eliminating Cade from the partnership altogether. Cade didn't really give a damn. In fact, in a perverse way, he was looking forward to it. An intellectual question would finally be answered.

Cade sat at the wheel. Porter was in danger. He intuitively knew this to be fact. Porter, the way Cade envisioned it, would arrive at the security station and Kapps' men would be waiting for him. After all, Kapps' warfare was mere playacting. Why should they bother to monitor it. Porter was too recognizable at this stage of the game. He and the others would walk directly into a den of awaiting wolves. The building would be swarming with church members. They'd spot the trio as ringers immediately. Porter didn't have the faintest chance of getting out of the compound alive unless...

"Unless the church members are occupied," Cade smiled to himself. What better to turn their attention to the outside world than an unauthorized van skidding across the Fountain Point grounds, making a beeline for the front gate? Cade looked at his watch. He still had three minutes to wait. Porter could lose his life in those three minutes.

Cade thought about Joanna. Perhaps time was his ally once again. Perhaps, it would allow him to accomplish something he truly desired before turning him loose into whatever dimension it was that Cade had avoided thinking about for years.

Cade turned the key and pressed the accelerator. The van moved forward. Noting that the road to the front gate was a curved one, Cade decided to pursue the most logical route. He stomped the accelerator to the floor. The van picked up speed. The shortest distance between two points is a straight line. Logically, the van flew off the road and onto the grass, accelerating constantly as it headed directly for the gate.

Cade vaguely made note of the shouting. He sounded the horn in a rare display of bravado. Splashes of light appeared around the windshield, illuminating the raindrops. They were shooting at him. He leaned on the horn. He increased the speed of the windshield wipers. A small bolt of light tore through the passenger's seat, burning a hole deep into the fabric. A section of the windshield melted, causing the windshield wiper to make a nasty, smacking noise as it made its pass.

The van continued to pick up speed.

The gate loomed less than a mile in the distance.

Guards appeared before him. Cade laughed aloud. The

guards dived out of the way of the vehicle, firing their rifles blindly as they did so. Their aim off, the shots hit high. Rain began to dribble in through several holes magically appearing in the roof of the vehicle.

Cade grinned, tensing his jaw. Perhaps he'd make it after all. No. He dismissed that small parcel of hope as soon as it arrived. His time had come. He no longer wanted to deal with the endless days and the sleepless nights. An unexpected bolt of light sliced through his chest from behind. Now where had that come from? It struck him just below the rib cage. He looked down at his torso. Blood was oozing through the security suit. A fairly clean wound, he noted. The pain suddenly flashed upward. No major arteries hit, he reasoned. Internal damage a certainty, however.

Much to his surprise, he found himself growing dizzy and sliding over in the seat. Damn it. He had never misdiagnosed before. What a time to start. Reaching deep into the recesses of his mind, he summoned up a vision of youthful agility and strength. Using the wheel as a crutch, he pushed his body upward and positioned it firmly behind it. He wrapped his arms around the steering mechanism, battling weakness, fending off unconsciousness.

Maybe when this was finished, he'd find Joanna waiting for him. He cackled to himself. He had found it ironic how his patients had always rediscovered religion on their deathbeds, and now, he was delving into spiritual slapstick himself.

He pressed his foot down to the floor. The pain welled within his chest. The van continued to barrel towards the gate. Cade, however, had no way of knowing that. In his vision, every action seemed to be coated in some sort of dimensional molasses. Rapid movements appeared to be slow motion travesties. Time was unraveling before him. He began to panic. Was this what death was like?

His right arm exploded onto the windshield as the windshield itself dissolved. Cade let out a shrill howl of pain that, in his solitary universe, thundered like the roar of a wounded bear. He hadn't expected that shot. Rain ricocheted off his face like bullets. His vision provided him with a blurred, kaleidoscopic view of the gate. He spotted a small loading ramp, used to drag dollies of supplies on and off the Point's vans. It was sitting, abandoned, near the side of the main roadway.

A glimmer of a plan tumbled through his mind as yet

another shaft of light plunged through the van. The light sliced into the back of Cade's brain. His forehead sizzled open, its interior mingling immediately with the torrent of rain. Whatever willpower still residing within the quivering mass of flesh somehow caused it to remain attached to the steering wheel.

From another vantage point, another time period, perhaps, the intelligence that had been Dr. Andrew Cade, experienced with satisfaction the distant, blurred sight of the small electric van hitting the metal loading ramp and sailing off into space. The van soared through the sheets of rain like an oversized arrow. It hit the front gate squarely, some ten feet above the ground. It knocked out not only the iron gate itself but also the four concrete posts holding it there.

The van hit the concrete road outside the Point and tumbled, cab first, over and over again. As the vehicle rolled nearly a half mile down the road, the tangled mass of humanity, which had once in operating rooms held court over life and death, seemed to mutter one last word as the thunder poured into its ears.

"Joanna."

7

Harry Porter galloped down the stairwell, taking two stairs at a time. His head ached. His lips were drenched with caked blood. His knee emitted a sharp snap of pain with each step. Saint-Crispen and Jessica West trailed silently behind, clutching their weapons. Something had gone wrong. They all knew it.

Harry rounded a corner badly, crashing into a bannister. He wanted to cry out in anger and pain. He couldn't shake the knowledge that the four of them were the only obstacles between a madman and the office of the Presidency. He didn't want that responsibility. He wanted to get his friends out of this alive. Period.

Harry listened intently. There was too much gunfire going on outside for his liking. That wasn't a good sign. He hoped Cade had been successful in reaching the federal agents.

The trio reached the bottom of the stairwell. Harry flew through the exit door and ran into the underground garage.

Sprinting, dazed and exhausted, beneath the overhead lighting, they headed for the sloped entranceway from which Cade and the van had departed only moments before.

Outside the garage, the gray light of an overcast day shone. It had stopped raining. Harry slowed his pace. He barely was able to make out the presence of a dozen or so men, armed with laser rifles, walking slowly into the underground chamber. Harry stopped in his track. The Saint and Jessica did likewise.

A chill racked Porter's body. There was no escape this time. The armed men marched down the exit ramp silently. Harry stared at their faces, illuminated from behind by the vague daylight. They were blank, expressionless. A sudden burst of hope flowered in the back of his mind. The intruders were not garbed in plant security outfits. The way they plodded along, they were either federal agents or lobotomy patients.

Porter placed his hands at his sides, allowing his rifle to point, barrel downward, at the floor. His two companions imitated his action. The dozen men surrounded the trio. Much to Harry's surprise, not one of the men bothered to train a weapon on them. It was as if they had known the trio would be down there, who they were and what they were capable of.

The ground fire outside slowly abated. A thirteenth figure appeared at the top of the exit ramp. Lightning flashed behind the presence, casting an eerie, elongated shadow down the entranceway. This was obviously the leader of the federal wolfpack. Pistol drawn, the well-tailored warrior marched stiffly into the garage. He made his way through the crowd of men. Harry remained frozen as the newest addition to the group stepped into the baleful light provided by one of the hanging lamps.

Vice-President David Reeves scowled at Porter. "You're a bigger fool than I thought," he said evenly. He turned to the men. "I want every inch of this station searched. You know who and where to find them. Bryant. You, Fielding, and Hooper remain below here. The rest of you, split into three divisions and hit the upper floors."

"Talk about arriving in the nick of time," Saint-Crispen breathed. "Tell him, Harry. Tell him what's been going on."

Porter cocked his head, regarding Reeves quizzically. The Vice-President smiled icily at Porter, his handsome features taking on a callousness. "Yes, Harry," Reeves said. "Tell me what's been going on here."

Harry stared at Reeves. Despite the politician's boyish demeanor, he struck Harry as the kind of guy who'd steal a fly from a blind spider. Porter felt a nervous twinge take hold of his upper lip. "You wouldn't believe me before, why should you believe me now?"

"Try me."

Harry took a deep breath and rushed through the entire plot, concluding with "the President that you or one of your icebergs will find upstairs is a bogus one. The real Walker is lying dead down here in a locker room."

Reeves almost collapsed with laughter. "I wish you could hear yourself," he chuckled. "You sound like a hyperventilating Hans Christian Andersen."

"Pity," Harry grimaced. "I was trying for Mickey Spillane."

"David! David!" cried a recognizable voice. "Thank God you've arrived!"

Harry glanced over his shoulder. President Sonny Walker trotted out of the stairwell and across the garage. "I managed to subdue the terrorists but these three vermin escaped!"

Harry clenched his fists, but otherwise, he remained outwardly calm. "Not bad," he said to Reeves. "He even sort of sounds like Walker, doesn't he?"

"Of course I sound like Walker! I am Walker!" the President growled. He strode over to Reeves' side. "These—these three traitors were part of the scheme! That girl is Hayden's strumpet. And Porter was just here to get himself a story. He didn't care if I died or not. That lowlife next to him is one of his lackies."

"What do you mean *one* of his lackies?" the Saint snapped before catching an angry glance from Harry.

"They were all trying to kill me, David! Assassinate me." Walker pointed a quivering forefinger at the trio. "The terrorists were never going to let me go. And these three knew it! They encouraged it! They wanted to see this country brought to its knees!"

"Come off it, Kapps," Harry replied evenly. "I just told Reeves the entire story. Everyone here can see through your charade." He hoped.

Reeves looked at Harry without expression.

Porter began to worry. "I mean, you *can* see right through this guy, can't you, Reeves? This isn't Walker. It's Kapps."

"Kapps?!" Walker replied, astounded. "Reverend Ashley Kapps? That's beyond lunacy, Porter." He placed a hand on Reeves' right shoulder. "David, you know what I look like. You know what I sound like. Am I Sonny Walker or not? Am I not your President?"

Reeves turned to Walker. "You're the President all right."

Porter thought his eyeballs would explode. "He's a ringer, I tell you! Check the locker room!"

One of Reeves' men returned from his search of the garage level. "Find anything?" Reeves asked casually.

"Naah," the federal man replied. "A few security guards stuck in a locker room That's all."

"They're not guards!" Harry declared. "They're members of Kapps' church. Were they wearing blue jump suits?"

"Nope," the agent replied. "Light brown security uniforms."

"Then they changed them! The locker room is full of uniforms."

"Sure."

"Did you find Walker's body?"

"He's crazy," the President interrupted. "He has a history of mental illness. The man is a dangerous lunatic. He tried to kill me." Turning to Reeves, he whispered. "If I had a gun, I'd kill them all right now. Prevent them from doing any further harm to the country."

"That should convince you!" Harry shouted. Think of it, Reeves. Would the real Walker ever be so decisive? Christ! He was a regular jigsaw buff. Whenever he had to make a choice he'd go to pieces. Now, here is the same guy, ordering the cold-blooded murder of three people!"

"You're tap dancing, Porter," Walker declared. "You're guilty and you know it."

Porter tensed his body. If he could leap to where Kapps stood and dig his hands into the syntheskin face, he'd show him up as a phony. He placed his left foot in front of him. His knee snapped and he almost found himself on the ground.

"Can this be the same Sonny Walker," he babbled, "who has fumbled his way through nearly eight years of office? The same 'good old boy' who has tripped over every speech, through every press conference and every public appearance he has ever been prodded into? Why all this tough talk, Sonny—or would you rather I call you Reverend?"

"Kill them!" Walker bellowed, shaking a fist at Harry.

Vice-President raised his pistol slowly.

He pointed it directly at Harry's head.

Porter knew better than to try to raise his rifle to defend himself. By the time he got it to knee level, two FBI men would have scorched him from behind. He swallowed hard and watched Reeves' reptilian orbs narrow to one, across-the-face squint. Did that expression denote amusement or malice?

Much to Porter's surprise, Reeves broke into a strange grin. He turned slowly and stuck the pistol in Walker's stomach. "I expect that we'll find Walker's body in one of the lockers, don't you, Kapps?" he asked nonchalantly.

"I don't know what you're talking about!" Walker cried. "Have you taken leave of your senses?"

"No, not really," Reeves replied. "But you've taken leave of your speech pattern. The real Walker would have been alternately whining about how hard it is to be President and screaming the word 'Treason!' over and over again right about now. He'd never hit me with a pristine line about my 'senses.'" Reeves motioned for two agents to take Walker away. Harry noted that neither man seemed surprised. "Take him to Simpson," Reeves ordered. "He'll know what to do."

"You'll pay for this, Reeves!" Walker cried, being strong-armed to the stairwell. "You'll pay."

"I gave at the office," the Vice-President answered.

Harry let out an audible sigh of relief. Reeves retrained his gun on Porter. "All of you. Place your rifles on the ground, please."

Harry, the Saint, and Jessica complied, none fully comprehending why they were still under guard.

"It's my sad duty to inform you that your troubles are anything but over," Reeves said with obvious malice.

"Porter," he said, moving closer to Harry. "You're a stubborn, self-righteous, pompous ass. I tried to keep you out of this. I tried to discourage you from putting your two cents in, but no, you had to grandstand. Well, here you are. How do you like the looks of your crypt."

"What the hell are you talking about, Reeves?" Porter blurted, his anger causing his cheeks to burn. "Are you crazy, too?" He began to feel queasy, the final pieces beginning to fall into place.

"Not at all," Reeves said cooly, keeping the gun aimed at Porter's quaking midsection. "You very nearly ruined a well-planned FBI maneuver. You see, Chief Hanratty and I have had an understanding for quite a few months now concerning the activities of Reverend Kapps. The bureau cracked his little suicide scam a half a year ago and sent a couple of their youngest field people into the church to monitor movements. It wasn't too hard to infiltrate Kapps' organization. The man was just too damned self-confident. He didn't use too much discretion in his recruiting procedures. Act depressed, angry, and alienated, and you were a must-have."

Reeves stared over Harry's shoulder. "Ah, Miss Thysson. You're uninjured."

The blond guard with the pigtail nodded and took her place next to the FBI agents lining the wall. Porter's stomach was in turmoil.

"We discovered Kapps' Presidential aspirations about four months ago," Reeves grinned. "It was a very clever idea, actually. As a matter of fact, to a degree, Hanratty, most of the cabinet, and I agreed with it in principle. As a President, Walker was the absolute nadir. The zenith of nadirs. I used the word 'was' because, I assume, according to your narrative that Sonny has gone to that great oval office in the sky by now."

"Yeah," Harry grunted. "Heart failure."

The blond with the pigtail nodded silently, confirming Porter's assessment.

"Sonny always did avoid explosive situations," Reeves mused. "At least he was consistent until the end. Oh, don't get me wrong, Porter. I didn't hate the man. In fact, a lot of us actually enjoyed Sonny's company. He was a good old boy, great at tall tales and short drinks. It was his leadership qualities we despised. In retrospect, it was his lack of leadership qualities that actually irked us. Not only was he taking the country down the tubes but, more importantly, he was also taking our party and our careers down with him. If we were to survive, let alone have the country emerge unscathed, we had to somehow get Sonny out of the driver's seat. When we found out about Kapps' plan, things simply got that much simpler for us. We decided to monitor Kapps' actions but allow him to succeed."

"Holy shit!" the Saint exclaimed. "You mean you and the feds stepped back and let some crazy guy deep six the Pres of the U.S. of A?"

Porter was stunned. "By letting Kapps play out his string until the end, you have effectively pulled off the first governmental coup in the history of the United States."

"Yes," Reeves acknowledged with pride. "Impressive, isn't it?"

Porter found himself speechless. Suddenly, he was wearing his intellect around his ankles.

Reeves was quite pleased. "It was good for the country. It was good for the party."

"It was good for you," Harry added.

"That goes without saying," Reeves smiled. "And I really and truly tried to keep you out of it. Only Hanratty and fifty of our most trusted field men shared the secret with me and the Cabinet. I tried to force you out of it. I had the locals stiff-arm you. The FBI put pressure on the police and the police tried to block your every move. I did everything I could do short of using physical restraint to dampen your curiosity."

"I don't believe this," Harry said, slapping himself on the forehead as if the motion could shake this reality harmlessly out of his ears. "Two groups of assassins after the same target! One group is trying to suck me into the plot so I can record their actions, and the other is trying to force me out of the picture in order to keep me in the dark. What do I look like, a Ping Pong ball?"

"A curious Ping Pong ball, unfortunately," Reeves stated. "As a result of your curiosity, I'm afraid that three more of you will lose your lives."

The impact of the statement didn't hit Harry for a split second. "More?" he finally repeated.

"There is a Dr. Andrew Cade lying outside with his head blown off, I'm afraid," Reeves sighed in mock anguish. "He rammed his van through the front gate in an attempt to reach us. Kapps' agents proved faulty marksmen. Since we couldn't leave Cade alive to tell his story to the world, my own men had to eliminate him. Sorry about that. A brilliant mind. Highly combustible, too."

Before Reeves could begin his next sentence, Porter's hands were around his throat. The move happened so suddenly that Reeves didn't actually see the reporter leap at him. "You bastard!" Porter yelled, his face twisted into a mask of demonic rage. "You rotten bastard. I'll see you in hell—"

A bolt of light hissed across the garage, slicing into the back of Harry's right leg. Porter cursed in pain and fell back onto the floor. His pants leg was smoking. Damn it, he grimaced. Why couldn't they have hit the bad leg.

The Saint and Jessica huddled protectively around Harry. His leg throbbed with pain. Blood had already filled his shoe. Overriding that pain, however, was a steady pulsating in his head. This was not the time for one of his migrains. Harry patted Jessica on the hand. "I'm all right."

"A temporary condition," Reeves smirked, rubbing his neck.

The bastard was actually enjoying this, Harry thought. Once a war hero, always a war hero. "What will you do with Kapps?" he asked the government man.

"You mean the President?"

"Whatever."

"The President is dead," Reeves answered with finality.

"But Kapps isn't . . ."

"Harry," Reeves said, squatting to place himself at eye level with the wounded journalist. "The nicest thing about syntheskin is that it can be peeled off as easily as it is applied as long as you act quickly, within four hours of application. After that time, you need surgical skills. At this moment, Kapps is being physically divested of his visions of grandeur by several of Hanratty's men. He will once again be wearing his own, saucer-conscious visage within the hour."

"Then what?"

"A touching denouement. The Reverend Ashley Kapps dies while trying to negotiate a truce between the government and the terrorists. The terrorists panic. Gunfire erupts. The President dies heroically while trying to save Kapps' life. The poor reverend stumbles into the cross fire. He dies a hero, Harry, a martyr for his faith. Hell. Every religion needs a couple of martyrs."

"And what about Vice-President David Reeves?"

Reeves' face brightened. "The soon-to-be inaugurated Reeves enters the fray with guns blazing. Backed by an intrepid force of crackerjack FBI agents, led personally by Chief Amos Hanratty, Reeves avenges his President's death, wiping out the terrorist army. At last, the United States has a hero in the oval office—a fellow with charisma, a fellow with leadership qualities . . ."

"A guy with the blood of innocent people on his hands," Harry pointed out.

"What's a war between friends?" Reeves asked. "Besides, no one will ever know about this."

"You've thought this out thoroughly, I take it."

"It's hitchless."

"What about Hanratty? Why should he keep quiet?"

"Come reelection I'll need a strong running mate."

"And what about us?"

"Harry Porter," Reeves announced, "bravely covering the incident, dies in the cross fire. Jessica West, an accomplice of terrorist leader Peter Hayden, is shot by federal officials during an attempted escape from the scene." Reeves motioned towards Saint-Crispen. "Several unidentified bodies, members of Kapps' church, most likely, are also discovered."

Harry squeezed his leg, noting that Reeves was not aware of Saint-Crispen's identity. "You just can't murder us," he stated.

"National security," the Vice-President smiled, getting to his feet. "No exceptions. David says."

Harry decided to take a gamble. He had very little to lose. "You won't try to harm us if you want to live long enough to see the White House," he sneered, using his good leg and Saint-Crispen's shoulder to raise himself to his full height. "Have any of your men gone up to the security room as yet?"

"I suppose so, why?"

"The whole room has been leveled."

"So what?"

"It was destroyed by mindpower, not firepower. My mindpower."

"Oh, come off it, Porter," Reeves laughed. "The wound is in your leg, not your head. Talk sense."

"I'm serious, Reeves," Harry said through clenched teeth, half in a show of bravura, half in pain. "Ask your men upstairs. Go ahead. Tell them to check the consoles. Ask them to see if the monitor screens blew up from within. Then ask them to run a quick scan of the room for the presence of any explosive devices or residue. Go ahead. It's your ass on the line." Porter glared at Reeves. He genuinely hated his guts.

Reeves' confidence faltered slightly, but enough. He raised a wrist communicator. "Ring?" he said.

"Yes, sir?" a voice from the device snapped.

"Have you been to the security center, yet?"

"Affirmative, sir. The place is a mess. Damndest thing I ever saw."

"What do you mean?"

"The room looks like it was flattened by an explosive, but

we can't find a trace of any. We have a few laser rifles up here that seem to have imploded. Most of the plastic and glass in the room is either shattered or fused into large wads. The metal has been welded into bizarre shapes and a wall of TV units are wiped out. It's like the place was hit by lightning traveling from fifty different directions."

"Thanks," Reeves said, his voice betraying an almost total lack of saliva in his mouth. "That doesn't prove a thing," he glowered at Porter. "Anything could have happened up there."

"Anything didn't," Harry sneered, attempting to affect a sense of swagger despite the pain in his leg and forehead. "But something did. I've already told you what."

"We'll have our experts run tests."

"Fine. It's your life you're toying with. Until you get the results of those tests, I'd advise you to tell your gorillas," he turned and faced the blond woman, "and gorillaette, to toss their joysticks down. That goes for you too. Your heads can all pop open as easily as those monitoring units did if I feel like playing around."

"What kind of story are you trying to sell me, Porter?"

"A nasty one, Davey. I'm a government-created mutant."

"Be serious."

"Ask the guards in that security office who were holding the laser rifles when they went boom. They'd tell you how serious I am, but they can't. They can't tell anyone anything anymore. I haven't exactly publicized my abilities because I like my privacy."

Reeves was wavering. Porter continued. "Do you remember that big stink concerning the space habitat a few years ago? Remember those genetic mutations that were caused up there in their greenhouse by conditions unknown?"

"Yeah. . . ." Reeves' eyes narrowed in either deep thought or suspicion.

"I was the one who covered that story."

"I know. I read the papers."

"What wasn't in the papers was the fact that those same 'conditions unknown' affected some of the more telepathically oriented space colonists. Some of the experts believed that it was cosmic radiation that caused the change in their mental processes. No one could say for sure, but there was a coven of homegrown telepaths loose up there. And, my tough-talking mental midget, I wound up on that spacescape following several months of parapsychotherapy. In other words, I reacted to that spacey effect like a sponge does to water."

"What kind of mutant are you claiming to be, Porter?"

"I'm a natural telepath, Reeves. An unsuspecting soul who was peeped one time too many before being shot off into space where god knows what took a liking to my unstable psychic condition and magnified it to King Kong proportions."

Reeves didn't move. He listened. Harry talked. "I've kept a low profile on my status for a couple of years for reasons of my own. I don't like to use my powers. It's almost self-destructive. It does strange things to my insides—but it does stranger things to the outsides of people it's aimed at. I mean, I could take apart this building, Davie, with you in it if you don't smarten up. You wouldn't have time to make it to one of your vans outside let alone the Oval Office if I turned the juice on. Think of that, David. And think of that room up there: twisted, melted, and gnarled."

Reeves regarded Harry with a mixture of hatred and fear. He considered Porter's story carefully before commenting. "Horseshit."

Harry couldn't betray panic. "All right," he shrugged, squeezing Saint-Crispen's shoulder. "Go ahead. Try to kill us. Maim us. See what happens. Try to lop off our heads like you did to Andy out there. What did you do, have your sharp-shooters train their lasers on his car before you gave the order to slice it to shit?"

Saint-Crispen's knees began to knock. The pounding in Harry's head became more pronounced. He glanced at Jessica. Her hand was already massaging her forehead. Saint-Crispen was beginning to panic. His cowardice was their last hope.

"How many times did you hit Cade, Mister Vice-President? Three, four, five times? Brave government trooper, having a fleet of agents slicing parts off the body of an unarmed man. Is that what you want to do with us, David?"

Saint-Crispen uttered a low moan. His eyes rolled back into their lids.

"Will you butcher us like that?" Harry yammered. "How will you destroy Kapps? Laser weaponry? Old-fashioned bullets? How much pain will your fed goons try to cause the three of us just for the fun of it? Will they play with us as much as our troops did overseas in our last undeclared war? What will you aim for first? The brain? The heart? Small organs?"

Reeves began to massage his forehead. "I don't... know what... you're talking about," he said uneasily. "We're not talking about torture... we're talking... talking about..."

"Cold-blooded murder!" Harry bellowed. "We're talking about death, David! Death. We're talking about you murdering all three of us!"

Saint-Crispen broke. "NO!" he screamed.

Harry's nose erupted once again, as did Jessica's. Saint-Crispen lapsed into a catlike howling, nearly knocking Harry to the ground. His brain on fire, Harry grabbed his friend and, linking arms, stumbled towards the Vice-President. He waved his arms dramatically, like a magician in search of a rabbit in a hat. Reeves saw Harry's theatrical approach.

Simultaneously, he was hit squarely by Saint-Crispen's ever-mounting fear. He was sent sprawling across the floor of the garage. Three FBI agents standing against the wall attempted to fire their rifles. Harry and the Saint spun around. The lasers began to smoke. The agents dropped them immediately. Clutching their heads, they backed into the wall and slid onto the floor.

Harry attempted to remain conscious. "Take it easy, Marion," he whispered in his companion's ear. "We've got them."

The Saint calmed down to a slow whimpering.

"Are you satisfied," Harry screeched, nearly sobbing under the impact of the Saint's agonized emotions.

"Yes," Reeves whined, writhing at Harry's feet. "Just stop it! Stop it!"

Harry stomped on Saint-Crispen's toe. The pain caused the Saint to mentally hesitate, refocusing his attention to his foot. "Damn it, Harry," he blurted. "I've got a hangnail there!"

Abruptly, Harry's head cleared. "Clumsy me," he smiled at the Saint. He winked at Jessica who was busily wiping her nose.

"All right, Porter," Reeves said, rising slowly. "You've made your point."

"Not quite," Harry smiled. "I haven't told you about the range I have with this power."

"How far can you project."

"So far," Harry smiled brightly. "The sky seems to be the limit. The more I practice, the further I go."

Reeves pondered that statement.

"What I'm trying to say to you, Mr. Charisma," Harry continued, "is that I fully expect you to lay off us now and forever. If I ever get the notion that you or any of your boys are putting the moves on any one of us, I'll think nasty thoughts about you in the Oval Office. I'll wipe your slate clean."

"That's scientifically impossible."

"So is what I just did here."

Reeves produced a handkerchief and dabbed the blood from his chin and ears. "I don't want you to print anything about what happened here today. Understand?"

"There's something in the Constitution alluding to freedom of the press, isn't there?"

"Look, Porter, I don't care how much power you have, think about the consequences. Aside from the fact that no one will believe your story, the tale could land you in prison on a conspiracy charge that I will personally instigate. I don't think you can wipe out an entire government with your powers, do you? I promise you that I'll have everyone possible on your ass."

"Let's say I remain mum. Then what?" Harry inquired.

"We'll write an officially sanctioned 'exclusive' for you. It will be delivered within two hours to your newspaper with your by-line on it. Basically, it will read like the narrative I recounted to you before."

"But we won't be among the fatalities," Harry added. "A small but important alteration."

"Does that meet with your approval?" Reeves snarled.

"For the time being," Harry sighed, "it suits me all right."

Reeves turned to Saint-Crispen and Jessica. "I must reemphasize the fact that national security rests upon your honoring the secrecy we have just discussed."

Jessica stared icily at the Vice-President. Saint-Crispen stepped forward, nodding vigorously. "Don't worry about me, your honor. I'm a real government man. I voted twice in the last election."

Reeves retrieved his handgun from the floor. It was twisted into a near 'u' shape. He gaped at the pistol and then at Harry. Turning his back on the trio, he motioned for his men to follow him. "There will be a van at your disposal when you decide to leave," he remarked.

"I'd like a doctor for my leg," Harry called. "And someone to take care of Andy . . . Dr. Cade."

"Consider it done."

"And remember," Harry shouted. "If you try anything, I'll

retaliate before you know it. The mind is quicker than the eye."

"You have my word, damn you," Reeves screamed, leaving the garage.

Harry gingerly sat down on the surface of the garage. "I'll hold you to it, too, asshole," he said through clenched teeth.

"You trust that guy?" Saint-Crispen asked.

"I have a choice?"

An ambulance appeared outside the garage entrance. The electric vehicle slowly made its way down the ramp. David Reeves remained behind in the sunlight, the twisted gun still in his hand.

"Well," Jessica said, helping Harry to his feet. "It looks like the country has finally gotten the leader it wanted."

"Yeah," Porter said, limping towards the ambulance. "As well as its first dictatorship."

8

The interweaving melodies of two acoustic pianos resounded through the small room. Mozart's Concerto in E Flat Major for Two Pianos, K. 365 was being played at deafening volume. Harry Porter, dressed in a newly purchased black suit, sat in the imitation leather chair situated before the video screen. He focused his eyes on the empty screen.

He vaguely heard the incessant ringing of the phone. For some inexplicable reason, Machine did not bring the phone to his attention. Somewhere in the back of his mind, he connected the ringing with the receiver and picked it up. The music, which dated back to 1779, automatically dropped in volume.

A naked woman appeared on the small videophone screen. "Harry!" Sybille DeVille exclaimed. "I can't believe you're home!"

"Oh," Harry said, nearly beating back the sense of distance which currently separated him from everything and everybody. "Yeah. I'm here. Hi, Sybille."

"Hi, Sybille?" the woman said, a look of consternation flickering onto the screen. "I've left dozens of messages during the past week. I'm due to leave town tomorrow. I call you again and again and again after you don't return any one of my last eight messages, and all I get is 'Hi, Sybille?'"

"Sorry," Harry said dully, "I haven't been home much. I've been working on a story."

"A newspaper story?"

"Uh-huh."

"Must have been a big one for you to ignore my calls."

"Fairly big."

"Too bad I don't read the papers, huh?" Deville grinned, returning to her original good humor.

"Yeah." Harry nodded.

"Can we get together tonight?"

"I don't think so, Sybille, I'm sort of tied up."

"That's exactly what I had in mind."

Harry smiled in spite of his lethargy. "Really. I can't. Maybe next time."

"Well, all right, Harrykins," the woman said amiably. "But cheer up, will you? You look as if you've just lost your best friend."

"You're very perceptive, Syb. Gotta go."

Harry replaced the phone on the receiver and returned to his marathon wall-staring binge. He didn't get too far into it when the doorbell rang. "Let her in," he told Machine.

Jessica West walked softly into the room. She wore an expression of intangible loss, wistful yet resigned. She sat on the arm of Harry's chair. "Isn't it time you slept?" she asked, placing a hand on his shoulder.

"I'm not tired."

"Well, how about getting out of those clothes then."

"I'm comfortable."

Jessica slid off the chair and dropped onto the new sofa with a sigh. "The funeral was yesterday, Harry. You can't sulk forever."

"I can if I want to," he replied. "And I'm not sulking. I'm mourning. There's a difference."

"Not the way you do it," Jessica snapped.

"Aww, hell, Jessie. There wasn't enough of Andy left to put in a closed coffin! Cremation! And what did he die for? He died for nothing. He died so some asshole could calmly take control of the government. My God! Nobody in this whole country is aware of what really happened up at Fountain Point! They don't know what a maniac Reeves is!"

"All right," Jessica said, the color rising in her cheeks. "It

stinks! Reeves is a monster! But your sitting there feeling
sorry for yourself because you couldn't stop him isn't going to
change one damned thing. It's not going to bring back Dr.
Cade any more than it will Peter. At least Dr. Cade had a
funeral, Harry. We've never even found Peter's body!"

The woman leaned forward in the sofa and, placing her face
in her hands, started to cry. It was silent at first, her body
rocking slowly back and forth. Soon, her sobs could be heard
clearly. Harry was shaken. He had never seen her cry before.
Feeling both ashamed and angered, he stood by her side.
"I'm sorry, okay?"

Tears poured from her eyes, dribbling down her cheeks
and onto the carpet. Her blue bangs shimmied with each sob.
Porter didn't want to deal with this. Any of this.

He ran a hand across his face. He hadn't shaved since
before the funeral. The clothes he had worn at Fountain Point
were still crumpled in the center of the living room floor
where he had tossed them two days before. The cane the
doctor had given him was broken in two nearby. He began to
hobble across the room, gesticulating wildly. "There are just
so many loose ends, so many victims unaccounted for. And,
now, with the government riding shotgun on the whole
incident, we'll never know what happened to all of Kapps'
victims.

"And the maddening thing about all this is that I'm coming
out of it looking like a goddamned hero! A man among men!
A patriot's patriot! Jesus! I feel like Patton or someone. The
phone calls haven't stopped since the story appeared. I'm an
instant celebrity!

"I mean, they're talking Pulitzer about this already . . . and
the gossip isn't confined to journalistic circles, either. I'm
being lionized all over the world! After all these years of
busting my chops trying to get the news across to people
accurately and fairly, I'm going to be canonized for a story
that not only did I not write but that is sheer fabrication.
How's that for poetic justice? If there's a patron saint of
ridiculousness, he's definitely in my corner!"

Jessica nodded slowly. "That corner is getting awfully crowded," she sniffed.

Porter turned around and looked at her. She had stopped
crying. He was glad for the company. The phone rang. Harry
glared at it before lunging for the receiver. "Hello!" he
barked.

"Harry," Leonard Golden said sheepishly. "DeWitt wants to see you on the double."

"Tell him to turn on his TV. I'm all over the networks."

"He says it's urgent."

"Nothing's urgent anymore. The teachings of Harry Porter."

"Please don't give me a rough time, Harry," Golden said softly. "This isn't my doing. I'm not calling the shots anymore. Those days are over."

"Sorry, Lenny. Where and when?"

"Mecoy's. Half hour."

"I'll be there." Harry hung up the phone. He hadn't been in Mecoy's since before the whole Walker mess had festered. He turned on his answering machine and walked into the bathroom without saying a word. The ridiculousness showed no signs of ending. Maybe it was his destiny to become a caricature of a cheerleader in a cartoon world. Hooray for the hero President. Hooray for the hero reporter. He splashed some water onto his face and gawked at himself in the mirror. He looked like hell. Fine. He felt like hell, too.

He decided against a shave, dried his face, and returned to the living room. "Wait for me, will you, Jess? This won't take long. Machine can regale you with stories of censored circuitry in my absence."

He limped out of the apartment, slamming the door behind him.

Jessica remained motionless in the chair.

Machine lowered the music. "So much anger . . ." it commented.

Harry waited for the elevator. The car stopped and the door slid open to reveal the presence of Dr. Jorge, hovering inside on crutches. "Meester Porter," he chortled. "Just ze man I vanted to zee. I'll ride down wiz you, all right."

"It's a free country," Harry said, stepping inside, "although you'd never know it in this building."

"Ha! Ha! Alvways making with the jokez. I just vant to compliment you your story. Vunnderful. Vunnderful. It just brimmed vit heroism, drama and, most of all, optimiskm. The power plant was savet. The President proved himself a brave man. And now, ve haf nothing to look forwart to but better tomorrows. It brought tears to my eyes!"

The elevator car slowed as it approached the lobby. "Maybe you just have an alergy."

"Vich brinks me to another point," Jorge said, floating out

of the car after Harry. "Despite this optimistic note, the recent transition of power in ze White House has sent the stock market into a tizzy. There's a fluctuation in energy prices again. I haf no choice but to pass alonk some of the burden to . . ."

Harry tuned the little man's voice out of his head and stepped outside into the rain. Since Cade's death it always seemed to be raining. Harry wasn't sure if that was actually a substantiable fact or not. Maybe it was just the way he felt. He might not have been noticing the sunshine, concentrating, instead, on the moods of nature that closely reflected his own. He hailed a cab and motored down to Mecoy's.

He shoved the driver a fifty-dollar bill for a twenty-five dollar fare and told him to keep the change. Hell, if a future Pulitzer winner couldn't be a spendthrift, who could?

Harry stood in the downpour and stared at the bar. It was as it had always been. Dignified but ramshackle, its awning in need of repair, the establishment boasted an appropriately dark and dank entranceway. The pedway in front was empty.

Harry stepped over the moving sidewalk and entered the saloon. A gaggle of guzzlers stood at the bar discussing sex, money, sex, work, sex, crime, and sex. Religion would have been considered bad taste. Harry nodded at Mecoy and silently walked past the debating club to the back of the room. He spotted Golden and DeWitt immediately. Much to his dismay, they were sitting at the table that Harry and Cade had frequented over a period of, what, years? Eons? An eternity or two?

Porter blinked his eyes quickly, half expecting to see Cade stroll in, a look of utter condescension on his face, and take his usual seat. That was not to be. DeWitt, the publishing world's answer to fungus, was perched sacrilegiously in Andy's chair. Porter caught Golden's eye. The editor, looking positively ancient under the strain of DeWitt's mindless effervescence, stared balefully at Porter.

Golden was beaten—a once-proud animal now reduced to the status of less than subservience, the family's third dog not even allowed second crack at the choicest bones. Harry took a deep breath and walked towards the table. He wished that Leonard had the guts to tell DeWitt off, to turn his heel and hit the streets. But Leonard would never do that. He had responsibilities. The remnants of a family. A home. A portfolio of bills.

Harry understood, the shadow of Dr. Jorge still hovering over his head like a vulture.

"Harry!" DeWitt beamed, getting to his feet. "Do sit down! Please! I have wonderful news for you!"

"Do we print any other kind?" Harry asked, pulling a third chair to the table.

"My point all along, remember?" DeWitt cackled. Harry looked at his knuckles. The guy was really suffering from I-strain. "As of today, Harry, you're being promoted to associate editor of the paper with a big increase in salary? How does twenty-five percent sound?"

"Like a quarter," he replied without enthusiasm. "What's the occasion?"

"My dear boy!" DeWitt chided, placing an oily hand on Harry's fist. "You must be joking! You're a shoo-in for the prize this year in hard news reporting. You must have heard already."

"Rumors," Harry shrugged.

"There's no way anyone can top this story!" DeWitt stated. "No way. Don't you understand? You will reap bountiful rewards for listening to your publisher. We have some good ideas at our side of the desk sometimes, Harry. Remember what I told you about positive journalism? Now, this is *exactly* the kind of situation I was referring to. You played it just right. The people out there in readerland deserve to know that there is a truly upbeat side to life no matter how dire the situation may seem!"

"I don't quite see your point," Harry said.

"You don't?" DeWitt was astonished. "My dear Harry, three days ago we were faced with a weak president, the possibility of a nuclear fiasco, and a reign of terrorist-inspired horror! Today, all the situations have reversed themselves. Your story has had a profound effect on the entire free world. Reeves is going to be able to walk into the fall reelection practically unopposed!

"Because of Kapps' heroic death, his religion of positivism is booming. You've chronicled the beginning of a new era, Harry. I credit this beginning, as a matter of fact, more to your observations than the hard news reported. There was a magnificent, swashbuckling flavor to your piece. It was positively inspirational. The whole country is caught up in Portermania! The suicides have stopped. The malaise has disappeared. You managed to turn a rather ugly escapade into a positive example of idealism triumphing over greed and violence."

Harry stared at the stranger in his best friend's chair. "A lot of people, innocent people, died up there."

"What are a few individual lives when the future of an entire nation is at stake?" A bright smile shone on DeWitt's face. He raised a glass in front of Harry's eyes. "Let's drink to the new era in America!"

Something that had been simmering within Porter suddenly came to a full boil. A strange laugh rattled from deep within his throat. He shot his left fist across the tabletop and caught DeWitt squarely on the nose. He heard the nostrils "click" upon impact. DeWitt cartwheeled backward out of the chair, tumbling seven feet across the floor.

"You drink to the new era," Harry said, getting to his feet and limping towards the door. "Drown in it for all I care."

DeWitt sat up, attempting to stem the flow of blood from his nose with his still-intact drinking glass. "You ungrateful has-been!" he screeched. "If it wasn't for me, you wouldn't be where you are right now! I forced you into this story! I should be taking all the credit!"

"It's yours." His fingers were numb from the collision.

"Damn right, it's mine!" DeWitt declared, crawling towards the table. "As of now, I'll let everyone know it, too. You're finished, Porter. You're fired! Do you hear that? Fired! And the world will know just why, too. You're an alcoholic, Porter. You're moody! You have no respect for authority. Your punctuation stinks, and you constantly misspell words! You'll never work on another newspaper again!"

"I'll survive," Harry grunted, stepping out into the rain.

DeWitt propped himself onto the table. "Golden!" he shrieked at the sad-eyed editor. "Do something! Stop him!"

Golden suppressed a faint smile. "Sorry, Mr. DeWitt," he said, finishing his drink before standing. "I can't do that. You just fired him." He handed DeWitt a handkerchief. "That doesn't give me too much leverage with the guy, does it."

"Awww, shit," DeWitt said, sinking into a chair. "Shit." He stared at the ceiling. "Shit."

"Let's try to have a positive attitude about this, sir," Golden smiled, patting the bleeding man on the head. He ambled away and stood at the bar.

Harry walked through the rain. The day seemed extraordinarily quiet. Manhattan seemed deserted. Something was missing. Maybe it was the warmth of the sun. A small twinge shot through his left hand. He clenched his fist and raised it before his eyes for inspection. The skin was broken. How Cade would have publicly abhorred Harry's crude response to DeWitt's hypocrisy. How Cade would have secretly enjoyed seeing that bastion of monied mindlessness topple out of his makeshift throne onto the barroom floor.

Porter stared at his bruised hand and laughed aloud. He started off once again. It was such a fine day, he decided to walk all the way home.

A block away, an electric vehicle rumbled to life. It followed Porter at a discreet distance.

9

A lone guitarist picked out an almost-melody on a seemingly ancient twelve-stringed instrument. Protected from the storm by the overhang of Gimbel's and Ahmet's on Eighty-sixth and Lexington, the young musician, a wiry young woman, played somberly. Her copper skin was taut and smooth. Her intense gaze almost spiritual. Each note reverberated under the overhang before wandering off into the wind and the rain.

Porter stepped beneath the covering to listen for a moment. Next to the young woman sat a bearded, bald, accomplice, a cup placed before his crossed legs for donations. Harry fished into his trouser pockets for a bill. He walked over to the cross-legged man and stuffed a three-dollar job into the container. The bearded man looked up from beneath a pair of large, dark glasses.

"Man, am I ever glad to see you," the bald stranger said.

"Are you talking to me?" Harry asked.

"Sure as hell I'm not talking to myself, Harry-boy," the man replied, uncrossing his legs and standing. "I may be 'luding' myself out to keep the mental resources in tow, but I haven't gotten totally punchy."

"Saint-Crispen?" Porter exclaimed, half in awe, half in relief.

"Dummy up, man," the Saint answered. "I'm incognito."

"What have you done to yourself?"

"Pulled a Whitmore. I've shaved my head, changed my skin pigmentation, and got hold of a fake beard until I have time to grow one of my own."

"What for?"

"Well, in case you haven't heard, Harry old pal, we're at the top of the President's hit list—with the accent on hit. As we stand here chewin' the fat, there is a car stocked with little boys from the Washington area about a block away trying to think of a way to arrange a one-way ferry ride down the Styx for both of us and make it look like an accident."

"You're kidding."

"Comedy has never been my bag, Harry-boy. Me and Red Bow over here are about one hundred dollars away from two tickets out of the land of the free and the dead."

"Where are you heading?"

"Yugoslavia. This is street fair season and we figure that between her charm and my business savvy, we can make a decent living over there."

"Decent?" Harry said, glancing over his shoulder.

"Don't lay any value judgments on me, Harry-boy. If you're smart and don't feel like walking down the street with your body whistling from laser holes, I'd advise you to take a lead from your old buddy here and split from the U.S. of A."

Harry stared out into the swirling rain. He was a dead man if he kept his part of the bargain with Reeves. He was a dead man if he didn't. Those were not the kinds of options he enjoyed dealing with.

"Government men?" he asked.

"Nope. Reeves kept his word about that. They're outside talent, privately employed. Local yokels who want to score big. If they pull it off, they can set up shop on either coast."

Porter shook the Saint's hand. "Thanks, Marion. I owe you one. Good luck in Yugoslavia."

"Hey, Harry," Saint-Crispen said, not relinquishing his grip. "You couldn't spare an extra fiver, could you? I mean, that information I gave you is worth . . ."

Porter emptied his pockets. Eighty dollars fell to the pavement. "That's all I have, Marion. Thanks for the tip." He turned and left the shelter of the awning. Pummeled by rain, he paused and turned to his friend. "Hey! What are you calling yourself these days?"

"Eric Von Arrowsmith."

Harry pulled a sour face.

"Hey," Saint-Crispen pointed out, "with Red Bow here bein' an Indian and all, my moniker will probably appeal to just about everybody once we get over there."

Harry nodded and trudged up Lexington in the rain. He made a left on Ninetieth and was hit by a sudden gust of wind. He was walking past the newly constructed high-rise row and abruptly realized why it was referred to as tornado alley. Fierce currents of air rushed down the sides of the buildings, hitting the pavement in a howl of power. In the background, Porter thought he heard the woman's guitar.

Harry entered the lobby of his apartment building. Dr. Jorge hovered across the floor, positioning himself between Porter and the elevator. "Meester Porter . . ."

Harry took the man by the arm and spun him across the lobby. "Later, doc."

He made it to his apartment door, his shoes squeaking from the rain. He placed his hand into the print lock and walked into his home. Jessica was still seated on the sofa, watching a video magazine on the overhead screen.

"That DeVille woman called again," she said casually as Harry dripped into the room. "She was rude."

"Lewd?"

"Both, really. I told her to go bounce her boobs somewhere else."

Harry walked into the kitchen and quietly retrieved a cup of coffee. Jessica seemed quite at home in his apartment. That both pleased and frightened him. After all, he didn't need any major commitments in his life right now, did he?

Stepping back into the living room, coffee in hand, he walked over to the couch, sat next to the woman, and announced: "We have to get out of here."

"You say the most romantic things," Jessica replied. "Why do we have to leave?"

"Two reasons, actually." Harry sipped the coffee. "First, I just quit my job. No money equals no rent for this apartment."

"I see."

"And, more importantly, the government has put out a contract on us."

Jessica's face turned ashen.

Harry continued to drink. "Insurance, I suppose. Reeves wants us dead to make sure that no one ever finds out what happened at Fountain Point. I'm sure he's especially nervous about the news hitting the fan before the fall elections."

"Are you sure about—"

"Yeah. If Saint-Crispen is actually running for his life, actually leaving the city, you can put money on the fact that something's in the air."

Jessica emitted a slow, exasperated sigh. "So, what do we do now? Run from the government the rest of our lives? If they want us dead, Harry, they'll arrange it no matter where we are. They can kill us for any reason they care to come up with. We can't prove a thing about Kapps or Walker or Reeves or..." Her face was growing flushed.

Harry got up from the chair and picked up the bundle of dirty clothes from the center of the room. "I wouldn't say that," he said, removing a small object from his shredded slacks. "Behold! A remarkable little instrument—a voice-activated tape recorder; a gadget I carry around with me at all times; those times included our whole stay with Kapps and Reeves." He scratched his head. "It's the sort of gizmo you don't really pay attention to, good backup for stories where people claim they've been misquoted."

"You've got everything on tape?" Jessica couldn't help smiling.

"Down to the last zzzap," Harry said, plopping onto the couch next to her. "I wasn't going to do anything with it for a while because of our deal with Reeves. But if he's reneging, so much for words of honor."

"You'll release the tapes to the world?"

"To the solar system if need be," Porter smirked. "But I would really like to be out of this country when things start perking. Do you still have that place in England?"

"The cottage? Sure."

"Feel like a quick transatlantic flight?"

"Love one," she said. "I'll go pack."

"Don't take too much," Harry cautioned as she left the apartment. "We don't want to arouse too much suspicion."

Harry sat alone in the apartment. Without being asked, Machine began playing Mozart's Concerto for Three Pianos, K. 242. Harry tilted his head back and stared at the living room camera. "You can shut that off, now." He paused as the music faded. "How long has it been for us, Machine? Three years?"

"Approximately," the unit answered. "Two years, eleven months, twenty days—"

"Okay. Just wondering."

"Fifteen hours, twenty-seven minutes, and fourteen seconds."

"And they said it wouldn't last," Porter smirked. "I can remember coming back to this apartment right after you were installed. God, how I hated you. You were pretty inflexible back then, you know: a regular mechanized martinet."

"I was programmed to act in your best interest," Machine pointed out as Harry walked into the bedroom one last time. "Human beings, being a frail species," the computer went on, "especially mentally, cannot always judge what is best for them . . . especially after going through as severe an emotional trauma as you had."

Harry tossed some clothes into a lightweight travel bag. "Bullshit," he laughed. "You were just playing the computer-ized curmudgeon back then."

"Your lowbrow analogies betray a penchant for bad examples of alliteration."

"Ah," Harry said, snapping the bag shut. "You'll miss me when I'm gone."

Porter was suddenly aware of how silent the apartment was. "Your absence will be duly noted," Machine replied after a twenty-second hesitation.

"Well," Harry said, reentering the living room and placing his bag near the door. "I'll miss you." He stared at the camera. "Damn. I never thought I'd ever say that to a piece of machinery." He shook his head slowly. "Well, I'm not ashamed of it. For your memory banks' benefit, Machine, I've grown quite fond of you. You're a stickler for rules, a thorn in my side, the bane of my existence. In short, you're my better half. We made a pretty good team, as far as man and machines go, don't you think?"

"We are, were, compatible in a strange way," Machine admitted. "Your departure from this place is final?"

The doorbell rang. Harry swung it open and faced Jessica. "Passport ready?"

Jessica smiled. "Uh-huh. I've already withdrawn most of my money from the bank here and had it transferred to a branch in London."

"Fine," Harry said. "I'll call Leonard and get him to run a phoney assignment wire to the *London Times-Mirror-Star* and have him transfer my severance pay to their office. If both of us tampered with our accounts simultaneously, we might be noticed."

"You're a genius." She kissed him on the cheek.

"Nope," Harry grinned. "I think on my feet. There's a subtle difference."

He picked up his bag and stood at the doorway. He turned, one final time, towards the camera. "Well, good-bye my marvelous Machine. You take care of yourself, okay? Remember me kindly."

"My memory banks will be erased to accomodate my next owner," Machine stated flatly.

Harry hesitated for a moment. "Too bad. Well, maybe keep a piece of all this swimming around in a stray strand of circuitry. See you."

The door closed slowly. The apartment remained silent. An elevator rumbled down the hall. The faint sound of a door sliding closed echoed in the stillness of the living room. Slowly, gradually, the sound of Mozart emerged from the wall speakers. "Good-bye, Harry Porter," Machine said softly. "Good luck."

The music grew in intensity. Before Mozart's three pianos could reach the Allegro, however, the door to the apartment burst open. Porter ran into the room.

"Since when do you listen to Mozart on your own? You old softy!"

"I prefer to keep the ambiance as normal as possible until I am undone," Machine said. "And I understood that you were on your way to the airport."

"I had a brainstorm in the lobby," Harry said, fishing through a kitchen drawer. Jessica appeared in the doorway with a smile on her face. "Actually, we *both* had a brainstorm," Porter pointed out. "Where's the screwdriver?"

Finding it, he rushed over to the wall unit in the kitchen where Machine had been initially installed three years ago. "How large are your memory circuits, Machine?"

"Not large at all," Machine pointed out. "All of my vital chips are housed in a small black box no larger than a mini-tape cassette. Most of the space is decorative, really."

"So, if I remove that black box and take it with us, I'll be carrying around your personality in my luggage, right?"

"Computerized household units do not have personalities," Machine informed him; "that is a human trait. However, you would be carrying around my essence, as it were."

"And I could hook you back up in any compatible system?"

"Correct."

"Fine," Harry said, unscrewing the small metal wall panel.

"I'm going to uncork your massive mind and tuck it into my little shaving kit. Give me some directions, here."

"Harry," Machine stated. "What you are proposing to do is illegal. Household units are rented to the individual home-owner or apartment dweller by the National Househelper Corporation. Theft of their black boxes is against the law. You can be fined or imprisoned."

"Would you rather have your memory circuits scrubbed?"

"The black box is the one with the two red screws and four blue screws. The additional pieces are decorative, designed to impress the human owner."

"Thanks," Harry said, removing the first large screw. "Now, just ⸝relax. When you wake up, you'll be in jolly old England . . . tending to the most wanted couple in America."

"Until t-h-e-n," Machine bade, its voice fading to a dull murmur.

Harry yanked out the box and stuffed it into his pocket. He picked up his bag and, giving Jessica a quick hug at the door, pointed to the elevator. "Shall we?"

Jessica laughed softly to herself. "I thought you hated that machine? Why did you go back."

"Had to," he explained, stepping into the awaiting eleva-tor. "Between you and me and this box of bolts, I figure we have the beginnings of a really solid nouveau nuclear family."

The door opened and Harry, Jessica, and Household Unit 487A trotted through the lobby. They jumped into an awaiting cab positioned outside the building. The rain had stopped. The pale yellow sun was fighting its way through a small range of rust-colored clouds. There was no sign of the car that had followed Porter earlier.

Harry smiled as the cab silently sliced past Gimbel's and Ahmed's. Saint-Crispen and the guitarist were gone. "Good luck, Saint-Crispen," Porter whispered to the back window. "Until next time."

In the distance, sirens wailed. Harry shut them out of his mind. He cranked down the window and inhaled the warm, moist air. He would learn to enjoy his life from this moment on. He would relish every minute. Every second. His lifestyle, he swore, would forever more be rooted in the present tense.

A police car and an ambulance roared by the cab.

Harry instinctively ducked in the back seat of the auto.

He had escaped the sirens today.

He couldn't be sure about tomorrow.

ABOUT THE AUTHOR

ED NAHA was abandoned by his gypsy parents while still a tot in a deserted Bohack supermarket parking lot in Elizabeth, New Jersey, a town famous for its thugs. Raised by wolves near the frozen-food loading door, young Naha immediately distinguished himself in the literary world by stalking several well-known authors and then gnawing on their legs while his unsuspecting victims attempted to purchase frozen TV dinners. As his creative juices began to flow, Naha found himself arrested and thrown in jail for long periods of time. In New Jersey, it is illegal to do ANYthing with one's creative juices...let alone having them flow in public.

Since his release from prison, Naha has gained fame by penning such classic works as *War and Peace*, *Crime and Punishment*, *The Greek Way*, *Mein Kampf* and *The Tell-Tale Heart*. Unfortunately, at present, his fame rests on the fact that, without exception, all of these works were written previously by other authors. This does not faze the budding genius. "Why tamper with a winning formula?" he is often heard to mutter. Today, the genius lives in a small ranch house located in Elizabeth, New Jersey, outside a frozen-food loading door. He is a bachelor, living with his parents, Lobo and Snowball.

But alas, most of this is unfortunately fiction. In truth, Ed Naha is a New Jersey-born writer living in New York City. Currently the senior writer at *Future* and *Starlog* magazines, two publications dealing with both science fiction and science fact, he has also penned both fiction and non-fiction and science fact, he has also penned both fiction and non-fiction pieces for *Viva*, *The Village Voice*, *Rolling Stone*, *Crawdaddy*, *New Ingenue*, *Playboy*, *Genesis*, *Swank*, *Gallery*, *More* and *Circus*. He is a contributing editor at *Oui* with a by-lined column appearing monthly. He is the author of three books, *Horrors: From Screen to Scream*, *The Rock Encyclopedia*, and *The Science Fictionary*. Formerly employed by CBS as a writer, publicist and A&R representative, he is the producer of the long-playing record *Gene Roddenberry: Inside Star Trek*. His previous Bantam book was *The Paradise Plot*.